GHOST
A John Spector Novel

Wayne Thomas Batson

Spearhead Books
Baltimore • New York • Seattle

Copyright © 2013 by Wayne Thomas Batson.

All rights reserved. No part of this publication may be reproduced, distributed or transmitted in any form or by any means, including photocopying, recording, or other electronic or mechanical methods, without the prior written permission of the publisher, except in the case of brief quotations embodied in critical reviews and certain other noncommercial uses permitted by copyright law. For permission requests, write to the publisher, addressed "Attention: Permissions Coordinator," at the address below.

Spearhead Publishing House
Street Address
City, State/Province Postal-Code
www.website-url.com

Publisher's Note: This is a work of fiction. Names, characters, places, and incidents are a product of the author's imagination. Locales and public names are sometimes used for atmospheric purposes. Any resemblance to actual people, living or dead, or to businesses, companies, events, institutions, or locales is completely coincidental.

Book Layout ©2013 BookDesignTemplates.com
Book Front Cover by ExtendedImagery, Carl Graves (designer)
GHOST/ Wayne Thomas Batson. -- 1st ed.
ISBN-13: 978-1490973456
ISBN-10:1490973451

Thursday, July 4th, 2013

This novel is dedicated to the Most High.
The principalities and powers of this dark world
serve only to make your light shine brighter.
…Ever your servant,
Wayne

Other Books by Wayne Thomas Batson

The Door Within
Rise of the Wyrm Lord
The Final Storm

•

Isle of Swords
Isle of Fire

•

Curse of the Spider King
Venom and Song
The Tide of Unmaking

•

Battle for Cannibal Island
Hunt for the Devil's Dragon

•

Sword in the Stars
The Errant King

{ Chapter 1 }

Nothing like waking up and not knowing where you are or how you got there. Unless of course you planned it that way.

Incandescent blue numbers glowed in the corner of the room, spectral figures, declaring the time 3:16, a.m. Something about the hour sparked a memory. I saw a flash-glimpse: gleaming, razor sharp steel. And blood.

I saw and I knew, but only for a moment. A great black wave washed the memory and my consciousness away. Memory Washing was pretty reliable. It took away the damaging things...and all the cognitive threads that might lead the mind back. It's thorough because it has to be. The mind is a restless, cunning thing. Leave even a trace of an image, and the mind will dig, delve, and deduce until it rips the scab off of the memory itself.

A full Memory Wash takes about seven hours, basically, a night. It takes away the agonies, the vivid disturbing images, the people and places of previous missions, but it leaves all the rest. The functional memory remains intact.

A dreamless vacuum of time later, the clock showed 6:23 in the morning. The sun knifed across a chasm of darkness between the blinds and the bed. I lifted my head a bit, and the bed jiggled. Waterbed.

I hate waterbeds.

I rose up on an elbow and looked this way and that. My movement sent ripples through the bed.

Immediately I felt nauseous.

How on Earth did I let myself fall asleep on a waterbed?

The room was unfamiliar, a complete blank. As my eyes adjusted to the low light, Roman columns materialized in the shadowed corners and led my eye to a vaulted ceiling with intricate crown molding. Nice touch, but expensive.

To my right, across the still undulating bed surface, stood a triangular rack of dumbbells. The weights themselves were brushed silver but likely cast-iron beneath. They started at 50 lbs. and went up from there. That's serious iron, even for someone like me.

Right of the weights, parallel to the overstuffed pillows at the head of the bed, stood a peculiar, black night table. It was shaped like a tree-ish hand and held a flat, silver-trimmed glass surface. A man's wristwatch lay there. An expensive one—TAG Heuer. At least three grand. There was also a pair of earrings, silver with some polished black stone.

I hoped the owner of the earrings wasn't the one who used those dumbbells.

On my left, in addition to the long, dark wood dresser with the clock and the wide, sun-separated blinds, was a full length mirror...one of those antique looking-glass-within-a-rotating-frame types. It seemed oddly out of place in the otherwise stylishly appointed bedroom.

There was a matching night table there on the left, half hidden by the pillows. A box of Kleenex rested there as well as a bride magazine, a pack of gum, and a hair band.

GHOST

Recently moved in girlfriend or newly married, I thought. *Guy used to his own space, but having to accommodate new tastes.* Confirmation sat on a dresser across from my feet: a wedding portrait. There was a handsome, square-jawed man, hugging the daylights out of his bride, a brunette whose eyes were green enough for me to notice from nine feet away in a dimly lit room.

Just then, I became aware of a muted *shooshing* sound...waves crashing. "I'm at the shore," I mumbled. I didn't remember being at the shore. I didn't know the couple in the picture either. I sat up, looked at my wobbling self in the looking glass. *What in heaven?*

I recognized my face: wispy, short blond hair, heavy, furrowed brow, slightly hooded gray eyes, square jaw, blocky cheekbones, and full, semi-frowning lips—but it all looked a little off. Like an incredibly skillful wax sculpture that had been in a hot room too long and melted just a little.

The sight made me cringe. No matter how many times it happened, I never got used to it. I needed a *resetting*. I needed it badly.

I needed new clothes also. The outfit I wore: some kind of trench coat, a black turtleneck, and blue jeans—were torn and shot through with holes. It looked like I'd shared a hug with a pipe bomb.

I touched a few of the holes in my shirt where my pale flesh showed through, but there were no open wounds...no blood. But the flesh was dimpled, raised, and coarse. Clearly, I had taken a beating.

What happened to me? I wondered. And why would I dress like this at the shore? I shrugged and flexed the stiffness out of my neck and shoulders. Sore, like after a hard workout, but without a clue as to why my muscles ached.

I heard a voice, outside the room, maybe even down a floor. "Ghost?" Man's voice. Deep, confident, used to being answered.

The bedroom door opened. The man from the wedding picture walked in. Looked like he didn't use the 50lb. weights anymore, but maybe the heavier ones.

I sat up, swung my legs around to hang off the edge of the bed. Again with the waterbed wobble. It was all I could do to hold back the hurl reflex.

"Cool, you're awake," the guy said. "Listen, I'm on my way to the office. The house is yours. Stay as long as you want. Shower's in there." He pointed to a door I hadn't noticed on my left. "Use the pulse setting. It'll help with sore muscles. And you might, uh...want to ditch those clothes. Help yourself to my closet. Seriously, I've got more clothes than I know what to do with, and we're about the same size. Take whatever you need."

I absently felt the shredded holes in my shirt. Needed the new clothes for sure. Then, I remembered having a suitcase, but it didn't have clothes in it. It wasn't that kind of suitcase.

"Thank you," I said. "I'll take a look."

"Least I can do." He shifted on his feet in the doorway a minute. "Are you going to stay?"

I said, "No."

"At least stay till lunch. Lise will be home. She wanted to thank you again, make you something special. That's how she communicates, you know? The language of food. I ought'a know." He patted his stomach as if he might have a little extra there. He didn't. "So, stay for lunch?"

"I can't," I said. "I have someplace I have to be."

He blinked and nodded. "Look, Ghost, you told me you won't accept money, but is there anything I can do for you?"

I asked, "Do you know where my case is? The silver one...looks medical or military or—"

GHOST

He laughed and shook his head. "Right here." He pointed at the foot of the dresser.

I saw it. Twenty-one inches long, fourteen high, ten thick. Silver hard shell, bulletproof, impregnable to anyone but me. I was glad to see it. No matter how deep a wash I went for, I would make sure I remembered my silver case.

The man drew closer to the bed and held out his hand. It trembled slightly. His confident expression melted. His eyes were sad, and there was a tremor in his voice. "I don't know what to say. I owe you everything. Everything—do you know what that means?"

I nodded and shook his hand. I knew exactly what it meant to owe everything. But I had no idea why he owed *me* anything. I almost asked, but he continued.

"A week ago, I was on the verge of losing it all," he said. "Then you showed up. Thank God for you, man. People just don't get involved like that. People don't help anymore, y'know? Listen, you ever need anything, you know where to find me."

I didn't know where to find him. Aside from somewhere near crashing waves, I had no idea where I was. But that didn't matter. I would never take him up on the offer. He was a thread of memory that would eventually be taken in the wake of the Memory Wash.

"Thank you," I said.

He let go of my hand. He laughed one of those half-annoyed, half-exasperated snickers. "No thanks to me. Thank you, Ghost. Seriously...thank you."

He left. I heard a door slam shut downstairs. A potent engine growled to life and purred out of a drive.

I stood up, headed for the bathroom, and again noticed the weight rack. "Just curious," I muttered. I went to the weights and selected a dumbbell with 120 lbs. printed on the side. I curled it once, twice, a third time. It felt good. I could have kept going, but what was the point?

I started the shower and stepped in. I checked my chest and stomach, finding numerous yellowing welts and a series of strange ribbed stripes...like cat scratches, long healed over. I put the shower head on pulse setting and turned to let the hot water soothe my back. The first steamy drops hit the top of my shoulder...and burned.

I winced and stepped out of the stream. I already knew what I'd find, but I reached anyway. Three wounds, three to four inches long, deep enough to not be fully healed—and stinging like hellfire.

"Careless," I muttered, watching the blood wash off of my fingers and disappear down the drain. *Shade for sure,* I thought. *Probably more than one, unless it was a Knightshade.* I shuddered and stepped back under the water. At last, the resetting began.

I felt the familiar tingle and closed my eyes. My flesh began to tighten, muscles filled with energy—everything about my physical body felt sturdier, tighter, and stronger. But, thanks to the dowsing in water, other abilities would be dampened for a time. That was something else I never let myself forget.

I dried off and went to the walk-in closet. The man was right. He did have more clothes than most people would know what to do with. Two-thirds of it looked hardly worn. All expensive brand names. Not that I'm into brand names. I'm not especially fashion-conscious either. Though, once I was told that I cut a dashing figure when I regularly wore a white waistcoat and a dark tailcoat. Still, I don't seek out the styles. I focus on the brands I trust.

GHOST

It's just when you've been around as long as I have, you get to knowing things. And the Memory Wash never takes away the functional stuff...or the trivial.

I slid into a pair of blue boxers and then selected a khaki pair of cargo shorts with more pockets than should be physically possible. I put on a black tank top that felt like it was made with silk and spandex. It clung to me like a second skin. Over that, I threw a white aloha shirt with browns and greens in a palm pattern. It was a Joe Tierney out of London. Silk and vintage rayon. Again, expensive, more than an average paycheck. The homeowner had seven pairs of Orvis Sperry boat shoes. I took one pair. They fit perfectly.

I checked myself in the mirror. My face looked right again: all the sagging skin, tightened into place. I looked like a man ready for a day at the shore which, in fact, I was.

When I reached for my suitcase, I found an envelope with "Ghost" written in ballpoint pen taped on one side. It was full of hundred-dollar bills. Must have been nearly three inches thick. I guess the man couldn't resist.

I closed the full envelope and put it under a pile of tube socks in the man's drawer.

I picked up the suitcase and went downstairs. Brilliant sunlight streamed in from a bay of windows. There was a crescent of pristine white sand outside and then endless turquoise water.

Gulf coast, I thought. *Maybe the islands.* I found a small phonebook on the black marble counter beneath the phone. It was a Grayton Beach directory. Gulf Coast of Florida.

I drank two glasses of V-8 juice, toasted and ate two cinnamon-raisin bagels, and left the house.

Already hot. Florida hot. I strode out from the deep carport onto the white sand and made my way to the beach. I wasn't sure what I'd find there. I only knew that this morning, I was supposed to go to the shore and look around.

It was happening again.

I felt the stirring in my chest and the itch on my shoulder blades. Not time for the Great Rest. Not yet.

Waking up from a Memory Wash was always the hardest part. The disorientation, the strange, nostalgic feeling of loss. But I had a night's sleep. I had breakfast. And I had my suitcase.

My memory was clear of hindrances. I remembered only what I'd planned to remember. I remembered that my name is John Spector, but everyone calls me Ghost.

I stepped onto the radiant sand and started walking. I didn't know where the steps would lead, but I knew that, sooner or later, there would be someone I needed to find.

Someone I needed to kill.

{ Chapter 2 }

THE MORNING SUN continued to beat down on me like a hammer. Florida heat can get to people fast, raining exhaustion and stress with each rising degree. But I didn't mind. I'd felt hotter.

A lot hotter.

The sand looked like powdered sugar. I took off the boat shoes and held them with two fingers of my right hand. I stepped on the sand. It felt like powdered sugar too.

I walked a path between wiry beach fences that held back the dune grasses and other tropical foliage. Little green lizards dropped from the fence as I passed and scrabbled into the plants. A few brown ones too. They change colors to blend in. A good tactic.

I found the beach mostly empty. Eight in the morning on a Tuesday was still early for vacationers. I saw a couple of joggers huffing along the wet, packed sand near the water. There was a guy with a metal detector in front of me. I could hear it ticking along as the guy waved its disc-shaped reader over the sand.

"Morning," he said. I made to avoid him, but he swung the metal detector in front of me like a gate. "Sorry," he said.

I shrugged. "Morning back at you. Found anything?"

He smiled like he'd been asked that question a hundred times but still liked to answer it. "Cans and bottle caps mostly. But yesterday, I hit somethin' cool." He tucked the metal detector under his arm, took out a grayish rag, and peeled it open.

"Silver dollar," I said.

"Not just any silver dollar. This is an 1878 Morgan Silver Dollar. See the seven tail feathers on the eagle? That makes it worth a lot of money. Maybe four or five grand."

As I leaned forward to look, the metal detector started making all kinds of noise—sounded like an electric zipper going up and down.

"You a coin collector?" he asked, pointing at my case.

Realizing what had set off the detector, I let my case drift back behind my leg. "No. Just some equipment I use. Have a good day and congrats on the silver coin."

"Thanks," he said, recognizing my dismissal. "Oh, hey, you might want to get some shades on. Sun off this sand'll make you blind."

I smiled politely, thanked the man, but kept walking. He was right. The sun was bright off the sand. But I'd seen brighter.

A few hundred yards later, I walked close to the water. Time was when I wouldn't have gone within a thousand yards of this much water. I guess you could say I have a pathological fear of drowning. Maybe not for the reason you might think, but it's real.

I've gotten over it, mostly. I even let the thin surf trickle over my feet. The water was warm like bath water, almost relaxing. And water was the key to a complete resetting. So maybe the best way to describe water and me is a love-hate relationship.

In the hazy hot distance, a fishing pier stretched out into the Gulf. But my objective was a mile closer. Massive, irregularly shaped stones had been piled up like a great cairn on the shore.

GHOST

Rocks stretched maybe a hundred yards out into the water, a massive skeletal finger pointing out to sea.

I didn't know what I'd find there, at the end of those rocks...only that I would find something or someone.

The footing wasn't as treacherous as I'd first thought it would be because a trail of sand and soil had been packed into the center of the stones all the way out. I stood at the opening to the path. The tide was coming in. Seaweed, driftwood, a red and white bobber, and a clear plastic bottle sloshed around near the shoreline. Orange fiddler crabs popped in and out of holes in the sand. I took a deep breath and started walking.

I was maybe twenty yards up the trail when a young man I hadn't noticed earlier stood up from the end of the rocks and walked toward me. No, not a young man. A woman. Long dark hair tied back nearly out of sight, slight build and willowy, but definitely a woman. Late thirties, early forties, she moved slowly, her movements very natural and kind of dreamy. As she drew close, I saw her eyes better. Gray-green like the Gulf under storm clouds. They were sad, but there were no tears. She passed me without a word, but a few seconds later she called to me.

"Fair skin like that, you'll burn you stay out here too long."

I turned and smiled. "Thanks, but I'll be okay."

"No, really," she said, glancing at my suitcase, "it's different down here. You ought to put on some protection."

"Again, thanks. But I won't need it."

She shrugged. "Suit yourself." She turned. I turned. We both walked away, but I heard her mutter under her breath, "You're gonna burn."

The woman didn't understand. In my family, only about a third of us burn, and I'm not one of them.

No, the heat of the sun wouldn't hurt me. Not to say it wouldn't affect me at all, however. I stood on the end of the rocky finger, sweat trickling down my temples, down the crease in my back. Even with the luau shirt over it, the black tank top was maybe not my best choice.

Out in the gulf, I saw a couple of dorsal fins appear and disappear. I watched them for a while...the way they surfaced, an arch of darkness following a perfect curve before submerging. It was like the fins were on some kind of wheel under the water. Dolphins are amazing creatures. Controlled, powerful, swift—much smarter than most marine life and, if threatened, even able to take on a shark. We were kindred in that way. Taking on sharks, that is. As I said, I'm not such a fan of swimming.

Beyond the dolphins, a few colorful triangles meandered lazily. Sailors are an enthusiastic lot, out playing even this early. A Sun Odyssey 42DS was heading south. It bore a sail splashed in purple, blue, and teal. On the hull, near the transom was a code of numbers and letters: FL 6606 KR. Some kind of marine registration number, that much was obvious, but I didn't know much more than that. Still, I notice numbers...and I remember them.

Behind the first ship and closing rapidly was a longer Hunter 50 with light blue sails, each emblazoned with a cream colored conch shell. Just before it caught the Sun Odyssey, the Hunter turned and went out to sea. I noticed its code too: FL 6589 BD.

A third yacht was much farther out. I thought it might be an Oyster. Maybe a 625, but I couldn't be certain. And I couldn't read its registration number. I stopped and blinked at the sun-dappled Gulf and laughed to myself. "Well, I guess I know yachts pretty well," I muttered. I'd had missions in coastal regions before, of course, but I couldn't remember why I would have become so experienced with marine vessels. Another Memory Wash casualty.

"What's this going to be about?" I whispered. Nothing came to mind. Whatever I was waiting for, it hadn't shown up yet.

I stood there for a long time, a little too close to a lot of water for my comfort. But I'd learned a long time ago that sometimes, the most intelligent thing a person can do is wait. Rash decisions ruin a lot of lives.

Other beachcombers came up behind me, stood and looked, and then left. Mostly I was alone there. I got tired of standing, and the climbing sun was beginning to remind me of other, hotter situations.

I wasn't getting sunburned, but it felt like my mind might boil. I sat down on the edge there and watched the sun flashing on ten thousand ripples. It made me think of the waterbed. I felt nauseous.

One of the flashes not too far away was different. There was a bit of color in it. Red.

A strange color for the Gulf.

It got closer to my rocky perch. It wasn't just the sun on a ripple. It was something metallic. And it wasn't quite red. More of a dark reddish purple. Definitely a strange color for the Gulf.

Soda can? I couldn't tell. But whatever it was, it was about to float right by. I stood up and meticulously shimmied down the rocks until I was as close to the water as I could get without falling in. I crouched low and reached, but the object bobbed still out of reach and it threatened to drift away. I clambered back up the rocks and cast about, searching for something useful.

In the water a few yards closer to shore, was a piece of driftwood. It didn't look long enough, but it was all I had. I grabbed it, ran back, and stretched.

My first couple of swipes were short. The driftwood plopped into the water, but hit nothing. I moved over a bit, put one foot on the submerged edge of a stone and tried again. I tapped the thing once. It was rectangular and solid. Not a can. But it was still just out of reach.

If it floated any farther away, I'd have to jump into the water. And I really—*really*—didn't want to do that. I glanced over my shoulder. About twenty yards back, a teenager sat on the edge of the rocks and smoked a cigarette. I thought maybe I could throw him into the water to fetch the item I wanted. It was a clear win-win. I get what I need, and put out the cigarette too.

But my next attempt with the driftwood hit the top of the object. It came a few inches closer. That was all I needed. A few tip-taps later and I chucked the driftwood away and grabbed the object with my bare hand. Some kind of electronic device, I thought. It had a screen—maybe a little handheld computer or a big MP3 player. But I was holding it backward and upside down. There was a lens and a viewfinder. *Digital camera. Duh.*

Vizica, not high-end, but not disposable either. I pressed the power button. Nothing happened. *Probably ruined,* I thought. Saltwater and electronics don't usually mix well.

Still, it felt like I had what I had come for...and I was hungry, so I left the beach.

* * *   * * *   * * *   * * *

I needed cash, so I found a Junior Food Store that had an ATM. I went behind the building, sat in some shade, and placed my suitcase flat upon the ground. I placed my left hand on the back left corner of the case and my right hand on the front right. I rippled my fingers on both hands in a well-practiced, rhythmic pattern and waited. There was a hiss of compressed air. The locking mechanism released, and the lid of the case came up about an inch.

Glancing both ways and convinced that no one was coming, I lifted the lid. My eyes met a whole host of tools. Some I had used before. Others looked new to me. There was a plain silver card in the slot nearest the handle. The silver card, I knew very well. I grabbed the card and closed the case.

In the store, I went to the ATM and put the card in the reader. My account opened up immediately. John Spector, total balance $1,614.00.

My portion.

I withdrew it all. My silver card let me empty the account. I knew I would need all of the money...to the dollar. And my first expense would be lunch.

The Junior Food cashier told me there was a little family owned pizza joint called Bambinos just around the corner. It looked quiet. Italian sounded good. I went in and sat down. A waitress came over. Maria, according to her name tag. Fifteen or sixteen, given the way she popped her gum while she chewed.

"What can I get for ya', honey?" Cute Southern drawl. Probably called everybody, *honey*. Sweet kid.

"Water with three lemon wedges. And coffee. Definitely coffee."

"You gonna eat?"

"I'm going to eat...a lot," I said. "I just need to cool down for a bit with the water. Can you give me a minute?"

She seemed visibly relieved that I was going to order. Better tip that way, I guess. She was back in a hurry with the water, and she kept it filled for me while I waited and cooled down. She brought the coffee a few minutes later. It wasn't stellar. But it was coffee...a blessed, wonderful thing.

I got extra napkins and wiped down the camera. I opened it up and took out the battery. I couldn't see any corrosion or damage, but a few beads of water had found their way inside. I twisted up a napkin and shoved it in. Then I wadded the camera up in a bundle of napkins and waited some more.

"Okay, sweetie," Maria said, appearing at my elbow. Her gum popped. "What can I getcha?"

"You recommend anything?"

"Depends. You like things spicy?"

I thought I did. "Sure."

"Pepperoni calzone," she said. "Ricotta cheese, peppers, our sauce—best around."

"Sold," I said. "And extra peppers please."

Maria smiled and scribbled on her note pad. She popped her gum again and was gone.

I alternated sips of ice water and coffee, and then I unwrapped the camera. It was as dry as I could make it. I pushed the battery in and hit the power button. To my surprise, there was a faint musical tone and the camera came on.

Its default mode was photography. The lens telescoped out, and the restaurant interior appeared on the screen. The image was a little grainy, but given the swim in the Gulf, it wasn't too bad. There was a silver knob on the back. I turned it until the lens sucked back into the camera. *Viewing mode.* I pressed a silver toggle to flip through the pictures—if there were any on the memory card…and they hadn't been corrupted by saltwater.

There were pictures. Eighteen of them by the counter icon. The first one was blurry, too close to whatever it was and too out of focus to tell the subject. The second picture slid into view. A beautiful young woman. Red hair; very pale, porcelain-perfect skin; thin ruby-red lips.

GHOST

A man stood behind her, but the top of the shot cut off everything above the tip of his nose. All I could see was his sturdy cleft chin, his full lips, toothy smile, and the tip of his nose.

It was a strange pose, and something about it bothered me. Their positioning, so close and intimate, faces so very near to each other, made me think of a carnival photo booth. But the photo lacked the silly spontaneity of a photo booth. And the smiles weren't pleasant. His was a sharkish thing, full of know-it-all guile. And hers was lopsided like that of a TV zombie or a stroke victim...unsettling.

The third shot, I froze.

The fourth picture, I stopped breathing.

The fifth picture...

My throat constricted, and I seized the edge of the table. I'd tensed up so much that the nearly healed wounds on my back stung. I retched and fought to keep from losing it.

"Sir?" Maria the waitress called from behind the counter. "Sir, you all right? You need a doctor?"

She was at the table in a heartbeat. I flipped the camera flat so she couldn't see the picture. "No doctor. I'm okay."

"You sure? You're about as pale as you could be. Paler than before, even."

"No, I'm good."

I stood up, shoved the camera in my pocket, and tossed a twenty on the table.

"What about your food? You want it to go?"

"No! No...thank you," I said, tempering my voice. I grabbed my case and headed for the door. "I'm sorry, but I don't think I'll be able to eat...for a while."

{ Chapter 3 }

THE CAMERA BURNED in my pocket. And, as I strode through the humid air up Highway 30, one thought haunted me: there were thirteen pictures left.

I am no stranger to blood. And I have experienced more of death than most, but the images I'd seen at the pizza shop hit me like sledgehammer blows to the gut.

Memory Washing cleansed me of these kinds of images, removing the specifics—the all-too vivid, mental videos of disturbing violence—from my conscious mind. But there was nothing I could do about the dreams.

Unbidden flashbacks while I slept: macabre images of torn flesh, gasping breaths, and lives seeping away in spreading crimson pools. These scenes of grief rarely failed to haunt my sleeping psyche. The nightmares left me no memories, but rather...an aftertaste, a faint reckoning of evil things. It was kind of like smelling the sickly sweet scent of decay in the woods. You don't need to see the dead thing to know that it's there.

But now, I had a cold sensation spreading in the pit of my stomach. Somehow, the kind of death I'd seen in the pictures was different...worse. It was a kind of intimate horror that hooked itself to my psyche and burned there. I couldn't shake it.

Could it be a prank? Hollywood make-up, special effects? I didn't think so. But I needed to be certain. I needed a base of operations, somewhere to analyze the photos in private. Somewhere to do research. For a moment, I thought...I thought I might have a place to go. Someone owed me a favor, maybe invited me—but that fast, it was gone. Gone in the wake of last night's Memory Wash.

I found an F-Trans stop and waited for about fifteen minutes. When the bus came, I paid my three bucks and asked the driver, "Any hotels in the area? Any on your route?"

The guy scratched between his collar and his curly gray hair. "Two or three in Destin. Holiday Inn Express and a Motel 6 for sure, right next to each other."

Motel 6, I thought as I sank into a window seat. *We'll leave the light on for you.*

It might sound odd that I could remember a commercial slogan and not remember what I did last night, but it's not. It's the way the Memory Wash worked. It was the way things had to be for me to keep doing my job.

So I remembered Motel 6, and I liked the slogan. *We'll leave the light on for you.*

Turned out, the Holiday Inn Express was the first place on the route. They had plenty of lights on and high speed wireless Internet in every room, but their business center was closed for remodeling. No good for me. I have many tools in my suitcase. But I don't have a computer. If the Motel 6 didn't have computers I could use, I'd have to buy one. I had $1,593 left. It felt like a computer would eat too much of that.

The Motel 6 was a little less expensive than the Holiday Inn, but their business center was open and well stocked—

computers, a printer, and a scanner. So, under the name John Spector, I took room 7 on the first floor. Sixty-seven dollars in cash.

I went straight to the business center, but there was an old guy in there playing solitaire on one computer. A little blond girl, his granddaughter maybe, was immersed in some panda bear maze game on the other. Too risky for what I needed to do, so I continued up the hall to my room.

I pushed in the key card, shoved open the door, and stopped cold.

The room looked clean, smelled clean. But it felt wrong.

There was a chill in the air, but not the kind any air conditioner could produce. The door whispered closed behind me and I scanned the room. I kept the lights off and my suitcase ready, just in case. Thunder rumbled outside. I moved slowly, making no sound the long roll of thunder wouldn't mask.

Nothing in the bathroom or the shower. Nothing in the closet or in the gap between the wall and the bed. It still felt wrong.

The curtains.

Both the room darkening panels against the window and the decorative drapes were pulled shut. Light flashed up near the curtain rod. Thunder, deeper and more menacing, crashed outside and rattled the building. The curtains billowed but not from wind.

Netherview, definitely, I thought. I willed the change in my retinas. The world changed before my eyes and I saw...really saw things beyond the curtain of the temporal. The four walls and furniture of the hotel room vanished. In its place, there was a stone chamber rendered like a negative photo image but in real time. On the far side of the chamber, beyond a device of tangled wrought iron that could only be for torture, I saw a large arched window with a broken pane of glass. And clambering in and out of the jagged opening was a Shade. It noticed me now and hissed.

Not taking any chances, I thought. I flexed the muscles of my neck and shoulders and slowly lowered my suitcase to the floor. I squeezed the handle with my index and pinky fingers. With a hiss, the u-shaped handle disconnected from the case. The particle nether emitters on either end shimmered a pale green. It was fully charged. I'd have two pulses or one maximum-strength burst.

I stepped toward the window. *It was just one, and a little one,* I thought. *But it might not be alone.*

I took another step. The remaining shards of glass rippled in the window frame. I lunged, sliding to one knee. But the roamer was very fast. I caught just a glimpse of a translucent limb sliding away from the upper left corner of the window frame. I fired, but too slow. The pulse of the emitter passed through the windowpane but struck nothing else.

Just one, thank God. They were known to collect in the strangest places, but usually in buildings older than this Motel 6. Unless something violent had happened here.

Or, unless they were sent.

That made me wonder if its presence in my room was related to the camera. I couldn't see how. I had just found the camera. And I picked the hotel and room at random.

No, the Shade was just a roamer. Still, I'd need to be watchful. Even if it was just a random thing, the Shade might be indignant enough to tell others of its kind. Waking up to a throng of Shades is no fun.

The eerie chill was gone. It felt like a hotel room again. I switched from Netherview back to Earthveil. After putting the handle back on my suitcase to charge, I opened the curtains as wide as they could go and enjoyed the spectacle of the storm.

GHOST

Fat raindrops pelted the window. Wind whistled and howled. Lightning, sudden and white-hot, crackled above. Thunder had its way with the high rise condos on the Gulf shore in Destin, reverberating from building to building. I wished I could see the Gulf. The storm would color the water a potent slate gray-dark green mix and whip up miles of whitecaps. There's nothing like a raging storm and a tempestuous sea.

Divine violence.

I turned away from the storm, took the camera out of my pocket, and sat on the edge of my bed. I found myself hoping the camera wouldn't work. Not impossible, considering that the camera floated in saltwater for, who knew how long. Even if the water hadn't damaged it, the battery might be dead now.

But no, I knew the camera had come into my possession for a reason. I was certain it would work.

I pressed the power button. The musical chime was a little louder this time. The screen on the back of the camera came to life. I passed the first photo, the blurry one, and came to the pretty redhead with the guy behind her. She wore a sheer white camisole that spilled down the contours of her body. The material was just a shade lighter than her pale skin. Her lithe arms were tight to her sides, and her hands were folded in her lap.

I took a deep breath and advanced to the next picture. The knife came into view. A very unusual knife. It was as long as a violin bow, but the double-edged blade was only four inches. The rest of the weapon was six inches of dark wood handle and at least a foot of a narrow brass sheath. Small studs ran down the shaft and three more dotted the handle. There was an odd knob at the bottom of the brass part. It was shaped like a butterfly wing, and I guessed that turning it would cause the blade to retract or extend from the sheath.

The man held the blade horizontally at the level of her collarbone. The woman smiled on. I blinked and cringed inwardly, knowing what was coming.

A twitch of my thumb, and the next photo appeared. He'd pressed the knife against her neck, the blade biting deep, and blood already flowing. Still she smiled.

The fifth photo, the knife had been pulled clean through. Her mouth had dropped open. Her eyes were rolling back. I hated to look, but I couldn't turn away. If I was going to track down this killer, I'd have to study these pictures. Starting now. Thirteen photos to go.

Picture number six, he had his hand in her hair and had yanked her head back. The wound was a crimson waterfall down her neck and soaking the cami. The woman's life's blood seemed nearly spent. In the seventh picture, he'd let her head fall forward, and her long hair covered the wound like the wispy limbs of a weeping willow.

The eighth photo was blurred. Not out of focus, but blurred by the captured motion. The man was three quarters turned, his right arm bent and rotated like he'd just hit a tennis forehand. Judging by the angle and rotation of the woman's head, the man had struck her...hard. I wondered why. At that point, she was already dead.

Photo nine was a peculiar collage of elements. The woman's left hand and about six inches of her wrist jutted in from the lower right corner of the shot. A small table had fallen in from the left, spilling its contents on the dark brown carpet: a clutter of silver coins, mostly quarters; a tall fast food soda cup; and a rolled up newspaper. Filling the rest of the photo was the bottom of a darkened doorway and a blur of gray and black. Recognition danced elusively for a few moments.

GHOST

Shoes. I was looking at gray slacks below the knee and black shoes. The killer's. And he was walking away from the camera.

The tenth photo showed the man's right shoulder, a bit of a low door frame, and a very peculiar wall. It almost looked as if the photo itself was distorted because the wall seemed concave, curling from the ceiling to the floor. Again, it might have been an aberration from the camera's lens or a bit of exposure error, but the low couch almost seemed to glisten as if it'd been shrink wrapped. It was disorienting.

Shot eleven placed the man, still walking, but now in a dimly lit, narrow hallway with a vertical band of light ahead on the right that seemed like it might be a doorway. The man was curiously missing from the twelfth picture and, at first, the perspective was disorienting. The photo seemed to be taken from just inside the doorway of a new area but captured only the upper half of the room. A conical lamp rose up in one corner like a large, electric tulip, its halogen light burning bright, and it too seemed to follow the odd curvature of the wall. A row of unevenly spaced track lights lit the room from above and glimmered like spider's eyes.

A theory about the setting had already begun to coalesce in my mind. It was growing stronger, pic by pic. But the next photo scrambled my thoughts and sent a chill creeping across my shoulders. There were doghouses, six of them, side-by-side. It was almost ridiculously clear that that's what they were. Red, shingled roofs and vertical white siding—even a big red bowl in front of each. These were much larger than the ones you might find in a suburban backyard, and yet someone had gone to a lot of trouble to make sure these doghouses fit the stereotype—

I froze.

There were chains leading into the first five doghouses. Something pale and white reached out from the arched entrance of the center house. It was an arm.

A human arm.

{ Chapter 4 }

BLOOD-RED NAILS adorned the fingertips of the curled hand. *Dead or alive?* There was no way to tell. The color of her skin could go either way: pale white from lack of sunlight...or exsanguination.

I knew one thing: I wouldn't need to look in a mirror to see the color of my skin. I knew it was red, furious red. I had seen the photographic evidence of one woman murdered in cold blood. And now, at least one more woman—a precious human being—housed and chained like a mongrel in a kennel. There needed to be an accounting, and I longed to be the deliverer of that collection.

I hoped it would be my mission. The way everything had fallen into place, gave me little to doubt. The digital camera could have washed up anywhere, but it had come to me. I released a deep, heated breath...and swallowed, urging the rage down into its proper place. It could smolder until the time came. This was just the beginning, and there were still four pictures left.

Movement. I wrenched my head around, half expecting to find a throng of Shades gathering at my window. But it was nothing. Just a couple of seagulls grabbing worms from the seams of the rain-drenched sidewalk and then taking flight.

The final five photos were nearly the same as the first two with the redhead. In each photo, the clean-shaven man with the sharp nose revealed only the bottom half of his face. He stood directly behind a woman. Each of the five women were attractive and smiling with the same lopsided, off-smile worn by the redhead as she was having her throat slit.

There was a woman with huge, almond-brown eyes and long, gossamer-fine blond hair. A dark-haired beauty with ice blue eyes came next, followed by a young woman whose dark auburn hair covered half of her face. A girl with sandy brown hair, a cute pug nose, and tiny, timid eyes appeared next.

The knife wasn't visible in those last five pictures, but the threat was clear. There would be violence to come.

*** *** *** ***

I sat in the Motel 6 Business center at 12:13 a.m., the very first time I found it empty. Amazing. The last guy was in here for five hours, on a Saturday night. Five hours straight. I figured he must have been a grad student doing research or some such. But the browser history showed he'd been visiting site-after-site, looking at exotic types of yarn. I kid you not. Yarn.

I guess some visitors to Destin, Florida lacked imagination.

I placed my silver case on the floor between my feet and sat down to the computer. After a few clicks, I arrived at the Federal Bureau of Investigation homepage. I clicked the link "Submit a Crime Tip" and waited. A dozen blank fields stared back at me. A cursor blinked in the first field, the place to type my name, like it was mocking me. *What are you going to write? John Spector? You think that's your real name?*

GHOST

I shrugged. But I had an answer. Glancing back at the door to the hotel lobby, I went to my silver case. I triggered the release. Compressed air hissed out. I checked the door again. If anyone saw the kinds of things I have in this case, I'd have some awkward questions to answer. And some questions I wouldn't be able to answer.

There were three perfectly molded indentations in the upper right corner of the lid, side by side like a Roman numeral three. Clicked into each space was a 21-exabyte storage drive about the size of my thumb. I plucked out the one closest to the edge of the case—the Z-drive—glanced at the side of the computer, and then selected a Firewire adapter so I could use the drive.

The rainbow pinwheel of death showed up on the monitor, but it wasn't frozen. It was just dealing with the weight of the vast new memory open to it. *21 exabytes.* That's enough memory to store the entire contents of the Library of Congress.

Seven thousand times.

Like I said, a lot of memory.

The pinwheel disappeared. I logged into the drive and selected a program I facetiously called Hal after the space movie computer that went murderously insane. I double clicked the icon, and a droll, little smiley face appeared in a corner of the screen for a moment. It rolled its eyes at me. *That Hal, what a kidder.*

Above the Hal smiley, three check boxes appeared. I clicked the one on the far left. I didn't need the full suite. Hal was an identity generator. If I needed it, one click of a button would send Hal scouring the Internet, hacking every necessary database to secure me a new alias, one that would stand up to just about any level of scrutiny. It would include: birth certificate, school transcripts, medical records, driver's license, passport—

pretty much whatever I needed to be visible and yet stay invisible at the same time.

But like I said, I didn't need the full suite this time. Just a real identity that would check out on basic levels. One more click, and every field on the Submit a Crime Tip page filled instantly. According to this, my name was Regis Willoughby from Scottsdale, Arizona. *Way to go, Hal.* What a stupid name.

Regis Willoughby, not Scottsdale.

I went to work typing the details of the crime as much as I could describe them. I told the FBI where I found the camera, its make and model. I zipped a file for all the photos and attached them. I pressed submit. I put my tools in the case and went back to my room for sleep. Depending on the FBI's response, I'd know what to do next.

* * *   * * *   * * *   * * *

There was no response by 7:54 the next morning. It was an Internet tip, so not sure what I was expecting but still, I was disappointed. Motel 6 was a nice enough place to camp, but I was ready to move out, to take action. Impatience has always been my enemy. And yet I knew I could not take this case until I knew for sure it was for me. And for that, I needed to hear from the FBI.

I left the business center for the hotel restaurant. I hadn't eaten since the bagels the day before, and I felt like I could eat. A lot.

Turns out, the Motel 6 restaurant wasn't a restaurant at all, at least not for breakfast. Just a dozen or so square tables with two chairs each. I frowned. There was a sign that read: Continental Breakfast! Please enjoy. That was just code for: *Go somewhere else to eat.*

So I did.

And that turned out to be a blessing.

*** *** *** ***

About two blocks from the motel, around a mountainous thatch of cypress trees, I found a Godsend of a restaurant, especially for someone in search of breakfast. Brick foundation, big windows, yellow siding with black letters spelling out Waffle House. For me, it might as well have spelled *HOME*. I hope I never become so desperate that I wash away my memory of Waffle Houses.

"Munchkin-sized cereal boxes," I muttered. "I don't think so."

I felt a little conspicuous carrying my silver case into the restaurant, but when I stepped through the door, I think each one of the five employees behind the counter greeted me. Friendly bunch.

I nodded and took a booth in the corner. I didn't need to look at the menu.

A waitress in a beige, brown, and orange apron appeared beside me. "What can I get for you, shugah?"

Her voice sounded light and happy, but her eyes seemed tired, almost vacant. I felt suddenly sad. I looked again, and I thought maybe she had been someone's sweetheart once. Maybe she had hope, but her knight in shining armor rode off and left her with a child. I thought maybe she had several kids now and worked a lot of double shifts just to make ends meet.

"You need a minute?"

I blinked. I hadn't meant to, but I'd been *reading* her. It's something I can do sometimes. I don't know why it happens when it does. I just get a blurred reading, a kind of visual summary of a person's situation.

"No, I'm ready." I pointed at the picture on the menu. "I'll have the bacon melt on Texas toast, but can you triple the bacon?" She nodded. "Crispy not chewy?" She nodded again. "And I'll have the hashbrowns with cheese and onions, but make that a triple order, please."

Her eyes widened. "You fixin' to feed an army?"

"Something like that." I smiled amiably. I could almost hear echoes of children crying when she spoke.

"Well, you look like you could put that away. What'chu, six-four?"

I nodded.

"Uhmm, hmph," she said. "We got us a man in here." Then, she stepped away from the table, stopped just behind the counter and called out to the cooks at the wide gray stove. "Triple bacon, Texas triple plate, scattered, smothered, and covered!"

I smiled, deciphering the Waffle House code talk. Scattered on the grill, smothered in onions, and covered in cheddar cheese.

I smiled even more as I ate. And like the lady said, I put it all away.

She brought the check and asked if she could get me anything else. I thanked her and said no. She slid away to another table. In spite of the warm satiation in my stomach, I felt heartbroken. I held the little yellow check in my hand and saw her name. Adelade. I looked at the charge for my breakfast. Even with a 30% tip, it wouldn't be enough to help her. She needed more.

$525.00 more. I knew.

I paid the check at the register and went back to the table. I went to the silver case for the extra cash, and left my tip hidden mostly under the plate. She'd see an edge of green and know I hadn't stiffed her. Then she'd pick it up and find something more. I left the Waffle House wishing I could watch her, but knowing I couldn't. She would ask questions. Questions I couldn't answer.

Then, I saw the Cypress trees and had an idea.

I'm fast when I need to be. I slipped around the trees and found a spot where I'd be well out of sight, but I could still see. I sighed. Best laid plans. There was a glare on the Waffle House's windows, so I couldn't see my booth.

I was about to head back to the Motel 6 when the Waffle House door swung open. Adelade ran out into the parking lot. She searched left and right and, seeing no one, her shoulders sagged. She looked up at the sky, mouthed 'thank you' and put a hand up to her eyes. She wept right there in the parking lot.

Like I said, the morning turned out to be a blessing.

***   ***   ***   ***

At 9:03 a.m., to my utter astonishment, I found the business center empty. I checked the secure email account Hal had set up for my Regis alias. There was one new message. It was from Special Agent John LePoast, FBI.

Mr. Willoughby, thank you for taking the time to report a potentially dangerous crime. However, the "Smiling Jack" cases, as they've come to be known, are an Internet hoax. The photos first appeared on a social networking site in the fall twelve years back. At that time, the Bureau launched a full scale investigation. We ran photos in all the major newspapers and on network and local news, but no one identified the alleged victims. After a massive nationwide search, involving hundreds of thousands of man-hours, no bodies were found. During the eight year investigation, no missing persons reports revealing the identity of the purported victims came to light;

there were no grieving family members searching for these women; there were no bodies ever uncovered, and, besides the photos, which reemerged online in various forms and on a multitude of sites, especially around Halloween, no additional clues were ever revealed. The Bureau has officially closed the case, recognizing "Smiling Jack" as an Internet hoax.

    We recognize the realistic nature of the photos, and we're sorry for the distress they may have caused you. But you can rest assured that these are Hollywood-quality special effects and digital retouching at work, not a serial killer. If, in the future, you run into anything disturbing like this on the Internet, try running it by Snopes.com. Snopes is an investigative company specializing in Internet myths, rumors, and urban legends. You'd be amazed how many kidnappings, killings, vampires, and UFOs get reported to the FBI each year, wasting the Bureau's resources that could be utilized for prevention and solution of real criminal activity.

Sincerely,
John LePoast
Special Agent in Charge

Check with Snopes, huh? I thought. *Leave the FBI alone so they can tackle real crime?* It sounded to me like Special Agent LePoast had maybe drunk a little too much coffee. Either that or someone took his favorite spot in the Bureau parking lot. It didn't matter to me really. I got what I needed: clear direction.

If the FBI was off the case, I was definitely on it.

{ Chapter 5 }

"THIS IS DIFFERENT," said Special Agent Deanna Rezvani, pacing in front of her partner's cubicle.

"It really isn't, Rez," LePoast replied tersely. He didn't look at her. He kept typing. Maybe she would go away.

"These are different women," Rez explained. "No matches to the women killed during the original investigation. Six...new...victims."

"So?"

Rez huffed incredulously. "So? So, Smiling Jack has gone active again. He's taken more women. We've got to act on this."

"Smiling Jack," LePoast coughed out the words. "There is no 'Smiling Jack.' Just some nutball with a lot of video tech gear and a sick sense of humor."

"You don't know that."

"And you don't know anything different. Plus, we've always had the pictures, Deanna! Where'd that get us?"

Rez ignored the question. "We've never had the camera before. The killer's prints could be all over it."

"Alleged killer, remember?" He sighed and thumped the delete key. Third time in a row he'd misspelled *reconnaissance*. Ignoring Deanna Rezvani wasn't going to work. It seldom did.

He swiveled his chair, banging his knee smartly on the desk. He spoke through pain-clenched teeth. "We've never had a missing persons report. No one recognizes the alleged victims. We've never found a body—there's no crime."

"You're a hypocrite, John," Rez replied. "And lazy."

He turned back to the keyboard and whined, "Oh, now I'm hurt. Mommy, make the bad woman go away."

Rez ignored the deflection. "When you first saw those shots, you said yourself they were real, that detail like that couldn't be faked."

"That was before I saw what CGI could do," LePoast replied. "That was before we mobilized almost the entire FBI and came up with zilch. Girls that hot, somebody would have missed them if they'd been killed. Can't be real, Rez. CAN'T BE."

"Girls that hot? You sexist, son of a—"

"Don't bother trying to flatter me, Rez."

"But these women—"

"Look, Rez," LePoast interrupted, "I know this was your first big case back in the day. I know it burns you that you couldn't solve it."

"It's not that!" Rez fired back. "We're talking the murder of twelve—no thirteen, now—maybe more to come."

"What's your evidence?" LePoast asked. "'Cuz, that's what this boils down to. Prove something."

"That's what I'm trying to do," she said. "We have new evidence now. We've got new pictures...and the digital camera that took them."

"Or maybe we don't," LePoast said.

The corner of the office where LePoast's cubicle was fell silent. He went back to typing.

"We could be missing an angle," Rez said. "Maybe this is more than murder."

LePoast stopped typing. "How do you mean?"

"It could be human trafficking," she said.

"What?" he asked. "Like sex slaves? But why kill off the women? That's his money train."

"Maybe it's something darker," she replied. "Weird fetishes or that kind of thing. A couple ATF guys I know were telling me about some sick stuff being brought in from overseas, Eastern Europe, I think."

"Overseas, huh?" he echoed. "Now, I'm confused. You think the sex slave kingpin from the Republic of Creep-istan is vacationing down in Miami—"

"Destin," Rez corrected.

"Whatever. So this sick pup is catchin' some rays in Florida and while he's coolin' off in the Gulf, he just happens to chuck his camera full of nasty pics into the water? Right."

That stumped Rez for a few seconds. "I don't have all the answers," she said. "But the loose ends are too promising to let it go. I could be right. The ATF guys know what they're talking about. It could be human trafficking. Maybe Smiling Jack's operation is overseas."

LePoast's fingers flew back to the keys. "Then, my dear Sherlock, it's not our concern."

She stopped pacing and huffed, "You're a piece of work, you know that?"

"That's me: John LePoast, a piece of work. Right you are. Speaking of work..."

"We should at least check out the camera."

"I bet the camera didn't even take the pictures. I'm tellin' ya,' Rez, it's just some kook who downloaded the photos from the Net. I mean, what kinda stupid name is Regis Willoughby anyway? That's totally made up."

"All the same, if it is a hoax, it could net us the guy who started the hoax in the first place. That would be worth something, right?"

"Don't pull that crap on me, Rez. I know how you feel about the Smiling Jack case. That's not your angle and you know it."

Agent Rezvani crossed her arms and glared. The buzz of the Hoover building, third floor, washed over them. Hushed conversations, phones ringing, keyboards, and old printers.

LePoast ran a finger under his collar and shrugged uncomfortably. He wasn't intimidated by her status in the Bureau. He had six years on her. And he certainly wasn't cowed by her size. She was 5'4" to his 6'2." But Deanna Rezvani had a presence about her—a mix of grace, confidence, and moxy—that filled up the room and made her partner a little nervous.

It didn't help that she was drop-dead gorgeous.

She had rich brown hair, burnished by the sun, curled naturally and tied back in a loose tail just above the nape of her neck. Big, brown, almond-shaped eyes under thin golden brows, cute nose, and full lips that curled impishly in the corners—and always iced with that dark plum lipstick. Her olive skin was smooth and lightly tanned, and she always rolled up the sleeves of her white blouse to the elbows. Even in FBI-acceptable attire, Dee Rezvani looked like a bronze statue of Venus. But LePoast was a married man, so he didn't notice such things.

Still, he squirmed a little under her expectant gaze. He felt a little like a bug getting roasted by the sun under some cruel kid's magnifying glass. "Whaddaya want, Dee?"

"I want to go to Destin," she said.

"Don't we all," LePoast shot back. "Some of the sweetest beaches in the world."

"You know what I mean. I want to meet this Regis, size him up. Something about this case...I don't know. I just feel like something's going to break. I want to be there when it does."

"The case is closed, Dee. Sheesh, it's not even an actual case. You wanna go to Florida, go to the Deputy Director."

***   ***   ***   ***

"Absolutely not." Deputy Director Ulysses Barnes looked like he'd been hewn from granite, or perhaps something harder. Fifty-nine years old, ex-Navy Seal, ex-Navy Seal Instructor, Barnes still exercised the equivalent of the Ironman Triathlon each and every month. At his desk, he sat with thick arms in front of him, knob-knuckled hands clasped. He was as rigid as could be, looking very much like the head of a sledge hammer. He just sat there, impassive and unyielding.

Deanna Rezvani waited, but she knew that game wouldn't work on the Deputy Director like it did on LePoast. Barnes had the constitution to out-wait anyone. As Deputy to the most powerful officer in the FBI, Barnes acted as a kind of physical filter for his boss—nothing short of a state of emergency got past him to the Director.

Once, a junior agent gave Barnes a wooden replica of former President Truman's "The Buck Stops Here" plaque. Deputy Director Barnes tossed it in the trash and said, "Truman was a wuss."

"Deputy Director, Sir," Rezvani said. "Please reconsider. The Smiling Jack case could be one of the worst serial murder strings in U.S. history. Twelve dead already, and now six more taken? If we can get something from this Willoughby, we might be able to rescue some of these women."

"Do you hear yourself, Agent Rezvani?" Only his lips and square jaw moved. "You're using phrases like 'could be,' 'if,' and 'might be.' That's because that's all Smiling Jack is. We never had anything besides those blasted pictures."

"We had twelve pictures," Rez said. "The same twelve, cycled through over and over again. This is a different set of victims. Smiling Jack is going active again."

"Or maybe it's not. I don't need to tell you what people can do with photo editing software, right? It's probably some Goth kid who's good with a computer, trying to make it look like Smiling Jack has a new set of victims. If there ever were any victims, that is. I'm sorry. You're a good agent and smarter than the Director and me put together. But you let your passions take you places you shouldn't ought'a go."

He went back to absolute stillness. Agent Rezvani waited a dozen heartbeats and said, "The answers are there, Sir. Destin, Florida. The killer screwed up and left something we can use. I feel it."

"You really want to go?"

"Very much, Sir."

"Then go."

Rezvani shifted weight from one foot to the other. "Sir?"

"...on vacation."

"Wha—?"

"You want to go to Destin, take vacation time and go."

"But, Sir, this is FBI business. Surely—"

"No, Agent Rezvani, this is not FBI business. Not for years now. This is a private hunch of your own. If it means that much to you, follow it on your own time. We spent years on this—*YEARS*—that and enough manpower to invade China on...this

'Smiling Jack.' We won't waste any more of the FBI's resources. My final word."

A bank vault's door slamming shut.

An avalanche of boulders thundering into the middle of the road.

A wrought iron portcullis crashing down to seal off the castle gatehouse.

Rez figured she could take her pick of the images. It was all the same when Director Barnes gave his final word. "Yes, Sir," she said. She spun on one heel and marched away.

"Agent Rezvani?"

She stopped, turned. "Sir?"

"If this turns into more than a hunch, call me."

{ Chapter 6 }

STATE OF THE ART.

Technology the way he liked it.

The computer flickered to life with a melodic chime and, as the drives and fans kicked in, the room seemed to thrum with possibility.

The encryption program launched at once. He typed in a long series of numbers, entered once, typed a three letter code, entered again, and then...typed his name.

Jack, he thought, rubbing the tip of his sharp nose. *Maybe not that ironic. After all, the killings were reminiscent of another Jack who used a blade. Still, a kind of irony. They know my name and yet they do not know it.*

He smiled. There was a singularly unique pleasure from understanding the details that others might never guess.

Jack glanced at the myriad of application icons, his eyes landing as they often did on Tournament Chess. *Business first,* he reminded himself. He clicked the Mixer icon. His custom coded browser went to work, and close to a dozen websites snapped open in orderly rows across the vast monitor. Beneath each homepage dropped a long scroll bar. Jack bounced from site to site, reading every visitor's comments and growing more and more convinced.

When he'd read them all, he rocked back in his chair and released a deep, huffing laugh. The comments ranged from sarcastic to sadistic, comical to creative. But none of the comments—not even one—captured the kind of passion required to violate Jack's theory. And none of the responses came from the proper audience either. *Hypocrites,* Jack thought. *Daring to condemn and then doing nothing.*

Jack closed the window and opened another. A dozen new articles appeared, and the headlines were not promising. He browsed several of his favorite sources and discovered that there had been no change in the recent legislation push. If something didn't happen soon, the law would likely be overturned.

"Blasted Justice Kearn!" Jack muttered. "Old man bowing to trends in the polls? Disgusting."

Jack thought about Molly. Surely the FBI could be more clever now. Surely the nation could be more clever...now. They would all make the connection, wouldn't they? But thus far, the evidence pointed to the contrary. Not a peep from the FBI, or any law enforcement for that matter. And the polls, the reports from Washington, the rumors suggested that, if anything, the opposition was gaining ground.

Chaos, Jack thought. *Bunch of Nazis. What will it take to get through to you? To get through to everyone?* Jack wondered, pressing the sharp nail of his index finger into the soft pad of his thumb. Any harder and it would bleed. He sighed. He'd always thought blood would make the difference. That people would come out of their collective stupor. It had worked the first time...and the second, hadn't it?

But the third time pays for all. The Supreme Court decision that loomed now threatened to change things more violently than anything before. And the change would last a very long time. Senator Esperanzo was almost a shoe-in to win the election in November, and he'd sure as heck make sure the court stayed conservative. This could not go forward. This could not be allowed to be. It was absolutely imperative that they got the message this time.

But maybe with all the blood and gore in the movies and even now on TV, people had become desensitized. They wouldn't care. Blood in pictures would no longer move them. Jack wondered again about Molly. Would she be wasted? Would her big moment come and go without so much as a ripple in the public consciousness?

Jack closed Mixer. He needed something else to tax his mind.

He double clicked the Tournament Chess icon. The program was a beast and took almost a full ten seconds to load. Jack had reverse engineered several of the market's most challenging chess software packages to create a personal Frankenstein program that harnessed only the best features of all the others. He searched through a listing of games in progress and eventually decided on Garry Kasparov. It had been over a year since Jack made a move against the computer simulated Russian Grandmaster, but he remembered the board as if they had been playing all morning and only paused for lunch. Cyber-Kasparov had offered an intriguing gambit, one Jack thought he just might accept. But, as with all such risks, there would come a time when payment would be demanded.

Jack shrugged and, as soon as the board materialized on screen, he moved his queen's pawn against his opponent's seemingly exposed bishop. Then the alarm on Jack's watch beeped. Though rather shocked that 4:30 had arrived already, Jack stood up so fast that he didn't even see Cyber-Kasparov's answering move. Time was everything to Jack, both a precious resource not to be squandered and a brilliant but rigid taskmaster not to be defied.

Jack went to the massive chrome refrigerator, withdrew one of a dozen meals he had prepared in the morning, and carried it to the elevator door near the study. He stepped inside. The doors closed. Jack didn't press the button for the loft or the basement. Instead, he inserted his key, twisted it a half turn left and a half turn right. The car descended smoothly, past the basement, and came to a halt on a very special floor.

The elevator opened to a spherical chamber ribbed with curving steel girders. Six yards away from the elevator, recessed into the wall, was a brushed aluminum door. Jack typed in a key code on the wall panel. The airlock separated with a hiss, and Jack entered.

He had barely closed the door when he noticed two very unfortunate things: a most unsavory smell and...whispers.

"Hurry up," one voice said. "Get back in."

"Shhh," a second voice warned, "he's coming."

Jack shook his head and sighed. He placed the meal on a shelf next to an assortment of black plastic canisters and then walked to the room he called *the kennel*. "I am terribly disappointed," he said, removing something from his pocket. "Pets are not permitted to speak until play time. Pets are not permitted to leave their homes until play time. And yet...I heard voices."

Jack paced in front of the *pet houses* and tapped each roof with a baton-like instrument. "Who was it?" Jack asked. "Lucinda?" Jack bent at the waist near the first house. "No, no, not Lucinda. Not kind, trustworthy Lucinda."

He came to the second house. "You know my discipline is just. You also know it will be more severe if you do not come forward right away—"

GHOST

A pale hand emerged from the doorway of the third house. "Ah, Pamela, I thought that was you," Jack said. "You've always been so social, so curious. Come out now. And who were you with? Midge?"

"No, no!" came an urgent whisper from the second house.

A hand slithered out of the fourth house. Jack sighed again. "Oh, Erica...and you were doing so well too. Come out, then. You and Pamela know better."

Pamela came out first, a lithe young woman with a shock of silk-fine, very dark auburn hair. Her skin was pale, and she wore nothing but a sheer white top and gray shorts that reached midway down her thighs. Erica emerged slowly and padded over to stand beside Pamela. Erica's skin was ivory white, and she wore the same scant outfit. But her sable hair was braided, drawn back, and tied at the base of her neck. Her blue eyes glimmered with tears.

"So that's what you were doing, was it?" Jack asked. "Braiding hair? It is beautiful." Jack caressed Erica's skin and let his fingers slide down one of the braids, off to her shoulder, and along the contour of her hip. There was a telling bulge in Erica's abdomen. Then, Jack understood the smell. "Erica, did you vomit?"

She nodded and blinked more tears. It gave her eyes the appearance of the purest ice, melting. "I'm sorry," she said. "I've felt ill all morning, and I dirtied my home. That's why I wanted the braids...to feel beautiful again."

"Pity you didn't wait until play time. Who came out first?"

"I did," Erica whispered.

"Very well," Jack said. "Hold out your hand." He grasped the end of the baton and pulled. It telescoped out until it about eighteen inches long. It ended in a small noose made of bent wire, looking something like a light bulb's filament.

He held out the baton and lay the wire on her palm. Erica closed her hand around it and shut her eyes.

*** *** *** ***

"Do you understand why I have done this?" Jack asked.

Erica and Pamela nodded, tears leaping from their cheeks to the cold floor. Neither of the young women could speak and they wouldn't be able to for several minutes.

"Return to your quarters, my darlings. I bear you no grudges. I will bring your meals soon. Lucinda is first today. Her turn. Oh, and Erica, see to it that your living space is cleaned."

She nodded again, half bowed, and disappeared into her quarters. Clutching her hand, Pamela slunk away as well. Jack spun on his heel and went to the first dog house. "Lucinda, my sweet, it is time."

A blond pixie of a woman crawled out and stood. Her huge green eyes glittered.

Jack took her by the hand and led her out of the kennel. "You've been crying," he said. "Were you feeling sorry for Pamela and Erica?"

She shook her head.

"You may speak."

"No, it's not them. I warned them they shouldn't disobey. They chose not to listen."

Jack gave a proud smile and led Lucinda into a room with a low ceiling, dim lighting, and a half-dozen quaint tables. The chairs were black wrought iron as were the decorative accents forming arches above the tables.

GHOST

He held a chair for her. "Our usual table." She sat. He sat and took her hands. "Your tears disturb me. If you do not weep for Erica and Pamela, what then?"

She blinked, starting new rivulets of silver on her cheeks. "I...I miss Molly."

"Shh, shh, shh, now. I am so sorry. But she chose to go and could not find her way back. Molly is lost to us now."

"I...I know."

"But what about Carrie?" Jack asked. "You know how she loves to brush your hair? She's nice, isn't she?"

"Yes," Lucinda said. "Carrie's very nice, but I miss Molly."

"You have many fond memories of Molly, yes?"

"I do."

"Cherish them. They enrich your soul. Learn and grow from them. And now, won't you eat?" He pushed the plate toward her.

"My stomach hurts."

Jack smiled knowingly. "I'll just be a moment."

He returned with a small tray. He wiped Lucinda's upper arm and shoulder with an alcohol solution and then dried her meticulously. Jack said, "I think this will help. It usually does." He peeled a still-smoking patch from its plastic contact sheet and then gently pressed it onto her shoulder.

"The chill feels good," Lucinda said. She smiled and ducked her head demurely. Then, she closed her eyes and let her head fall back. "Oh, I think I could eat now."

Jack smiled. "So very glad to hear it. Perhaps later, if you're feeling up to it, I'll send Doctor Gary to come and see you."

"At play time?" Lucinda asked.

"Of course."

***   ***   ***   ***

At exactly six o'clock, Dr. Gary came home. He placed his briefcase on the floor by the antique coat rack. "I have news, Jack."

"So do I," Jack replied. "But you go first."

"All right. We've accepted Stricker and Lends' contract. It's final. They are throwing a huge party. All the surgeons are invited."

"Sounds wonderful."

"It will be," Gary said. "You'll need to dress the part, of course."

"Of course," said Jack.

There came a sudden knock to the kitchen door. "Expecting someone?" Dr. Gary asked.

"No, not today," Jack said. "It's Saturday."

"Still, you should change."

Jack disappeared down the hall, and Dr. Gary went to the kitchen door. He glanced through the draped window and saw a harried looking woman with very curly hair and very thick glasses. He recognized her at once and opened the door.

"Ah, Mrs. Bell," Dr. Gary said. "Sophie's mother, correct?"

"It's Karen," the woman said, glancing around nervously. "I mean yes, I'm Sophie's mom, but call me Karen."

"What can I do for you, Karen?" Dr. Gary asked.

"It's about Thursday," she said, trying to peer over Dr. Gary's shoulders. "Is Jacqui around?"

Dr. Gary kept the door semi-closed but called over his shoulder, "Sweetheart, Mrs. Bell is here," he called. "Are you free?"

Jack appeared a moment later, wearing a floral sundress and flats. "Hi, Karen," Jack said, taking the door and sliding between Dr. Gary and the visitor. "What brings you here on a Saturday?"

GHOST

"Well, I was a half hour late," Mrs. Bell said. "So I owe you a check, but I was wondering if we could...could we just push it to next week's payment? We're a little tight right now."

Jack smiled and said, "I see. Well, you're usually so timely...sure, just apply the penalty to next week."

Mrs. Bell offered a great deal of thanks and said goodbye. Jack shut the door.

"You handle them so well," Dr. Gary said.

"Not so different from the children," Jack replied. "Or the pets."

"All require more patience than I have." Dr. Gary strolled about the kitchen, making a show of sniffing the air. "What do I smell?"

"Prime rib, slow cooked with scallions and garlic," said Jack.

"My favorite. What's the occasion?"

"It is bittersweet, I'm afraid. That's the news I mentioned. We're going to need to lose Lucinda."

"So soon after Molly?"

Jack nodded. "Like you said, the tide is turning. I fear for the court's decision. It doesn't look good."

Dr. Gary shook his head. "It's all we talk about in the clinic," he said. "But tell me, why Lucinda? She's always been so complacent."

"And obedient," Jack said. "But she has festering attachment for our departed Molly. She won't let it go, and you know how the temperament can spread."

"I understand." Gary cupped Jack's chin in his hand.

Jack pulled away. "Erica will need a procedure," he said.

Dr. Gary let his head roll backward on his neck. "I suppose I should not be surprised," he said.

"No," Jack said, his voice high and clipped. "You've spent too many occasions *playing* with our pets."

{51}

Dr. Gary made a clicking sound in his throat, then said, "You've never had a problem with it before. You are welcome to indulge as—"

"You know it's not the same for me," Jack whispered.

"Yes, yes, I know," Dr. Gary replied. "Well...I will take care of the procedure in the next day or two." He cleared his throat and changed the subject. "And what of our little message in a bottle plan, any response?"

"Nothing yet." Jack sighed. "Ten cameras and not one law enforcement hit."

"Give it time. Rome wasn't built in a day."

"But time is running out. The ruling could come in less than two weeks, maybe sooner." Jack looked plaintively at Dr. Gary. "I'm afraid we'll lose."

"Jack," Dr. Gary said, softening the gravely tone in his voice, "we cannot lose this fight. The stakes are too high. We are on the right side. We will not lose."

{ Chapter 7 }

I BOOKED ANOTHER NIGHT at the Motel 6. Another sixty-seven dollars in cash to keep my base of operations in Destin, Florida. I slept fitfully, dreamed horribly, and awoke feeling pretty much like road kill.

Though I'd miss the hash browns scattered, smothered, and covered, I didn't go back to the Waffle House. I might see Adelade again. She might ask questions. Worse, she might give me the credit for helping her.

A block inland, I found a little greasy spoon called the Echo Inn Diner. $12.50 for a heaping plate of food. The home fries were tossed with onions and red peppers and then cooked in bacon grease. I also had a delicious crispy meat called scrapple. I asked the waitress what was in it. She said I didn't want to know.

When I returned to the hotel, I found the same old guy and his granddaughter occupying the hotel's business center. I waited just outside for three hours. The whole time he played, he looked irritated, and she looked bored. I wondered why, on such a beautiful day, they didn't go enjoy Destin outside, especially the powdered sugar beaches.

I finally got on the computer around noon. I had business, but I couldn't resist. I looked up scrapple ingredients. The waitress was right. I really didn't want to know.

The contents of my stomach still roiling like a dryer full of cinderblocks, I went to work on the case history. A simple search on "Smiling Jack" netted me close to 30 million hits. I knew that roughly 29,999,800 of those were worthless mentions in Tweets and blog articles. So I went to the major news sources first: *NY Times*, *Washington Post*, CNN, etc. The first was a ten-year-old article from The Times that chronicled the appearance of the first "victim" photographs. In a matter of hours, the story went viral. The Internet flooded with chatter, mostly public outcry and fear. The FBI set up a task force, and local authorities mobilized. But no bodies had been found, no one identified the victims, and no one knew where jurisdiction began and ended.

The case name "Smiling Jack" had been coined by a blogger and gained momentum by February that same year where it appeared in a *Washington Post* page one banner headline. The murder weapon in each of the photographs had been the same strange blade that I'd seen used on the young redheaded woman.

Nico Mendle, a hobbyist and blogger interested in history's serial killers, noted that the murder weapon resembled a surgical knife of the kind purportedly used by Jack the Ripper. I clicked on the link and a jpeg of the "Don Rumbelow Blade" taken at the Museum of London in Docklands appeared. It did indeed look similar to the weapon used in the photographs. There was no brass sheath, however. And the cutting edge was four times as long as the weapon used in the Smiling Jack photos. Mendle had noted the ghoulish smiles on the killer and all the victims and coined the phrase "Smiling Jack."

The door to the business center swung open, startling me, and there stood the old man who had been playing solitaire all morning. The little blonde girl hid behind his leg. I minimized the knife window and turned just in time to hear the old guy say, "Sorry, Carri-boo, we'll have to come back later."

Caribou? That didn't sound like a very nice thing to call a little girl. I pictured the shaggy reindeer of North America and shrugged.

Over the next hour, I read dozens of articles spanning the next six years and, to the FBI's credit, the content of the national news spelled out everything just the way Agent LePoast had. The "Smiling Jack" photographs had appeared on thousands of websites. There seemed to be an influx of new blogs dedicated to "the case" every month. And the popular buzz seemed to intensify each October, especially around Halloween.

The investigation was spearheaded by techies who used every trick in their collective Web-crawling bag to trace the originator of the photographs. This proved beyond daunting because so many sites—true crime, missing persons, blogs, voyeurs, social media, and news—had posted some or all of the photos. The FBI focused on the earliest posts and even unofficially enlisted the aid of Homeland Security. But the cyber-trail was a dead end. More like a loop, really. An infinity loop.

The photos' first posting turned out to be a link from another posting of the photos, one that came chronologically later. One site digitally referred to the other as the originator, which shouldn't have been possible. But, Smiling Jack—or some associate of his—had found a labyrinth of code to make it work. I made a mental note to find out just how many folks had the technological know-how to pull something like that off. I suspected it might be an uncomfortably high number.

Beyond the "office agents" working on the digital trail, thousands of law enforcement personnel had participated in an international manhunt. A list of "interesting persons" from the web postings had been generated. Slowly, each one had been investigated. The list narrowed until no stone had been left unturned. In the end, no evidence other than the photographs had been uncovered. No missing persons. No bodies. The FBI officially closed the case, and for four years, no other photos surfaced. Until now.

I peeked out of the business center to make sure no one was about to walk in on me. It was all too easy to imagine the old man coming back. If he saw anything in my case, he'd have plenty of questions, especially about my tools. Pressurized air hissed as I opened my silver case. I kept the lid up just long enough to get what I needed, this time, the X-drive.

The Z-Drive, Hal included, was all finesse. It captured all the physical requirements for every kind of identification and recreated them for me. The X-Drive, on the other hand, was the equivalent of a digital bazooka. All muscle. If there was a barrier, the X-drive blew it up. If there was a fire wall, the X-drive knocked it down. If there was a back door or a trapdoor, or any door at all, the X-drive would hack, blast, and gouge until it found a way in. I had two searches in mind for the X-drive this time.

First, I took the original "Smiling Jack" web link, the one that sent the FBI into the infinity loop, and ran the X-Drive on that. Five minutes went by. Ten. Up popped a red error message. This did not bode well. Whoever Smiling Jack really was, he was absolutely brilliant. From what I could tell, it hadn't so much kept the X-drive out, but rather had let it through...an easy slide but only to useless places. It was like opening a locked door for a pursuer but greasing the floor so that he slid right on by.

Jack, or whoever Jack employed, had written a code that managed to stonewall the X-drive. I'd bet all $934 of my remaining dollars that the FBI wouldn't be quite as successful.

Law enforcement agencies rarely release all of the details of a case to the press. It was one way to filter crime tips. Anyone who knew something about the case that had not been revealed to the general public would be taken very seriously. Surely the FBI had withheld something. Maybe it wasn't enough for the FBI to keep the case open, but it might be enough for me. I needed everything they had.

I brought up the FBI home page. Naturally, the ultra powerful, ultra secretive law enforcement agency would keep their internal databases walled off from their public face online. But most webpages, most servers, most anything networked and connected to the Web, had a back door. Garden variety hackers wouldn't find those back doors. Even Digital Age industrial spies might not find the back door if the system of encryption was sophisticated enough. Fortunately, the X-drive was very good at backdoors.

Five minutes later, thanks to an obscure digital trail—an order of drinking straws for the FBI cafeteria—I had access to one of the Bureau's mainframes. Cases didn't have searchable titles like "Smiling Jack," so I had to find another way. The problem was, the FBI had built-in monitors for sensitive information. They'd created beneficial viruses to trace and capture invading algorithms and domains. The X-drive posted a red bar graphic showing that I had three minutes before my information was captured. If it was, the FBI would know my X-drive's identifiers. If they back-doored into my X-drive, they would discover some things. And then...they would come looking for me.

As I searched frantically, the red bar graphic continued relentlessly on.

*** *** *** ***

FBI Special Agent Dee Rezvani began her *vacation* by stepping off a plane at Panama City Beach Airport. The humidity hit her like a wet towel, and she knew immediately that she hadn't packed enough full changes of clothes. *Welcome to the Florida Panhandle,* she thought, pulling at her blouse so it wouldn't stick to her back.

Like the flight, she paid for a rental car on her Visa card. Everything had to be on her own dime. Assistant Director Barnes hadn't left her any choice about that. Rez shrugged and slid up onto the high seat of the Nissan SUV. She'd saved enough money over her seven years in the Bureau to live comfortably without new income for quite a while. She cranked the engine. Six cylinders—decent power. Better than the heap she drove around in D.C.

Even with a decent salary, Rez didn't treat herself to much. No sprawling condo with pool and tennis privileges. No new car. And, other than an occasional filet mignon from the grocery store, no high-end groceries either. In fact, Rez didn't allow herself much of anything aside of work.

She had no family, which wasn't really by choice. Not a lot of friends. No husband or boyfriend, certainly not from the Bureau. The male agents fell into two camps, neither of whom appealed to Rez in the least. Some were too strong: cocky, overpowering, or even slimy. They saw her as an entitlement or achievement, someone to ogle and tell dirty jokes about later. Other agents were too weak: unnerved by her looks or intimidated by her abilities. Rez was looking for a secure man who would love her, respect her, and challenge her. Special Agent Dee Rezvani had hunted and captured dozens of criminals, but she'd yet to get so much as a sniff of the man she really wanted.

Not that she'd spent much time actively looking.

Too busy in school—MS in forensic science, MA in law—led to too busy in career. Through diligence and laser-sharp attention to detail, Rez had risen from recruit to field agent to special agent in just three years. Her work eventually led to the capture of Sid Hain, the killer known as "the Scientist" due to the horrific experiments he'd performed on his victims. Rez had been made a Violent Crimes Division Leader and moved to D.C. where she'd flourished ever since. And that all left little time for personal or romantic life.

Which was why she was taking a vacation to find a serial killer.

Rez sighed, put the SUV in gear, and pulled out of the rental lot. She headed west on Route 98 toward Destin. Vacation or not, she had a suspect for the first time in the Smiling Jack case. His name was Regis Willoughby.

***   ***   ***   ***

The X-Drive's red bar graphic told me I'd already used up two and a half minutes to find any "Smiling Jack" files. I had to search out the web addresses of some of the original blogs to cover the murderous photographs. I figured the FBI tech guys would have scoured those websites for anything useful. They'd have put their findings in a report. They had, and within the first file, I found links to others.

Several thousand others. I'd let my X-drive have at those as soon as I could, but I had to get them all first.

I had all of 30 seconds left to gather information from all those pages. I clicked from link-to-link, frantically clicking link copy commands. The red graphic bar showed me I had just a few seconds. I captured 3 more pages of data and clicked the kill button. The connection was cut. The backdoor trace failed.

I breathed again.

The next order of business: the camera. I doubted the killer left a paper trail purchasing the camera he'd used to take his ghoulish photos. Still, the camera's history might give me something I could use. I found the Vizica homepage easy enough and then the model. It was a Vizica Sport with an 8 megapixel resolution, 200X zoom, and 50GB built-in memory, enough for thousands and thousands of photographs. The killer had taken only 18. One other problem: the Vizica Sport was virtually waterproof. That explained why the camera still worked.

I removed the battery from the slide hatch on the bottom of the camera and found the serial number. I tried plugging it in to the Vizica website and found I couldn't get in without a password. I reconnected the X-drive, submitted the web address, and waited for the algorithm to do its thing.

The door opened behind me, and I heard a breathy version of the word, "dang." I closed the case with one hand, and saw the old man standing in the doorway with his hands on his hips. He let out a little exasperated sigh. The little blond bounced hopefully by his leg.

"How much longer?" he asked, wearing an I-just-sucked-a-lemon face.

"Some time yet," I said, keeping my wrath in check. "Why?"

"Well, the third computer's blinky. I want to get back to my solitaire, and my little Caroline wants to play Cookie Munchers." He stared at me as if, by sheer force of will, he could make me vanish from existence.

"I have a fair amount of business to attend to," I said.

"Business? What kind of business?"

The kind of business that is not yours. But what I actually said was, "I am a headhunter."

He paused, chewing on the word like a piece of suspect beef. "Oh, like you find people for jobs, that it?"

"Something like that."

His expression turned slightly triumphant. "Heh, heh, heh, guess I won't ever be givin' you a call. Retired. Plenty of time for my granddaughter now."

And for solitaire, I thought, turning around. "I'm afraid I'll be needing this computer for some time."

"I'm sorry, Carri-boo," he told the little girl. "Looks like we'll have to wait some more." He adjusted the thick framed glasses and scratched the unruly thatch of gray hair near his ear. "Mister, can ye' at least gimmie a time you'll be off?"

I took a deep breath. "I wish I could, but my work is a bit...indefinite. You're perfectly welcome to take the other computer."

His face morphed back to lemon mode. "I told ye' already that computer don't work right." He muttered something I couldn't understand, but the little girl gasped, and I saw her hand fly to her lips. Then they both were gone. Maybe now, he'd do something that promoted togetherness with his granddaughter, rather than parking her in front of Cookie Munchers all day.

Back to Vizica. The algorithm battered down the firewall, and I learned that the camera had been shipped to a distributor in April and then to a Walmart just outside of Panama City, Florida...not far from Destin. Not far at all.

Back to the web browser. I needed access to Walmart's sales records. As I suspected, that information was not normally accessible via the Internet. One of the applications on my X-drive told me that I could, however, access sales through their internal server. I clicked the "GO" button and waited.

And waited. The search and decipher program raised the internal temperature of the X-drive six degrees and took eight minutes to break through. I'd hacked national defense servers faster. Good for Walmart.

What I discovered didn't give me much, and that didn't surprise me. The scarlet-colored Vizica Sport had been purchased from the Walmart in July, paid for in cash, and was a part of a larger order that included five other cameras. That worried me.

Next up: the sailboats I had seen that day from the shore. If the camera had been purchased in Panama City and I found it floating just off Destin Beach, it was a good bet that the killer dropped the camera in the Gulf, somewhere in between. Maybe Smiling Jack was a sailor. Maybe he lived on a boat. Maybe the concave walls in the photographs were actually the inner hull of a ship as I suspected. Maybe the killer made a mistake and the camera went overboard.

But the Vizica was waterproof.

Maybe Smiling Jack wanted the camera to be found. After all, he'd been posting photos of himself in the act of murder...for years. And yet, no one had come close to catching him. Maybe Jack's upping the stakes a little by throwing out some physical evidence.

I'd seen several sailboats out on the Gulf that morning. I remembered them pretty well, even their registration numbers. Maybe if I found the right boat, I'd find the killer.

A few clicks, and I found out the Sun Odyssey 42DS was a French craft built by a company called Jeanneau and sold through American dealers. The base price was just over two hundred grand. I needed to know who paid that kind of money, so I set about using the X-drive to try to discover who had purchased the Sun Odyssey with the registration code: FL 6606 KR. A few moments passed. I didn't get the name of the purchaser, but I did discover the name and address of the dealer: Spinnaker Sales in Miramar Beach, just a few miles up Emerald Coast Parkway.

Just then, the door to the business center opened again. And there again was the old man and his granddaughter. And this time, he brought a friend.

"Excuse me, sir," the man said, swallowing to get his full voice. "I am Donald Granderson, the Motel 6 Manager on Duty, and one of our guests, Mr. Havacamp here, says that you've been on this computer for well over an hour." I nodded. He went on, rocking on his heels as he spoke. "If you'll note on our business center rules..." He pointed to the plaque on the wall. "...there is a one hour limit if people are waiting."

I stared at the old man. He stared back triumphantly. Fortunately for him, I am not easily provoked.

"No problem," I said. "I'll be very careful to observe the rules. I'm sure Mr. Havacamp has something very important to work on. I'll clear out at once."

The manager looked surprised and more than a little relieved. "Thank you, mister, uh?"

"Willoughby," I said.

"Right, Mr. Willoughby. Room...?"

"Seven, just up the hall."

"I'll be sure that you get some meal vouchers for being so cooperative."

That's me, Mister Cooperative.

I force-deleted all the browser histories, disconnected my X-drive, took my silver case, and left the business center. I was mulling the fact that I didn't get a chance to search for the other sailboats, the Hunter 54 and the Oyster 625, when I realized my mistake. I'd booked the motel room under John Spector. And now, I'd just told the manager my name was Willoughby, the alias I'd used with the FBI.

I had a feeling that was going to come back to haunt me.

{ Chapter 8 }

DEE REZVANI BECAME SUSPICIOUS when things were too easy. In her personal and professional experience, things were never easy. People were never what they seemed. Oil changes turned into $1600 repair bills. Home improvement projects that should've taken minutes were measured in days instead. The open-and-shut case turned, with a single clue, into a dizzying maelstrom.

So looking at the Motel 6 in Destin, Florida made her nervous.

She sat in the parking lot at three minutes to 4:00 and wondered about Regis Willoughby. Was he just some innocent guy with an unfortunate name? Someone who found the camera and wanted to do the right thing?

Or was he something much darker? The Bureau kept statistics on almost everything related to violent crime. In most cases the killer was either family or knew the victims. And a very high percentage of killers purposefully contributed evidence that led to them getting caught. Was that what Regis was doing?

Was Regis really Smiling Jack? But this killer had pulled off a series of perfect crimes. No digital trail. No forensic trail. No missing persons. No real suspects. He wasn't stupid, and didn't seem the least bit interested in helping anyone catch him.

So why would he come to the FBI now, after all these years? And why would he use a traceable public computer that would take all of the guesswork out of it? The most logical theory was that LePoast and the Deputy Director were right: this is a copycat...a hoax of a hoax.

But Rez wasn't okay with that. Her investigative intuition was practically screaming that this camera and this Regis fellow would be the first real leads in the Smiling Jack case history.

Maybe the killer's angry that we're so inept, she thought. *Like playing a game of "hide and go seek," and sitting in a hiding spot that's so good for so long that you begin to worry the others have all given up.*

Agent Rezvani's gut told her that there was something here, that Smiling Jack was more than a hoax, and this might just be her chance to nail him. As she left the SUV, she chambered a 9 mm round in her Sig Sauer p226 and secured the weapon in the shoulder holster beneath her jacket. The FBI had switched over to the Glock, but Rez figured she was on vacation, she'd bring her own gun. Plus, she kept a Glock 27 "pocket pistol" in a special holster in the small of her back.

She had two extra clips on her belt. 45 rounds of 9 mm Parabellum ammunition. *Parabellum,* she thought, her impish smile curling. The bullet's name was derived from the Latin *Si vis pacem, para bellum.* If you seek peace, prepare for war.

"Regis Willoughby," she whispered, "come out, come out, wherever you are."

*** *** *** ***

GHOST

Say what you want about public transportation, but around the Florida beaches? They got things right.

The F-Trans bus arrived right on time. Ten seconds after 4:00 and I was on my way to Panama City Beach Hospital Center. As the bus trundled faithfully on, I held the FBI screen captures in my hand and stared down at the analysis of the murder weapon. The knife was fourteen inches long, though only two and a half of those were blade. It had a wooden handle, studded with brass like a steak knife, but the body of the weapon was enclosed in nickel plate—not brass. The blade was twin sided, likely surgical steel, but very old. FBI's analysis said the blade would have been used by turn-of-the-century thoracic surgeons who would use the added length to cut deep inside the chest cavity. Of course, all they had were still photos of the murder weapon, so all of this was conjecture. Informed conjecture, but conjecture nonetheless.

One thing for sure, it was a very unusual weapon. I needed a second opinion. Who better to ask than doctors to get a second opinion, especially concerning a blade?

Thunder rumbled out over the Gulf. Storms were like clockwork in parts of the deep South. Almost every day between 4:30 and 4:45, you could count on the heat and humidity to bubble over into a mess of roiling dark clouds. Wind, torrential downpours, plenty of thunder and lightning—and it would all clear out in less than an hour.

I never grew tired of storms...the more powerful, the better. Looking at the black sky churning behind the hospital, I knew this storm would pack a wallop when it opened up. I hoped to be finished with my business so I could watch.

Yellow pastel facade with orange stucco shingles on its roof, towering palms scattered about the grounds, and all manner of bright, tropical flowers bursting from manicured beds—the hospital looked more like a resort, I thought. Cool, climate-controlled air washed over me as I entered. I found myself staring up into a beautiful atrium enclosed with massive sheets of glass. It felt like walking into a hollowed out prism. Colored light spilled down onto the marble floor and bathed patients and visitors alike. Three stories up hung a tall sculpted cross surrounded by winged cherubs and doves, all in brushed silver.

The angels looked like naked toddlers. I shook my head and went to the receptionist.

She was a fifty-ish woman with hair the color of dark chocolate with ribbons of caramel. Frosty clear blue eyes looked out from behind stylish black framed reading glasses. She smiled and gave me a look like she knew everything there was to know. I held up an identification card and shield, aside from money, the only contents of a wallet from my silver case. The credentials didn't say I worked for the FBI, CIA, or NSA. But hardly anyone looked closely enough to know for certain. I flipped shut the billfold and asked, "You have cardiac surgeons?"

"Best cardiac docs in the U.S.," she replied. Her accent, deep south, rolled off her tongue: one part brilliant, one part honey. She didn't question my identity at all. Picture ID and shiny shield. Works every time.

"I'm looking for a certain kind," I said. "Male or female, it doesn't matter. Someone who has been around the field for a long time but still sharp."

"They're all like that," she said. "Most heart cutters are sharp."

"Point granted," I said. "But I'm looking for someone who's as clever as they come, the type who sees around corners, if you take my meaning."

"Doc Shepherd's who you want. Chief of Surgery, the best cutter bar none, comes from a family of surgeons." She lowered her glasses a little. "What do you need a surgeon for? Anyone in trouble?"

"No, no, nothing like that," I said, giving my best *It's just standard procedure* shrug. "I need an expert's opinion about a surgical instrument."

She smiled as if she understood completely. "Cardiology's third floor, Gulf side. Ask the nurse if Doctor Shepherd is free. Oh, and you'll need this." She handed me a clip-on Panama City Beach Hospital guest card.

Photo ID, shiny shield, and now a hospital badge. Nothing could stop me now...or so I thought.

***   ***   ***   ***

The charge nurses upstairs weren't quite as friendly as the receptionist. They looked like photocopies of each other, except one had hair dyed blonde and the other, hair dyed black. I told them I needed to see Doctor Shepherd. They told me to sit in the waiting room.

The waiting *room* turned out to be an uncomfortable bench in the middle of a hallway. And it's relatively safe to say that waiting is not one of my finer qualities.

Twenty minutes later, I heard muted thunder. I went to the desk again and held up my badge and ID. Neither of the nurses looked up. "I'm sorry to trouble you," I said. "But I'm investigating a serious crime. I really do need to speak to Doctor Shepherd."

The fake brunette said, "Doctor Shepherd is in surgery. I don't much care what your badge says or what you're investigating. No one rushes surgery."

"So, unless you're God," the fake blonde said, "and you're planning a miracle, I suggest you take a seat or make an actual appointment during Doctor Shepherd's office hours."

The nurses glanced at each other, and I could see high fives in their eyes.

Thirty more minutes on the bench later, and I couldn't hear any more thunder. I missed the storm.

"Ah, there you are."

I looked up and found an amiable gentleman standing there. He had dark gray, close-cropped hair and matching sideburns. Wire-rimmed glasses framed his owlish, gray eyes. He wore a blue bow tie and a smile. His handlebar mustache looked perfect for twirling, and I thought maybe he did twirl it as his genius intellect worked.

"They kept you in the hall, all this time?" he asked with a subtle gesture towards the charge nurses.

I nodded. "I understand you were in surgery."

"Oh, nonsense. It was just a routine aortic stent." With a humorous pigeon-toed gait, he strode to the nurses station. "Nurse Brandywine, Nurse Pelagris, how could you keep this fine officer waiting on this ridiculous bench?"

The brunette looked carefully indignant. "He didn't make an appointment."

"Oh, don't be obtuse," he said. "Crime doesn't make an appointment. This man has work to do. You should have at least let him wait in my office." He cast a surprisingly stern glare at both of them and then motioned for me to follow.

*** *** *** ***

Covered by so many matted diplomas, certificates, awards, and special recognitions, the office had almost no visible wall space. Apparently, Dr. Shepherd was very good at what he did. Either that, or he was an egotist.

He sat backward at his desk so he could face me. "So tell me, detective, how can I help you?"

"You know I'm a detective just from looking at me?"

"No, no," Dr. Shepherd replied. "I'm no Sherlock Holmes. Carol—receptionist in the front lobby—left me a message, said you had a badge and some questions."

I decided not to correct the good doctor's notion of my identity and nodded. "I was wondering if you could identify this instrument." I handed him the photocopy.

He held it in both hands for a moment. Then he leaned back in the chair and used one hand to twirl his mustache while he stared on. Genius at work, just as I suspected.

"Surgical steel," he said quietly.

"You're sure?"

"Young man, I refuse to speak unless I'm sure. This is a steel-chromium-nickel alloy—surgical steel. Look here." He held the photo and gestured from the blade to the handle. "Notice there's no corrosion on the blade. None at all. The handle and casing, however, all show signs of many years of use."

I nodded affirmation and then offered, "Some have claimed that this is the type of blade Jack the Ripper used."

Shepherd laughed and cleared his throat. "Jack the Ripper, mmhm. The Rumbelow blade, eh? No, this blade is quite different. Of course, no one really knows what weapon the Whitechapel killer used. Is that what this is...a murder weapon?"

I ignored the question. "How is this one different from the Rumbelow knife?"

"It's longer for one thing." He went back to the mustache. "In fact, that's the most curious aspect of this instrument. It's so long. We have sales reps roll through here all the time. They buy us lunch or pastries and show us their new state-of-the-art equipment. I've seen any number of strange implements. Long, short, curved, backward—you name it. But few bladed instruments this long. I can see why some might compare it to the Ripper weapon. It's quite old. Turn-of-the-century, maybe."

"Why do you say that?"

"The casing for one thing," he said, tracing his finger along a seam in the metal. "It's not very streamlined, is it? The housing would be completely sealed on anything made in the last forty years. But I think this is older than that. Notice the brass knob? That's old school. Very old school."

"What's it for, the knob?"

"You ever use an X-ACTO knife?" I nodded, and he went on. "It's like that. Turn the knob and the blade slides back into the housing."

"Would a surgeon need that feature?"

He smacked his lips and shook his head. "Not likely. Not these days. We don't need to adjust the length of the blade. We just ask for a different blade. I'm rather wondering if this instrument might be something other than surgical in nature."

"Like what?"

"I'm not certain." He gave the mustache a few more twirls. "And so..."

"You won't say till you're certain."

"Right." He raised an eyebrow wryly. "I might know someone who could tell me. Can I keep this photo for a few days?"

I sighed inwardly. "If it will help."

"I can't promise you much," Shepherd said. "But I'll look into it and get back to you with whatever I learn. What's your cell number?"

"I'm staying at the Destin Motel 6."

"They leave the light on for you?"

Funny doctor. "I'm in room seven. Just leave a message at the desk."

"For?"

"I'm sorry," I said, feigning embarrassment. I hesitated a moment. I'd rented the room under one name and given an alias as well. Better to stick to basics. "John Spector," I said, standing.

He stood and offered his hand.

We shook and he said, "You never explained what kind of crime this was related to. Murder, I presume?"

"The victims were all young women," I replied. "The killer used the blade in the photo to cut their throats."

"It would certainly work for that." He had what looked like an involuntary shiver. Then, he frowned.

"What?" I asked.

"Well, any surgical blade would do for cutting a throat," he said. "One this size would be harder to manipulate, a bit more ungainly. Makes me wonder. With all the sharp blades out there, why this one?"

I sat up a little straighter in my chair. "Thank you, Doc," I said. "That feels like a very important question."

He nodded but looked uncomfortable. "You'd think that being a surgeon, I might not be bothered by something like that. But I am." He removed his wire glasses, and his eyes looked even more owlish, owlish and sad. "You look like you've been at your job for a long time," he said. "Not that you look old, Officer Spector. Just seasoned. What I mean is, after all you've seen, does it...does it still bother you?"

"Yes," I said. "It bothers me very much."

{ Chapter 9 }

THE HOTEL MANAGER, Mr. Granderson, was so startled by Deanna Rezvani that he stepped backward into the old room key cubbies.

"FBI?" he said, his Adam's apple bobbing. He rubbed the back of his head, then removed his glasses and wiped sweat that instantly beaded on his forehead. "I...I don't understand. Has something happened? Big Dave's not going to like this."

"Big Dave?" Rez echoed, slipping her ID back into her suit pocket.

"He's regional manager. If something goes wrong here, it's my head."

"Mr. Granderson, please, relax. Nothing has happened in your hotel, but there might be someone with information pertaining to a crime renting a room here. Do you have a renter named Regis Willoughby?"

Granderson flew to the computer keyboard and clacked way. "I know I've heard that name. Not a name to forget. Kinda stupid-sounding, y'know?" He pressed a few keys and shook his head. "Wait, now that doesn't make sense. There's no record of anyone by that name. I thought sure I'd—wait. The guy in the business center."

"Go on."

He wiped more sweat from his glistening forehead. "There was a guy hogging a computer in the business center. He said his name was Regis Willoughby. Big guy, kind of creepy."

"But he's not on the registry?"

"No, not in the computer, but I remember now. I checked the guy in." He let out a breath full of despair. "This is awful. What is he anyway, a drug dealer? Aww, this will never work. I rented a room to a drug dealer wanted by the FBI."

Dee took a deep breath herself. To avoid smacking him.

"He's wanted for questioning," she said. "That's all, Mr. Granderson, but if he is still in the motel, would you please tell me what room?"

"Oh, right." Granderson went back to the computer. "He said he was in room seven. Here it is, John Spector. Paid in cash day before yesterday. He's booked through tonight. Come to think of it, I was supposed to send him some meal vouchers, y'know to smooth over that I booted him from the computers."

"I'm going to need a room key," Rez said, holding out her hand.

The manager opened a drawer, fished out a magnetic stripe card, and plunged it into the encoder next to the computer monitor. He handed her the card key. And then froze. He'd seen a flash of the gun under Rez's sports coat. "You're not going to shoot anyone...are you?"

Man, this guy is wound tight, she thought. She reached across the front desk and put her hand on the man's shoulder. "No, of course I'm not going to shoot anyone. Just questions, that's all. I promise."

"Good," he replied, nodding like a bobble-head doll. "Good, good. That is such a relief." He looked up at the clock. "Come on nine o'clock. Daddy needs a mimosa."

Rez turned to leave but couldn't resist. "If I do need to shoot someone," she said, "I'll be sure to do it outside."

Mr. Granderson turned sheet white.

***   ***   ***   ***

John Spector, Rez thought. *Better than Regis Willoughby.* She passed the motel's business center. There was an old guy in there playing solitaire on one computer and a very bored-looking little blonde girl.

Rez came to room seven and rapped on the door. "Regis Willoughby?" she called. She waited and got no response. "Mr. Willoughby, please come to your door. I'm Agent Rezvani from the FBI. We'd like to ask you a few questions." She knocked again.

No answer. No frantic rustling from the other side. Rez glanced up the hall toward the front desk and back the other way. Then she pulled the Sig Sauer out from beneath her coat and put the key card in the door. The tiny green light said the door was unlocked. Rez held her gun vertically a few inches from her chest and slowly opened the door. Cold air leaked out, giving Rez an instant chill.

The room was dark except for an incision of light between the curtains. She eased the door shut behind her. It clicked. Rez stood very still, just listening. No sound at all. Not even the room's A/C unit.

A big guy? she thought. *Not too many places for a big guy to hide in a small hotel room.* She tried the bathroom first. The shower curtain was drawn. Rez's heart rate climbed a notch. Still, the curtain was semitransparent, and the shower lining was some light color, cream or off white. Someone standing in there would be easily visible...even in the shadows. She looked behind the curtain anyway. No one there.

Light flickered in the bathroom mirror. Thunder thumped the motel, rattling the windowpanes and vibrating the walls.

Rez swallowed, and thought, *Holy smokes, that sounded like a bomb!* She waited for her heart to slow and then stepped out of the bathroom. She took in the rest of the room: mini-fridge, microwave, entertainment center with a dresser beneath, vacant flat screen TV, two double beds, an easy chair, a tall lamp, and a long desk by the window. But she couldn't see around the near corner. Someone could hide there.

Gun raised, she spun around the corner and found no one. That left the curtains guarding the window, but there was no figure-sized hump. She holstered her weapon and threw open the curtains. Gray light bathed the room. Rain splotched the glass. Thunder rumbled. Rez didn't care much for storms. She looked away from the glass just as lightning flashed.

The room looked empty. The bed was made. There was no luggage. All the trashcans were empty. All the towels were hung neatly or stacked. None of the plastic cups had been set free of their cellophane wrap. Either the housekeepers were amazing, or Willoughby skipped town. She sighed and wandered over to the dressers. No clothes in the drawers. Just a Gideon Bible. It looked well used...doubtless the accumulation of wear from hundreds of occupants, if not thousands.

She went to the desk next. There was a hotel directory and a Destin area phone book. She opened the thin drawer beneath the desktop and found a few Motel 6 pens and a stationary pad. She removed the paper and held it up to the light from the window. There were definite imprints there, from someone with a heavy hand.

"Haven't done this since high school," Rez muttered, taking one of the pens and shading lightly over the page. "Still works though." When she was finished, there remained a grainy blue cloud on the notepad. But the ink didn't fill the shallow crevices of writing. *PCB Hospital* had been written there, as well as a phone number.

"Panama City Beach Hospital," she said. "Probably not the guy I'm looking for. Still..." She tucked the notepad into her coat pocket.

Thunder cracked so loud that she involuntarily ducked. She felt sudden cold wash over her and shivered. The A/C unit had not come on.

She felt a weight on her back and shoulders as if someone was watching from the window. As she spun on her heel, her hand flew to the holster beneath her jacket, but there was no one in sight. The rain continued to splatter the glass. Rez sighed and left her Sig Sauer alone. But she still couldn't shake the feeling.

She stared at the glass and, among the spatters of raindrops, found the beginnings of a shape. Irregular rivulets of rainwater seemed to be organizing, spilling into each other, forming something. Staring intently Rez recognized the trickling outline of a slight female figure. "What the...?" she mouthed. It had to be some trick of the glass and rainwater. But there it was: the outline of a flowing dress, long arms, slender fingers...a soft, slightly open mouth and horribly vacant eyes.

Lightning flashed. Thunder shook the building. Rez jumped.

"What are you doing in my room?" came a deep male voice from behind. Rez jumped again and turned in a blink.

In the doorway stood a very tall man with door-spanning broad shoulders. His skin was pale, and wisps of blond hair were pasted by rain across his forehead. He held the door with one hand and held a silver suitcase in the other. Rez glanced back at the window. Lots of rain splotches, but no discernible pattern, no spectral figure.

"I'm Special Agent Deanna Rezvani of the FBI," she said, struggling to lace her voice with authority. "Are you Regis Willoughby?"

He nodded.

"Or are you John Spector?" she asked.

He didn't blink, but faint lines appeared around the corners of his eyes, and he smiled grimly. "I'm both."

Rez's mind raced. Was he admitting his alias because he was certain he had the upper hand? Was this his trap all along? Her hand slid away from her side to the small of her back and the Glock 27 hidden there. "Mr. Spector, why are you using an alias?"

"Can I see some ID?" he asked.

Dee frowned. She had to use her gun hand to get to her badge. She held it up, wide open, so he could see the big blue letters, FBI.

"It's not that I don't trust you," said Spector. "I just have a thing for picture ID's and shiny badges."

Rez put away the ID. Some unguarded part of her registered the humor, but not for long. Danger alarms blared from every other corner of her mind. "Mr. Spector, I'm asking again, why are you using an alias?"

"Ghost," he said.

"What?"

"People call me Ghost."

The tension in Rez's neck threatened to spark a migraine. Rez couldn't let that happen. Not now. It might be fatal. She flexed her trapezius muscles and let them relax. She took a deep, very measured breath. "Mr. Spector...Regis Willoughby...Ghost? Why the aliases?"

"Bad habit," he replied.

He hadn't moved yet, not an inch. He filled the doorway and looked as if nothing short of a bulldozer would get him out of the way. Or maybe a bullet. She let her hand drift back to her Glock.

"Are you arresting me?" he asked.

"No. I just wanted to ask you a few questions." He still didn't move. Rez stared at the silver suitcase. It looked like something out of a sci-fi movie, like maybe it was full of chemicals, an advanced sniper rifle, or a bomb. Involuntarily she took a step backward toward the window. She felt like the walls were closing in, making the room into a narrow hall with a potential killer blocking her only escape.

"I thought the FBI wasn't interested in the case," Ghost said. "A hoax."

"Not everyone at the FBI feels that way."

Ghost nodded. "Agent LePoast indicated years of searching turned up so little that the case was dropped."

"Again, not everyone dropped the case." Rez grew impatient. "I need to ask you some questions."

"Shoot," he said with a momentary glance at her right arm. "With questions, I mean."

Rez hesitated. So, he knew the gun was there. *Good,* she thought. *Let him know that I'm armed.* "Outside," she said. She wanted to question him but not on his terms or in his room.

"Whatever you want," he said, backing up. He held the door for her. "Lobby?"

Rez said, "Fine."

***   ***   ***   ***

The manager, Mr. Granderson, fidgeted behind the desk, his eyes darting thirty times a minute toward the FBI agent and the suspect sitting in his lobby. A group of tourists stood a few paces back from the sliding glass doors. They were much more intent on the rain blowing in sheets than the pair sitting in the burgundy arm chairs near the window.

"Interesting line of storms," Ghost said. "Big one blew through yesterday. But this one's pretty potent too."

Rez nodded but said, "That's an interesting suitcase."

"You aren't much for small talk, are you, Agent Rezvani?"

"The suitcase?"

"My equipment."

"What do you do for a living?" she asked.

"I find people," he replied. "People who are hard to find or hard to get to."

"So, you're like a private detective."

"You might say that," he replied.

"Tell me about the photos."

"I was out at the beach, Grayton Beach, like I said in the email. I found the camera floating in the Gulf, just offshore."

"May I see it?"

Ghost picked up his case, moved his hands strangely, rippling his fingers in certain places. He had the case open, the camera out, and the case closed in a flash. Rez hadn't seen a thing except for the gleam of silver.

He held the burgundy camera out to her. She took it by the corner. "I'd like to dust it for fingerprints," she said. "Would that be all right?"

"You'll get mine," he said, looking sideways at the camera, "and now a few of yours...but not much else."

"How do you know that?"

"The camera was floating in the Gulf," he said. "The camera's got a polymer case, not metal. In hot saltwater, prints wouldn't last for long."

Rez blinked. The man knew his stuff. She placed the camera in a plastic evidence bag and dropped it into her purse.

"Mr. Spector," she said finally, "did you post the pictures from this camera anywhere else?"

"Just the Feebs," he said. "Sorry. FBI, I mean."

"No blog posts or websites?"

Spector shook his head slightly. *No.*

"Did you send the photos to anyone else? Even to another law enforcement agency?"

"No," he said. "You do realize you now qualify as insane?"

"I'm sorry," she said. "What?"

"Doing the same thing, the same way, and expecting a different result? That's one definition of insanity. You keep asking me the same question."

"But not exactly the same way," she countered.

"Okay," Spector said, the smile flattening into a grim frown. "But I am telling you, I did not send the photos ANYWHERE else. Just the FBI. And that was with pretty stiff encryption, so I don't think anyone hacked me. Why are you asking?"

"The photos are all over the web now," Rezvani explained. "One day after you sent them to us, they wind up on every serial killer hobbyist site, blog, Pinterest, you name it. Just like before."

"I didn't know that," Spector said. He folded his hands on the table and waited. They sat without speaking for some time. His eyes never left her, and she studied him.

In the "Smiling Jack" photos, the killer had revealed only the bottom of his face: chin, jaw, most of his nose. Rez saw some similarities, especially the cleft in the chin. But the width of

Spector's jaw seemed wider and the general shape was more square.

"Agent Rezvani," said Ghost. "The FBI has already wasted years on this case. Seems to me, you might not want to waste any more time."

"What do you mean?"

"You think I'm the killer."

"I never accused—"

"You're an honest person," said Ghost. "I can tell. So don't try to deny it. You didn't fly all the way down here to look at the same pictures I already sent you. You didn't break into my room to surprise me with flowers. And you're packing enough heat to take down a rhino. Shoulder and small of the back, right?"

Rez laughed in spite of herself. "I didn't think they showed."

"So Agent Rezvani, I want to save you the trouble. Don't waste your time or resources on me."

"You think you've got me figured out?"

"I've been around awhile," he said. "I know a lot. But I will never claim to have figured out a woman."

She laughed. "Touché."

"There is one thing I don't understand. For a murder case this dangerous, I'm wondering why you came alone."

"Don't leave Destin, Mr. Spector," Dee said. She stood and walked slowly toward motel's exit. "I may have further questions."

"Aren't you going to answer my question?" Spector called after her. "Hey, that's not fair."

Agent Rezvani paused, looked over her shoulder, and said, "I'm a Special Agent in the FBI. I don't need to be fair."

{ Chapter 10 }

S PINNAKER SALES, I thought. Cute name for a dealership. They were open until 8. Due to my unexpected meeting with Special Agent Rezvani, I got there at 7:45. The showroom was massive, the ceiling five stories up—everything glass and lights. Everywhere I looked, sleek water craft and brilliantly colored sails. Just standing in the showroom made me feel richer.

The manager stood at a computer behind a tall metallic blue counter. I could tell he was glad to see me when he looked up...and snarled.

"Do you carry Sun Odyssey?" I asked, leaning on the counter like a regular.

"This is Spinnaker Sales," he said, licking the tip of a finger and slicking one of his perfectly groomed eyebrows. "We carry all the finest boats. Please don't lean on the counter."

I ignored him. At least he was telling the truth so far. On the way in, I'd seen Sun Odyssey, Hunter Marine, Oyster—they did carry it all. Probably ten million worth of sail craft in this one showroom. "What about the 42DS?"

"The 42 is one of our bestsellers," he said. He stroked his goatee, cut immaculately to the quick. He looked like a suit model from Jos. A. Bank. Silk shirt, woven royal purple tie, gold Rolex. His hands were perfectly manicured, but he'd bitten some of the nails down. Nervous habit, probably. "You realize it's ten minutes to closing."

"I'm interested in the 42DS," I said, nonchalantly placing my silver case on the counter. "What do they run? 225K? 240?"

He regarded me a little differently now, stood a little straighter. "We can talk price later," he said, holding out his hand. We shook. He walked around the counter. "I'm G. Alonzo Vasquez, but my friends call me G. Would you like to see the 42?"

"Yes, I would," I said. "I knew I'd come to the right place."

"Of course you did. Spinnaker Sales is the number one dealer on the Gulf. Right this way, Mister...?"

I sighed. Forget Willoughby. "Spector...John Spector."

We strolled through a dizzying array of over-lit, sparkling yachts and came at last to the Sun Odyssey 42DS. It had a single mast that reached almost to the vaulted ceiling. Its twin sails formed a white isosceles triangle that looked like it could catch—and hold—hurricane force winds. The hull was held in some kind of bracket rigging that kept the fin-like rudder and keel off the ground.

"Would you like to go aboard, Mr. Spector?" G asked.

"Are you sure you have the time?"

He smiled like I'd just asked if sailboats float. "At Spinnaker Sales," he said, flashing a million dollar smile, "we always have time for our customers."

A moment ago he looked at me like he'd just eaten a roach sandwich. Now it's all grins, I thought. People are funny that way.

GHOST

G moved the rope chain for me, and I climbed aboard the yacht. He was noticeably nonplussed when I ignored the impeccably designed deck and went straight below. But I couldn't care less about the mast, the multiple benches, or the massive captain's wheel. I needed to see if anything from the Sun Odyssey's interior reminded me of the setting in Smiling Jack's photos.

Ducking below the top of the hatch, I descended a few steps and found myself a little disoriented. Granted, I hadn't walked the perimeter of the craft, but it didn't seem possible that so much space could exist within its sleek hull. While G prattled on about things like berth, keel, and hull displacement, I absorbed the cabin. A kitchen fit snug on my right, a small bathroom on my left. Behind me, through a door, were a pair of beds—each with two pillows as if four people could sleep there. I thought maybe I'd fit if I slept horizontally across both of them.

Scanning fore, I noted a beautiful entertainment area with two C-shaped couches and a collapsible table between them. Beyond that was a door leading to another small bathroom and another bed. "Amazing interior space," I said, interrupting a grand speech about lightweight polymer materials used in the couch cushions.

"Every inch has been maximized for comfort."

"If I didn't already know better, I would swear that this is more than forty-two feet. It feels like more."

"Genius of design. You know this is a Lombard-Garroni design?"

I didn't reply. I was thinking about Smiling Jack. The 42 was certainly a similar confined space with the concave walls and the compact furniture—just like in the photos. But there wasn't a narrow hallway, not really. Just a doorway to the master suite. And the windows were different from the 42 I'd seen out of the

Gulf the morning I found the camera. "How much of the interior can be customized?"

G turned on me like I'd just suggested that his mother worked the local red light district.

"One does not customize a Lombard-Garroni design," he said, coming dangerously close to a hiss. "Each one is a custom design."

"The cat's eye windows," I said, pointing. "They're a little too...nontraditional for me. I was thinking of a series of porthole type windows. Could that be done?"

G scowled like I'd just suggested that the rest of his family worked the local red light district too.

"Portholes? Really, Mr. Spector? No, the Sun Odyssey will not be equipped with portholes."

I trilled my fingers on my silver case and said, "That's too bad, really. It's what I had in mind, G. And when I get something on my mind, I just can't rest until I take care of it." I turned abruptly and climbed the stairs to the deck.

I was back on the showroom floor before G caught up with me. "Of course, of course...once you have the boat in your possession, I'm sure you could find a craftsman willing to do the job." G motioned for me to follow. I did.

"I might have a card," he said, back behind his counter. "There are...rare...occasions when a customer needs to add a feature that is to his liking. Ah, here, Cecil Wright." G handed me the business card. "Mr. Wright does good work by all accounts. But he's very expensive."

I pocketed the card. "Money's not really a problem," I said. And that was true. I had precisely $934 left to spend, and no intention of purchasing a boat or customizing it. No problem.

GHOST

"Now, before we get down to business," said G, flipping through a sheaf of forms, "I am curious. Most people positively adore the cat's eye windows. Why portholes?"

"I was out at Grayton Beach the other day, and I happened to see a Sun Odyssey out on the gulf. It had portholes. I liked the look." I put the silver case up on the counter and scratched my chin. "I wonder...Spinnaker Sales being the number one dealer on the Gulf, I wonder if perhaps you sold the Sun Odyssey I saw the other day. I wonder if you might be able to tell me who the customer was? I could then contact the customer and find out who did his portholes. Do you think you could do that for me, G?"

"That is a strict violation of customer privacy," G said.

I tapped the silver case. "It would mean a lot to me."

G licked his finger and did both his eyebrows. "Well, in the interest of new customer satisfaction, I suppose I could at least check if we sold the boat you saw. Of course, if you contact the owner, you could never mention where you obtained his information."

"Of course," I replied. "The registration number is FL 6606 KR."

G nudged the mouse to wake his computer, clicked a few links to get to the right page, and then dutifully typed in the code. "Ah, I am sorry, Mr. Spector, but that number isn't correct—not a craft we sold anyway."

I leaned in and looked at the monitor. "You put a one in there, but it's not 6616; it's 6606."

"Did I? Well, let's try it again and see." A quick glide of the mouse. The click of four digit keys. Then, the whole world changed.

G's ubiquitous smile faltered...just a little. "Again, no luck," he said, gesturing dramatically with his right hand. "It would

{ 89 }

seem that some other lesser sail craft dealer sold that boat. That is, if you yourself got the number correct."

"I'm very good with numbers," I said.

"Of course, of course." G's smile returned to full vigor. He straightened a stack of papers. "Now, then shall we discuss terms and payment for the Sun Odyssey? Spinnaker Sales offers a tremendous financing package."

"That won't be necessary."

G's eyes darted toward my silver case. "You wish to pay in cash then? Mr. Spector, I—"

"I wish to think about it," I said, noisily sliding the silver case off the counter. "A man in my position can't make such a purchase on a whim."

I watched the dollar signs drain out of his eye sockets. He blinked, the smile returned as warm as ever. "Just so, Mr. Spector...just so. Nonetheless, Spinnaker Sales appreciates your confidence in us." He held out a hand. The gold Rolex dangled a bit on his wrist. We shook, and then he asked, "Do you have a business card, Mr. Spector?"

"All out."

"What about a contact number?" G tilted his head. "I will make a few calls, see if I can find out which dealer sold your porthole yacht."

"Thank you, G," I said. "I appreciate that. You can reach me at my hotel in Destin." I gave him the number. Then I left.

***   ***   ***   ***

The testosterone years.

Deanna Rezvani smirked, remembering the phrase she used to describe her first three years in the Bureau. She'd met a dizzying array of men during that time. She looked away from her laptop's screen and laughed. A few of them were more memorable than others.

There was enigmatic Rolf Cursade, the genius criminologist who'd cracked the "bloodletting code" of a ritualistic killer who called himself the Serpent. Rolf was nearly as much a predator as the killers he chased, and he wanted everyone to know it, especially the ladies. He wore a choker necklace adorned with sharks' teeth and carried a knife big enough to shame Crocodile Dundee.

Rolf could flip a switch and get inside a killer's mind. And while in "whack-mode," as his somewhat creeped out colleagues called it, Rolf could often plot the killer's next move well in advance. Some thought Rolf was crazy, but everyone thought he was brilliant. But Rolf wanted trophies, Dee remembered, not girlfriends.

Dee's study partner in the academy, Nathaniel Petrikin, was another memorable man. When he was just five, Nathaniel had promised his beloved Momma he would join the Bureau because he knew an Eff-bee-yie man had rescued his grandfather from a bunch of clansmen intent on a lynching. Nathaniel had been true to his word. First in his class at the academy, he'd breezed into the Bureau. But at every turn, even with all the Bureau talent spotters trying to recruit him for leadership roles, Nathaniel stayed in the field. He wanted to fight crime at ground level where things can get dirty. His mother's rosary in one pocket, a tiny Gideon Bible in the other, Nathaniel was a good man. A good man who got married halfway through his first year on the job.

Special Agent Gerard Stephen Harris was another sort of man. Granite jaw, glinting blue eyes, and a chiseled physique, Agent Harris was stunningly handsome. The man had a way of shaping himself to get what he wanted, a chameleon with an approach for every person and every situation. He cowed other field agents and bulled through jurisdiction disputes. He talked training with Deputy Director Barnes and spoke politics with Director Peluso. And even though Rez thought of him as slimy, she had to admit, Agent Harris was smooth around women. Charismatic, statuesque, and bold, he could walk into a room full of beautiful women and take his pick with no more effort than selecting a peach in the produce aisle. Cursade, Petrikin, Harris—they were remarkable men.

But Dee had never met anyone like Ghost.

Putting her finger on exactly why proved a daunting task. He wasn't strikingly handsome. Certainly not homely though, thought Dee. Aside of his imposing size and curiously pale skin, there really wasn't anything unusual about his looks. But Ghost carried a powerful presence. It was as if the man had a kind of inner might that radiated from him, even when he was still and silent. And when he spoke, his words echoed stark white purity...innocence. He seemed without pretense, without guile, and utterly unafraid. Toward the end of their time sitting in the Motel 6 lobby, Dee had found herself trusting him, in spite of her initial suspicions.

Dee shrugged, turned back to the laptop, and let her eyes linger for a moment on the horrid Smiling Jack photos. Blade. Blood. Ghastly smile.

Work thoughts, Deanna. Think work thoughts.

She'd already dusted the camera, inside and out, and sent digital renderings of the prints to the Bureau for matching. She'd just begun to upload the photos from the camera's memory and clicked over to see the status bar. Taking longer than usual for a handful of pictures, she thought.

She watched the status bar and listened absently to the muted ramblings from CNN on her room's TV: something about conservative Senator Karch Ridgeway's bid for the Presidency and for the upcoming Supreme Court decision on abortion. But CNN scarcely registered in her conscious mind.

There was something else about Ghost, something that wouldn't let Dee put aside her doubt completely. Maybe it's my imagination, Dee thought. Something about the way he walked...or maybe the intensity in his green-eyed gaze, just shy of ferocity. He seemed coiled like a spring, or like a sleek panther ready to pounce. Dee had no doubt that this man could be dangerous. She had no doubt that he could kill if he had to. And she felt certain that he had killed before. Was this Ghost the killer they called Smiling Jack? She'd thought so before they'd met. He'd altered her opinion somewhat, but she wasn't foolish enough to dismiss the possibility.

She blinked, brought back to focus by movement on her screen. The PhotoScan icon bounced in the sidebar dock. Rez clicked it to stop its bouncing. The photos had all uploaded. Rez scanned down the list of files...and then froze.

***   ***   ***   ***

I had a lot to think about on the bus. I had underestimated G. He was good. Good enough to fool most people. Just not good enough to fool me. When he typed in the correct registration number for the yacht I'd seen, his smile lost a little of its charm. For just a moment, there was a subtle change in the tension in the corners of his mouth. There was a peculiar stillness in his eyes also. It reminded me eerily of the change in someone's eyes when they die.

But G had recovered swiftly, and his next move was genius. The flourish of his right hand almost distracted me enough to miss him turning his monitor with his left hand. It was like a cruise ship magician holding up a gold coin for the audience to see while slipping something from his coat pocket. I almost missed it. Someone had purchased that Sun Odyssey 42DS from Spinnaker Sales. But whoever it was, G didn't want me to see his name.

***   ***   ***   ***

"I don't know," said G into his cell phone. "He said his name was John Spector. But he asked about the boat."

G listened for a moment and then replied. "He's staying at the friggin' Motel 6 in Destin. I should have known he wasn't buying. He didn't look like the sailing type. White as a ghost, definitely a snowbird, but I couldn't place his accent. Big guy too, looked like a bouncer."

Shouts erupted from the phone. G held it away from his ear until the yelling died down. "No, no way. I didn't give him anything. He doesn't know Jack! He's not a local cop, that's for sure. White as white—you should'a seen him. I don't think he was FBI either. Didn't try to scare me with a shield or anything. One weird thing, he had this silver case. Looked like something from the movies: a sniper case or nuclear detonator, some crap like that."

More shouts from the phone. G endured them and said, "He had the registration number, said he'd seen the 42 on the Gulf. Now that's legit. He knew about the custom windows. He didn't say any more. Uh, huh, Destin Motel 6. As far as I know, he's alone. Hey, listen, you're not angry at me, are you? You know I wouldn't cross you. Okay, okay. Sure." G pressed the red button on his cell and ran a finger under the collar of his shirt. It felt suddenly very tight.

GHOST

***   ***   ***   ***

I walked into the Motel 6 lobby at quarter past nine, and I was thinking that I ought to switch hotels soon. I decided to give it the night. Mr. Granderson was at his usual post behind the desk. He looked up, saw me, and backed up a step.

"Oh, Mr. Spector, uhm, or is it Willoughby?"

I definitely needed to switch hotels. "What's the problem?"

He squinted like he was bracing for a punch. "The-there's no problem," he muttered. "It's just that you have messages. Two of them." He handed me two slips of paper. I thanked him and walked away. The first message was from Doctor Shepherd at the hospital. The second was from the FBI agent, Deanna Rezvani. Both were marked: Urgent.

{ Chapter 11 }

I PASSED THE BUSINESS CENTER, half expecting to see the old man ignoring his granddaughter again, but I found it empty. Maybe he finally figured out that little girls like to go outside and play.

My room felt empty too—thankfully—not even a trace of Shade-vibe, so I put my case on the bed and picked up the phone. Dr. Shepherd first. Got voice mail. Agent Rezvani next. Voice mail again. So much for urgent.

I took a shower, making the water so hot it stung. Steam enveloped me. I let my head rest on the shower wall. The resetting began. I felt my flesh tighten. Everything about me began to feel sturdier and stronger.

But I was still angry. I'd been at it two days now, and while some of the evidence I'd turned up was promising—especially the sailboat dealer—I still hadn't rescued anyone. Those women in the pictures were still out there, kenneled up like beasts. I pounded the wall with a taut fist. *Inexcusable, unfathomable, egregious—evil.*

A flash of images—the blade, the creepy smile, the kennels. My stomach lurched, and I almost lost it. Those women...precious, precious lives being degraded like that and snuffed out. Beautiful children with hopes and dreams—each life of inestimable value—suddenly gone. I thought of the killer. I pounded the wall, caving a square of fiberglass inward.

"Ignorant, bloodthirsty, fool!" the words blasted from my lungs. I came that close, but I caught myself before it was too late. There'd be a time for unleashing all of the pent up indignation, the righteous anger, the collective fury of retribution—the rage. But for now, I needed to think clearly. It started and ended with the photos. What was I missing?

The FBI files revealed that the original Smiling Jack photos had been released over a span of four years. In the earliest photos, there were always shots of the victims to come, threats that he would continue to kill. The second batch of photos began to appear four years after the last photo of the first series. And, it had been four years since the last photo of the last series before the photos I'd discovered on the camera. What was it about four years?

The photos I'd obtained on the camera continued the pattern. And now, according to Agent Rezvani, the shots were all over the web. Jack was making a new power play. He'd murdered the woman with red hair, and rubbed it in our faces. But there were young women still alive. Five, if the number of doghouses meant anything.

Until more photos surfaced, I couldn't know for certain. But, I needed to operate under the assumption that every day I delayed, was another day of hell for women who were still alive. I wondered about that.

What is their existence like? Being treated like animals, degraded, and likely abused—I dared not imagine the potential variety of horrors. And yet, in the photos, the women wore that same ghastly, contented smile. Drugged? But what sort of drug would keep someone grinning while her life's blood drained away? That would be another question for Dr. Shepherd.

The steaming water poured down either side of my neck. For a moment, I imagined it was my own blood draining from a gaping throat wound. I shook the thought from my head and pounded my fist once more. Then I stood still. The moment I'd struck the wall, I thought I'd heard something. It wasn't the fiberglass cracking. It was a kind of dull thump. I thought maybe it was the shower pipes behind the wall. I turned off the water for a moment to listen. I didn't hear anything. I put the water on again and heard nothing more.

The heat and the steam soothed my muscles and helped me think. The resetting was complete. And yet, I lingered in the hot water a little while longer. Perhaps the greatest nagging mystery was how women such as those in the photos, attractive women by this society's standards, could be abducted without anyone reporting them missing? Maybe foreign slave trade or prostitution, maybe the bowels of the pornographic industry could provide such victims. The FBI had looked into those possibilities, hadn't they? Or were they handcuffed by international law? But it had to be something like that. You don't just give up on a loved one. I told myself that, and I almost believed it. But the FBI had given up. Maybe some of the victim's had family who had given up too. But not one family member had ever come forward to identify a victim. I shook my head. That just didn't seem possible.

And why the display? Was Smiling Jack simply saying, "See what I can do?" Was he flaunting his god-complex and daring the world to catch him? Or was there something more?

It happened again. I shut the water off. This time I was certain I'd heard something. Not a thump, more like a melodic trill. The room phone.

I crashed out of the shower stall, whip-cracked a towel around my waist, careened around the bed, and snagged the phone mid ring.

"John Spector."

"Mr. Spector, this is Doc Shepherd from PCBH. I have some information about the surgical implement you showed me."

Doc Shepherd, I liked the way he said that. Like the Old West, Doc Holliday. "That's very good news," I said. "What have you discovered?"

"I think it best if we talk in person. Could you meet me again at the hospital?"

"Name the time."

"I've got procedures all morning. How about 2:30?"

"I'll be there. Just make sure—" Something was wrong. The room had gone cold, and it wasn't just air on my wet skin.

I heard the worry in the surgeon's voice. "Mr. Spector?"

"I'll have to call you ba—" The wire dropped past my face, bit into my neck, and jerked taut. I took a deep breath as I dropped the phone. I tried to wedge my arm beneath the attacker's wrist, tried to grab his hand, but he was beastly strong. I couldn't breathe.

I could last longer than most, but without air, my muscles would soon burn with lactic acid. I'd lose strength. I'd lose vision. This mission would come to an end, and those women would never leave those horrid kennels alive.

It came. All the rage, barely controlled before, erupted within me. Even after the recent resetting and the diminished ability that came with it, the rage infused me with a surge of ferocity and strength. I threw my arms back, leaped, and used the bed to explode backward into the attacker. The killer had been using his considerable might to constrict and pull back, expecting all my effort, all my fight to be clawing and resisting the wire. So when I launched backward, my force joined his force. We became a two man missile and crashed into the entertainment center. Wood cracked, the television imploded, and glass showered us as we fell.

All my weight came down on the killer. He groaned, and the wire went slack. I slipped out from under it and rolled off. I tumbled to the window side of the room and turned. I expected to see the assailant writhing in agony. His head and neck had taken the initial impact, and I'd fallen upon him with rib-cracking force. I thought it was over. But I was wrong.

The man had gotten to his feet just as I had. He shook his head, blinked his vision to focus, and then cracked his neck to either shoulder as if to say, *Is that all you got?*

I could see the blood glistening in his dark hair, matting the back of his head. And something about his fighting stance was off. His right leg, flexed behind him, was a bit akimbo. It was like a marionette's leg, in the right place but looking not quite alive.

He reached backward and his hand returned with a slender blade that ended in a wicked sharp point. It looked like a boning knife. He flexed, looking ready to spring. I couldn't believe it. This man should be unconscious. Then, I saw his eyes. And I understood.

Under dark, unruly brows—already standing out on his sweating mad face—the man's big brown eyes changed. His sockets grew huge and, just for a moment, I saw twin black holes in his fierce stare. Whirling, sucking darkness, empty but for a tiny orb of fire in each eye. It was then that I knew the man had been taken.

And I also knew, I was in serious trouble. The resetting had left me vulnerable, weaker and slower than I could normally be. I needed my silver case. Keeping the killer in focus, I searched around the room for my case, saw it on the other side of the bed, between the bed and the wall. I could dive across the bed for it, but he'd be on me with that blade before I could grab the suitcase handle.

I'd have to take him hand-to-hand.

I lunged, leaped and planted both my feet into his chest. He crashed into the wall behind him, and I fell to the floor. I rolled backward to a crouch, and he rebounded and came at me with the knife. I slammed an inside-out forearm into the wrist of the knife hand to keep the blade at bay. Then I rotated my waist and flexed my upper back and rear shoulder muscle to drive my elbow into his jaw. I heard the crack of bone and a shriek. Then, I felt the blade.

The knife plunged into my gut, sliding with little friction through the stomach muscle. I felt the pain and shock radiating from the new wound. I elbowed him again, fell backward over the bed, and stumbled to my feet.

He stood there, blood dripping out of the corner of a ghastly, misshapen grin. He still held the knife, and blood glistened on the blade. My blood.

I wasn't too worried about the stomach wound. The recent resetting would slow the healing process, but it would heal. That is, it would heal if I didn't let the assassin hurt me further. And that was a pretty big "if." The tearing of the stomach muscle had weakened my core.

The killer moved laterally to his right, giving me limited options. I countered by moving away from the bed, crunching TV glass as I went. He moved the knife side-to-side hypnotically like a pendulum. I watched it.

There were three sharp bangs at the door. A voice. "Mr. Spector! What's going on in there?" It was the manager, Mr.

Granderson. "I've gotten three calls about the noise. Mr. Spector?"

The killer was distracted for just a second. It was enough. I swooped in and, with both hands, grabbed the man by the neck, and flung him headlong into the wall by the window. Inverted, he slammed into the large duck painting, and then slid down the wall to rest in a heap on the floor.

"MR. SPECTOR, I demand that you open this door!"

I heard fumbling at the lock, a key card swipe. I vaulted to the door, dead bolted and chained it. "Uh, I'm sorry about all the noise, Mr. Granderson!" I ground my teeth, fighting against the burn radiating from my stomach. "There won't be any more...noise...tonight. I promise."

"Wha-what are you doing in there? It sounds like World War III!"

"Would you believe aerobics?" I asked, suddenly feeling like Maxwell Smart.

"Aerobics? No, I wouldn't believe that. I heard glass breaking."

"Well, it was kind of like combat training," I said. Technically, it was true. "Like Tai-Bo, just...uh, more so. And things got out of hand." Technically, that was true also. "I'll pay for damages."

"I expect you'll be leaving this motel for good in the morning, as well?"

"Yes, yes, you won't have to worry about me any longer." I turned a few moments too late.

A translucent form—long, sinewy muscles, claws, and gnarled wings—was emerging from the killer's body.

I leaped for my silver case, knowing I'd miss the chance to blast it. The Shade gave me a black glare and then surged through the window into the night. I'd never catch him. And I needed to let my gut finish healing.

"I'll expect full payment, Spector," the manager said, his voice trailing off. "Just tell me you didn't break the TV."

I looked at the TV. Shattered glass, twisted and cracked frame. *Oops.*

Then, I heard a groan. I went to the killer. He was a mess of blood and broken bones, his head angled awkwardly to the wall. But...he was still breathing.

I eased his head to the ground. His breathing was shallow and coarse with blood. He was dying. I couldn't prevent that, but I could delay it. I hurriedly popped the clasps on my case, slid an internal latch, and lifted out one compartment. I found a vial full of bluish fluid, removed the cap, and replaced it with a pressurized flange seal. Then, I jammed the seal against the man's neck and watched the blue fluid seep into his flesh.

He groaned and sucked in a harsh breath. His eyes fluttered and became a little more focused. I had a hundred questions, but I couldn't ask them all. There just weren't enough heartbeats left, and I didn't want to let him die without giving him The Offer.

"Who sent you?" I demanded.

He made a kind of guttural noise and moved his ruined jaw, wincing repeatedly. Still, he kept smiling that ghoulish grin, and blood trickled over his lips and down his cleft chin. Cleft chin. I looked at him, and a thrill swept through me. Smiling Jack.

With the damage to his jaw and skull, it was impossible to know for sure. And I was running out of time to find out.

"Where are the women you took? Where are they?"

He mumbled something, making more of those garbled sounds.

GHOST

"Don't you understand?" I growled. "You are moments from death. Tell me where they are!"

"I...don't know," he muttered at last. "Women...?"

"The women you took, the doghouse...the pictures..." I stopped that line of questioning. I could see in his eyes. He didn't know. This wasn't Smiling Jack. The giant blinking question mark in my mind...if not Smiling Jack, then who sent the assassin? The answer came immediately, but I couldn't waste the precious few seconds remaining. The man was dying, and I needed to make The Offer.

"Look at me!" I commanded, my voice dropping several octaves.

The killer looked up, his focus crystallizing.

"You have suffered," I said. "Your life is littered with deep wounds and your soul is marked. But you made choices all along the way, and you will stand before the Throne and face judgment. But there is one choice remaining for you. This is your final offer." I knelt close to him and whispered The Offer.

He coughed out a laugh, and more blood dribbled over his lips. He cursed me and spat. Then, he died.

I looked at the dead man and sighed. It is these times that I feel as if the earth's gravity has increased tenfold. The man had made his choice—*the wrong one*—and departed. But, in spite of the fact that he had tried to kill me, I had been the one to send him on his way. He was not my mission, but perished at my hands anyway. I stood up and shook my head.

A quiet, metallic voice distracted me from the corpse. "*If you wish to make a call, please hang up and...*"

The phone still lay on the carpet and was trying to persuade me to please hang up or dial the number again. I hung up.

I wondered what Doc Shepherd had to tell me. I'd see him at 2:30 the next day. Before that, however, I figured to go visit G

{ 105 }

at Spinnaker Sales, see if he knew how coincidental it was for me to be attacked by a professional hitter right after my first visit with him.

Special Agent Rezvani owed me a call as well. She might even want to meet again. But all of that would have to wait for tomorrow.

I had a lot to do in the meantime. I had a room to clean and a body to get rid of.

{ Chapter 12 }

"WHAT...WHAT TIME IS IT?" Lucinda asked dreamily.

Jack knelt at the arched opening of her kennel home and shone a penlight against the inner wall. "It's very late," he said.

"Why are you waking me up?" she asked, no anger in her voice...just half-awake curiosity. "You've always said how important our sleep is."

"Oh, it is, Lucinda, very important." He took her hand and led her out of the house. "But for some special occasions, we may go without."

"Special?" she echoed.

"Shhh, yes, but quietly, dear Lucinda. Quietly. You'll wake your sisters, and that would spoil the evening. Understood?"

Lucinda nodded solemnly. With her sleep frizzed blonde hair and gossamer nightgown, she looked even more like a faerie. "I'll be good," she whispered.

"I knew you would," Jack replied. With deft touch, he unlocked her neck collar and the shackles on her wrists and ankles.

He placed the chrome chains next to Lucinda's house, making barely a tinkle of sound.

Lucinda shivered a little, and Jack put his arm around her and led her into the hall. "Now then, Lucinda," he said as they walked, "I want to ask you something. You've spoken often of Molly these past weeks. Why do you think that is?"

"I miss her," Lucinda replied. "She is my favorite sister. I think about her every day."

"I thought so," he said. He paused by a door. "And who could blame you? Molly was a very special young lady."

"Is."

"What?" Jack asked.

"You said Molly *was* a special young lady. You meant *is*, right?"

"Of course," Jack replied. He forced a broad smile. "You are so very perceptive, Lucinda. Here, go into the powder room, brush your hair, and make yourself up like I've shown you. I've laid out some new clothing for you."

"New clothes?" Lucinda's eyes danced. "What for?"

"You're going on a trip, my dear."

"A trip?" she asked. "But I've never been on a trip. Where will I go?"

Jack flipped on the powder room light and directed Lucinda inside. Then he answered her at last. "You are going to see Molly."

***   ***   ***   ***

"I get more than one?" Lucinda asked as she peeled the small round patch off the contact sheet.

"This is a special occasion," said Dr. Gary. One lens of his thick-framed glasses appeared from behind the camera. Half of his bright white smile appeared, as well, and he said, "But put it on your other shoulder, dear. And try to relax."

Lucinda reached under the wide neckline of her blouse and affixed the patch to her right shoulder. She took in a sharp breath. "Oh, it feels so good. It's like my birthday all over again."

"Very much like your birthday," said Dr. Gary.

"And I get my picture taken again?" Lucinda asked, her head swaying.

"Not just your picture," he replied. "But a movie as well."

Lucinda's eyes fluttered open and she smiled. "A movie? Me?" The doctor nodded.

"Oh, thank you so much," she said. "I've always wanted to be in a movie."

"You know Molly was in a movie," Jack said, entering the room. He walked casually across the plastic and stood behind Lucinda. "Molly's movie was very important."

"Oh, Molly, Molly, Molly-kin," said Lucinda dreamily. "So beautiful. So right for a movie. But...why didn't I get to see Molly's movie?"

"Why spoil the surprise?" Doctor Gary asked. "This way, you'll experience the movie just like Molly did."

"Will anyone see my movie?" she asked.

"If we have our way," Jack said, rubbing the cleft in his chin, "millions of people will see it."

Lucinda smiled, arched her back, and groaned with pleasure.

"The cameras are ready," Doctor Gary said. "This resolution is so high, they'll be able to watch it on an IMAX screen if they want. They'll have to be in utter denial to brush this off as a fake."

"I'm not a fake, doctor-woctor," Lucinda purred. "Fake, wake, take..."

"I think she's ready," Dr. Gary said dryly.

Jack nodded. He sat on a high stool directly behind Lucinda. "Gary, the plastic slipped off the laptop," he said. He waited for the doctor to make the adjustment. "That should cover it well enough. Size us up. Are we good?"

"Lower your stool a little," the doctor said, squinting at the digital viewfinder. "I can't even see your chin right now. There. Perfect. That works."

"Okay, Lucinda, my sweet," Jack said, petting her silky blond hair. "We are about to start the movie. You'll have to open your eyes and smile."

Lucinda obeyed.

Jack pinched the thin skin on her neck between his nails. "Did you feel that?" he asked.

"It tickled."

He pinched harder. "How about now?"

"It feels good. Do it some more."

"I will," Jack said.

"Will I get to see Molly soon?" she asked.

"Very soon," said Jack. "Smile pretty." He nodded to Doctor Gary. The camera began to roll.

Jack continued to pet Lucinda with his left hand. He leaned forward a bit so that the back of Lucinda's head rested lightly against his chest. Then, in his right hand, he lifted the blade. He looked straight ahead into the camera, though he knew that only the lower portion of his face was visible. By feel, he found the dimple on Lucinda's neck, below her ear, below the corner of her jaw. He applied just enough pressure to the blade and began to cut.

Jack likened it to a symphony, and he was first chair cello. His hand moved fluidly, and the blade glided over flesh. As the blood came, Jack smiled for the camera.

GHOST

*** *** *** ***

"I've got to go now," said Doctor Gary, slamming the hatch of his black sports utility. "This hour I shouldn't have any trouble."

"So you'll be going straight from the marina to the hospital then?" Jack asked.

"I'll need the time," he replied. "I'm going to take her farther out, almost to Pensacola. Then I've got to be at the clinic for a procedure at ten, three more in the afternoon. But, ah..." He hesitated.

"What is it?" Jack asked.

Dr. Gary plucked off his work gloves and tossed them into the backseat. He shut the door, leaned against it, and sighed. "Shame about Lucinda. It felt rushed."

"I'm worried," Jack said. "But not about Lucinda."

"About Erica? I don't think she's too far along. I doubt very much that she has any idea—"

"Not about Erica," Jack said. "You'll take care of her problem this weekend. No...I'm thinking about the elections."

Dr. Gary rubbed his temples. "I don't believe they will get enough votes back to take the big chair. Especially not after our messages become...more public."

"Polls aren't exactly looking favorable," Jack replied. "And they've already got the court in their back pocket."

"But surely not the Senate?"

"How many times will we tread this same ground?" Jack hissed. Then, with some effort, he moderated his tone. "If they get the Presidency, the House, and keep the Court, the Senate will be worthless. I'm beginning to fear that our work these many years is coming to naught."

"Don't say that!" Dr. Gary whispered urgently.

"But subtlety isn't working, not this time," Jack said. "In fact, we have become largely irrelevant. You were right all along about the desensitization of America. If we do not find a way to generate enough buzz with Lucinda..." He glanced at the black bag in the back of the SUV. "Well, the only thing left to do is reveal."

"We always knew it might come to this," Dr. Gary said.

Jack's shoulders fell. He nodded slowly.

Dr. Gary said, "You understand where this will go? If we reveal, there will no longer be any hiding. No safety. No future plan."

Jack smiled gently. "In every revolution, in every just cause, there are martyrs. Future generations are more important than...than our survival."

"Yes, yes they are," Dr. Gary said. "But listen, Jack, you need to relax." After a pregnant pause, he went on, "I think we need to go out tomorrow."

"You'll be too exhausted after work—"

"I won't take no for an answer," Dr. Gary said. "Come, we'll visit our favorite place. Not a late thing. We'll go right after I get home, say about five o'clock. Can you swing it?"

"I...I think so," Jack said. "The parents will understand. After all, I offer them favors of convenience, and I almost never close the daycare early."

{ Chapter 13 }

I HAVE MANY HELPFUL ITEMS in my silver case. But one thing I do not have is some liquid or spray that would dissolve a corpse. *Body-B-Gone* or maybe *Abracadaver*.

Something like that would have really come in handy the night I was attacked. Sure, I could've just called the police, explained how a killer broke into my room, how I fought him off in self defense, and killed him. After due process, I'd certainly be acquitted. But the women who'd been abducted by Smiling Jack didn't have time for due process.

I certainly didn't find that camera so that I could wait in a jail cell for local cops to figure out how innocent I am. And if they did any in-depth research into my identity, I'd be in for more than due process. In fact, there was enough material in my silver case to have me shipped to a top secret government lab for a long, long time.

So I had a body to get rid of.

I thought about dragging him out through the lobby as if he was a good friend who'd passed out from too much to drink. But even if I managed to wash the blood off the killer, there's something different about a human body when it's no longer animated. Rigor mortis begins to set in, stiffening places that are usually fluid and flexible. Every part of the body becomes utterly dead weight. Someone would notice. Probably Mr. Granderson; he was already suspicious. He might put two and two together and make a whole lot of trouble.

Then I had an idea. It might even kill two birds with one stone. So to speak.

***   ***   ***   ***

The killer had no ID on him. He did have a single, nondescript car key and a gold money clip with several hundred dollars in it. That would help pay for damages. I figured he left the ID in his car. I needed a car for what I was planning, but I'd need to hurry. Being on the first floor turned out to have a few perks. A window large enough to climb in and out of was somewhat convenient...though it had been the killer's source of ingress, I reflected. The window slid open easily, and I slipped outside.

A pro wouldn't leave his car in the motel's parking lot. He'd park nearby but on a shadowy side road where a police car could drive right by it nine times and never remember seeing it there. Someplace where he could leave in a hurry, with easy access to the main drag. A block away, I found the road. Then, I found the car. Netherviewing let me see the residual warmth of the four cars parked on the curb. But I needn't have bothered. Black and sleek, a low slung sports coup—typical image prop for a killer.

Using the killer's key, I opened the car and sat behind the wheel. I found his ID in an overhead compartment. Gerrard DiPietro was his name. 32 years old from Panama City Beach. A local. *Killers-R-Us,* I thought sardonically. *An office in every town.*

Beneath a tarp in the back, I discovered a treasure trove of Gerrard's tricks of the trade: a dozen slender blades like the one he used on me, two automatic rifles, two silenced 9-millimeter pistols, and, sitting innocently in a Tupperware container, a block of plastic explosives. Semtex, military grade.

I thought about this hoard. Gerrard wasn't some movie-watching, assassin-wannabe. He was a big hitter. I blew out a sigh. If the guy was less discreet, he might have blown up half the Motel 6, taking out a score of innocent folks. Thank God Gerrard was discreet...and confident enough to make it personal. That gave me pause as well. *Personal.*

Someone *really* didn't like me sniffing around. Whoever it was wanted me out of the picture urgently enough to put down hard cash for a real pro, someone who wasn't likely to screw up the job or leave loose ends. Too bad.

Gerrard screwed up. And I'm a pretty big loose end.

I turned the key in the ignition, and the sports car purred to life. I drove back to the motel and parked in the open slot next to my room. I spent the next two hours cleaning blood out of the carpet and off the walls. Using a few ounces of a powerful epoxy from my case, I repaired the entertainment center door. But the TV and the duck painting were history. I'd leave the killer's wad of cash for the replacements.

I put Gerrard's body under the tarp in the back of his car and locked it up. Then, with the sun already airbrushing the horizon pink, I climbed back into my room and went to sleep for three hours.

***   ***   ***   ***

I passed by the business center just as the old guy and his granddaughter were going in.

"But, Grampy," she mewed, "I wanna build a sand castle. I wanna go to the beach. You said we could. You s-a-i-d!"

I shook my head and waited in line to check out. When I stepped up to the counter, Mr. Granderson bounced backward. He wasn't quite as bold when there wasn't a locked door between us.

"Checking out?" he gurgled.

"Yes." I handed him two key cards just like everything was normal. Just Mr. Happy Customer, checking out after a pleasant stay.

Mr. Granderson cleared his throat and said, "Any additional charges...or damages?"

"I'm afraid I've destroyed the TV and one of the paintings. This ought to cover it." I handed him a sum in excess of $800, more than enough to replace the stuff. The TV wasn't exactly state-of-the-art. And the duck painting wasn't a Rembrandt.

I turned to leave, but then I had an idea. "Do you have any lollipops?"

Mr. Granderson almost laughed. "Lollipops?"

"Yeah, you know, a stick with a hard candy on the end? We give them to give kids?"

"I know what a lollipop is," Mr. Granderson quipped. Then he seemed to remember he was terrified of me. He held up a little bowl full of red and white striped candies. "Will peppermints do?"

"Perfect. Thanks." I left without taking a mint. They weren't for me.

I stood outside the business center and watched as, once again, the old guy was at the solitaire, leaving the granddaugh-

GHOST

ter playing with a doll on the floor. I entered, stood just inside the door, and glared at the man.

"You'll have to wait your turn for the good computer," the old guy said, barely sparing me a glance.

"S'okay," I said. I knelt down by the granddaughter. "Pardon me, little girl, but the manager at the desk said he has some candies for you."

"For me?" She was all smiles, bright blue eyes, freckles, blond pigtails. Adorable. She looked from me back to the old guy. "Can I, Grampy?"

"Go ahead," he replied without turning around.

I waited until the little girl was gone. Then I grabbed the back of the old man's chair and spun him around to face me.

"What are you—"

"Neglect," I said, hammering both syllables. "That's what you're doing. I don't know who you are and I don't know your story. But that little girl's worth more than every computer game in this world. Now here's what you're going to do."

"Who are you to tell me—" He sucked in a harsh breath. He'd seen my eyes as I began to Netherview.

"Don't speak again," I commanded, the bass in my voice reaching subwoofer levels. "When she comes back, you're going to tell her you love her, and you're going to turn off that stupid game and take her some place nice. Take her to the beach to build a sandcastle. Take her to a water park. It's going to be a hot day. Let her swim for you. Watch her do tricks in the water, and tell her how great she is. And don't you ever take her for granted. You don't know how many more days YOU have left. Do you understand?"

The old man swallowed and blurped out some kind of affirmative noise. I turned and left just as the little girl came back.

She was smiling and one cheek was puffed out with a peppermint. She had at least seven more clutched in her fists.

* * *   * * *   * * *   * * *

It was already 87 degrees by 10 a.m. in Panama City Beach. Not the best conditions to be riding around with a corpse. The smell made me gag several times on the short trip.

I pulled into the Spinnaker Sales parking lot, sliding to a stop in the pristine white gravel. The showroom didn't open until eleven. I figured I had maybe twenty minutes until G showed up. I didn't know what kind of top level security technology they used. It didn't much matter. I had my silver case.

* * *   * * *   * * *   * * *

G. Alonzo Vasquez arrived at 10:55. He was the only one on the floor at Spinnaker Sales until one o'clock, so he took the liberty of getting a long overdue manicure on the way in. He wasn't worried. The showroom was immaculate, lit with inner fire from the Gulf sun, like a diamond with perfect color, cut, and clarity. *Shining like my future,* G thought, a jaunty spring in his step as he strolled to the showroom's doors.

G was smugly expectant because he had a very important appointment coming in that morning, one that could dwarf the rest of the weekend's sales by comparison. Sir Drystan Pembroke, the captain of the Royal Welsh Yachting Club was coming to Spinnaker with the intent of updating his fleet. If all went well, his lordship might drop eight digits on Spinnaker that day.

What a party I'll throw, G thought, imagining his commission from such a sale. When G turned off the security system and entered the showroom, he shivered. "A/C's a little high," he muttered, striding to the control panel by the main sales office. And indeed it was. Set at sixty-two degrees, much—much—lower than usual. G turned it back to a more comfortable seventy-one degrees and made a note on his legal pad to call the A/C people.

G put on hot water for his vast selection of gourmet teas. Surely Sir Drystan would find one to his liking. Perhaps Glengettie or Murroughs, specialty teas that G had imported from Wales. G smiled and rubbed his hands together. *Yes,* he thought, *today will be a day to remember.*

G booted up his office computer. Then he stiffened. He'd just caught a meandering wisp of something unpleasant. *No,* he thought. *Not today.* He raced into the restrooms and looked around. Nothing had backed up. Nothing had been left...unflushed. The smell of the room was sterile if not fragrant. Back in his office, he sniffed around, but did not detect the odor again.

Thus, G continued his usual bustle around the showroom. He flicked on all the hanging lights and polished anything that looked the least bit smudged or dusty. By the time his lordship Sir Drystan appeared, the diamond of G's showroom had been polished to the epitome of luster and class.

When his lordship's chauffeur opened the showroom door, G was waiting. But Sir Drystan did not enter alone. A ravishing young woman stood at his elbow. She was raven-haired and had large dark eyes, dark enough to get lost in for a very long time...if one were so inclined. G was definitely so inclined.

Had he been a cartoon character, his tongue would have rolled out of his mouth, over his chin, and half way across the showroom floor. This woman wore a stark, royal blue dress with a wide pearlescent belt. She was curvy but not tawdry. In every way, she seemed poised, mannered and wise beyond her apparent years.

"Ah, Mister Vasquez," Sir Drystan Pembroke said, extending his hand. "So good to finally meet you."

G shook his eyes off the woman and shook the master yachtsman's hand. "Sir Drystan, you are kind to grace Spinnaker Sales with your presence." He paused and nodded graciously at the woman. "Is this your wife?"

"Ah, you old letch," Sir Drystan said, reddening. "This is my daughter, Cambriard."

G took her offered hand and bowed over it. "My pleasure, Ms. Pembroke."

"All mine," she replied. She turned to Sir Drystan. "Daddy, you never said he was so debonair."

"Tut, Cambie," he replied. "We're here for boats not boys."

"You're here for boats," she murmured.

"I'm afraid we're in a bit of a time crunch," said Pembroke with a sideways glance at his daughter. "I wonder if we couldn't see the models we discussed?"

"Of course," G said. "You won't find a more complete selection anywhere in the world."

"Very good," he replied. "If your inventory is as complete as you indicated in our previous discussions, this shouldn't take long at all."

G led his lordship on a flourishing tour of the best racing yachts Spinnaker Sales had to offer. He knew he'd impressed father—and daughter—with his voluminous knowledge of each boat's details: draft, keel, fuel capacity, overall beam, water displacement, etc. Facts and figures, delivered with shark cunning, and a few devastating winks for Cambie—G thought sure he'd made the sale. *Ha,* he laughed to himself. *Made the sale. I'm charming without even trying.*

But at the edge of his senses, every now and then, an odd, unpleasant odor made itself known. Neither Sir Pembroke nor his gorgeous daughter seemed to notice it, but G did. He wondered if perhaps a gull had found its way into the building's ventilation system and summarily died. *Most unsavory,* he thought. *And bound to get more unsavory.*

Still, Sir Pembroke and his daughter were all smiles as they boarded boat after boat. "I must admit, Mr. Vasquez, I didn't really expect your selection to live up to your rather glowing description." Pembroke paused a beat. "But honestly, I have never seen anything like this. So much quality at my fingertips. I should like to flood your showroom and take each and every hull out for a spin."

"Thank you, Sir Drystan," G said. "There are still more to see, if you wish?"

"I believe we've seen more than enough to close the deal. I'm going to add four additional hulls to my order," Pembroke said, giddy with the purchase and the assets he had which allowed the purchase. "And Mr. Vasquez, I am very good friends with New Zealand's captain, Charles Draper. I plan to recommend your establishment—wait a moment." Pembroke stared behind G. "That's a Jeanneau frame if I've ever seen one."

"Ah," G said, "the 42DS."

"Is that the one, Daddy?" Cambie clutched her hands together and bounced.

"I believe it is," Pembroke replied. He leaned conspiratorially towards G and whispered, "I promised Cambie I'd get her a 42 if you had it in the showroom. Well done, Mr. Vasquez."

"Would you like to go aboard?" G asked, winking at Pembroke and taking Cambie's hand.

"Yes, oh, yes I would," she said.

They covered forty yards of showroom floor in an instant. "Watch your step," G said, giving the shapely daughter a hand up. He let Sir Drystan board next and then clambered up after them. The moment he set foot on deck, G knew something was wrong.

The odor was there, like a wall. From the sour look on Sir Drystan's face, it was clear his lordship had scented it as well.

Apparently, Cambie wasn't too worried about it. "I'm going to go below," she said.

"No, wait," G called after her. "Let me..." But she was already down the stairs.

G let out a dreadful sigh. He was greatly fearful that she'd find a dead seagull. When he heard her scream, he felt sure she'd found something worse.

Lord Pembroke ran to the below-deck stair just in time to catch his daughter as she leaped and tripped over the hatch. Her eyes bulged and she could barely breathe. "Blood," she gasped.

"What in the world?" Sir Drystan exclaimed as she dragged him to exit the deck. "What did you see?"

"Wait!' G cried. "I'm sure there's a misunderstanding. Wait for me at the front desk. I'll see to this!" G bounded down the steps and saw nothing at first. He looked in the bedroom behind the stairs and found nothing. There was nothing amiss anywhere in the main cabin. The smell was another matter. Each breath was like being hit with a sickly sweet, scented hammer.

G knew where it was. The fore cabin, the master bedroom. G stepped around the small dining table, passed the galley, and stumbled into the room. Sprawled across the king bed was a very bloody corpse.

It was a man, someone G had seen before in the company of one of his "private" clients. But this man's skin was seven shades of vile. Blood had pooled on the bed beneath his skull. And his arms and legs were spread as if he had died while making a snow angel.

G doubled over and heaved on the floor. He clambered out of the room, vomiting as he lunged toward the stairs. He needed to get containment on this, but he had no idea how he could. Pembroke and his daughter had seen the body. What would they tell the authorities? Maybe, just maybe, G thought, he could put a spin on the whole thing and persuade his Welsh visitors not to go to the police. Let G handle it, he would say. After all, it would be a Spinnaker Sales affair.

But worse than that task was the circumstances around the body itself: how it had gotten there, why it had been left there, and who could have so thoroughly dispatched such a capable...employee. As he descended the ladder to the showroom floor, G cringed inwardly. He thought of the big guy with the silver case. *Spector.*

His stomach already roiling, G found no one at the front desk. Pembroke and his sexy kitten of a daughter...had gone. Things were spinning out of control. It was a vortex, and G felt he was caught in its relentless pull. He stared at the phone. He had a call to make, but he knew very well it could be his last call. His employer didn't like loose ends.

He punched in the number but hesitated to hit send. In the span of just a few minutes the vision of his mega-commission party had vanished. Pembroke's car was long gone. He took a deep breath and hit send. Losing a commission paled in comparison to other things he might lose.

{ Chapter 14 }

THE FAKE BRUNETTE and the fake blonde charge nurses sang a different song when I entered the Cardiology wing this time.

"Dr. Shepherd's procedure is running a little long," said Nurse Pelagris, the blond. "But please wait in his office."

"Can I get you a coffee...soft drink?" Nurse Brandywine asked. She wore her lustrous brunette hair in a decidedly grandmotherish bob.

"Yes, thank you," I replied. "A Dr. Pepper, if you have it."

I was barely in Shepherd's office five minutes before Nurse Brandywine showed up with a large cup of ice and a tall Dr. Pepper.

"Here ya' go, officer," she said. Technically, I'm not an officer of anything. Not in the sense she was using the word. But I was okay with her flawed assumption.

I was also okay with her change in attitude. There wasn't a hint of resentment in her manner, but I knew she had to be feeling it. Doc Shepherd must have had a few more words with his charge nurses after I left the last time. I hadn't known the good doctor for very long, but what I'd learned of him so far, I liked.

I sipped my soda and scanned the quilt of awards and diplomas on the office walls. I noticed that the dates on most of them were current, this year even. I considered all the recognition, all the awards, etc. I felt sure it wasn't ego-stroking. Not for Doc Shepherd. The guy seemed about as humble as can be. Old school humble.

I laughed to myself. I should have figured it out sooner. After all, I was sitting in the office of a heart surgeon. Those diplomas, certificates, and awards weren't for Doc Shepherd at all. They were decorations of comfort for his patients. If someone was going to have a doctor cut into his heart, it would be more than a little peace of mind to have a surgeon as qualified as Doc Shepherd. Each one of those framed pieces of paper was a security blanket.

The office door opened. "Ah, Officer Spector!" Doc Shepherd shook my hand. His bow tie was bright red today. He wore a traditional white lab coat, and his mustache was waxed into a gleeful curl. "I'm dreadfully sorry about the delay."

"Complications?"

"Not with the procedure," he said. "Laser angioplasty is fairly routine. The problem was the Westing excimer laser was not the one I requested. Those Westing catheters are unwieldy as heck. I much prefer the Irwin implement and had to wait close to thirty minutes for its delivery." He instantly realized he'd gone over my head and smiled. "All jargon," he said. He closed the office door and waddled over to his seat behind the desk.

He folded his hands on the blotter and stared thoughtfully. "I must confess I was a bit worried about you," he said. "All that ruckus on the phone and then the abrupt disconnect...I almost called the police. Of course that would be redundant, wouldn't it? And you look none the worse for wear."

"Unexpected visitor is all," I said. "He thought it would be funny to jump out and surprise me. Joke's on him, I guess."

He twirled his mustache. "Quite."

"The blade," I said, wanting to divert his keen eyes and keener mind. "You know something about it?"

He blinked. "Yes, yes I do. More than I ever wanted to know, in fact."

I leaned forward, rested my forearms on his desk.

"I didn't waste my time with database queries," he said. "Coming from a long line of surgeons, I had much better primary sources, my Uncle Timothy being the best. I sent him a scanned image, and he called me straight along. Surgical steel, he confirmed, as I suspected he would. Somewhat inferior grade cutting steel of its day, but nonetheless effective given its use."

"What kind of instrument is it?" I asked. "What's it for?"

"Well, it's the length of the instrument that gives it away...that and the retractable blade. It was used mainly in the late 1800's and is probably one of a very few still in existence. My uncle recognized it from a particularly gruesome assortment called the Grisham Collection. It is called Cain's Dagger, and it was used for abortion."

Abortion. The word sat hard in the pit of my stomach. I swallowed down bile and drifted back in my chair. For the moment, all association with the Smiling Jack case disintegrated.

Beyond all sunrises and sunsets...beyond all magnificent storms and the myriad intricacies of life in the natural world, there was nothing so beautiful and precious as a child. I had held a newborn once, a baby girl. I cradled her protectively in my arms and stared down at her in awe. Barely a handful and yet, a person. A thinking, feeling person. One who would work and play, hope and dream, love and weep.

And not just priceless for what she might become but for what she already was. From the most minute cells and their organelles to the major body systems, respiration, circulation, even the spectacular nervous system...all designed to work synergistically—she was a miracle of life. And yet, how many like her had been carelessly destroyed? Public and private industry measurements make the number at approximately 42 million children slain worldwide through abortion.

But my sources were more accurate, and I knew the number was higher. Much higher.

I squeezed my eyes shut and felt the rage surge begin to bubble up inside me. I can abide all manner of ignorance, but not this kind...and not with so much at stake. Those who would scream to heaven for justice if someone broke into the Louvre and slashed paintings or took a hammer to the sculptures—those very same—would smugly affirm that murdering an unborn child was some kind of right.

How I longed to visit wrath on any who commit such crimes. Maybe, someday I could. And yet, I knew that behind this scourge was a foe beyond my means. One who, perhaps more than any other, deserved the hand of judgment, and yet I had not the power or authority to render the due sentence.

"Officer Spector, are you all right?" Doc Shepherd asked. "You...you're shaking."

"I'm fine," I said, but my voice was so tight and clipped I was sure Doc would know otherwise.

He stared at me and twirled his mustache. Finally, he said, "I'm fine too."

I took his meaning instantly. More points for Doc Shepherd in my book.

"We swear to do no harm," Doc Shepherd said, muttering as if I wasn't even in the room. "Hippocratic Oath, it's what doctors are supposed to stand for. Some of us still do." He fell silent, and his eyes took on a level, faraway stare.

I shook my head at the madness of it all. There was a black-soul out there somewhere killing young women with a 19th century abortion knife. A theory about the killer's motive began to emerge, but I was reluctant to go there.

"Can you tell me anything else about the blade?"

He nodded, seemingly relieved to exit a room full of dark thoughts. "The knife is old," he said. "And a far cry from modern quality. But this was no crude instrument used in back alleys on prostitutes who found themselves pregnant. The Cain's Dagger was used by surgeons on anyone who could pay. And this was high-end technology, at one time, of course."

"Surgeons," I repeated.

"Surgeons."

Again, the motive whispered at my door. I had to go there this time. "Some sort of religious statement?" I asked Doc Shepherd. "Some so-called Christian...killing with an old abortion knife to show that abortion is murder?"

Doc Shepherd leaned forward and raised an eyebrow. "Not sure it's as simple as that."

"I don't follow."

"The age of the instrument," Doc Shepherd said. "Why not use a modern abortion device? There are plenty to choose from, unfortunately."

The freight train of motive I'd been growing more certain of...just derailed. Actually, it slammed into a brick wall.

"I suppose it's not out of the question for Pro-Lifers to use violence to make their point," Doc Shepherd continued. "There are hypocrites everywhere, of course. Do you happen to know if any of the victims were abortion docs, surge-techs, or any kind of clinic employees?"

"Not that we're aware of," I said. "But we can't rule it out."

"I see," Doc replied. He made a thoughtful humming sound and twirled the end of his mustache. "Officer Spector, are you at liberty to share the number of victims so far?"

I nodded. "Thirteen to date."

"To date?" Doc Shepherd echoed.

"It's complicated."

"It might be," Doc Shepherd said. "Increasing the number of variables can do that. But, once a connection asserts itself, the variables have a way of falling into tidy columns."

"Doctor Shepherd," I said, edging my voice. "Do you have a theory about these killings?"

"Like I told you before," he said, "I don't care to speak in theories. I like to be sure. But I like to ask questions."

I almost laughed. "I'd be very interested in hearing your questions."

"Very well," he said. "We'll begin with, why do the extremists use violence?"

"To shock people...to frighten."

"Or?" Doc Shepherd waited patiently.

"Or...to get attention."

"Precisely," he said. "So who gets attention from these killings? Thirteen grisly killings, and yet, I've not heard anything in the news."

Actually, I thought he probably had heard of these murders before. The Smiling Jack case had created a media frenzy several years back. If I connected those dots for Doctor Shepherd, there was a good chance he'd know the FBI had declared the case a hoax. There was a good chance Doctor Shepherd would accept the FBI's assessment. And, there was a very good chance, Doctor Shepherd would wonder why a law enforcement officer

GHOST

would be looking into a closed case. It might even be enough to get Doctor Shepherd to question my identity.

"Serial murders make for good TV ratings, unfortunately," Doctor Shepherd went on. "But given the absence of such coverage, I am led to wonder: are these murders getting the attention the killer thinks they deserve?"

"I doubt it," I blurted out.

"Why not?"

"That," I said, "I am not at liberty to share."

"Well, then, I suppose the question becomes: who does the killer expect to provide the attention?"

"Explain that."

"Right," he replied. "So let's assume the killer is a deranged Pro-Lifer. If he kills abortion docs and clinic employees, who's supposed to notice?"

"The other abortion docs," I replied. "The other clinic workers. Scare them. Make them think twice about coming to work."

"Certainly," he replied. "And?"

"And...uh...I suppose the public conscience. Open eyes to the horror going on behind the scenes."

"Yes," Doc Shepherd said. "And if, the victims aren't abortion clinic employees or surgeons who perform abortions?"

"Then, the intended audiences shifts."

"Seems likely," Doc Shepherd said. "Do the victims have anything in common?"

"Young women, early twenties...that's all we've got so far."

Doc Shepherd twirled his mustache.

"What?"

"All young women," he said. "That...that's problematic."

"How so?"

"If you murder young women with an abortion knife...it certainly seems like you're trying to scare off other women...women who might be considering abortions. Still...the age of the knife doesn't fit with that."

"At the very least," I said, thinking aloud. "the killer has to be trying to send *some* kind of message...something related to abortion."

"Oh, he's sending a message all right," Doc said. "He wouldn't be using Cain's Dagger if he wasn't."

"So what's the message?" I asked absently.

Doc Shepherd winked. "I suppose, Officer Spector, that's what you need to figure out. But, I would begin with the intended audience. Discover the nature of who's supposed to pay attention and you are very close to motive. And once you establish the motive, I suspect, you will find your man."

"Thank you, Doc," I said. "I don't know that I could have gotten this information anywhere else."

He fluttered a hand like he was brushing off the comment. "Officer, as you no doubt recognize, this blade is no common instrument in this day and age. It would be something of a collector's item today. A very disturbed collector, that is. You might consider that thread as well."

I stood. We shook hands. "I appreciate the help. You've given me a lot to think about."

"If I can be of any further assistance, don't hesitate, young man."

"I won't," I said. And I had the strange fleeting thought that, even should this case become blindingly disturbing, I might have to give serious thought to keeping my memory of Doctor Shepherd.

I turned to leave, but Doc drew me to a halt when he asked, "You a Dickens fan?"

"Dickens?"

"As in Charles Dickens, the writer."

GHOST

I shrugged. "He had a keen wit," I said. "Had a way of capturing the human condition that was better than most. I guess, you could say I'm a fan."

"My favorite author," Doc said, twirling his mustache reflectively. "Y'know, I think Dickens had it right when the Ghost of Christmas Present told Scrooge to beware of man's offspring, Ignorance and Want, but especially Ignorance."

I nodded, deep in thought. And it dawned on me what Doc meant. I quoted Dickens, "For on his brow I see that written which is Doom..."

"Be careful out there, son," Doc said. "There's no end to the wickedness of mankind."

"There will be," I replied as I left. "For some sooner than others."

*** *** *** ***

Walking out of the hospital into the wall of heat some people in Florida called air, I was thinking that my day couldn't possibly get any more interesting. Then, I almost literally ran into Special Agent Rezvani.

"You checked out of Motel 6," she said.

"You noticed."

"I *am* with the FBI," she said. "They pay me to notice things. Not much, but they do pay me."

"How'd you know to come to the hospital?"

"You'd written it on a stationary pad...left an imprint."

"Clever," I said. "From the other day, when you were in my room."

She nodded. "Speaking of your room," she said. "I went by there about a half hour ago, and it looked like a train wreck. Mr.

Granderson was having a major hissy fit about it. Care to tell me what that was all about?"

"That depends."

"On what?"

Cicadas in the palms chirped more loudly. I raised my voice. "Depends on what you wanted to talk about...and whether or not you plan on trusting me."

"Mr. Spector," she said. "I want to trust you, but professionally, it would be ludicrous to do so. Do I have to explain why?"

"No, I guess not. But you did come looking for me. Should we sit down and talk somewhere?"

"Out of the heat," she said. "This is oppressive. Come on. I'll drive."

***   ***   ***   ***

We settled on a little hole-in-the-wall Mexican place a few miles from the hospital. The waitress didn't speak much English except for what was on the menu. She brought us a basket of chips and three different salsas. One of them green, one dark red, and the other a viscous, angry orange. She pointed to it and said, "Hot."

I wasn't too worried. I loaded a chip with a glob of the so called hot stuff and wolfed it down. I blinked a few times. Beads of sweat popped up on my forehead. My throat burned. My stomach churned. And, I think my heartbeat became a bit irregular.

"This..." I said, swiping up the glass of ice water and gulping it down, "this really is hot."

Agent Rezvani booted her laptop, plugged a power cord into an outlet below the table, and hooked up a pair of ear buds.

When the desktop appeared, she opened a video player and said, "You aren't going to want to eat after this."

"More photos?" I asked, swabbing my forehead with napkins.

"No." She typed in a username and a password. "A video. The camera you found had a two minute video clip on its memory card. Did you know?"

The hair on the back of my neck stood up. "No, I didn't." I slid the chip basket to the windowsill. "Does it show something new?"

"You tell me."

Agent Rezvani gave me the ear buds and pressed play. There was no ambient sound. No voices. No scrape of a chair. But there was a dreadfully out of place cello piece. It was a deep, thrumming melody that—coupled with the expected content—turned my stomach almost immediately. The young woman with lush red hair sat in a chair like before. She wore the same ghoulish expression, but it was far worse seeing it in motion: the subtle sway of her head, the languid leer in her eyes, the lips moving, curling into that sickly smile. The killer stood behind her as before, face visible only from the bottom of his sharp nose down. The blade came up, touched her throat. A bead of blood appeared. The cello raced on. She smiled through the whole cut.

After her head fell forward, the screen flickered. There was the long dark hall and the strange glow up ahead. The unsteady camera bounced along, showing the killer from behind as he walked. The brightness of the light from the doorway burned away the killer's face, except for a brief flash of the eyes. The camera passed through the doorway, panned left, and found the room full of dog houses. The screen went dark.

"There are two killers," I said.

Special Agent Rezvani nodded. "No doubt about it. An accomplice at least. Easy enough to set up a camera for the still pics. He could put it on a tripod during the murder. But it followed the killer, and the picture bounced with each step." She shut down the video software and pulled up email. "What else?"

"I think they're killing the women at sea."

"Why?"

"The camera's zoomed in tight on the victim, but you can see everything's cramped in there. The ceiling's low and arched, like a ship's cabin. The doghouses are in another section, but again, the walls are concave."

"You've done this before," she said. "Investigated, I mean."

"A few times," I admitted. "Have you sent this to the Bureau?"

She tapped a few keys. "Last night. Nothing back yet."

"Think it'll make a difference? Think they'll reopen the case?"

She looked out of the window, her eyes reflecting the glowering gray sky outside. Another storm. Like clockwork. "No," she said. "I don't think they will."

"But you're going on," I said. "You're still on the case."

Agent Rezvani's dark eyes smoldered. "If what we've seen is real, there is another young woman dead. The bastards have five left, keeping them in dog houses. But they aren't going to stop."

"That's where you're wrong."

"What do you mean?"

"I'm going to stop them."

"You'll have to get in line." She glared at me, and I couldn't tell if it was her way of sharing the anger over what was happening or if she was letting me know that she had priority on this case. Either way, there was power there. Something I couldn't ignore. Special Agent Deanna Rezvani was going to be a factor no matter what I chose to do.

"You going to tell me what happened in your hotel room?" she asked.

"I will. But there's something I want to check out first."

"Where can I reach you?"

"Nowhere yet. You have a card? I can call you."

"You really should get a cell," she said, reaching into her purse. She handed me a card. "Not all technology is evil."

"That's the truth," I said, tapping my case, then wishing I hadn't. Never provoke an investigator. I stood up, let the case fall to my side, and changed the subject. "Can you drop me back at the hospital? I left the k—left my car there."

***   ***   ***   ***

The sky was darkening, storm blowing in from the west this time. We'd traveled in silence, but when I stepped out of the car in the hospital parking lot, back out into the wall of heat, I said, "There's one more thing I picked up from the video. Maybe it will help your friends at the Bureau open their eyes."

She stared at me, exasperated, hands gripping the steering wheel way too hard. "What?" she demanded. Lightning flashed.

"The victim," I said. "In the video, her lips were moving. I think she was talking. Maybe someone in the FBI can read lips."

"Son of a—" She peeled away from me so fast that the momentum slammed my passenger door for me.

Lightning flashed again. Thunder cracked and rumbled. I'd counted seven seconds. The storm was getting close.

Divine violence. I was about to bring a little of that myself.

{ Chapter 15 }

THE LATE AFTERNOON THUNDERSTORM was raging, and Spinnaker Sales was hopping by the time I walked through its glimmering doors. The showroom floor was packed with clusters of smooth-talking salesmen like G and saleswomen too, though they had a decidedly different approach to luring customers. Apparently, it was working. I'd never seen so many rich people grinning with the prospects of a new toy.

I found G near the back of the showroom. His back was turned. He was staring at a clipboard. His head bobbed slightly, and his jaw was working, apparently counting. Probably figuring out how many thousands of dollars he'd made that afternoon. He looked smooth as ever and in charge. He didn't look like someone who'd recently found a corpse.

"How were sales this morning?" I asked.

G must have jumped ten inches off the ground. He spun around, and even his carefully controlled expressions couldn't hide his shock. It was something close to panic. "Wh-what are you doing here?"

"Is that any way to speak to one of your valued customers?" I asked.

"You're no customer," he said, drawing back a measure of restraint. Then, forcing out a little superiority, he shot, "You were staying at Motel 6 for crying out loud."

"What?" I asked. "They left the light on for me. It's a good chain."

"Get out of here, or I'll call the police."

"Really, G? You're going to pull that card out this early? We haven't even gotten started." I drummed fingers on my silver case. Amazing how each new context inspires the imagination so very differently.

G swallowed. He gazed around the showroom, maybe hoping an associate would come to his aid. Maybe looking through the glass at the outside and wishing he was standing out in the storm. Or maybe just searching for a rock to hide under. "What...what do you want?" he wheezed.

"I think...I think I want to help you, G."

"Help me?" he spluttered.

"The way I figure it, whoever you're protecting didn't like me poking around about his special Sun Odyssey."

"I don't know what you're talking about."

"Spare me." It was my turn to look around the showroom. "You have a manager's office somewhere? A place we can talk without this going public?"

G swallowed. I guess he thought about the body...put it all together. "You...you're not going to kill me, are you?"

"Not unless you attack me first," I said and then added, "That's what the other guy did, the guy you found in the boat this morning. What'd you do with him anyway, G?"

"Shut up," he hissed. "Back here." He spun on his heels, marched back behind the counter and down the hall.

He opened the door to a tidy little office. There was a small desktop computer, a filing cabinet, a couple of chairs, and a large window. The desk was more of a counter that fit two sides of the square room.

Soon as we entered, I put the blinds down. I shut the door and said, "Sit down." I put my case on the counter so he could see it...and wonder. "Now, I'm going to tell you some things. And I'm going to ask you some things. You're going to tell me the truth. If you do, you'll walk out of here, and you'll have my protection."

"Wait, I...you said you weren't going to kill me."

"G, I don't have to kill you. I can do other things. Now, are you with me?"

He swallowed and nodded.

"You had the registration number of the Sun Odyssey on file. You lied about it. It was there. Right?"

He nodded.

"Good so far," I said. "After I left, you called the owner. And the owner put a hit on me. Did you know that?"

G nodded again. "I mean, I called him, but...I didn't know...didn't think about the hit."

"Of course you didn't, G. You could care less if someone takes a dirt nap as long as it's not you. But I'm going to go out on a limb here and guess that, maybe you're a little worried about your own skin right now. Now that the hitter's in a box, and I'm still walking around, your boss is liable to get nervous. Maybe he's thinking you're a loose end. Am I close?"

G suddenly became a bobble-head doll. "He...he sent some men, for the body you left here. He wasn't very happy about it."

"Now, I can take care of this for you," I said, stepping so close to his chair that my shadow fell over him. "Your boss has done some very bad things, and he'll keep on doing them unless someone makes him go away. I can do that, G, but I need some information."

He wiped a trickle of sweat from his forehead and gave a tentative nod.

"Let's start by you telling me who he is and where he is."

He cursed and shifted on his chair like he had noose around his neck and any moment the floor was going to drop open beneath him. "Don't...don't know his real name."

"That's okay, G. You just give me whatever name he gave you. Give me his port. Give me his phone number. Everything you got."

"Forget this!" G tried to stand up but ran into my chest like a brick wall. He cursed again. "You don't know, man. This guy is nuts. He'll carve you up and throw you to the sharks! No way I'm crossing—"

I smacked him, open palm...hard. He blinked up at me with that wide-eyed shock most men get when they get hit, really get hit. All the memories of childhood beatings come flooding back in. He blinked again, and I could see the indignation and defiance coming back.

"Look, G, I don't have time for this petty arrogance. I need to know where I can find this guy. He's hurting women. Did you know that?"

"So what!" G spat. "Who cares if he smacks around a few b—"

"I do." My voice dropped two octaves. I couldn't hold it back. The room darkened and my skin went white-hot until I was the only light in the room. White light. Searing, pure phosphorescence. There was the sound of rushing wind, deep and ominous, like an approaching tornado. Papers whirled wildly. G's immaculately combed hair blew around his face.

At once, I willed myself to unmask partially while, at the same time, triggering a Netherview. The office was still there, but so were other things: the stone and mortar walls of an ancient chamber, cobwebs shrouding every corner, and creeping lichen spread across many patches of stone. I watched the membranous lichen, remnant shreds of iniquity, spark to whitish-green fire and burn away. And then, I saw G for what he was. I read his real name. I saw his heart, saw the fear and all the lies he'd told himself for a lifetime. I saw his inner man. It was an ugly, shriveled thing. I almost had pity on him.

Almost.

"Gimoaldo Alonzo Vasquez! Tell me what you know!" my voice boomed, but only between the two of us—my mind to his. If someone had been listening at the door, they'd have heard nothing.

G shook in his chair. "F-F-Four Seasons Marina!" he blurted. "D-don't know the berth. It's under Dyreson Industries."

"His name?" I thundered.

"I...I don't know. He called himself Gray. That's it—don't know if it's a first name or what. Just 'Gray.' He has an accent sometimes, maybe...maybe South American, I don't know. He doesn't explain a lot. All I know is him and his partner sail outta Four Seasons."

I ended the Netherview. Wise not to use it for too long at a time...unless I wanted to go to war. A Netherview attracts things. Unpleasant things like Shades...and worse.

The overhead light came on. My voice went back to normal. "I'm going to see him tonight," I said. "After tonight, you won't have to look over your shoulder anymore."

"Not tonight, man," G said, still shaking. "He doesn't go out 'til Friday night. That's when he takes the girls out, y'know?"

"Where is he now?"

"I don't know, man. I swear!"

"I believe you, G." I turned and reached for the door. "You won't call him...warn him."

"No, no, I won't, no freakin' way." G swallowed. "Wh-what are you, man?"

"G, I'm going to give you some advice," I said. "The best advice you've ever gotten in your life." I leaned down and whispered next to his ear.

When I backed away, G looked like he'd seen a ghost.

Maybe it's wrong to feel this way, but I love messing with people's categories.

*** *** *** ***

"With all due respect, Deputy Director," Special Agent Rezvani argued to her cell phone, "you told me if my findings became something more than a hunch...that I should call you. I'm calling now. We need to reopen Smiling Jack."

She listened to his response, then yanked the phone from her ear, and glared at it like she was going to take a bite out of it. "But, Sir," she growled into the mouthpiece, "We've got new evidence. No, I know we still don't have a body...look, Sir, it's video footage. We have Smiling Jack's latest kill on video. What do you mean? It is NOT more of the same. It's—"

Rez's mouth snapped shut and she listened for another three minutes straight. Finally, she'd heard enough. "Look, I know the Director doesn't need the Bureau getting another black eye right now. Opening a case, especially one like Smiling Jack won't look good, but Sir, we're talking about the lives of at least five more women. Just give me—"

He'd interrupted her again. And now her blood was really boiling. "Excuse me, Sir, but have you mentioned the possibility to Director Peluso that the FBI doing nothing to prevent five more Smiling Jack murders would be much worse for her administration?"

Rez had to hold the phone away from her ear to avoid the blistering string of angry counter arguments salted with enough expletives to EVAC a shipyard. The Deputy Director ended with a very pointed career question for Rez.

She ignored the question and almost managed to restrain herself. "I have plenty of leave, Sir! I'm not certain when I'm coming back to D.C. I'm on vacation, remember?" She couldn't have pressed the red button on her phone any harder. She screamed at the hotel room and slid her phone across the desk. It hit the side of her purse and bounced back a few inches. Just then, the throbbing began.

"No, not now!" she hissed. But her migraine headaches didn't listen. And this one came pounding in as if someone was repeatedly shoving a javelin into the back of her skull. She grabbed her purse, snapped the cap off her pills, and dry swallowed them down. Then she stumbled to the bathroom and splashed some water into her face. It didn't help. She clutched her head with her hands as if trying to prevent an explosion. She glared at herself in the mirror and wondered if she'd just thrown her career away.

The phone trilled and vibrated in the other room. Rez darted to it. She didn't look at the number, flipped it open, and said, "Sir, I'm sorry, Deputy Director. It's just that—oh, Mr. Spector. No, I was expecting someone else. Yeah, yeah, I can meet. Now's fine. I need to get out. Maybe get a drink...or three. I don't know the area. Wait, just a second."

Rez put the phone down and grabbed the hotel's "Amenities and Attractions" booklet. A few pages in, she found something and picked up the phone. "There's an Italian place called Pompano's off Emerald Coast Parkway on North Walton. Say in a half hour? You need a ride? No, okay, see you then."

Wayne Thomas Batson

*** *** *** ***

It was only fifteen minutes to the restaurant, but the hotel room felt confining, so—head still throbbing—Rez left right away. The Miracle Strip, as the Panama City locals called the main beach drag, stretched along ten miles of the whitest shores in America. Towering resorts, condos, and hotels lined both sides, and there were more clubs and hotspots than you could shake a swinger at. Even on a Wednesday night, the strip was hopping.

Rez wished she knew the area a little better because her directions took her out of the modern touristy area into a slightly seedier part of town. Still, seedy for a beach town wasn't so bad. Rez wasn't too worried when she found that Pompano's didn't have its own parking area, but rather shared a little lot with the adjacent strip mall and apartments.

Latin music pounded from one of the little clubs nearby. *That's all I need,* Rez thought, pressing her fingertips into her temples. Night insects made their own music. Rez left her car beneath the only streetlight that worked in the parking lot. Huge palmetto bugs dove beneath the light. One landed on the roof of the car right next to Rez. She cringed and flicked the thing away. Call it what you want, but it looked like a giant roach.

Rez clambered up the single flight of concrete stairs that led out of the lot and took a look at the shadowy alley ahead. Blank wall of the strip mall on the right, four-story apartment complex, complete with black iron fire escapes, on the left.

I can take the alley, or I can traipse all the way around the apartments. Rez decided on the alley. Superior grades in hand-to-hand combat in the Bureau, a black belt in Taek Soo Do, and private lessons in Brazilian Jiu-Jitsu told her she could take care of herself. Carrying two guns didn't hurt either.

Still, she thought, *overconfidence in closed in spaces could get someone killed.*

{ Chapter 16 }

I WAS GETTING MORE than my money's worth out of the assassin's sports car. It still had a quarter tank left when I parked in the lot a hundred yards or so behind the strip mall where Agent Rezvani and I were to meet.

A sensory assault awaited me when I got out of the car. Half a dozen delicious smells haunted the air: basil, cayenne, garlic, also something sweet, like a rich barbecue. Gulf Coast summer humidity hit me also, and it occurred to me that I'd probably need to spend a little of my remaining money on a change of clothes.

But the loudness of the music was the most striking. It seemed like two or three different apartments were having parties, and the little club across the street was competing decibel for decibel. But, alas, the mixture of Dubstep, Heavy Metal, and Salsa music wasn't working.

I grabbed my silver case and shut the car door. I hopped up three steps and stopped. The music had really built to a cacophony. One of the singers was just brutally discordant, screaming the lyrics. I'd heard some pretty awful death metal in my time, but this was—I suddenly realized—this was not music at all.

Someone was screaming and grunting up ahead. I sprinted up the stairs to the alley just in time to watch a dark shape slam Special Agent Rezvani up against the alley wall. She dropped her gun and slumped to the pavement. The assailant flashed a knife.

I grabbed his wrist, squeezed until he dropped the blade, and then spun him around. I planted all four knuckles of my right hand onto his left cheekbone. I'd downed dozens of men with that punch. Out. Cold.

But not this guy. The impact turned his head, but he used his torso momentum and planted a snap kick into the center of my chest.

I landed hard on my back and stared up at the fire escape for a heartbeat. Then, I rolled toward my silver case and grabbed the handle. I had a feeling he wouldn't give me time to get the case open, that he'd grab up his knife, and come after me. But I was wrong. He didn't grab up his knife.

He pulled a gun instead.

I saw the muzzle flash, felt something like a hot coal on the right side of my chest, and...and my next breath caught in my throat. I looked down, touched the bubbling wound, felt the liquid warmth on my fingertips. And, while I know this won't win me any intelligence contests, it was honestly the only thought I could muster: *He shot me.*

I blinked and looked up at the man. So many details poured into my mind: he was Latino, about 5-9, stocky but not buff. The muscles on his arms looked ropey but strong: the kind of strength an old sailor had after a hard life. His stringy hair was salted with gray, and heavy bags lay beneath his eyes.

The eyes.

Taken.

GHOST

I could see that he'd been Taken a very long time. He wasn't a professional, but he'd killed before. The blood of six people stained this man. I was so focused on reading him that I almost didn't see him move.

He raised his gun and fired again. The slug careened off of my silver case. His turn to blink.

I slid inside fast, captured his gun arm at the elbow, clamped in my own armpit, wrenched upward, and heard the joint pop. I slammed my silver case into his gut. When he doubled over, I slid in behind him and found his spine. I dug my fingers in, depressed the three critical vertebrae in the thoracic region, and felt him go limp.

I eased him down against the alley wall and then darted over to check on Agent Rezvani. Her pulse was strong, her breathing normal. Beyond a stunning headache, she'd be fine.

I went back and stood near the killer. He shifted his head just a little to look up at me. The *still touch* leaves a person conscious and lucid, but paralyzed from the neck down.

"What...what did you do to me, man?" he asked in heavily accented English.

"I want you to listen very closely," I said. "Your life depends on it. Your life and a great deal more."

He cursed at me. It was a vile, venomous blast that seemed to ricochet up the alley.

I ignored the curses and figurative instructions and said, "I've triggered a release of neurotransmitters in your body. It's kind of like the paralysis that happens when you're in a deep sleep. By itself, it's not harmful, and it will wear off. But you need to understand something: by your own decisions and actions, you stand condemned. I am going to offer you one...last...chance."

"Mannn, what the...? What you mean, my last chance? You think I'm some kind'a punk—"

I swooped in beside him. I spoke the offer low and clear, words just for him, directly into his ear. When I stood up again, he looked up at me and for the briefest, split-second, I thought I saw just a glimpse of hope in his expression. But a steel curtain of hatred fell, and he cursed me again. He told me what I could do with my offer.

Then, he did something that surprised me.

He moved.

Not just his head. He started to get up.

In very rare cases, the power of the Shade within a man can overpower the man's physiology. He flashed to his feet with shocking speed and gave a brutal palm thrust to my chest wound. I grunted and stumbled drunkenly backward into the opposite wall.

I'd seen so few men overcome the still touch that, all I could do at first, was blink stupidly at him. He called my stupid blinking and raised me one slackjawed grin, reminding me horribly of Smiling Jack's victims. I was getting pretty tired of crooked smiles.

The taken man had only one working arm, but, as I'd just discovered, he had augmented strength. His left hand found the knife in his belt. He lunged.

I exploded upward and drove an uppercut beneath his chin. He staggered and dropped the blade, but this time, I didn't let him fall. I dropped my case, and with a lunge, hooked my hands into his armpits and thrust him bodily into the air. I drove his head between iron rungs of the fire escape. I turned him and then, using my upper body strength and weight, gave him a swift yank. I heard and felt the vertebrae crack as they pulled apart and separated. I stepped a few paces back and watched the body sway for a moment.

The wound on my chest throbbed, but I was pretty sure I got the better end of the deal. In fact, I was certain of it. He'd had a chance. He'd had *The Offer*. In death, as in life, he had chosen...poorly.

"You killed him?" Agent Rezvani asked from behind me. I heard her slow approach, her heels making a gritty sound on the pavement. I think she still had her gun out. I think she had it trained on me.

Staring at the corpse I couldn't help but notice how weathered and shriveled the man looked now. His shell looked so utterly wretched and sad—it made me long to wash my memory clear. I shook my head and whispered, "He's gone."

When she spoke again, her voice was hardened with law enforcement steel. "He came at me from a window well. Up there. Just dropped down like some kind of mountain lion. Still, I would have liked to question him."

"Trust me on this," I said. "He wasn't the cooperative type. After he shot me, I—"

"He did shoot you," she whispered, gasping out the words. "But he missed, right? Had to miss. You were lucky."

"I don't believe in luck." I turned. I was right. The FBI woman had a Sig Sauer pointed at my chest. The big gun wavered. She was uncertain. "You don't need that," I said. "I'm no threat...to you."

Her arm and the gun fell to her side, but she didn't reply. Her jaw went slack and her eyes widened. "No...he didn't miss," she said. "Mr. Spector?"

I followed her line of sight to my chest. The bullet had punched a nasty hole in my shirt and into the flesh of my right pectoral muscle, beneath the collarbone right where the pec tied in with the shoulder. The shirt had absorbed a lot of the blood, but the wound still leaked freely. Any second now, it would change. *This won't be easy to explain.*

"Your blood," Agent Rezvani said, her lip quivering. "It's glowing."

I said nothing. Her mind was reeling too chaotically to grasp any explanation I could give. Then, I felt a familiar inner pulsing, a tremor of muscle and flesh washing up from my legs, in from my arms—all converging on the bloody gash. *This isn't going to help.* I turned my back.

"Freeze!" I heard the Sig Sauer's hammer cock. "Turn around—SLOWLY."

"You might want to cover your eyes," I said. The pulses met at the broken skin. Involuntarily, I arched my back. Pure white light blazed from the gunshot wound, wavering and flashing like the bubbling gleam of a welding torch seen from the other side of a metal plate. Sound bled away to a ringing silence. I felt a familiar tingling itch, like hundreds of tiny strands of thread were being drawn through seams in my flesh. The mangled bullet pinched out of my chest and fell at my feet. The light burned away, leaving a slightly luminous scar. The lightwash was over. Now the hard explanation.

I turned around. A cool breeze swept up the alley behind me, but I didn't think much of it. I locked eyes with the FBI agent. She lowered the gun again and stared at my chest. "That's impossible," she said.

"Uncommon," I said. "But not impossible."

"I saw the wound," she whispered. "I saw the bullet...it freaking popped out! How did it...how could you...heal?"

"It's a long story," I said, reflexively locating my silver case. It was near the apartment building wall, a few feet from the hanging body. I glanced at the dumpster in the back of the alley and said, "Would you like to get a cup of coffee?"

"Coffee?" she echoed absently. "Cof...fee?"

She'd just blown a fuse. Somewhere in the multitude of mental pathways formed by each and every experience of her life, Agent Rezvani had just hit a wall. There was no frame of reference for what she'd just experienced, and it left her unstable. I was about to say something when I felt the cold breeze again. It wasn't natural, and I thought maybe the Shade was taking its leave. But no, there was something different here. Something foreign and very, very dangerous.

I held up my hand. The hair on my neck stood up. I heard a predatory clicking behind me. I hadn't heard the sound for some time, but it was unmistakable. "Agent Rezvani," I said. "You need to run...right now."

"I'm not leaving you without an expl—"

"RUN! NOW!"

She backed away a few steps, and something hit me hard from behind. I pitched forward, rolled to a crouch and almost lost consciousness. I felt a combination of burning and numbness on my back. Either an especially large Shade or the more lethal Knightshade, I wouldn't be able to tell without a Netherview. But my vision swam, and I couldn't focus enough. I heard movement.

It was coming.

I leaped up, grabbed the fire escape, and—hoping to let it pass beneath me—kicked up my legs. The thing slammed into my heels, launching my torso into a backward swing. Nearly inverted but still holding on, I crashed into the fire escape's lowest landing. I lost my breath and my grip and fell headfirst toward the pavement. If only I'd hit the pavement.

Whatever it was grabbed my ankle out of the air and flung me cartwheeling toward the dumpster. I heard a deep metallic thud, felt the jolt of my body slamming into the metal, and then collapsed to the pavement. I coughed hard and spat a bloody gob. Then I heard the clicking and sharp scrapes on the street. I blinked, saw my case, and made a desperate grab.

In a clumsy, painful dive, I sprawled toward the case. The thing took hold of my leg and started to lift. I snatched the handle of my case, released the catch, and twisted around. I fired both streams of netherwield, the powerful agent used in any particle nether weapon. I prayed I hadn't missed.

There was a grating shriek. I fell back to the pavement and snatched up my case. I needed to know what I was up against, so while I reached around inside the case, I constricted the thin muscles around my eyes, and attempted a Netherview.

The alley fell into twilight. Where there had been buildings and fire escapes and sidewalks, there now stood a thicket of ethereal trees, swaying gently near a stream's bank. A weed-strewn walk of cobbled stone curled from my position up to a pair of massive hoofed feet. My head pounded, and I couldn't stay focused. The nether flickered, and I saw that the shade wore a black crown. A Knightshade. The netherwield surged on his massive arm and he flexed his fingers, trying to regain motor control. Then he turned to me. My focus wavered. The last thing I saw was the Knightshade removing a huge hammer from its back hanger.

A brimstone bludgeon.

"Blood and thunder!" I exclaimed, scrambling through the contents of my case for my favorite dagger. I found it, the corded grip sliding into my palm. Then I leaped into the dumpster and tried to brace myself.

GHOST

The Knightshade growled. The right panel of the dumpster collapsed inward, and the whole thing slewed farther back into the alley. Before the next blow, I leaped back out of the dumpster, cracked my knee smartly against the side of the red building, and limped up the alley.

There was a heavy crunch of metal and another shriek behind me. I flexed my eyes, trying to penetrate the nether and see the thing. It was running toward me again.

"Spector, what's going on?" Agent Rezvani yelled. "I can't see what—"

"You're STILL here?" I bellowed. "RUN, NOW!"

I saw into the nether just in time to witness the bludgeon wheeling toward me. I ducked and fell backward, and the fiery weapon crashed into the side of the building causing a hail of brick shrapnel. Tiny fragments sprayed into my eyes as I tried to crab crawl backward.

I was lifted bodily three feet off the ground. It had me by the neck and began to squeeze. I swiped with my dagger, but it must have been holding me at arm's length...like a bully teasing a smaller child. I gasped and choked and felt my senses starting to leave me. Then I heard a click. Agent Rezvani had ignored my command. Of course, she wouldn't know the threat. I had an idea. After all, the Sig Sauer was a respectfully powerful weapon.

I grabbed the Knightshade's arm with my free hand, strained the muscles around my eyes, and channeled all my strength into Netherview. Amazing how much power you can find when you're about to have your throat crushed. The sight of the Knightshade was nearly blinding from my perspective. Every feature within the nether burned with white hot intensity, and I knew that slowly...some of it would become visible in Earthveil.

From the place where my flesh touched his flesh, the Knightshade began to materialize. I groaned and struggled, feeling dizzy and faint. But I groaned out a last measure of strength. The Knightshade's shoulder and neck melted into existence. Finally its head. "Now!" I screamed.

Agent Rezvani fired, putting a hollowpoint parabellum slug right into the Knightshade's eye. It dropped me. I pivoted, leaped, and plunged the dagger into the thing's throat. I twisted the blade, jagged it to the right, and then tore it out. The Knightshade gurgled out a final shriek and fell to the pavement. In seconds, any visible part of it melted from Earthveil back into the nether.

I heard a sound behind me, turned, and found Agent Rezvani breathing in gasps and wheezes. The gun was still raised and it shook in her hand. "Here," I said, "let me help you lower this. Just take your finger off the trigger. Good. Now breathe, Agent Rezvani. Breathe slowly. You're hyperventilating."

I eased her down to sit on the curb. For a second, I thought she was going to lose it. Her lower lip trembled. She was still breathing way too fast. "That...isn't real...can't be real." Then she vomited.

"You should feel a little better now. It's shock. You'll get past it. But, Agent Rezvani, we should leave now. We're as far from prying eyes and ears as we can be in a city, but someone's bound to have heard the dumpster crashing around. And there's still a body here."

She blinked and nodded.

"Where'd you park the rental?"

She pointed out of the alley. That was a start. I helped her up and started walking. It was probably the longest walk of her life. At the end of it, I knew I had some decisions to make.

GHOST

*** *** *** ***

Something like liquid shadow poured over the edge of the roof of the apartment complex near Pompano's Restaurant. It ran swiftly down the side of the building, momentarily snaking around the drain pipe, seeping into cracks, and diverting past window frames. Without a sound, it was lost in darkness at ground level. And then, a man was there. He stood directly beneath the fire escape and about ten yards from the dumpster. He was very still because he was studying the trash strewn alley, the cracked slabs of sidewalk, and the no loitering and neighborhood crime watch signs. But he saw signs that other men could not see.

He saw nether.

And in that surreal twilight, he saw the remnants of a Knightshade. He smelled brimstone. He thought he could just detect the faint echo of a final shriek. He removed black hands from the folds in his vaporous garment and he knelt on the glistening pavement. Something like a hiss came from the man. Then a triumphant grunt.

He stood and began following the trail of his prey.

{ Chapter 17 }

SOME SAY COFFEE is an acquired taste. If that's true, then I acquired that taste at the moment I was created. The smell of it. The warmth of it. The color of it—it all just makes me happy.

Special Agent Rezvani looked like she enjoyed a good cup of Joe as much as anyone, but right now, I doubt she could taste much of anything. She was in shock. For how long, I didn't know. It's different for everyone.

She sat across the little round table and stared down at her mug. Steam wafted up right into her face. I'm not sure she noticed.

We'd driven in silence to a coffee house a safe distance from the alley. Beasley's Grounds & Sounds. They had a nice selection of brews and blends from all over the world. A couple of guys with guitars had just arrived and were unhurriedly setting up on the shop's tiny stage.

I wasn't in a hurry either. Agent Rezvani might need a good, long while. I waited, smelled the coffee, and waited some more. She looked up, chewed on her bottom lip a moment, and asked, "I don't understand what I just saw."

"Where do you want to start?" I asked.

"Who are you?"

"My name is John Spector, but people call me Ghost."

"Is John Spector your real name?"

I tilted my head, narrowed my eyes a bit, and smiled. "It's my real name here."

"Here?" she echoed faintly. "More riddles. How's that different from just another alias?"

"I like this name."

She shook her head. "Whatever." Then she lowered her voice. "You were shot in the chest. At first, I thought he missed you, but..."

"He didn't miss."

"How...could you heal from that? I mean, that's a punctured lung, muscle damage. Gah, would've put most men in the hospital...or killed 'em."

"I am not like other men."

She laughed, but her mirth was laced with pain. "I'm a Special Agent in the Federal Bureau of Investigation. I have degrees in Criminology, Forensics, and Law. Given my in-depth training, I was able to figure that much out, thanks. How'd you heal yourself? What was it...some kind of stem cell serum? And the light...crap, what was that?" She put her head in her hands and seemed to be staring through her fingers into her coffee.

"It's who I am...how I was made. I heal fast. I can take a beating and keep going strong. It would take a lot to end me."

She glanced beneath the table. My silver case was there. When she looked back up, I could see the wheels turning. "I...I get it," she said, thinking out loud. "You're government too, aren't you?"

I said nothing.

"You're some kind of genetically engineered soldier. That's why you're so strong. That's why you healed like that. I bet you've got all kinds of advanced gadgets in that case of yours, don't you?"

"You have no idea."

"So who are you working for? You're not FBI. Or maybe, you could be some rogue division no one's supposed to know about." She waited. I said nothing. "No? Not the Bureau? I didn't think so. So what, then? CIA? NSA?"

I shook my head.

"Delta Force? Seal Team Six? Some super black ops unit reporting to the President himself?"

"Higher up."

"Higher up than the freaking Executive Branch?" She whistled.

I shrugged.

"What about that guy in the invisibility suit? He was huge. I didn't see his face very well, but what was he, some kind of terrorist?"

"You might say that." I sighed relief inwardly. She hadn't seen as much of the Knightshade as I'd feared.

She wiped her forehead. "Unbelievable. You mean we've got enemies who can just appear and disappear?" I nodded, and she asked, "Well how do we stop them?"

"The same way we just did."

"Okay, so tell me this: why are you on the Smiling Jack case?"

"Following orders."

She leaned back in her chair. "It all makes sense now." She shook her head and laughed. "That's why Barnes was being such a moron."

"Who's Barnes?" I asked.

She stared at me. "You're kidding, right? Ulysses Barnes?"

I shook my head.

Agent Rezvani let out an exasperated sigh. "He's the freakin' Deputy Director of the FBI. He's also the reason I'm down here on my own. Now, I understand why. He's probably catching all kinds of heat from the higher ups—your higher ups. No wonder the FBI won't reopen the case. Whoever you're working for is probably clamping things air tight." She was quiet a minute. I saw her glance furtively over her shoulder. "So...your superiors...they don't mind me working this case...working with you, I mean?"

"So far, so good."

Special Agent Rezvani took a long overdue sip of her coffee, smiled at the taste, and nodded.

This was going a lot better than I expected. It was always best to let people answer their own questions. Answers they could come up with on their own were much easier for them to accept. But, as shrewd as Agent Rezvani seemed to be, I wondered how long her answers would satisfy her. Probably not long. She'd remember some detail from the attack in the alley, something she wouldn't be able to reconcile. And then, she'd come asking again. Good investigators always do.

"Smiling Jack posted the video," Rez said absently.

Back to the case, I thought with relief. "The woman with red hair."

Rez nodded, and I thought I saw a hint of despair in her eyes. "But there was a second video too," she said. "Another victim."

"Tell me."

"A young blond woman, very slight, shorter than the other. Almost angelic...and he killed her. She was in the pictures on the camera...you know?"

"We're moving too slow," I said, my voice tight. "He's killed two of six already, but...but I think I've got something."

I told her about the ship I'd seen the day I found the camera. I told her about Spinnaker Sales, G, and the knee-jerk hit someone had put on me. I told her about Gray at the Four Seasons Marina and about the berth registered under Dyreson Industries. Finally, I told her that I was planning a little visit Friday night.

"You could have told me some of this before," she objected. "The yacht, the hitman..."

"I've just learned all this myself," I said. "Besides, you thought I was the killer before."

She shrugged. "It's my job to be suspicious." She glanced outside, then back at me. "I'll do some checking on Dyreson Industries."

I nodded. "I'm going to the marina. G said Gray takes the girls out Friday nights."

"Count me in," she said. "There anything else?"

"The reason I was at the hospital the other day was to find out about Smiling Jack's murder weapon," I explained, sipping my coffee. "I met a cardiac surgeon, Doctor Shepherd."

"Doctor Shepherd?" she echoed. "Tell me he looks like the guy on *Grey's Anatomy*."

"Grey's what?" I asked.

"Never mind."

"Uh...okay. Anyway, Doc Shepherd thinks the blade was originally used in the nineteenth century for abortions."

"Abortions?" she echoed thoughtfully. "We have experts in the Bureau—that wasn't their take. They ran it through every database known to mankind, called historians and medical professionals, and the consensus was that the blade was for abdominal surgeries—old, yeah, but for a very different purpose. You sure about this Doc Shepherd?"

"Doc Shepherd's as solid as they come. Has enough diplomas, awards, and commendations to wallpaper a room. He's a top of the line heart-cutter from a family of surgeons. One of 'em collects surgical instruments. This blade is pretty obscure. Maybe only a couple just like it. It even has a name: Cain's Dagger."

"Ominous ring to it," she said.

"Agreed."

"If he's right," she said, "that changes things."

"I agree, but what's your take?"

"Well, we've gone from a very methodical, very intelligent killer to a very methodical, very intelligent killer with a mission."

"I thought so, as well. Go on."

"First of all, the killer's going on camera. That says, 'Look at me. Look what I'm doing.' Or maybe it says, 'Ha, you can't catch me.' But now, if what your surgeon says is right, well, it's not like Smiling Jack just happens to have this kind of rare blade in his kitchen. He's using it to make a point. Probably one of those far right, Christian fundamentalist whack-jobs."

I waited a few beats, then said, "I'm not certain yet. Doc Shepherd wasn't either."

"What? Why not? Those Pro-Lifers have killed abortion doctors before."

"This isn't the same." I had a feeling I knew where this conversation was headed. A gurgle of rage began to make itself known in my gut.

"Wait," she said, her eyes narrowing, "you're not a Pro-Lifer, are you? If so, I didn't mean to offend—"

The rage gurgled again. "You mean, you're -*not*- Pro-Life?" I asked. "What happened to Protect and Serve?"

GHOST

Agent Rezvani scowled. "That's local law," she said. "FBI is Fidelity, Bravery, and Integrity."

"Okay," I said, "But what have you got against life?"

Her mouth snapped shut, opened and shut twice more before she said at last, "I'm not getting into this with you. Keep your views; I'll keep mine. But, if your Doc friend is right, I think it's a virtual certainty that Smiling Jack is trying to send a message that is in -*some*- way related to abortion."

"Agreed." She was right...up to a point. But her take on the Fundamentalist as whack-jobs as Christians? People take the name of God and do a lot of horrendous things. But that doesn't make them Christian any more than a bumper sticker does. Smiling Jack and his accomplice, whoever they really were, somehow I just didn't think they were screwed up Pro-Lifers. But, then again, I couldn't entirely rule it out. The eternal battle between how we want things to be versus how they really are. I gave a growling sigh.

We sat in silence long enough for the coffee to stop steaming.

"Look, Spector..."

"Call me Ghost."

"Ghost...fine. Look, I know whatever secret organization you're working for, I know you can't say much, but there's something I don't get."

Uh, oh. Here it comes.

"I mean, if you're some special op military outfit, I could see you going overseas and nailing some terrorist leader. I could see you being in Florida here to take down a drug cartel. But Smiling Jack? Why take on a domestic case that no one believes in? Why throw a man with your skills out here to put this killer behind bars?"

"Because he's got to be stopped," I said, keeping my voice low and even. "But, Special Agent Rezvani, there's something you need to understand: I don't plan on putting Smiling Jack behind bars."

* * *   * * *   * * *   * * *

As a Special Agent tasked with solving violent crimes, Rez had seen her share of peculiar events. She'd been the first on the scene to uncover a serial killer's "trophy room." She'd witnessed terrorists being virtually disintegrated by advanced tactical weapons while hostages remained unharmed. She'd even seen an ultra-secret surveillance drone aircraft in action, a sight that had left her breathless and precipitated more than a hundred UFO reports to local law enforcement. But she'd never seen anything like what she'd witnessed in the alley earlier that evening.

This Ghost character, John Spector, or whoever he really was, had fought with virtuosity against a murderous foe cloaked in invisibility. He'd healed from a chest wound that would have disabled most others. And he claimed to work for someone higher than the Executive Branch.

Anything at that level, she knew, was ultra-classified and meant to stay that way. But she couldn't just drop it, couldn't just *not* investigate. *Besides,* she thought, *I've already rankled all my superiors. Might as well push it up the line.*

She opened her laptop, clicked to the Bureau site, and went through the ten step sequence that would grant her access to the classified databases she wanted. After half an hour sifting of names and info, she found exactly zero information about her John Spector. Ironically, the FBI employed a man named Jon Spector. But he was 5 foot 3, with a thinning black comb-over, coke bottle glasses, and enough spare tires to outfit a Humvee.

Weighing the risks for at least three seconds, she decided to go a little deeper. There were other government databases she could access from the Bureau site. She had the clearance, barely. But some of these agencies were known for being obnoxiously protective of their records. Knowing the next three clicks would leave an indelible digital trail, she clicked anyway. *I hope this doesn't come back to haunt me,* she thought, rolling her eyes at the pun.

The 'weighted search' began. A gray pinwheel appeared in the center of the screen as the computer worked and the internal protocols and calculations used by the databases checked and rechecked Rez's query. After five minutes of supercomputer convolutions, the application came back with two hits. Both were marked Top Secret and carried Directive 7 Restriction, thankfully just within her reach.

The first file concerned a captured French spy nicknamed Spectre. He'd run a high end brothel in D.C., and many of his *employees* had gathered some pretty embarrassing intel from certain government officials. Eyebrows raised, cheeks reddening, she thought, *Interesting, but not what I was looking for.*

The second file seemed more promising. It concerned a special operation in Afghanistan, codenamed: Ghost. In 2009, the US had sent an elite unit into the Khyber Pass in the Safed Koh Mountains where a particularly aggressive al Qaeda leader named Khalid al-Maghreb was rumored to have built his center of military operations.

Rez looked at the dossier and the only photos provided. One of the men in the unit might have been John Spector. He was taller than the others and very pale. Behind sunglasses and camouflage BDUs, it was impossible to tell for sure. Apparently, the team carried out its mission, leaving al-Maghreb buried in the rubble of his own base. But before the team could be extracted, they met unexpected resistance and fled into Pakistan. And there, on the outskirts of a town called Landikotal, the team had been ambushed by al-Qaeda sympathizers...and killed. There were no survivors.

Rez sighed. Not only had she struck out but she'd absorbed a ton of information she wished she'd never read. Bleary-eyed and exasperated, Rez clacked the keys ten times harder than she usually did and performed a simple web search. The results flashed onto the screen. Rez sat up straight and leaned toward the screen. Having come up empty on the classified pages, Rez couldn't believe what she saw.

867,000 hits. Some of the pages were duds, just compilations of ghost stories and hauntings where people had misspelled specter as spector. But the third page of links had his name: John Spector. Rez clicked the link for realghoststories.weebly.com. It looked like some of the others, a combination of text entries and peculiar photos. She almost clicked back to the search page, but froze as she read one of the accounts dated just the previous year.

It told the story of a low income family living in the worst part of South Central Los Angeles. Their youngest son had been kidnapped by a drug lord. The scumbag held the five-year old captive to force the family to work for him. Worse still, he'd gotten the child addicted to heroin, basically enslaving him and his family to his product and his employ. A man named John Spector showed up. He bought everything the family had to sell...and destroyed it. Then, he went and got their son back. In the process, he'd killed the drug lord and more than a dozen of his bodyguards. And he'd done it all with little more than his silver suitcase.

Rez froze. This was her man. She read post after post, some going back ten years or more. Each one told of the pale stranger who showed up at just the right time...and came when no one else would help. He did extraordinary things for people in desperate need. Whatever the problem was, Ghost solved it...often closing the case with a lethal exclamation point.

An answer to prayer, some called him. A modern knight in shining armor. A teenager called him "one scary dude." There were links to other pages, a forum, a blog, pictures, requests. It was crazy, almost like a fan page. Then Rez noted something odd about the photos: she couldn't see his face. There was a shot with Spector standing in front of an orphanage in what looked like an Eastern Bloc country. His face was completely obscured by a wide-brimmed hat. In another photo, he was standing behind a police car in front of a convenience store. He was looking away, staring into the shattered front window of the shop. Still another, Ghost knelt by a woman on a stretcher. He was holding her hand, but the IV bag hid his face.

Several of the shots showed that silver suitcase of his. His build was right too: just short of pro-wrestler mass and tall. It had to be him. There was a whole page devoted to photos. Rez started clicking on the thumbnails. The image jumped to full screen. Rez got chills. It was the perfect shot. John Spector, his shirt torn and bloody, was just turning toward the camera when the shot had been taken. There was nothing in front of his face. But his face was gone. It looked as if the air in front of his face had been distorted as if by intense heat, like the vapors on a desert highway. But you couldn't see his face with any clarity, just warbled, almost molten features. Rez clicked through a dozen more photos. It was the same thing every time.

She rubbed the gooseflesh on her forearms. The hotel room seemed so much colder now. She went to the AC unit by the window and went to turn it to a warmer setting, but it was off. Completely off. Rez had a flash of the strange image she'd seen in Spector's hotel room. With a shudder, she shut down the laptop. After getting ready for bed, she snuggled beneath the covers like she did when she was a little girl. She went to flick out the bedside light, but thought better of it. In fact, she switched on the television and went to sleep to the Cartoon Network.

{ Chapter 18 }

"I GOT HOME AS SOON as I could!" Dr. Gary said, his voice as taut as surgical stitches. "Where is she?"

"She won't leave her house," Jack said, stepping into the elevator, inserting the key. "There's a lot of blood."

Dr. Gary got in. Jack turned the key. Half turn left, half turn right. The doors shut.

"You're angry," Dr. Gary said, reaching for Jack's shoulder.

"Of course, I'm angry," Jack said, shrugging him away. "You botched the procedure. You rushed. I told you it could wait for the weekend."

"Why does it matter?" Dr. Gary asked. "To you, I mean? You take no real pleasure from our pets. Or has something changed?"

"You bastard," Jack hissed. "How dare you—"

The doors opened. Dr. Gary grabbed Jack by the shoulders and slammed him against the side of the elevator. "You...need...to...calm...down!" he said, his voice powerful and grating, like the grinding of stone against stone. "We cannot afford to lose our grip, not now with so much at stake."

"I know," Jack whispered. "I...know. It's just I saw the blood, and Erica...she doesn't look good."

"I did not botch the abortion, Jack," Dr. Gary said. "There's always a risk. You know that better than anyone." He released Jack's shoulders, stepped back, and straightened his tie.

Jack stared at the floor and nodded. "I just don't want to see anyone wasted."

"And I don't intend to waste anyone," Dr. Gary said. He shrugged quickly out of his lab coat, rolled up his sleeves, and snapped on a pair of latex gloves. "Now, let's see to Erica."

Jack led the way to kennel. There was weeping. Someone cried out, "Why are you fighting?"

"We're not fighting, Midge," Jack consoled. "It's just that this is an important time. Don't you worry. I'll give you a new patch later."

Dr. Gary looked at the blood smears on the floor outside of one of the houses. "Erica, Erica, do you hear me?" he called.

"Dr. Gary?" came a weak reply. "Oh, you've come...you've come...I knew you would." There was a pause. "I hurt. Please...please save me."

"I will, dear," he said. "I will."

* * *   * * *   * * *   * * *

"How bad is it?" Jack asked.

Dr. Gary shook his head. As he brought the coffee mug to his lips, his hand was shaking. He swallowed. "She won't make it through the night."

"Isn't there anything you can do? Can't you...can't you open her up?"

"Not here. At the hospital, maybe I could save her. But we don't have the equipment here."

"This shouldn't have happened," Jack muttered.

"Look, I did my best. I tried—"

"But all the new implements, they were supposed to be the safest yet."

"I understand your sensitivity to this," Dr. Gary said. "I've got the best record in the clinic, but sometimes...it happens."

Jack grit his teeth and wiped the corner of his eye. "What now?"

"We're losing the battle," Dr. Gary said. "I don't think we can wait another cycle to be...to be more overt."

Jack sighed. "By the time this litter is of age, the courts could overturn everything."

"We're going to change things. We're going to change things, tonight." Dr. Gary's pronouncement hung in the air.

"What do you mean?" Jack asked, a trembling smile appearing on his lips. "If Erica's dying, how can we—"

"We will give up her body," Dr. Gary said, putting his hand on Jack's. "Erica will send the most telling message of all."

"Are you sure we're ready for this step?" Jack asked.

Dr. Gary laughed. "In every revolution...there are martyrs? Isn't that what you said?"

Jack nodded. "It won't take long, will it?"

"As foolish as they've been over the years," Dr. Gary replied, "they aren't fools, not really. Once they find her, I imagine we've got a few weeks, maybe as much as a month."

"Will it be enough to complete the Manifesto?" Jack asked.

Dr. Gary looked down at his coat. He touched a dark spot, and his finger came away glistening crimson with Erica's blood. "It...it will have to be."

Jack's expression became very grim. "Where will we take Erica?" she asked. "Where will we make...the reveal?"

Dr. Gary nodded. "I've been doing some research. I know the perfect place."

***   ***   ***   ***

Four Seasons Marina wasn't nearly as posh as I expected it to be. Maybe thirty or forty years ago, it would have been. It sprawled in a vast letter L shape, raggedly covered berths and deep jetties next to an aging, high rise hotel with the same name. Music sauntered out of the restaurant's tri-tiered decks that looked to need a good sanding and staining. Colored lanterns hung from the eaves and dressed the place up. Sort of.

At the crook of the L, just at the edge of the parking lot, a two story gatehouse waited. Other than climbing a rickety-looking chain link fence, it was the only way in that I could see.

I made sure Agent Rezvani's Glock was invisible under my nifty new sports coat. She and I had spent an hour on Thursday shopping for some much needed new clothing. Turns out, she had definite opinions on my wardrobe choices. That was a special time, I can tell you. And I spent $240, leaving me with just $694 for the rest of the mission.

"How do you want to play this, Agent Rezvani?" I asked.

"Call me Rez," she said. "Not by flashing my badge."

"Are you sure?" I asked. "I'm kind of fond of the shield-in-the-face technique."

Rez laughed, a musical, girlish sound I hadn't heard from her before. "Don't think I don't enjoy throwing the *big letters* at perps," she said. "But Smiling Jack and his partner are too smart not to employ someone careful at the gate."

"Agreed. How, then?"

"We blend in. Guests of another yacht owner."

Ah, I thought, *that would explain the need for the sports coat.* "If they're that smart," I said. "Still, they won't let us in just because we dressed nice. We don't know any of the other yacht owners."

"I have that covered," she said. "Walk behind me like a friend, not a date. Just follow my lead."

I followed her lead.

I was relatively certain that when Agent Rezvani strolled the hallowed halls of the FBI in Northwest D.C., she didn't wear outfits like the summer dress she wore tonight. It revealed her upper back and shoulders...toned, very feminine, and bronze tanned. If there was a guy in that security gatehouse, he didn't stand a chance.

I kept my eyes on the shadows as we rounded the gatehouse. If Smiling Jack and his murderous partner had been using this marina for some time, they would have attracted Shades. And maybe worse things. In fact, it was near a certainty that one or both of the killers had already been Taken or perhaps even Seared. I switched momentarily to Netherview and was surprised to find the gatehouse clear of supernatural evil. But there were two guards.

Both male.

I switched back to Earthveil. Unfortunately, they weren't rent-a-cops. The taller of the two sported red hair, buzzed high and tight, and a jowly bull-dog face. He had a coiled "Don't tread on me" snake tattooed on his forearm and a Marine Corps eagle and anchor ring on a finger of his right hand. He wasn't bulky, but the edgy muscle he did carry made him look hard enough to break a board on just about any part of him.

On tip-toe, the other guard wouldn't be as tall as the Marine's shoulder. He had dark, shifty eyes and black, slicked back hair. He was clean-shaven and had olive skin like a first generation Italian with weeks of tan on top of that. Everything about him looked smooth. He seemed like the sort of man who could duck behind you in an instant and put blade between your ribs.

But, I repeat: they were men.

Agent Rezvani changed the way she walked as she approached the booth, and I was immediately glad that I let her handle this part. Hollywood itself couldn't have conjured up a more perfect breeze off the water, just enough to ripple the sheer dress and delicately toss the burnished curls of her hair on her slender neck and toned shoulders. She smiled sweetly at the guards, and they moved closer to the sliding window and smiled back. She dangled a tiny plum-colored purse from one wrist and made a big show of fingering through it. That purse might as well have been a hypnotist's watch swinging on a chain.

"Hey, there, miss," Mr. Smooth said, his hand gliding to a pen while simultaneously opening a thin blue notebook. "What can Four Seasons Marina do for you this fine summer evening?"

"Yeah," Red-buzz said, "what can we do for you?" *Not too original, that Red-buzz.*

Agent Rezvani tilted her head and raised an eyebrow, and I'm certain, I saw both guards rock backward on their heels.

"It *is* a fine summer evening," Rez replied, her voice velvety-Southern. *Where did that come from?*

"My *friend* and I"—she emphasized 'friend' and waved over her shoulder at me—"have a private dinner cruise with our good friends the Adderlys. Only been here once before, but I've forgotten the berth. I know I wrote it down, but I think I put the card in my black purse."

She was a damsel in distress. The *perfect* damsel in distress. I'm reasonably sure, if she asked the two men to fight with aluminum baseball bats for the chance to help her out, that they would instantly beat each other senseless.

"Adderlys' berth, eh?" said Mr. Smooth. "I think we can find that for you."

Rez reached over and touched Mr. Smooth's hand as she said, "I cannot thank you enough."

Mr. Smooth didn't look so smooth anymore. He paled a bit and swallowed. "It's really no trouble."

"Yeah, no trouble," Red-buzz said.

Rez lifted her hand, leaned forward, and cast a blinding smile at each man in turn. "Honestly, some places these days forget all about the common kindnesses that mean so much."

"Uh, Applebees—I mean, Adderlys, got 'em right here," Mr. Smooth said, tapping a finger on the notebook page. "Berth 22A." He pointed out over the jetties. "Just take the left side, go past the covered berths. It's about a hundred yards out."

"Again, my thanks," Rez said. She turned with a wink to me.

When we were far enough away, I asked, "How'd you know about the Adderlys?"

"I am FBI," she said. "I have sources. Their berth is pretty close to the one rented by Dyreson Industries."

I handed her the Glock I'd held for her under my sports coat. "Thanks," she said. "Kinda hard to hide that under a dress."

"G didn't say what time this Mr. Gray takes the women out," I said. "We should hurry."

Rez looked me up and down. "What about a weapon? You have something in your case?"

I smiled. "I have what I need."

***   ***   ***   ***

"I feel good," Erica said as Jack helped her from the dock onto the yacht. "But I also feel strange."

"That's perfectly all right," Dr. Gary said, stepping lightly over and taking her arm. "You can rest when we get you down below." He looked up to Jack. "Cast off as soon as you can. Once we're out in the Gulf, make for Pensacola. We'll need to start filming right away. I don't know how much longer..."

"Are we making a movie?" Erica asked. "I like movies."

"Yes, we are," Jack replied. "And, Erica, it's your turn to be the star."

***   ***   ***   ***

Berth 22A, the Adderlys' berth, was just a few yachts away from the berth owned by Dyreson Industries. But the Sun Odyssey was gone. Smiling Jack had already left port. The Adderly's yacht, *The Sirocco*, however, bobbed gently on the Gulf.

"Ahoy!" a pencil thin man called from the cabin. "Can I help?" A much younger woman emerged at his elbow. She was blonde and curvaceous, wearing a bikini top and cargo shorts—and sunglasses, even though it was dark.

She wobbled a little, held onto his shoulder, and said, "You look all dressed up and nowhere to go."

"Is it that obvious?" I asked. Then I played a hunch. "We were late for a party cruise with Mr. Gray here, berth 22D. Didn't think he'd leave without us."

"He left all right," the man said. "Maybe half hour ago. Sorry 'bout that."

"You didn't happen to hear where he was heading?"

"Nope, sorry," he said.

"Hey, Paul," the blond said, tugging on the man's shirt. Her speech was a little slurred. "I thought I heard them say something about Pensacola. They walked right by me."

"Thanks, Darcy," he said. He looked at us and shrugged. "Well, there you go."

Rez raised an eyebrow. "Miss, did the Gray's have any women with them?"

"Oh, yeah," she said. "Three or four."

"Probably real lookers too," Paul said. "Don't know how he does it. New babes all the time."

"Paul!" Darcy slapped his arm playfully.

Rez looked at me. "Badge?" I was already getting it out of my coat pocket.

"Are you Mr. Adderly?" she asked.

"That's me," he said, hopping gallantly up onto the pier. A blonde like that at his elbow, and still he literally leaped to Rez's call. *Amazing.*

"Do I know you?" he asked.

"No, sir," Rez replied. She held out her badge. "Mr. Adderly, I am Special Agent Deanna Rezvani of the FBI." She held out her badge.

"Wow," he said, staring at the ID. He turned back to Darcy. "Babe, this is real."

"The FBI parties!" she hooted, pumping a fist.

"Well, that's not exactly why we're here," Rez explained. "We never were invited to a party cruise with Mr. Gray. We're actually investigating him. He could be involved in some very dangerous business."

"What sort of business?" Adderly asked.

"We can't go into specifics, you understand," she said. "But Gray's wanted for questioning in at least one murder investigation. We got a tip that he berths here. But we missed him."

"Never liked the arrogant jerk," Adderly grumbled. Then, he frowned, seemingly chewing on an idea. His eyes went wide and he grinned, an industrial strength light bulb appearing above his head. "You want us to take you out on the *Sirocco* and catch the bum?"

Rez and I exchanged glanced. "Yes," she said. "Yes, we would."

"Climb aboard, Special Agents," Adderly said. "The *Sirocco* is a JMV hull, custom built in Cherbourg, France. With my regatta team, we took her to 40 knots." He paused and looked at the sky. "We won't get near that with these winds, but we won't need it to catch up to Gray's *little* boat."

*** *** *** ***

Adderly could flat out sail. In just a few minutes, we were way out in the Gulf. I didn't know the Gulf of Mexico as well as some other bodies of water, but Adderly apparently did.

"Keep a northwesterly track from here and we'll run right into Pensacola," he crowed. "If that's where he's headed, we'll catch 'em."

"I'll keep an eye out for his lights, love," Darcy said, sauntering towards the foredeck. "He's got more red lights than most."

"Red lights," I muttered to Rez. "Mean anything to you?"

She shook her head. "I don't know anything about ships." She turned to Adderly at the wheel. "Mr. Adderly, do you know why Gray might have extra red lights?"

"He's supposed to have four lights," Adderly said. "A red and a green at the bow; a white at midship and at the stern. Darcy, where are his extra red lights?"

"Up on the mast," she called, her voice stuttering with hiccups. "He's got two ex—two extra—red lights. One of th—them—at the top; one half way. Middle one's not always on though. Both were t—tonight."

"Mean anything to you?" I asked Adderly.

"Not regulation," he replied. "But...if you wanted to signal someone without calling too much attention to yourself, you might use red."

I looked at Rez and met her thoughtful gaze. We were likely both wondering the same thing: who might Smiling Jack be signaling?

***   ***   ***   ***

"Erica, you need to stay awake for a little longer," Jack said, brushing silky black hair out of her eyes. "Just a little longer."

"But...I...mmmmm, so tired." Her head swayed.

Dr. Gary moved away from the camera and looked beneath the table. Blood pooled at Erica's feet. "We'd better do this now," he said.

Jack nodded. "Erica, sit up, darling. It's time to make your movie."

***   ***   ***   ***

We'd been blessed with a bright, nearly full moon. And with the *Sirocco's* speed, we'd managed to intercept one shy of a half-dozen yachts on the way to Pensacola. But drunk and disorderly was the worst of the crimes we encountered on those ships, and we hadn't caught the Sun Odyssey.

"This is a needle in a haystack," Rez whispered to me at the port rail. "Gulf's a big body of water. They could be anywhere."

"I'm used to long odds," I said. "If he's out here, we'll find him."

Rez stared at me. "You're not just being cocky, are you?"

"Not in the least."

"Maybe we should go back to the marina, back to the berth, and wait. He's gotta come back to port."

That made sense, but I wasn't ready to go to plan B. "Thing is about waiting...another young woman could die."

"There's a sail!" Adderly called from the wheel.

The boom was in the way. I ducked under and stared over the undulating, moon-dappled water. It was hard to tell from the sails. Seemed like too many sails for a boat that size.

"Two red lights on the mast!" Darcy called.

Yes, I thought. *Yes, there are.* The hull profile was right too. Then, I saw the windows. Porthole windows. "That's it!" I called out. "That's Gray's ship."

"I think you're right!" Adderly yelled back. "But there's another boat there."

I looked again. There was another ship directly behind Gray's. I couldn't tell the make because the Sun Odyssey was between us, the two ships moored side-by-side. "Can we cut all our lights?" I asked. "And bring us in slow to about 100 yards."

"Will do," Adderly replied. Every light on the *Sirocco* went dark.

"Darcy, do you have any clothes aboard?" Rez asked. "This dress isn't going to cut it."

She lifted her shades at last and frowned. "Mostly just beachwear. Oh, but we've got some scuba stuff. Wetsuits. You'd fit in mine."

"Even better," Rez replied, disappearing with Darcy below deck.

Adderly looked me up and down. He said, "No way you'll fit in mine."

He was right. I'd have to manage swimming in what I had on. I tossed the sports coat onto the forecastle. The real problem was my silver case. It's airtight, and it would float. But it would slow my swimming. And it would be too reflective in the moon's light.

I went below deck, passed a closed door, and found the restroom. Inside, I opened my silver case. Light from several sources within illuminated the tiny room. Only God knew what I'd find on that ship...human and otherwise. I lifted one tray out of my case. There was a compact handgun recessed into the second tray. The stock was a little bulbous and a little longer than a standard 9 mm. That's because this weapon didn't hold bullets. Not the traditional kind anyway.

This pistol held pulses of particle nether, concentrated in vapor-locked capsules within titanium casings. The Particle Nether Pistol, PNP, could hold three-shot clips, and each shot would absolutely ruin a man, ruin in such a way that no hollow-point .45 handgun or even a big-bore rifle shell ever could. Along with the PNP, I selected a slender silver tube. It was only a foot long, but with the push of a button, it would telescope into a very lethal weapon. It had a long, complicated name, but I simply call it the *Edge*.

I closed the case. And went back topside. Rez, black from neck to ankle with neoprene, waited for me at the rail. Adderly had maneuvered us close, a little more than a hundred yards, I thought. Better safe than sorry.

"Right ship?" Rez asked.

"Undoubtedly," I replied. "But the other ship troubles me. It's a variable we'll have to handle on the fly."

"Story of my life," Rez muttered, half to herself.

"Hey," Darcy said, slinking over to the rail. "You want us to radio the Coast Guard for back up or something?"

"Only if you don't hear from us in an hour," I said. "Once we're aboard Gray's ship, things are going to move fast. If you don't hear from us in an hour, there's a pretty good chance we'll be history."

Rez and I slipped silently into the water.

{ Chapter 19 }

"I LIKE MOVIES," Erica cooed. She raised her chin a little and swayed.

Jack readied his blade, took his position behind Erica, and waited. Dr. Gary started the camera and then nodded. Jack held Erica's chin. He could feel the pressure in his palm, the dead weight. She was fading fast. He pressed the knife blade to her throat...but pulled it away sharply.

There'd been a sound somewhere on deck. A muffled thump.

"What the heck was that?" Dr. Gary asked.

"I don't know," Jack hissed. "Go, go check."

Dr. Gary stopped the camera, went to a drawer, and withdrew a compact, brushed metal handgun, a Ruger SR1911 .45 caliber. "I'll be right back...but I don't think she's going to last."

Erica mumbled a string of unintelligible syllables, ending in two clear words: "I'm sorry."

*** *** *** ***

There were lights on inside the cabins of both ships. But fortunately, for our boarding purposes, the upper decks were shrouded in shadow. We clambered aboard at the aft rail of the Sun Odyssey, past the name *Company Gold*, written ornately on the transom, and now crouched on deck a few feet from the cabin steps.

"It's going to be close quarters in there," Rez whispered. "Not a lot of room for missing."

"I'll go first," I said. "I can take a few rounds if need be."

Rez frowned. "I know that. I saw. But I'm talking about the women. If Smiling Jack and the accomplice have the women aboard, an errant shot will kill them just as dead as Jack's knife. We can't afford to miss."

"Point taken," I said. "But I'm going first. I know this ship's layout and...I don't miss."

"I've heard that before," Rez replied. "From a former partner. Listen, Ghost, what do you expect me to do, shoot under your armpit? You're wider than the ship's doorway."

"Once I'm in and things happen, you'll have room. I'll make sure."

I tucked the Edge inside the waistband of my soaked khakis and reflexively checked the load of the PNP. The meter showed three green bars. It was ready.

I was ready.

Or so I thought.

My fingertips had barely brushed the handle of the door when the handle turned and the door flung open. A paunchy man with dark, short-cropped hair, frosted blond, gawked at me for just a few split seconds less than I gawked at him. In those few seconds, I tried to place the man's face with Smiling Jack. It wasn't him, but it might have been his accomplice. There was no way to know.

My hesitation proved costly. Frosty put a knife blade into my upper arm and struck a nerve. I dropped the PNP. He drew back the knife to strike again, but this time, I was faster.

I drew the Edge, depressed a switch, and heard the hiss of pressurized air as the emanation rod extended. About as long and as thick as a fencing rapier, the Edge crackled to life. Alternating serpents of blue and white energy spiraled instantly up the rod until reaching the fusion cap. The rod pulsed electric blue and emitted a warbling buzz. The Edge had reached battle charge in two heartbeats. By the third heartbeat, I'd severed Frosty's arm at the elbow. The limb—hand still holding the knife—fell at his feet with a muted splat, like a dead fish.

There'd only been a spattering of blood because the Edge cauterized the blood vessels and flesh almost instantly. Mouth hanging open with incomprehension and shock, Frosty reached down for his severed limb. I almost felt sorry for him. Almost.

I slammed my knee under his chin and heard several sharp snapping sounds. He sprawled backward against the forecastle and crumpled into a messy heap.

"Go!" Rez shouted.

She was right. We'd made too much noise. Smiling Jack wouldn't be surprised like his accomplice, and every second that passed could be life's blood.

***   ***   ***   ***

Jack put down the knife. No pulse. No point. He began to lower Erica's body to the cabin floor. SLAM!

Something hit the boat. Hard. Jack picked up the knife again and stared hard at the cabin door. He heard footsteps on the deck. Then, the cabin door burst open, and a dark figure dropped to the floor.

*** *** *** ***

I leaped down into the cabin, and saw a man crouching on the floor next to a reclining woman.

A knot of three other men and several women were tangled in the cramped room beyond. They began to untangle and guns came up.

"FEDERAL AGENTS, PUT DOWN YOUR WEAPONS!" Rez screamed behind me.

They fired. The doorjamb splintered. Rez fired, and I actually felt the heat of the gun's discharge beneath my arm. One of the men went down, cursing in Spanish. I wheeled right, flung one of the women behind me and put all four knuckles of one hand into another shooter's cheek. He was out cold before he hit the ground. The women were screaming now. I took my eyes off the other two guys and took a slug in my shoulder.

Rez's Sig Sauer barked once, and the man fell back into the compact sofa. He uttered a string of obscenities so vile I wished I didn't understand Spanish. Blood leaked from his shoulder, but he tried to raise the gun. I slashed the Edge and took his hand off at the wrist. His pistol sailed backward over the couch.

The last man dropped his gun, raised his hands high, and yelled for us not to shoot—in English, this time. Rez was on him instantly, producing cuffs, and slamming the guy against the cabin wall. It was then that I noticed the cameras. Two of them, expensive HD video recorders, on tripods aimed at the couch from different angles. Drug paraphernalia littered a low rectangular coffee table, and a mixed puddle of spilled drinks grew larger by the moment.

I heard a muffled cry from topside and then an engine.

GHOST

"You good?" I called. I didn't wait for Rez's answer. I knew she would be. I snatched up my PNP and thumped up the steps. I reached the deck in time to watch the ship that had tied up along side the *Company Gold* race away into the darkness. I steadied the PNP and fired once. The expelled charge raced soundlessly away. There was a flicker of bright white light on the back of the ship. But I'd likely only hit a rail or a hatch. The ship sailed on.

I went back down below. The young women were wrapped in blankets and huddled in the ship's master bedroom. And Rez had all four assailants zip tied and seated on the couches. Two of the men were still out cold. The man who'd lost his hand was awake but making fish faces, clearly in shock. Rez stood behind the only man who was still conscious and lucid. She nodded me over to the corner by the wet bar, and I knew what Rez would tell me before she said a word.

"We got the right ship," she said, "but the wrong criminals. These guys are sex traffickers. La Compañía, Cuban mafia."

I stared through the door at the women. Two of them looked like they could still be in high school. I shook my head at the innocence lost.

"That's right, La Compañía, you pathetic cop bastards!" The man on the couch crowed. "You know what that means?"

I took a step toward him. Rez put a hand on my chest. "Don't," she said. I pushed past.

"You Gray?" I asked.

"Stupid cop," he replied. "You don't know my name do you? I will tell you something: you will know my name. I'll have it carved into your lily white, cop chest. You'll be whispering it through bloody bubbles when I have you gutted. La Compañía! You don't know who you're—"

I was around the couch and loomed over him, my face just inches from his. I held back the full-blown Netherview, but let my eyes do their thing. The irises went from pale blue to jet black. The pupils shrank to a pinprick of light, but I knew they blazed like distant stars going nova.

"Now you listen to me," I said, my voice, deep and menacing, spoken right into his mind. "You might cow teenagers with this lame Al Pacino, Scarface shtick, but I can see you. You are a miserable little boy. You've been lost for a long, long time, and the way out has become so narrow, it's barely there. I hope you find it. Because if you don't, I might come for you."

Just then, white light flared from my wounded shoulder.

Gray sat back and gaped. If I'd filled his mouth with dish soap, he'd be blowing bubbles.

Rez stared as I approached. "Holy smokes, Ghost! Gray went from arrogant wise guy to zombie. What did you say to him?"

I avoided eye contact with Rez and said, "It was something he needed to hear."

Rez waited a beat, probably hoping for more details. I didn't offer any. She huffed out a breath. "Still, Ghost, be careful. La Compañía isn't something to be trifled with. They're heavy hitters down here. Watch your back."

I said, "Someone already is." She smiled. I think she thought I meant her. I didn't correct her. "Take the young women to Adderly's ship. Get them some decent clothing if you can, maybe some coffee. I'll babysit these guys."

She started to leave but paused. "You aren't...you aren't going to do something to them are you?"

I shook my head. "Tempting, but I'll let due process handle them for now."

Rez disappeared. I knew she'd contact the Coast Guard. I knew there'd be questions. And I knew the Feds would probably get involved. I was glad for the bust, but it was a costly mistake. I just didn't know how costly.

*** *** *** ***

"What's the matter with you?" Jack screamed. "Dropping down like that? I almost had a heart attack!"

"I'm sorry," Dr. Gary said. "I knew what a hurry we were in with Erica...and...oh, she didn't make it."

"No," Jack muttered. "She bled out while you were gone. What took you so long? And what was that crash I heard?"

"Driftwood," Dr. Gary replied. "Half a tree by the look of it. The current slammed it up against the bow, port side. We're going to need new paint."

"What about our plan?" Jack asked.

Gary looked down at Erica's body and shook his head. His eyebrows knitted tightly a moment, then relaxed. "We can't film her expiring," he said slowly, thinking. "Do her throat anyway. Then, get her wrapped up and come topside. I'm going to pull anchor."

"What are you thinking?"

"Later," he said, "when we get to the fort."

*** *** *** ***

It had been a grueling six hours with the local police and the Feds who had choppered in out of the Jacksonville field office. Agent Rezvani was my shield, vouching for me as a local private detective and hiding my silver case far from prying eyes. Maybe their eyes would have pried a little more if they hadn't been so overjoyed by the break in the La Compañía organization.

Mr. Gray's real name was Ernesto Guevara Ramírez, and he was a major player in the Cuban mafia's local sect. He was known on the street as the man who could make anyone's sexual fantasies—no matter how perverse—become reality, for a price. He was a confirmed violent misogynist, but slippery as an eel, he had been impossible to put away for long. The Feds thought that might change now, and that was probably why they didn't pay as much attention to me.

With one exception. A field agent out of Jacksonville named Culbert was a little too curious about the severed limbs. He had wiry, curled white-bond hair that reminded me of a kitchen scrubbing pad. He wore thick glasses, and seemingly had been born with a permanent, incredulous sneer.

"You mind telling me, Mr. Spector," his voice whiney and grating, "how you cut off one guy's arm at the wrist, the other at the elbow? Clean as you could want and cauterized too?" He exhaled loudly. "What'd you do, torture them? What kind of blade did you use?"

Rez appeared instantly and took Culbert aside, but not quite out of earshot.

"Look, Culbert," she said, "I know you're just doing your job, but you need to leave this guy alone. He broke this case open. He's on our side."

Culbert's sneer became even more lopsided. "Agent Rezvani, I don't know how you do things in D.C., but down here, these aren't the kind of details we leave as loose ends. Did you see those wounds? Whoosh! Right through flesh and bone and sealed right up like a surgeon. What kind of weapon does tha—"

"Leave it alone, Field Agent," Rez warned, deepening her voice. "Mr. Spector is above your pay grade."

Culbert bristled. "What the heck does that mean? What is he, a spook?"

Rez looked both ways as if to make sure no one else was listening in. "CIA, NSA are dark right?" she asked. He nodded. "Okay, so Spector belongs to something darker. Leave it alone or expect a visit from the guys in black suits and sunglasses."

"Crap," Culbert muttered. "But we're supposed to be the guys in dark suits and sunglasses!"

Rez shook her head. "You have no idea." Then she walked away, leaving Culbert in stupefied silence.

They were loading one of the La Compañía gunmen into an ambulance and he yelled to Culbert, "I'm tellin' ju, mannn, he's like a freakin' Jedi Knight, yo. Arrest that dude...'fore he cut off somebody's head with dat lightsaber!"

Culbert didn't even look at the Cuban. "Save it for your lawyer."

***   ***   ***   ***

"You want to get breakfast?" Rez asked, turning into the strip mall parking lot where I'd parked the dead hitman's car. "The sun'll be up in an hour."

"Thanks, no," I replied. "I need to get some sleep, or...at least rest while I think about things."

She took my silver case from her backseat and handed it to me. Then she handed me something else. "Take it," she said.

"What is it?"

"Duh, it's a cell phone. You're the only guy I know who doesn't have one. It's prepaid for a year. My number's preprogrammed in there. Call me if you need to."

I smiled. "You mean, it's so you can call me when you want to."

"That too."

I pocketed the little black electronic candy bar and said goodbye. I drove to the nearest hotel outside of Panama City Beach proper, a local place called The White Sands Inn. It wasn't a Motel 6, unfortunately, but it was clean...and cheap. I paid $42 in cash and fell into the bed in my new room. The mattress was hard, but it didn't matter...not really. Sleep would elude me until my mind quieted down. And that didn't look to happen for some time. My thoughts raced...running laps around the same maddening reality:

Smiling Jack and his accomplice were still out there. And our best lead had come up empty.

*** *** *** ***

I woke with a start to a blaring, loud rendition of *I Feel Pretty* from West Side Story. Whoever the last occupant of the room was, I guess they liked to wake up with a heart attack. *I feel pretty, oh so pretty...*

I hit the snooze button on the alarm a little too hard. The brick-sized alarm skidded off the bedside table and dropped to the floor with a crash. But the dreaded music wouldn't stop. I rolled out of bed and fell to all fours, scrambling for the alarm. I found it, but I wasn't familiar with this alarm at all, and there were a lot of buttons and switches. I tried flicking every switch in rapid-fire combinations, but still the music played on. If anything it was even louder now, seemingly right in my ear.

I feel charming, oh so charming, it's alarming just how charming I feel!

I didn't know how much more of this I could take, so I pulled the little alarm clock's plug.

But the music didn't stop. *What in the...?* Then I realized: battery backup.

Such a pretty face. Such a pretty dress.

I was half tempted to get the PNP from my silver case and blast the thing. But I found the battery compartment, flicked out the two double A, Duracells, and started to grin at the sudden peace—

But the music didn't stop.

I feel stunning and entrancing, feel like running and dancing for joy!

At last, it dawned on me that the music wasn't coming from the alarm clock at all. The phone. It was coming from the phone Rez gave me. I dug into the pocket of my new sports coat, grabbed the little black phone, and hit the glowing green button.

"What took you so long to pick up?" Rez growled.

"I thought the ringtone was the alarm. I didn't—"

"Never mind. I need to you to get to Fort Pickens National Park in Pensacola. There's a body here, and Ghost...I think it's one of Jack's."

***   ***   ***   ***

I pushed the sports car past the speed limit on US Route 98 and stopped only once, filling up with gas at a little middle-of-nowhere station called Isaiah's Gas-n-Go. Fifty-nine dollars later, I was back on the road to Pensacola Beach.

Two and a half hours later, the sun was already climbing, humidity hugged the coast like a wet wool blanket, and I was staring down at the lifeless body of a young woman.

Fort Pickens was built between 1829 and 1834 and was the largest of four forts built to defend the naval yard at Pensacola Bay. It was a pentagonal structure with strongholds at each angle and ten concrete gun batteries spread along its perimeter walls. It had served with distinction becoming one of only four forts in the South never to be occupied by Confederate forces during the Civil War. But after World War II, weapons technology had made the fort obsolete, and the Army abandoned it.

The U.S. Park Service occupied the fort now and apparently took some professional pride in posting historical fact signs like the ones I'd read as I walked the two hundred yards from the parking lot to the fort interior. The Park Service also ran tours of Fort Pickens' narrow stone halls and cramped bunkers, no doubt recounting the few historical details not emblazoned upon the signs.

The young woman's body had been left at the end of one of those narrow halls, the one at the pentagon's point just a few hundred yards from the glistening Gulf of Mexico. Fortunately, an early-bird park ranger by the name of Slemner found the body prior to any tour group full of grandparents and impressionable grandchildren. The scene would have haunted young memories and nightmares for many years, as they would mine...if I let them.

The woman was a young brunette who, in life, must have had very little exposure to sun. Her skin was ivory white and flawless but for the wounds that had killed her. She wore a white camisole similar to the one worn by the red headed victim from the camera I'd found. The cami was stained bright red as were the sheer white shorts she wore. She lay on her side, very much in the fetal position, but her head was turned to stare at the ceiling. Her throat had been cut fiercely, deep enough to reveal bone.

Rage surged up within me. The killers had kept this poor young woman kenneled like a dog and then slaughtered her. And they had been out on the Gulf last night, after all. We'd found a boat, the very one I'd seen the morning I received the camera. We'd stopped a crime, and for that I was grateful. But Smiling Jack and his accomplice were still free...still alive.

Finding whatever ship the killers used out on the open Gulf at night would have been a needle in a haystack. But none of the excuses mattered. I had not stopped the killers in time, and another young girl was dead.

"What's he doing here?" Culbert poked me in the shoulder. I saw him wince and discreetly shake his hand behind his leg. I think he felt a little too close to me in the narrow stone hallway because he backed up quickly.

Agent Rezvani again came to my rescue. "I called him. Mr. Spector has been working the same case. I've invited him as a consultant."

"Consultant, huh?" Culbert said, his sneer lifting into a ridiculous smile. "What exactly do you do, Mr. Spector?"

"I consult." I stared at him hard, and eventually he got the hint and backed down.

Other agents and local law scurried in and out of the tunnel. Rez took me around a corner and led me to a dimly lit stone alcove. I could easily imagine old cannons and barrels of black powder stored there.

"This changes things," she said.

"I understand."

"I'm not sure you do." She exhaled as if what she was about to explain annoyed her but maybe there was nothing she could do about it. "The body changes things. She's one of Jack's. She was in the last batch of photos to hit the web. I'm sure of it. Her body will bring a cloudburst of Federal intervention. Remember, we spent millions on this case the first go round. There are dozens of higher ups still cleaning the bird crap off their shoulders. They'll be itching to put this to bed so they can report to John Q. Public and claim the win."

"I don't want credit," I said. "I want the killers."

"I know that. But my superiors won't be scared off like Culbert. Unless you flex a little muscle from your agency, you're going to be left out."

I said, "I don't think so." Rez put her hands on her hips and sighed. I decided to change the direction. "The body also means new leads."

She ran with it. "From her, we'll get prints, dental records, blood type...maybe, if we're lucky, we'll get some physical evidence from the killers. If not that, at least we'll get next of kin, maybe someone who knew her."

I nodded. "I'll need that information, Rez. Will you give it to me? Or will you cut me out too?"

She laughed. She actually laughed out loud at me. Then she slugged me in the shoulder, some kind of martial arts punch full of force and plenty of angst. It hurt a little, but I didn't flinch.

"Why did you do that?" I asked.

She looked like she was considering a second punch. "Y'know, for a smart guy, you seem to miss a lot. What kind of ungrateful hack do you think I am? You gave me my first real leads in this case and believed when everybody else told me to go fly a kite. Oh, and you saved my life. That counts for something in my book." She leaned in close. "But once my superiors show up, you'll have to disappear."

"I'm pretty good at that."

"I'm sure you are," she said. "Just keep the phone I gave you handy."

"About the phone...the ringtone?"

She stared at me, and I got the feeling that if we weren't at a crime scene, she would have burst out laughing.

"I guess you didn't care too much for that one. Give it here."

I handed her the phone. She tip-tapped buttons and slid the touch screen this way and that. Then she gave it back.

"That should do the trick."

I smiled and put the phone in my cargo shorts pocket. "Thank you."

Rez motioned for me to follow. "ME said he was almost finished."

We went back to the body, and the ME was just leaving.

Rez stepped into his path. "What did you get?"

The medical examiner was a short, roundish fellow who reminded me of a dark-skinned version of the Penguin villain from the Batman comics. But instead of a monocle, he wore wireframe specs with rounded rectangle lenses. Behind the glass, his sharp green eyes scanned Rez up and down, not ogling. More like assessing...analyzing. "Sorry, Special Agent Rezvani," he said. "Can't say 'til I get d'body back to d'lab."

There was a hint of the islands in his speech, Aruba, maybe. West Indies for sure.

"Off the record?" Rez pressed. "We've been working this case for some time. Cause of death? Time?"

"Off d'record, dee cause of death be exsanguination, but not 'ere. D'er eese not enough blood 'ere."

"From a cut throat?" Rez asked, incredulous.

"Mebbe," he replied. "But d'ere eese also dis wound in d'vaginal canal, and so I cannot rule out 'til I get back to d'lab."

Rez swore, not at the ME, but at the news. "What about the time?"

"From d'flesh temperature, I estimade d'time of death to be 'bout ten hours ago. Tree in d'marnin'...'bout."

Her eyes darted at the man's plastic encased ID. "Dr. Abbott, is there anything else you can tell us?"

"No'ting more, now if you'll pardon me, I 'ave much wark to do."

She handed him her card. "I'll call you," she said, "but if you get anything else before, please call me right away."

The ME nodded and walked away. Dr. Abbott, the West Indian Penguin. He even had a slight waddle to his gait.

"What now?" I asked.

"We hit the beach," she said. "She wasn't killed here. If they did this out on the Gulf and then brought the body here. There should be some sign on shore. Sand is pretty good for keeping footprints."

"Unless the tide washes them away," I said.

Rez gave me a fretful stare. I wondered if she was thinking the same thing I was.

We might be closer to finding the killers than we'd ever been. But would we get them fast enough to keep them from killing again?

{ Chapter 20 }

WE WERE ON THE BEACH for an hour, talking to the agents who were scrutinizing a twelve-foot wide path staked off from the waterline to the fort. As the waxing afternoon sun raged down upon us, we learned pretty much what we expected to learn. The killers had likely anchored in deeper water and come to shore in a Zodiac or some other small craft. Two sets of footprints led from the water. There were spots of blood along their path and occasional depressions where they might have rested the body. The scene technicians had taken impressions on the prints. We'd likely get a definitive identification of whatever footwear the killers had been wearing.

The techs gave us what they could so far. One of the killers had larger feet and was heavier than the other. The techs estimated one in the 180-240 range; the other 150-175. Not a lot to go on. But it was more than we had before and likely all I was going to get from the FBI for a while.

"Rez!" came a voice like an avalanche. "Culbert told me you got some hotshot consultant?" A sweaty hot older man in a way-too-dark for Florida suit charged across the sand. He had a jaw like a wedge of granite and proceeded to spew a list of invectives that would have sent an Army drill sergeant to therapy.

"Oh, crap," Rez hissed. "What's he doing here?"

"Who is he?"

"Deputy Director Barnes," she whispered. "I had no idea he'd come himself."

"Is that bad?"

She nodded. "It shows you how important this case is to the Bureau. And I don't think he's going to like you very much."

"Should I leave?"

"Too late," she said.

"This the guy?" demanded the blocky, muscular Deputy Director of the FBI.

I held out my hand. He ignored it. "John Spector."

"Never heard of you," Barnes said. "But if you know anything about law enforcement, you've heard of me. Ulysses M. Barnes, Deputy Director of the Federal Bureau of Investigation. Can you or Agent Rezvani please explain to me why you are present at a crime scene?"

I started to speak, but Rez cut me off. "Deputy Director, Sir, he's here because I invited him."

"Invited him, what in the—"

She cut him off too. "Mr. Spector was the one who sent us the photos from the camera he found, remember, Sir? He's also the one who broke the Cuban mafia's sex-trafficking ring. He's proved an invaluable ally and consultant in all my efforts investigating Smiling Jack. He's the only help I've had, Sir, since I'm working during my vacation."

"Touché," Barnes replied. He glanced down. "What's with the silver suitcase?"

"Tools," I said.

"Uh, huh." Barnes looked like I'd just spat a glob into his bowl of cereal. "He needs to leave."

"But, Sir, he's—"

Barnes held up a hand. "My final word."

***   ***   ***   ***

Mortified and angry, Rez had offered a variety of apologies and promised to call and keep me in the loop. I tried to reassure her. Honestly, I preferred to work from the outside. Teaming up with Rez was one thing, but working in concert with dozens and dozens of FBI agents and higher-ups, well...that wasn't a very good idea. The fewer people who knew anything about me the better.

I drove back to Panama City. While waiting for any new leads the FBI's best and brightest could find, I wasn't about to sit still. The condition of the body, the wounds...they led to questions, questions that maybe Doc Shepherd could help answer. In fact, Doc Shepherd suddenly seemed like an underutilized asset. I'd turned over a stone, but not dug down deep enough to find what I was looking for.

The killers had been sending a message all along. Only now, they were sending the message louder. And somehow, I still wasn't getting it.

***   ***   ***   ***

The sun was setting beautifully over the western corner of the Gulf, soaking the towering pillars of clouds billowing to the far north. Maybe my awe of creation was why I didn't pick up the tail until just a few blocks from Panama City Beach Hospital Center. It was a black SUV, but I wasn't sure of the make. One of those Hummer wannabes, for sure. Blocky military body, wide axles, and tinted glass.

I guess the FBI couldn't just let me walk away. I shrugged and pulled into the hospital's visitor lot. The pseudo-Hummer drove right on by. They'd turn a block down, circle back, and park just in time to watch me disappear through the revolving door. They'd be waiting for me when I left, and I made a mental note to spot them quick. I'd also need to get my car out of sight so I could check it over for tracers or bugs. Of course, maybe the agents would be so bold as to run a check on the car. If so, they'd likely mistake me for a hitman. The irony was not lost on me.

But still, I could not afford the time or the hassle an arrest would cost me right now. I entered the hospital, strode beneath the atrium's moronic cherubim, and boarded an elevator. No one stopped me. No one asked me for a badge. Perhaps it was the expression on my face. I'd been told on one occasion that my "angry and determined face" could break a mirror...and the wall behind it.

"Is Doctor Shepherd available?" I asked bleached-blond Nurse Pelagris.

"One moment, Officer," she said. "Actually, yes. He's just finished a consultation and doesn't have any procedures until this evening. You remember the way to his office?"

I nodded and found my way to Doc Shepherd. He welcomed me into his office with a broad smile and a glint in his pale blue eyes. Nothing about his expression said he was surprised to see me.

"Officer Spector," he said, gesturing to the chair across from his desk. We both sat, and he asked, "So, any progress on the case? Were you able to track down the blades? Cain's Daggers that were bought or sold in the past ten years?"

"I haven't had a chance," I replied. "Things have...things have escalated."

"Oh?"

"It's why I've come back." I told Doc Shepherd about the recent murder. As I explained the details, I watched the color drain out of his face and then return a few minutes later, darkening to angry red.

When I had finished, Doc asked, "So the ME believes the young woman bled out, but not necessarily from the throat?"

I nodded.

"Are you certain this was one of the women in the pictures?" he asked.

"Positive. Why?"

"Correct me if I'm wrong," he said, "but none of the other victims had vaginal trauma."

"No," I replied. "Not that we're aware of."

"That's a very puzzling thing for you to say, Officer Spector," Doc said. "You mentioned several previous victims...I'm assuming they were all thoroughly examined."

Things were about to get dicey. "Doc Shepherd, can I count on your discretion in this matter?"

"Of course."

"Have you ever heard of the Smiling Jack Murders?" I asked.

It wasn't so much that his expression changed but it was as if the skin on his face tightened instantaneously. He didn't answer my question. "Go on," was all he said.

"Until now," I said, "there haven't been any bodies left behind. Only pictures."

"Uh, huh," he said, twirling his mustache in a most dispirited fashion.

{ 207 }

"The latest victim is indeed one of the young women from the Smiling Jack photographs," I said. "It's the first physical evidence we've had to go on."

"We?" Doc Shepherd asked.

I hadn't realized I'd used that particular pronoun. "The FBI," I said.

"I thought the FBI dropped the Smiling Jack case," he said. "In their professional assessment, it was a hoax."

"It wasn't a hoax," I said. "They just weren't smart enough to find the clues they needed."

"They?" Doc Shepherd asked.

Speaking of *not smart enough.* I wanted to hit myself, preferably with something large and blunt. "The FBI," I replied.

Doc Shepherd folded his hands on his desk. "You know, Mr. Spector," he said, "I find myself wondering a great deal about you and your involvement in all this. When I met you, I thought everything about you spoke of professional law enforcement. But now, I'm thinking that was because Carol told me a cop was coming up to see me. But now, I hear you say we, implying you're part of the FBI, and then they, implying that you are not. You aren't actually with the FBI, are you?"

"No," I replied, feeling ridiculous.

"You never did correct me when I called you officer," he said. "FBI would go with agent, I believe. Still, now I'm wondering if you are even with the police. Well, are you?"

"No," I said, "I am not."

"Mr. Spector," he said, his voice taking on an edge I had not heard before. "I'll accept that I made all the assumptions here, that I alone am at fault for being wrong about you. But you allowed me to carry on with those assumptions. You accepted my help under false pretenses, no matter whose fault those pretenses were. In my book, that's a violation of trust."

Guilty as charged. He had me dead-to-rights, but he did not understand the whole picture. I don't know how he could. "Doctor Shepherd," I said, "Trust is a precious commodity in this world and, for what it's worth, I never intended to mislead you. However, I did allow you to believe those things about me because...well, because the truth would be harder to believe."

He blinked, and I could tell that, behind that blue-eyed gaze, tens of thousands of possibilities were racing in the circuitry of his mind. "Try me," he said.

I took a deep breath. I'd been through this before. How much could I reveal? How would he react? What greater damage could occur? I made up my mind, and I was about to give him some information when his desk phone rang.

He took up the receiver. "Shepherd," he said. He listened intently for a few moments and then, his voice suddenly full of command, he said, "Tell Nurse Cathy to get down to the blood bank. Uh, huh, right...all the A-positive we can get. I want the bypass ready and waiting when I arrive. And get someone to the freezer to wait. If I can't create something internally, I'm going to need something PDQ." He hung up the phone and stood.

"Emergency?" I asked.

"I'm afraid I need to cut this conversation short," Doc Shepherd said. "A man is dying upstairs, and I'm on the clock."

I stood up and started to speak, but he held up a hand.

"Don't say anything more," Doc Shepherd said. "Not now. We're both in a hurry, and liable to make mistakes. But, Mr. Spector, if you want any additional assistance from me, you'll need to level with me. And God help you if your involvement in the murders of these young women is anything but noble." The threat lingered in the air even after Doc Shepherd left the office.

I'd learned nothing more to help me, and I may have sealed off a very important source of information. All in all, not a stellar effort.

***   ***   ***   ***

When I passed through the hospital's sliding exit doors, it felt like leaving an airlock for another planet. The heat seemed to boil up from the pavement and broil down from above. The heat must have triggered a hallucination because I suddenly heard a bouncy tune full of violins, bells, harps, and flutes—a tune that couldn't possibly have clashed with my mood any worse than it did.

I am sixteen going on seventeen
I know that I'm naive.
Fellows I meet may tell me I'm sweet...

"No," I muttered. As I fumbled in my coat pocket for the cell, I finally realized I'd been had.

I am sixteen going on seventeen, innocent as a rose...

An older married couple walked by just then, whispering and snickering merrily as I came up empty in the two outer pockets.

I need someone older and wiser,
Telling me what to do...

Finally, I snagged the phone out of the left hand inner pocket. I smashed down the green button and growled, "Liesl's song from The Sound of Music...really, Rez?"

I thought I'd have to endure peals of triumphant laughter, but when Rez spoke, her voice was uncharacteristically stiff...robotic and tersely professional. "Mr. Spector, I'm calling you on behalf of FBI Deputy Director Barnes."

"What can I do for you, Agent Rezvani?" I replied, playing along—though I had no idea what game we were playing.

"Mr. Spector, I am calling to inform you that the case, hitherto known as Smiling Jack, is exclusively the domain of the FBI."

Hitherto? Who talks like that?

"And so, Mr. Spector, you are advised to cease and desist all activities that may relate to the case." There was a pause, and I heard a gruff male voice say something unintelligible in the background. "In fact, Mr. Spector," Rez went on, "if you involve yourself in the Smiling Jack investigation—in any way—you will be arrested and charged with felony interference in a federal case."

"Felony interference?" I echoed. "Are you sure there is such a thing?"

"I hope you understand the gravity of the situation, Mr. Spector," Rez said, her voice sounding pained and raw. "Lives are at stake."

"I understand completely," I said, wondering how much of this she really expected me to honor. And how much of this would she honor?

"From this point on, Mr. Spector," she said, "we will have no further contact. Violations of any kind will result in my dismissal from the FBI and your incarceration. Please reply to indicate that you have understood this official warning."

I had to fight down a bile-filled wave of rage. I'm not sure I succeeded entirely. "Let the record show," I said through clenched teeth, "I have been so informed."

"Goodbye, Mr. Spector." She hung up. Just like that.

{ Chapter 21 }

I DROVE THE HITMAN'S CAR away from the hospital and didn't care if I still had a tail. If the FBI wanted to play cat and mouse with me, fine. They'd figure out in short order which one of us was the cat. And this cat was in one serious bad mood.

In the past six hours, the biggest lead in the Smiling Jack case had been laid out in front of me...and then snatched away. The FBI had cut me off. Doc Shepherd had cut me off. And, in spite of her previous pledge, Agent Rezvani had cut me off too. Of course, it was my fault for trying to collaborate, but that was not the predominating thought in my mind at this moment.

I thought sure Rez would have called me back, maybe when she got out from under the blazing glare of the Deputy Director. But I'd driven around for an hour without even so much as an "I am sixteen, going on seventeen," warbling out of the phone.

So I already had a chip the size of a garbage truck on my shoulder when I happened to drive by a billboard sign. "Great Progress Clinic for Women," it read. "Where a Woman's Choice is Held Sacred." There was a phone number and the exit listed as well.

I should have known better. I should have looked away and driven on. After all, I needed a new base of operations for Internet research. Like I said, I should have known better.

But, after spending the afternoon wallowing in disgust over my lack of progress and all the dead ends, I found myself taking the exit for the clinic. I parked on a side street about a hundred yards away from the front doors. Great Progress Clinic for Women looked like a giant spider built from steel, glass, and stone. Its hub was a blocky, two-story structure capped with a bluish dome, and its appendage-like wings sprawled out all around it.

I told myself I was there to think about the facts of the Smiling Jack case. The murder weapon was, after all, a turn of the century abortion instrument. Smiling Jack chose the weapon because he has a message to send, and maybe if I spent some time at an abortion clinic, a new angle might present itself.

But that was just psychological slight-of-hand.

The truth was, I had come to the clinic because I was angry. The rage had been building for days now, and I needed an outlet soon, or bad things would happen. So I'd come to the clinic to turn it loose.

I had a clear line of sight to the clinic's front doors. I willed the Netherview to begin. The road vanished. The sidewalk, the trees and shrubs, the mailbox, and the street signs—all dematerialized in moments, becoming a sunless twilight full of phosphorescent elements. And I saw pretty much what I expected to see hidden in the nether at an abortion clinic.

A formidable, gothic-styled iron fence surrounded the property. The Shades had claimed it as a stronghold, and it would remain theirs until taken by force. Beyond the gate, a few agonizingly twisted, leafless trees stood guard like sentries in front of a faintly luminous structure. This stronghold was a castle in theory, but there was nothing at all romantic about this place. The towers leaned. The parapets were angled and framed by jagged merlons and gouged crenels. The gatehouse was misshapen, and the portcullis looked as if it had been made to tear flesh. It was an utterly ugly structure, but it was home to my quarry.

Shades, and lots of them. Roamers, nesters, prowlers, haunts, and thorns meandered across the property and were more heavily clustered at the stronghold. I didn't see any Knightshades, but I expected them to be inside. Unwilling to reveal my presence for too long, I snapped off the Netherview. The clinic and its property reappeared.

I'd never attempted to storm a stronghold this well-fortified, but today, I just didn't care.

I'd called ahead: the clinic closed up at 5:00. It was quarter till. I probably should have come right after closing, to save myself the wait...and avoid the thoughts I'd have to deal with. I drummed my fingers on my silver case and watched the clinic. The moments ticked by like molasses.

Smiling Jack had used a turn-of-the-century abortion instrument to kill his victims.

The message seemed clear enough: Abortion is murder. Was that it? I cringed inwardly. I'd been given this mission specifically, but I didn't want it to turn out the way it seemed to be heading. Could it be as simple as a deranged Pro-Life activist going to severe lengths to show the reality of abortion?

While the news media took every chance it got to make all Pro-Lifers seem like violent, fringe psychopaths, I knew better. But there were a few. And that was a few too many. Those who assaulted abortion docs or shot up clinic windows were doing nothing to help a very just cause. And the worst of these were the ones who committed crimes and claimed to do so in the name of God.

I glanced up at the clinic and shook my head. Trouble was, I completely understood the motive. Children had been slain in places like this...by the millions. It was a holocaust that no one had the courage to recognize and stop. All the terrible dangers of the world: disease, sickness, famine, weather, etc.—things that could take the lives of the very young—and yet, mankind had the despicable temerity to murder its own. And then call it a *right*.

My blood was already boiling at six minutes to closing, when the clinic doors opened. I sat up a little straighter. A male nurse with very hairy forearms came out, slowly pushing a woman in a wheelchair. I couldn't tell how old the woman was. She had her head buried in her hands, and her hair made a curtain around her face. Her head bobbed slowly, and I felt my heart breaking. It was clear what she'd been through. And I knew what she'd have to face in the time to come.

The male nurse had wheeled her about half way down the front walk when a brown SUV left the clinic parking lot, pulled into the circle, and parked at the curb. A big man got out of the vehicle. He was barrel-chested, dressed in a too-tight black t-shirt and military-styled camouflage pants. His hair was a disheveled, rooster feather mess, and a trail of gray cigarette smoke followed him to the curb. He stood there, glaring at the approaching woman. And, I could scarcely believe it, but the man was actually tapping his foot.

I wanted to go over there and leave a four-knuckle tattoo on the guy's jaw, but that kind of thing was mostly outside the purview of my mission. I pushed down the rage, reminded myself that I had bigger fish to fry, and did my level best to be patient. In a few minutes, the clinic would be closed. A few minutes after that, the doctors, nurses, and assistants would clear out, and then, I could go in.

The woman in the wheelchair screamed.

I snapped to attention, thinking maybe the cammo-jerk had smacked her, but she was still twenty yards away from him. She seemed frantic, shaking her head and swinging one hand around. That's when I willed my Netherview once more.

The scene changed, and I knew instantly what had the woman so distraught. Shades surrounded her. Two roamers and a half a dozen thorns whirled about the woman. They darted in and out slashing at her with their talons and claws. These were not physical wounds, I knew. They were spiritual...many times more dangerous than damage to the flesh. The Shades were taunting the woman relentlessly. They were tormenting her.

That was more than I could take.

I opened my silver case. I withdrew my three favorite tools: the PNP, the Edge, and the Cat. I locked the case in the car, put the Edge and the Cat in my two deepest pockets, and tucked the PNP into my waistband where it would be hidden by my coat.

I strode towards the woman, and I can only imagine what I must have looked like to them. Big guy, bulging pockets, mad at the world, stomping up the sidewalk. But I couldn't be deterred by anything. I was taking a big risk in more ways than I could count. I had to be purposeful.

And absolutely lethal.

I switched back and forth between Netherview and Earthveil as I approached. The Shades so far were too busy making sport of the woman to notice my approach. They would notice soon enough.

The male nurse looked up first. "Excuse me, sir, can I help you?"

I thought fast. "John Spector, United Health Services," I said, holding out my badge and shiny shield. "I'm sorry I'm a little late for the observation." I flicked on Netherview. The Shades were tangled in the woman's hair. They were biting and scratching.

"Could I see that badge, sir?" Back to Earthveil.

"Of course," I replied, handing him the badge. The second he took the badge and his eyes left me, I flipped to Netherview and found myself glaring at a gaping roamer that was half entangled in the woman's hair. Its face was human...if you took a human's face and yanked strategic features with a pair of industrial strength pliers. I pulled the PNP from my waist band and let the big nasty roamer have it right in the kisser.

I pulled the PNP trigger, and in Earthveil, in strong daylight, all anyone would've seen is a little wavering shimmer in the air, and all they might've heard is a kind of a muted click. In Netherview, there was a flash of green light and a thunderous roar. The PNP launched a disc filled with particle nether, a pulsing, lugubrious substance. It was an incomplete recreation of the fabric of the spiritual world, but because it was incomplete, it would instantly consume anything spiritual that it contacted.

The roamer's face melted like the Wicked Witch of the West at her baptism. Its headless carcass fell away, and its essence—an oddly beautiful mist of sparkling crimson and deep purple—began to whirl in a vortex, being drawn inexorably back to the Abyss. Another roamer leaped at me. It took a PNP round in the groin. I didn't watch how much of the creature disintegrated. All I know is, once the pieces started flying, I switched back to Earthveil.

The male nurse handed me back my ID and shield. He hadn't seen any of the spiritual action. "I don't actually see United

Health Services on here," he said, looking hesitant, like maybe he didn't want to take chances with his job. "But...uhm, I'm not sure, I mean there wasn't supposed to be...anyway—can you tell me what this is about, sir?"

I subtly slipped the PNP behind my back and into the waistband of my shorts, grabbed up my billfold with a flourish, and said, "Again, sorry about the delay. I got called back to the office, and then traffic was a bear."

He didn't say anything at all but waited for me to actually answer his question. I'd stalled as long as I could. Every second of Earthveil was a moment the Shades could advance without me tracking them.

"Nurse Griggs," I said, noting his name tag and adopting an attitude of vast superiority. "You realize the recent legislation demands that you inform each patient of the potential physical and emotional side effects that may result from this procedure. You have signed documents, correct?"

"I...well...I, I..."

I took his babbling for a pause, switched to Netherview, just as two thorns burrowed into the flesh of my cheeks. Thorns are winged creatures about the size of a man's palm. Trust me when I say you do not want these things burrowing in your flesh. Shades of this ilk grappled quickly for tendons and bones.

The nurse wouldn't be able to see the things, of course, but I turned away briefly out of reflex...and to hide the pain. I managed to pluck the creatures free, but not before they had gouged and shredded a few things. My smile would be a little off until I found some time to reset. The thorns wriggled furiously in my hand, tearing at my fingers in a vain attempt to get free.

I crushed them, one in each fist, letting their remains slip to the concrete. Three, maybe four seconds had passed. I spun around quickly just in time to see the two remaining roamers disentangle from the woman's hair and launch toward me. But I could hear the male nurse's voice as if from a memory.

"Hey, bro, you okay?"

I had to go back to Earthveil, but the roamers were a heartbeat away from knocking me off my feet. They left me no choice.

I yanked the Edge from my pocket and switched it on. Its ethereal blade buzzed to life. In the same moment, I turned my vision back to Earthveil.

"Dude, you looked really strange for a minute there," the nurse said. "Hey, why are you smiling like that?"

I lifted the Edge, slashed it forward in a couple of quick cuts and then made like I was pointing over the tree line in the distance. "Sorry," I said, wristing the Edge back and forth. "I just remembered I left some important equipment back in my office. See? That gray building over there?" I made a real show of pointing.

All the male nurse saw was a peculiar silver baton in my hand. In broad daylight, the blade itself wouldn't show but a glimmer. I'm sure the roamers saw quite a bit more.

"Anyway," I said, retracting the blade and slipping the Edge back into my pocket, "I'll have to come back another time to complete the inspection."

"Whatever you say, man," the nurse replied. He wheeled the woman past me.

I nodded and willed back Netherview. The sidewalk was littered with the carved up remains of the roamers. I'd dispatched them blindly, but efficiently. And, for now at least, there were no Shades troubling the woman in the wheelchair.

In Earthveil, I saw her sitting up a little straighter. She was putting her hair up in a ponytail. I hoped that my efforts would afford the woman a little peace though I knew all too well that it would be merely temporary. She bore a Soulmark.

GHOST

I'd seen it in Netherview, a small but virulent red gouge in the center of the woman's forehead. It was shaped like a comma, and it meant the woman had been hurt. Not hurt physically, not necessarily, though it might have been. No, this was a wound to her identity, a wound to the essence of who she was, a wound to her soul.

It's like spiritual scar tissue. Without redemption, the Soulmark would fester and begin to leak tendrils of agony and guilt. Like blood in shark-infested waters, the Soulmark would attract Shades to the woman. And they would torment her again. I had no idea what circumstances had led the woman to the abortion clinic, but I knew the damage done to her was far more than physical. I'd given the woman a few hours of relief. Nothing more.

I let out a long, tired sigh. I'd come to the clinic to spend my rage. And I'd spent it. I was wounded and tired and wanted nothing more than to get in the car, drive back to a motel, and get a long shower. But resetting would have to wait. By slaying a handful of roamers and thorns, I'd just walked up to a Shade Stronghold and rang the front doorbell.

They'd seen me in my Netherviewing, and they'd seen my deadly handiwork. If there were Knightshades inside the clinic, they had no doubt been notified of my presence. *No,* I corrected myself. *I hadn't rung the front doorbell. I'd thrown a rock into a hornets' nest.* I could get in the car and drive away, but it wouldn't matter. They would follow.

I walked slowly back to the car. I'd need more clips for the PNP and a few other tools from my silver case. The rage had subsided, but I had little choice but to face the stronghold.

When the last of the clinic's employees left for the night, I'd go in. And then, all hell would break loose.

{ Chapter 22 }

THE SUN HAD GONE DOWN rapidly, almost as if it were getting clear for the events to come.

I watched red tail lights flash angrily as the last clinic employee drove away. That was my signal. I left the car.

And no being choosey this time, either. I took the entire silver case, and I was ready to use each and every weapon inside. The Edge, the Cat, the PNP, Slammers, and more—an arsenal in the right hands.

I was ready to go to war.

Netherview is incredibly vivid at night. All the luminous elements of the spiritual realm take on an eerie brilliance. I looked up at the abortion clinic, but saw only the Shade stronghold with all its wicked angles and jagged edges. A cluster of Shades waited near the ethereal gatehouse.

That surprised me.

I thought the moment I switched to Netherview, I'd find myself surrounded. But no, they hung back. I guess they figured they didn't need the element of surprise. It was their home turf. They knew how to protect it.

I took off in a lunging run toward the stronghold. A sleet storm of winged thorns raced out to meet me. They would cut me to ribbons if I let them get close enough. I didn't.

I almost wrenched my shoulder out of socket, throwing down the Slammer grenade. The lemon-sized incendiary device hit the ground, burst, and sent a fountain of blue sparks into the path of the oncoming thorns. The impact of the weapon was much like that of a shrapnel grenade...only worse. Every blue spark that contacted a thorn began to burn its leathery flesh. Each wound became a patch of spreading white fire, hungrily devouring everything but bone. Blackened Thorn skeletons fell from the air and crackled on the ground.

I leaped over their remains, dove over a charging prowler, rolled and came up firing the PNP. I hit the prowler in the back of its neck, and as I spun for the next target, I noted the prowler's head bouncing awkwardly off the walkway.

A second prowler leaped right in front of me. Its razor-sharp nails raked my chest and grazed my forearm. I saw the spray of my own blood. I swept the silver case, a hard outside in jag, and sent the roamer sprawling. Then, I simply raised the PNP to the creature's exposed back and pulled the trigger. The impact blew out the creature's spine. What was left of the prowler was spread all over the ethereal pavement.

I backhanded an approaching roamer, darted past its remains, and fired two PNP charges into a clot of thorns. There was a choral shriek and then a faint clattering of tiny bones hitting the ground. I slammed home my second PNP clip and continued toward the stronghold's gate.

At this point, the Shades got a little smarter. They stopped coming a few at a time and opted for a high volume, multiple angle attack. I cracked off two PNP rounds, sending a ham-fisted nester—the ogre-like dumb muscle of the Shade world—one flaming piece at a time, to the Abyss.

WHOA!

I ducked, and a corded, sinuous arm swept overhead. A prowler. I threw myself into a roll to put some distance between us. Prowlers are lethally capable grapplers. Shade Safety Tip 101A: do not get into a wrestling match with a prowler. There are no pins or tap-outs. They will twist you and tear you and break you. And...they cheat.

I came up from the roll, drew a bead on the gangly Shade, fired, and turned the thing inside out.

But that had to be it for the gun. Only one clip left—definitely needed to save it for the Knightshade. I tapped open the silver case, chucked the PNP inside and snagged the Edge. I lashed out, driving myself forward into a glut of Shades barricading the stronghold's main gate. Shade limbs flew as I whirled among the creatures. I hammered my elbow into the jaw of a roamer, spun, dropped to one knee and eviscerated a prowler that had been about to grab me.

A searing hot blade carved into my upper thigh, the pain instantly reminding me that the Shades were not weaponless. I grunted, lost balance, and sprawled to the ground. But I didn't stay down. I grabbed the scaly hind leg of the Shade who had cut me, and used its weight to pull myself up. I slashed the Edge at its midsection, but it parried that away with its brimstone blade. It tried another stab at my legs, the weapon just missing what would have been a crippling blow. I managed to spin away just in time and planted the Edge into the creature's hip socket. The Shade collapsed upon itself, blocking the path of another Shade that had been charging my way.

Something heavy hit me in the shoulder, knocking me off balance. It forced all my weight onto the wounded leg. I promise you: the sound I made in that instance was not a high-pitched, feminine scream. It was a guttural roar. It was. Really.

I bounced from the leg to an awkward landing on my knees and elbows. The Edge clattered from my hand and deactivated. That was bad. But when I heard the shriek, I knew I was in trouble.

Haunts.

In the realm of Shades, Haunts are the shock troops. They aren't as big as Nesters, nor as powerful as Knightshades. But they make up for it in sheer ferocity and fright. Haunts have the ability to shift in shape, but in their regular state, they resemble great, black hounds. They have blazing, blood-red eyes, long tapering jaws full of irregular sabers of teeth, and thick, club-like paws. Being on the ground with haunts around is not good at all.

Haunts like to go for the throat.

The first one pounced on my back and flattened me to the ground. Another barreled into me from the side, flopping me over. I had a split second to throw a hands-and-arms defense up to guard my neck and face. The haunt tore into me, teeth shredding flesh and striking the bone of my hands and arms. Blood spattered my face and dribbled into my eyes. I heard jeering laughter and haunt howls all around me. The other shades thought I was done for.

Not yet.

I felt the Haunt's jaws close on my wrist, felt the pressure build as it clamped down. As I knew it would, however, there came a moment when the pressure let up...just as the haunt was about to release its jaws and bite down again. I took a chance and yanked at my wrist, but not to pull my hand free. Instead, I shoved my fist into the beast's gaping maw and grabbed the thing's tongue. It felt like squeezing a leathery piece of steak. Only disgusting. Much more disgusting.

The haunt's jaws snapped shut on my arm and that, of course, was the correct countermove. If it could by blunt-force-trauma snap my bones and shear off the hand, I was pretty much done. But I held on to that tongue. In fact, I began to squeeze. I made such a tight, clamping fist that my fingers began to dig into its flesh. The haunt didn't seem to know what to do about the pain inside its mouth. The harder it bit down, the harder I squeezed. The ethereal hound squirmed on my chest and tried to yank itself away. But I held on.

The haunt gave a powerful pull. I used the beast's force to curl upward—just in time to see a big, slant-eyed nester standing over me with a brimstone sword held high in a two-fisted grip like an executioner. The blade came down. The haunt shrieked.

With the torn out haunt tongue to pad my palm, I slowed the brimstone sword's impact enough to avoid an unwanted amputation. The blade had sheared through the meat of the tongue and gone straight to the bone of my thumb. My right hand radiated agony, but at least I was free to get to my feet.

Left handed, I reached into my case and pulled the Cat free. Its housing was identical to the Edge: a silver, metallic baton with no noticeable features. But when I activated it, a cable of crackling purple electricity snaked out. With a flick of my wrist, the Cat snapped in the air with a sound like a thunderclap.

The Shades edged away from me in unison. But I didn't let them get out of range. I swung my flail weapon in a loop around my head, creating a giant, luminous halo above me. Then, I tore into the Shades. My first stroke was a wide backhanded arc that gutted a foursome of roamers that just couldn't get out of the way of each other fast enough. I snapped the Cat back and tore the face off a prowler. I dodged a leaping nester and gave a little wrist snap. The whip responded, snaking out to take off the nester's hind legs.

Finally, the haunt whose tongue I'd kind of ripped out lunged at me from the left. Another of its kind dove at me from my right. They didn't know it, of course, but they had just set themselves up for my favorite move with the Cat. I took one step backward and, at the same time, sent the whip whistling towards Tongueless. At the end of the Cat's whip-like cable is a cluster of tiny blades, the scourging elements. These dug deep into the haunt's neck. Then, with all my might, I hauled the whip toward the other oncoming haunt. The scourging elements had found solid purchase, and so the tongueless haunt was propelled bodily into the other haunt. The collision was terrible...for the haunts.

They hit head first. There was a tremendous cracking of bones, the wet crushing of a skull, and the heavy *whump* of the two bodies. I watched them for a moment to make sure they weren't going to get up. They didn't. I let out a deep breath and turned to look for the next threat.

The few remaining Shades did not attack. They vanished into their stronghold. I thought they retreated...that they went to the one place they were certain I wouldn't follow.

I couldn't have been more wrong.

***   ***   ***   ***

I deactivated the Cat and slammed it back into my case. Then, I cast about and found the Edge under one of the dismembered Shades. It was a bit messy, but I couldn't do without it. I wiped the Shade-goo off on my shorts, and turned to the gate.

GHOST

If I'd been in Earthveil, I couldn't have entered the abortion clinic without sawing through the locks and setting off the alarms. But in Netherview, there was no clinic. It was a spiritual stronghold held by the Shades.

I found myself facing a very sturdy-looking iron door. *The Shades went in this way,* I thought, grasping the handle, *but they've no doubt locked it up tight—*

The door fell open.

That should have been a clue, but I ignored it. No sooner had I stepped inside the stronghold, than the iron door slammed shut behind me and locked. I wanted to beat myself over the head with a bat. The Shades hadn't been retreating. They'd been baiting the trap. The temperature dropped enough that I could see my breath...as well as...the puffs of breath from all the Shades that lined both sides of the long corridor that stretched out in front of me.

"He is a foolish Guardian who sets foot in Sintryst," a deep voice rolled out from the darkness far ahead.

The Shades hissed ominously. It sounded like the corridor was filled with hundreds of vipers.

"Advance," the voice commanded. "But make no sudden movements. My minions are a bit...anxious...after your doings outside."

Knightshade, I thought. And given his sense of authority, I was guessing he was pretty high up on the local food chain.

Stepping forward didn't seem very promising. But neither did trying to dust it up with the Shades, at least eighteen of them, maybe more. Outside, I might have tried it. Room to maneuver. But not in here. In this narrow corridor I would be the lone fish in a very small barrel. Besides, it would be decidedly foolish to make a move before I knew what sort of Knightshade I was dealing with.

I strode forward, the case in my wounded hand, the Edge ready in my left. The Shades' hissing continued. I briefly considered smacking a few of them as I walked by, but...that might be seen as an act of provocation, so I resisted.

I stepped over a threshold and found myself in a vast chamber. Two grand staircases descended from an upper story and met at the foot of a massive throne.

An honest-to-goodness throne.

Either this Knightshade had delusions of grandeur, or I'd just stepped into a nightmare. When I focused at last on the being seated on the throne, I knew.

Definitely nightmare.

The Knightshade on the throne was massive. Thick slabs of muscle covered his chest, shoulders, and stomach like armor plating. His lower torso was thick with fur all the way down to his cloven feet. His immense wings were folded behind him, and he rested his chin on one of his fists.

"Tell me, Guardian," the Knightshade said, "Why have you come? The woman you...meddled with...earlier, she was not one of yours."

"Are you certain?" I asked.

The Knightshade laughed, and I felt suddenly like a little boy playing chess against a grandmaster. I'd offered up what I thought was a good move and, knowing how he'd crush me, he'd just smirked in my face.

"The woman and so many others who come here, are in my care," the Knightshade said. "Sintryst is my domain...one of *my* domains. I am Forneus."

I tried to keep myself from reacting. I locked out my knees so they wouldn't buckle. I kept my hands in my pockets so they wouldn't shake noticeably. I even widened my eyes to keep from

GHOST

blinking. But my body still betrayed me. I sucked in a sharp breath.

"Ahhhh," Forneus said, a very deep rattling in his voice. "I will accept your compliment. I am pleased to find that you know of me."

Know of him? Forneus the Felriven...Forneus the Despoiler...Forneus the Spirit Prince—pick a name. All of them were bad news and far above my pay grade.

"You realize now, your mistake?" Forneus asked.

I nodded. Inwardly, I felt the rage building up. But this time, it was rage towards myself. I'd been utterly careless, and now it was going to cost me this mission. More than that, it would cost other young women their lives at Smiling Jack's blade.

Forneus stood up. With each step, the chamber literally shook. I saw a long black sword at his side.

I saw my end...and cursed myself for a fool.

Forneus towered over me, his chin three feet above the top of my head. His wings rose even higher, spreading behind him like a vast shadow. He drew the sword and held it for me to see.

"Do you recognize this sword?" he asked.

I swallowed hard. The hilt, haft, and pommel were made of an otherworldly metal that was somehow both iron gray and bloody crimson at the same time. But it was the blade that held my eye and sent an icy chill skittering down my spine. The blade was made of pure sabelin, a misbegotten miasma molded from the pool of the world's transgressions. The blade was a Soulcleaver.

If Forneus struck me down with this blade, he would end me, and the mission would be lost.

"You are at my mercy," Forneus said, his voice oddly matter-of-fact. "And given your affront to me by coming to this place and rather rudely dispatching so many of my lesser colleagues, I should cleave you from this world."

I thought about trying something with the Edge but, in this case, I thought discretion might be the better part of valor.

"But, Guardian," Forneus went on, "I have not risen to this position without occasionally granting a mercy." He laughed as if this were some grand joke that all the world should know. The Shades all around me joined in the laughter.

Forneus said, "I am going to spare you, Guardian."

That's when it finally hit me. He'd been calling me Guardian all this time, and I'd been so terrified that it hadn't sunk in until now. Forneus thought I was a Guardian. And I wasn't about to correct him.

Forneus let the tip of the Soulcleaver fall to the floor. "I will withhold this consequence, for now. But I require of you a service. You will deliver for me a message."

I swallowed again. "Who should get the message?" I asked, sick to my stomach over the quiver in my voice.

"One of your superiors," Forneus replied. "Anthriel is his name."

I knew the name. Anthriel wasn't my immediate superior because I belong to a completely different area, but he was a superior, and far superior to me in every way I could think of.

"You must deliver the message promptly," Forneus said. "Can you do this?"

"Yes," I replied. "What is the message?"

"It is not for you," Forneus said, his yellow eyes narrowing to reptilian slits. He held up his hand and black tendrils began to grow out from the flesh of his fingers. They intertwined again and again until a shape in black ash appeared. He blew into his hand, and the ash dispersed in a dark cloud. A scroll rested in the palm of his hand.

"This is the message for Anthriel," he said, handing it to me. "Deliver it soon, Guardian, or I will need to come and find you. And then, nothing will hinder my blade. Have we an understanding?"

"Yes," I said evenly, doing my best to make eye contact.

Forneus scanned me shrewdly, and I feared he might somehow recognize me. But no, he had something else in mind. Something that would all but cripple me.

"You seem awfully fond of that silver case of yours," the Senior Knightshade said, a glimmer in his sickly yellow eyes.

Instantly, I became very nervous.

"A kind of toolkit," Forneus went on. "Place your weapons within the case."

He said it so casually, and yet, I could literally feel the force of his ancient will bearing down on me. Every syllable of his command was weighted with Soulcleaver venom. To resist in even the most minute fraction would result in unyielding agony...and the end of my mission. I lowered the case to the ground. And while the Shades nickered and snickered all around me, I put the Edge and a few Slammer grenades inside the silver case and closed it. I stood, knowing what would come next.

Forneus reached down—a long way down for him—and half-crushed my fingers as he wrapped his massive hand around the case's handle. He took it from me as if I were a disobedient child and said, "I will hold on to this for now...as collateral. Return to me once you have delivered my message, and I might return it...that is, I might consider sparing you."

He gestured for me to leave, and believe-you-me, I took the hint and started walking. But just before I reached the iron door, Forneus' voice rumbled out of the darkness once more.

"Guardian," he called. "Give the message to Anthriel only. If you give it to any other of your order, they will end you instantly."

{ Chapter 23 }

THERE'S SOMETHING ABOUT BEING THREATENED with annihilation that can really rattle a guy.

I'd driven away from the abortion clinic/Shade stronghold and spent the first fifteen minutes in an absolute thoughtless haze. I don't know which roads I took or what places I passed. I'm reasonably certain I followed the traffic laws, but beyond that, I didn't know much else. After all, I'd just narrowly survived a run-in with a legendary Senior Knightshade, keeping my existence only in exchange for running an errand that would almost certainly turn out to be epic-level evil.

When I finally snapped out of my fog bank, I came to the realization that I'd rarely been to the end of my rope like this. Not only was I #1 on Forneus the Felriven's hit list, but I still hadn't come close to completing my mission. Smiling Jack and his accomplice were still out there. Innocent young women were still in danger. The FBI was back in and, as far as they were concerned, I needed to be out. Even Agent Rezvani, with whom I'd shared a kind of tacit partnership, had been browbeaten into disowning me. Did that mean I really was out? It was somewhat standard protocol for me to be involved only when no one else could be...or more often, would be. And yet, I did not get called to a mission by mistake.

Ever.

And yet, here I was at a virtual dead end. I had a lot to think about. I needed wisdom. I needed direction. But, at least for the moment, I needed coffee.

I'd driven aimlessly past a dozen strip malls. Why I stopped at Miracle Strip Shopping Center, as opposed to any of the others, I have no idea. But, it seemed like in this area, you could drive five minutes in any direction and you'd be sure to run into a marvelous coffee shop.

I sat down at a place called Nightgrounds. It didn't look like much from the outside, but the interior was a sight to behold. In one corner stood an honest-to-goodness iron maiden. Shackles and chains hung from the left hand wall. A flickering candelabra rode a barely visible wire back-and-forth between jagged, black chandeliers overhead. A leering stone gargoyle sat on the front counter. *Dungeon Feng Shui.* The tables even had little coffin-shaped containers to hold the sugar and sweetener packets. *Groovy.*

The waitress who came to my table was, of course, as Goth as she could be. Seriously, she made Morticia look like Snow White.

"Welcome to Nightgrounds," she said amiably. Though it was hard to read *friendly* from lips and eyes so darkened by makeup.

She started to hand me a menu, but I held up a hand. "I'm not eating," I said.

"This isn't for food," she replied.

"Then, what is it for?"

"Coffee," she said. "Duh."

"I already know what I want."

"But you're not a regular."

"How hard can it be?"

"We have 177 blends."

"I just want coffee. Black."

"Black we got," she said and spun on a platform heel.

She came back with a mug. It wasn't a mug really. More like a stein or a tankard—ten inches tall at least. And the thing was decorated like Dracula's castle.

I gave the waitress a look like, *Really?*

She sneered and stalked away.

But at least the coffee was good. It was the darkest black I'd ever seen. Crude oil black. Tar black.

It was bitter, sharp, strong, and...delicious.

I sat, sipping my coffee, and thinking. A stream of pedestrian traffic moved by.

Downtown Panama City Beach isn't like downtown New York City or downtown Chicago...or even downtown Albuquerque. It's not skyscrapers and taxicabs. It's not designer suits and briefcases. It's casual. Even at night when the party crowd comes out, the place is low key and smooth.

So when a certain man turned the corner and sauntered to my table, I actually raised an eyebrow. He wore a black, three-piece zoot suit. I kid you not—a zoot suit.

The long coat was buttoned at his chest only, draped back behind his arm, and a hoop of gold chain dangled from his pocket down to his knee. He tipped a black fedora with a red feather sticking up out of its satin band. He straightened a jaunty yellow tie and flashed a blinding white smile.

"Mr. Spector," he said, words rolling off his tongue like jazz. "I believe I have come at just the right time...as usual."

"Do I know you?" I asked.

He smiled and took a deep breath. "I see," he said. "One would think, with all the oh-so-timely assistance I have provided, that I might just *merit* remembering."

I shook my head.

"Apparently not," he said.

He stared at me. His face was perfectly tan, but his skin had a waxy look as if he was one of Madame Tussaud's figures come to life. He had eyes darker than my coffee and a sharkish nose. That knowing, chalk-white grin never left his face. And I still wondered how he knew my name.

Then he actually removed a gold pocket watch from his billowing slacks' pocket. With a smooth flick of the wrist, he flipped open its lid, glanced, and pressed it closed again. "I really must impress upon you," he said. "My time is not unlimited, you know. I have other appointments to keep."

I sipped my coffee. Then I laughed and said, "Don't let me keep you. I'd just as soon be alone anyway. Lots of thinking to do."

The pocket watch disappeared with his hand into the deep pocket. "A shame really," he said. He spun with a flourish of his pinstripe coat. As he walked away, I heard him say, "Too bad though. I do believe Smiling Jack is about to get busy again. A shame."

The wrought iron chair scraped loudly on the stone floor as I thrust myself up to my feet. "Wait!" I called.

He stopped and spun back. "Yes? May I be of service...after all?"

I gestured to the second chair at my table and cleared my throat. "Sit," I said. "Please."

The way he moved, weaving his way between the other tables, and coming to rest lightly in the chair—it was New Orleans cool. Liquid velvet.

GHOST

"I am so glad you reconsidered," he said. "But still...you really don't remember me, do you?"

"Look, cut to the chase. How do you know me? What do you know about Smiling Jack?"

The Goth waitress decided to appear at that moment. She handed my new guest a menu. And I'll be boiled in pudding if he didn't take his sweet time. I watched his eyes travel the coffee menu, line by line.

"Hmmm, mmmhmmm," he mumbled with a languid drawl. "Mephisto. I am most reasonably certain this blend will satisfy my discerning palate."

"Whatever," the waitress replied. She whisked the menu out of his hands and left abruptly.

"Insufferable youth," he said. The easy smile disappeared for a moment. Only a moment. Replaced for a blink by something close to violent hatred. But it was gone so fast I had to wonder if I'd really seen anything at all.

"Who are you—"

"I do know you, John Spector," he said. "I know you very, very well. I know how you work, how you play, how you operate. And, as always, I am here to help you. Why, yes I am."

Another casualty of my most recent memory wash, I thought. If I did force-forget him, I'm pretty sure I knew why. I don't like folks beating around the bush.

He sighed. "Well, though it seems to me a travesty to be required to remind you, I suppose you should know my name. Scratch is the name. Mr. Scratch. Say my name and strike a match and I'll come calling."

"I didn't say your name. I don't carry matches."

He waved his long fingers. "A triviality," he said. "I am not without a heart, my dear Ghost. I saw that you were in grave need."

I slammed my fist on the table.

"Should I come back?" the waitress asked, holding another castle-tankard.

I waved an apology and shook my head.

Scratch accepted the coffee, breathed in its scent, and closed his eyes. Then, he exhaled deeply. "I do believe I made a most excellent choice." He drank from the mug. He drank for a long time. I saw the steam rising and wondered how he didn't scald his throat. When he put down the coffee, it was more than half gone.

Just before he spoke, he adjusted the cuff of his dress shirt, sliding it out of his coat sleeve to cover his wrist. But I caught a glimpse of wounded flesh, the white marbling of a burn scar. I frowned, thinking that maybe I had a faint memory of something similar.

"About your friend, Smiling Jack," he said. "You are most certainly barking up the wrong tree."

"What do you mean?"

"Don't get me wrong," he said. "You've most certainly resolved a few issues. But lately, you've been most willingly blind. You dig?"

I shook my head.

"You sure that memory trick you do doesn't take a few of your most clever thoughts away too?"

I thought about taking something out my silver case, something that would alter Scratch's sense of humor. That's when a lightning bolt hit me: I no longer had my silver case. No wonder I'd been in a mindless haze after leaving the clinic. Being without my silver case was like losing an arm. Maybe I should have just given myself over to the rage and taken a crack at Forneus. *Right.* I might have managed to put a dent in his ancient, armored hide before he hacked me asunder with a thunderous flourish. I squeezed my fists so tightly that my knuckles cracked.

"Did I say something wrong?" Scratch asked.

"Let's just say I'm feeling a little unsettled right now."

"Interesting," Scratch replied, taking another gulp of his coffee. "Well, now see how splendid it is for you that I am here. I've come with such timely advice, and I've even brought you a little gift."

I watched, flinching involuntarily as Scratch reached beneath the table at his side. When his hand came up, I fully expected to see a big black handgun...but he had a silvery baton instead. He slid it across the table to me.

The Edge.

"How...?" I stammered. I usually make it a point not to stammer, but here it was more than appropriate. "How could you get...I mean, my case won't open for anyone but—"

"And now, for the advice," Scratch said, cutting me off and standing. As he waltzed away, he said over his zoot-suited shoulder, "Sometimes the way forward is the way back."

***   ***   ***   ***

"'Sometimes the way forward is the way back.' Great," I muttered, driving the assassin-mobile toward Grayton Beach. "I'll just put that on a bumper sticker. Super."

And who was this Scratch cat anyway? See what I did there? I called him a "cat." That's hipster talk...I think. Anyway, I had no clue what to make of him. Apparently, he knew me quite well. He even knew about the memory wash that I had apparently used to wipe him from my memory. If he had helped me before, why did I erase him?

What really cooked my noodle was the Edge. Number one: no one could open that case except for me. Forneus could have batted it around like a piñata with his black blade and not left a scratch. And yet, Mr. Scratch had gotten it open. Number two: how on earth had Mr. Scratch gotten past Forneus to get to the case in the first place? My mind went wild with possible scenarios: was Scratch in league with Forneus? Was this all a ploy? Was Scratch a kind of spy for the Enemy?

And how, out of all the coffee joints in Panama City Beach, did Scratch happen to walk into mine? I realized absently how close I had just come to quoting Rick Blaine in Casablanca. This is how disheveled I get without my silver case.

Then my cell phone rang, belting out *I am sixteen going on seventeen, innocent as a rose...*

Rez.

I answered quickly. "I wondered if I'd hear from you. I—"

"What in blazes is the matter with you?" Rez growled.

"With me?" I pondered aloud.

"Don't play dumb, Spector," she said. "I was expecting a little help here."

"O...kay," I said slowly, keeping my voice even. Anything to avoid ratcheting up the tension. "Maybe you could refresh my memory. Last I heard from you, you were reading me the FBI's official get-lost speech."

"That was all Deputy Director Barnes, and you know it. He's always by the book, always firm, but I've never seen him like this. He's putting clamps on every loose end—including you—suddenly and with extreme zeal. The veins on his neck and forehead are sticking out. He's gone maniacal on this, and I don't dare cross him."

"I still don't understand how I could help you with that."

GHOST

I heard a muted snarl from the phone and, when Rez spoke again, her words were clipped with seething frustration. "You told me that you work for powers-that-be, powers well beyond the FBI. Higher than the Executive Branch, for cryin' out loud. Why didn't you put in a call to your superiors? Why didn't you pull rank and tell the Deputy Director to back off?"

I was speechless for several seconds. I didn't have a good answer, not one that she'd be willing to accept anyway. "It doesn't work like that," I said lamely.

"Oh, c'mon," she said. "Don't give me that line. You've got to have some kind of code word, right? You just mention the word, and the Deputy Director goes all bug-eyed and sucks in a deep breath. Then he apologizes and rolls out a red carpet for you...or at least gets out of your way."

"No," I replied bluntly. "It doesn't work like that. Look, Agent Rezvani, my protocols include avoiding all notice by the usual law enforcement agencies. As it is, I've already stepped too far onto the FBI's radar. Pulling rank, as you put it, would just throw a great big spotlight onto me and my activities. I cannot afford to let that happen. As much as I appreciate the assistance you've provided so far, I'll understand if your hands are now tied. I'm used to working alone."

When Agent Rezvani spoke again, there was a subtle shift in her tone...just for a few words, but enough for me to discern it. She was hurt. "This case is important to me," Rez said, and then her voice hardened once more. "And whoever you work for, you're a heck'uva good investigator. Honestly, I thought you were our best chance of finding Smiling Jack. Now...now, I'm not so sure."

The line went silent for several moments. I listened, absently realizing that I'd left Panama City Beach proper, and taken the exit for the White Sands Inn. Then, Rez said, "But, Mr. Spector...just so that we understand each other: you are Federally blocked from interfering on the Smiling Jack case. Any interference from you, any evidence that you are pursuing the case, any theories you withhold from the FBI—all of the above and more—will constitute a felony violation of the law. You will be arrested, jailed, and tried."

"I understand," I replied. "But, Agent Rezvani, there's something that you need to understand as well: while we both want to keep Smiling Jack from killing again...our intended methods of accomplishing that are very different. I have a mission, and I intend to see it through."

Agent Rezvani of the FBI ended the call. I drove on in silence. Ordinarily, I felt pretty confident in my decisions, especially when they led me to working alone. But this time, I couldn't shake the feeling that I'd made a mistake.

A mistake that, like an undersea quake, would send ripples into the future, unseen until they form a catastrophe.

The mission already felt like a catastrophe. In the past 48 hours, I'd managed to cut myself off from Doc Shepherd and Agent Rezvani, I'd attracted the murderous attention of an ancient Knightshade, and I'd lost my silver case. Oh, and I'd promised to deliver an undoubtedly treacherous message to one of my superiors, a superior so far up the chain of command that my actions might be construed as high treason. All in all, I'd had better weeks.

I pulled into the White Sands Inn parking lot. I had my hand on the door handle, and that's when I remembered: all my money was in the silver case.

The silver case lay now in the custody of a ridiculously powerful Knightshade.

GHOST

I restarted the car and parked it in a space facing east so that I'd wake with the sunrise. Then, I cut the engine, eased the seat back, and closed my eyes. I'd slept in worse places.

{ Chapter 24 }

IT WAS JACK'S TURN at the downstairs computer. He noted with a pang of guilt that his partner had logged sessions on their Manifesto four times since Jack last had. This wasn't about second guessing. Jack was as clear on their mission now as he was nearly twenty years prior when he and Dr. Gary met, learned each other's secret passions, and recognized that they had a role to play in changing the world for women.

No, the lack of effort on the computer was not about doubt. The hesitance came rather from the finality represented by the Manifesto. To complete and release this document, Jack knew, would spell the end of their efforts in this great battle. But not just that; it would mean the end of a very fulfilling relationship with Dr. Gary.

And, it would mean the end of their lives.

The thin line of the cursor blinked contemptuously at Jack. *Such is life,* Jack thought. *Thin, mercurial, gone in an instant, and ultimately meaningless.*

Meaningless for the individual, Jack corrected. But to leave something important for those who would come behind, well...that was something.

Jack nodded and stared back at the blinking cursor. Since he had special insights that Dr. Gary could not rightfully claim, the rationale section was left for Jack to complete. But thus far, that had proven difficult. Digging that deep into the past meant tearing the ragged scabs off old wounds.

Jack heard whimpering from down the hall. *Pathetic whimpering.* Jack snapped closed the silver laptop, a bit harder than he'd meant to, but the simpering cries grated on his nerves. He went through the door and a few steps down the narrow hall and aimed his voice at the kennel. "Why are you crying?" he yelled. "You've been fed!"

"We miss you!" a voice cried out. Jack thought sure it was Pamela. Only Pamela had the nerve to speak up like that. There were muted sobs and other voices: Midge and Carrie.

"I am so very sorry," Jack called back, softening his tone. "Dr. Gary and I have important business to look after."

"But we're important, aren't we?" Pamela asked, her voice tinged with more confidence than Jack had heard. "You haven't played with us for three days!"

Jack was tempted to get the prod, but the process of discipline took a lot of time. More time than Jack could spare today. Of course, they didn't understand the change in schedule. *They don't know I had to close the daycare. They don't know the number of procedures that are piling up for Dr. Gary. They don't know anything, really.* "We will come play with you again soon," Jack said. "I promise."

"But you promised us before," came mewling whine, punctuated with sobs. Midge.

"You shut your mouth!" Jack screamed venomously. "Don't you dare stand in judgment over me!"

"I'm sorry! I'm sorry...sorry," Midge cried back.

"I miss Lucinda," came a third voice, huskier, but frightened. Carrie. "I used to brush her pretty hair. And Erica, I used to braid her hair. I want them back."

Jack swallowed back the heated bile that had risen in his throat. He mastered his tone to placate...to coddle...to reassure. "Please don't be sad, my pets. Don't you know how very special you all are? Each and every one of you, so very precious to me and to Dr. Gary. Destined for big things like your sisters before you. And you will join them soon enough."

"We will?" Pamela chirped. But then, she said, "You've been saying that forever."

You soonest of all, Jack thought. "Yes," he said. "You will join your sisters very soon."

"I can't wait," Carrie said.

Midge just cried, but it sounded less like misery and more like relief.

"There now," Jack said. "You see? All will be well again soon. Now, please be silent. I have terribly difficult work ahead, and I will...not...be...disturbed...again."

All sound from the kennel vanished. Jack returned to the kitchen, his soft chair in the corner, and the waiting laptop.

He opened it up, scowled at the blinking cursor, and went to work.

When free will is corrupted, he wrote, *life is compromised. In fact, without the human imperative of choice, there can be no humanity...no life whatsoever. It is incumbent upon a just government to protect this, the greatest of all human freedoms. And no agency, public or private, may be permitted to interfere. For any dark act by such agency that hinders the will, will in fact call for drastic, secretive action. Dark things begin to occur.*

Jack deleted the last sentence. It sounded too primitive, almost sensational. But it was true.

How he railed at me, Jack thought, images of his father coming unbidden and unwelcome. *Nothing I could do was satisfactory because I was unsatisfactory to him. I was never strong enough to do the farm work. I was never 'man' enough to do anything right. He almost killed me...but instead, I was reborn.*

Jack remembered that incredible, liberating day so long ago...how sore he'd been from his father's beatings over the weekend. And that particular day, school had held a book fair. Jack had used the money his mother had given him and bought the usual tripe. But he'd used his own hard-saved money for one particular book that he never showed his parents: *Lizzy Borden, Fact & Fiction* by R. Stewart Grady.

By the time Jack was twelve, he'd already imagined killing his father. But until finding the book, he'd never thought he could be smart enough to pull it off without getting caught. Lizzy Borden had done it, and she hadn't been very smart. Her alibi's were weak. She hadn't put enough time or cleverness into planning. And the follow-through had been utterly sloppy. But she had gotten away with murder, and that had been enough to inspire Jack's plan.

The pieces had been in place all along. He'd grown up on a boggy, half-wooded farm in rural Massachusetts. Jack's father was a drinker. He'd cheated on Jack's mother dozens of times and had a history of disappearing for weeks unannounced. While waiting for the spring thaw, Jack had spent months planning. He'd seen to every detail, predicted every investigative angle, and invented brilliant solutions. He chose not to force it, but rather plotted out potential opportunities. The weather was key. He needed an inbound deluge, a heavy, drenching rain. In Massachusetts, in late April, there were many such storms.

When the spring thaw began, Jack found the perfect sinkhole forming several hundred yards into the patchy pines that splotched the property. Five perfect storm fronts came and went before Jack was finally able to coax his father into position. But finally, it all came together. Jack's mother had gone to visit her sister. She'd be gone for days. Jack's father had spent the afternoon with a bottle of gin. He was moderately plowed when Jack approached with the story:

Jack claimed to have discovered evidence that Bill Ash, their hated neighbor, had come hunting again on their land. Jack's father had just about burst a vein in his thick neck when he'd heard the news. He'd grabbed his shotgun and demanded that Jack show him the evidence. Jack was only too happy to oblige. With a mantle of dark storm clouds looming in the east, Jack and his father took the utility vehicle and traversed the property, arriving at last at the sinkhole. And there was the four-point buck, shot through with one of Ash's compound bow arrows.

Jack's father had worked himself up to a seething rage at the edge of that sinkhole. But Jack wasn't going to let his father vent that anger. Never again. Jack kept himself behind his father and at an angle. His father never saw Jack remove the ten pound sledgehammer from behind the nearest pine. Jack had thought about using an axe—as an ode to Lizzy Borden—but refused to repeat her mistakes. With his father close enough to the sinkhole's edge to be pushed in, Jack wheeled the sledge with all his might and slammed it between his father's shoulder blades. Jack had heard a satisfying snapping crunch of bone. His father's muffled cry was smothered by the pines. Jack's father toppled into the sinkhole. He'd spun sideways in the fall and crashed down upon his own leg. Jack had heard the snap.

But his father hadn't felt the leg. The damage done to his spine had paralyzed him. He stared up from the sinkhole, eyes roaming...frantically searching for help that would not come.

His mouth gaped open and closed like a fish. Jack stood at the edge of the hole. Not too close, but near enough for his father to see him standing there.

Jack watched for a few moments. It had turned out even better than expected. His father would likely stay alive long enough for the storm to unleash its rage. The water and mud would pour in, and the sinkhole would swallow Jack's father alive.

Jack had driven the utility vehicle back to the farmhouse. He'd planned it all out. He'd known that the storm would wash away every single trace of his journey back from the sinkhole.

At age fourteen, Jack had gotten away with his first murder. It would not be his last. Not by a long shot.

There came a mechanized hum from the elevator shaft, and Jack checked his watch. "Home early again," Jack whispered. He looked guiltily at the Manifesto. "I haven't gotten much accomplished."

The elevator doors opened and shut. "Jack, Jack, where are you?" Dr. Gary called, urgency in his voice.

"Kitchen!" Jack called. "Why, what's wrong?"

"Not what's wrong," Dr. Gary said, his smile an alabaster trench beneath the heavy mustache. "What's right?"

"I could use some good news," Jack said, glancing sidelong at the laptop.

"Ah," Dr. Gary said. "Words coming slowly again?"

"My thoughts are heavy," Jack replied. "Each word I write, each sentence, feels like closer to the end. Makes it harder."

Dr. Gary nodded thoughtfully. "I'm sorry," he said. "I can help you with that, if you think it would help." He waited. Jack said nothing. "Well then, let me lighten your load. The FBI has finally reopened our case."

Jack felt the tears coming on. "Erica served her purpose then," he said.

"Yes, in a mighty way," Dr. Gary replied. "The Deputy Director himself flew in to Pensacola. My friend Marc Jacobs—"

"He runs security at the clinic, right?"

"That's right," Dr. Gary said. "He told me we've got agents from Jacksonville and Mobile swarming into town."

Jack sighed and put his head in his hands. He tried to fight the sobs, but they came shuddering through.

"Hey, hey, now," Dr. Gary said, sitting down. "I thought this would be good news."

"Don't you see," Jack said. "This is really it. The FBI will be on us and soon."

"Not so soon," Dr. Gary said, cupping Jack's chin in his hand. "We've been very clean, and the trail they need to follow to find us will be very, very long. And in that time, we must not falter. We must not fail to make our message clear. Millions of women are counting on us. All that we've done, all of our planning and efforts, it has all been for this moment. And so, I think, we need to make our message clear. Even before we release the Manifesto."

"Another body?" Jack asked, tears already drying.

"Yes," Dr. Gary said. "I think we must make her count in an increasingly profound way."

"May I choose?"

"Of course."

"Pamela."

"Excellent," Dr. Gary said. "She has changed of late, hasn't she?"

"Yes, and not for the better." Jack sneered. "When?"

"Not tonight," Dr. Gary said. "I have planning to do. I have the location, but I need to figure out the arrangement. And...I want to give you time to work on the Manifesto. Do you think you can finish the rationale this evening?"

"Yes," Jack replied, looking at the blinking cursor. "I will finish."

Dr. Gary leaned down and kissed Jack full on the mouth. "Don't forget, we have one more grand party to attend."

"I won't forget," Jack said.

Dr. Gary stood up to leave, but paused with his hand on the corner of the wall by the elevator. "Tell me something, Jack," Dr. Gary said. "Do you blame your father or your mother for all that you have become?"

A chill ran up Jack's spine. The question had so many layers. But Jack had explored every nuance ten-thousand times. "I don't blame my father or my mother," he said. "I hate them both for what they did to me, but I do not blame them. I live for much, much more than revenge."

Dr. Gary smiled proudly. "I could not have asked for a better partner in life," he said. Then, he disappeared around the corner.

* * *   * * *   * * *   * * *

The cursor still blinked on the same line.

Jack had gone deep into his mind, remembering Dear Father and Dear Mother...and tracing the steps that led to today. He'd lied to Dr. Gary. Jack did blame his parents...for everything. They had warped him body and soul. Jack thought about all he'd been through, how it had shaped him utterly. In fact, how easily the pronouns flowed, even in thought: he, him, his...

But it was all an act. From Father on down the line, they thought they could take identity away, force identity to their own wishes, and by brute force turn fantasy into reality. But all they had ever really done is turn reality into fantasy.

GHOST

Jack slid her hand across the material of the flannel shirt, felt the bulge of her breasts, painfully flattened by the gauze, but still there. Then, she reached down and let her hand rest lightly on her right thigh. She would never have a child of her own.

They had taken that away. And they would likely take her life in the end. But Jack shrugged. It would all be worth it if she could make them all understand. Then, maybe, no one else would have to suffer under the iron grip of a society that took everything away from women...even their most sacred, private choices.

Having finished her rationale, Jack closed the Manifesto. The more she considered the title, the more she hated it...but approved of it all the same.

A Reditum Ad Tenebrosi Temporis

A Return to Dark Times.

{ Chapter 25 }

SOONER OR LATER, I'd have to face Forneus the Felriven. I need my silver case, and not just because I was hungry. Though to be truthful, one hour after sunrise, I was ravenously famished. It didn't help that I'd passed three Waffle Houses as I'd driven north on Route 231. I stared straight ahead, until each of the black-lettered yellow signs passed behind me. I may have mentioned I have a weakness for hash browns.

Food money aside, my silver case had all of my tools—except for the Edge. Without those tools, my chances of success on the Smiling Jack case were exponentially diminished. But if I went back to Forneus without first delivering the message, I'd likely lose the silver case and the mission. Even if I delivered the message to Anthriel as directed, there was still a reasonably high chance of me ending up...ended.

I was mindful of the possibilities related to Forneus' message. The ancient Knightshade hadn't been given his names—Felriven, Despoiler, Spirit Prince—by accident. Whatever the contents of the scroll, it would likely cause epic-level chaos. But what kind of message would lead others of my own order to end me if I delivered it to anyone but Anthriel? Had I done something, something I'd washed from my memory? No, the message wasn't likely about me. Forneus didn't know me from a Guardian.

Was it some top-level secret that I wasn't supposed to know? Something that would necessitate a superior ending me? And what would such a message mean to a warrior of Anthriel's level? I would warn Anthriel, of course. And then, good-or-ill, I'd find out my fate.

Unfortunately, Anthriel wasn't a local. And the nearest Waypoint was several hours north in Jackson County, Florida. I glanced over at the mile markers. I was still about thirty miles away from Sweet Deliverance Cemetery and the Waypoint hidden within. That's when I noticed the tail.

In highway traffic, I don't much like to cruise in the fast lane. I prefer to find a car in the right lane, one doing reasonable speed, and then I just fall in behind him. But, on this journey, I ended up stuck several times behind cars going just south of slothful. It was the darting in and out of the fast lane to get around such pedestrian drivers that helped me spot the tail.

Gray sedan with silver trim; very sporty, aquiline features for a big luxury car. Headlights were slanted like snake's eyes and stayed on, maybe due to the overcast skies. The windshield was as dark as the shadow beneath a storm's mantle. And it didn't seem to cruise on the highway, but advanced rather with a relentless prowl.

So far, the sedan had mirrored my traffic moves. I saw a rest stop up ahead and decided to test my theory. If I was right, I wouldn't pick a fight there. Too many innocents could get in the way. But, I couldn't very well have them follow me to the Waypoint either. This might call for a touch of creativity.

GHOST

I slipped into the far right lane and drifted into the exit. The rest stop was packed. Tour busses lined up like fat caterpillars on the east side of the building, the roof of which, oddly enough, was shaped like a leaf. The rest of the parking lot burgeoned with a technicolor mix of tractor trailers, cars, campers, and utility vehicles. I slid the assassin-mobile behind a hulking U-Haul truck and slipped quickly out onto the sidewalk.

As I walked to the restrooms, I kept half an eye on the gray sedan and watched it pull into a spot about ten cars away from my U-Haul. I wondered if they'd leave the car or just wait for me. I figured it depended on their purpose.

If it was the FBI, as I suspected, they'd likely just want to keep tabs on me. But maybe they'd play it safe and send someone inside, just to make sure I didn't disappear. No big deal. If it was someone else, well...anything was possible, including violence. I looked around. There were kids everywhere. I would not let a fight go down here...even if it meant I had to run. And I am not fond of running.

I passed by the restrooms without going in. I thought I might slip around the flank of the building and see what I could figure out about my pursuers. I had to wade through a thicket of travelers—mostly kids—at the snack machines. The smell of every chip ending in -itos hit me like a salty bat. I watched a teenager rip the top off a snack-sized bag of Cheetos and dump the contents into his mouth. That's where the creative spark hit me.

I'd never been called the Prince of Nonviolence, but hey, there was always a first time. If I could pull this off, it would eliminate the threat of violence and keep whoever it was from following me.

I slid around the backside of the building as planned, but instead of finding a hiding spot for spying purposes, I waited. A couple of truck drivers emerged from the restrooms. As they joined the crowd departing that side of the building, I blended in beside them. We walked past the rows of cars, including the gray sedan. When we came to a couple of vans parked next to each other, I slid between them.

Five minutes later, I circled back around the building and emerged from the front side as if I'd just used the facilities like any other traveler. I stopped in a sunbeam that strayed through the cloud cover, and I made a big show of stretching and yawning. I wanted to be certain they saw me. I got in the car, backed up, and drove slowly away.

I watched in the rearview mirror as the gray sedan backed out of its spot. *Wait for it,* I thought. *Wait for...it.* The driver of the gray sedan let a family cross the parking lot in front of the car. Then, he pulled forward.

I watched intently. Ought to be right about...now.

The back end of the gray sedan suddenly dropped about a foot. One of the back wheels, a stub of axle still attached, wobble-rolled away, and the car came to a grinding halt. I watched the driver and two passengers practically leap out. Not FBI, not in those designer threads. La Familia, more than likely.

It didn't matter. They were out of play, and I had a cemetery to visit.

***   ***   ***   ***

Sweet Deliverance Cemetery sat upon 25,000 acres of prime Florida real estate. I pulled through the high arched gates and noted the horn-blowing cherubs worked into the wrought iron fence decor.

"Right," I muttered, shaking my head and creeping along the winding cemetery road. I passed perfectly manicured gardens full of perky flowering shrubs and a manmade lake where seagulls, ducks, geese, and peacocks wandered. Yes, peacocks. Complete with spectacular sprawling plumes of tail feathers. The grass was lush, immaculately cut, and greener than any grass grown in Florida heat had a right to be. It was the perfect, peaceful place to live.

Ironic, I thought that the dead had better property than most of Florida's living.

The sun had scarcely appeared all morning, and given the thickening mantle above, I figured I wouldn't be seeing it again anytime soon. It threatened rain but seemed to me more like the all-day soaker kind of storm. No thunder and lightning. No divine violence.

I soon found myself in an ocean of grave markers: tall, stately crosses, headstones of granite or marble, blocky crypts, saintly blank-eyed statues, and mausoleums the size of summer homes. Like I said: ironic.

I'd been to Sweet Deliverance only once before, but it had been a very long time ago. I thought I still remembered the way to the Waypoint, but even if I got mixed up, it wouldn't take me long to spiral in on it. It would be the mausoleum that the Shades stayed farthest away from.

Anthriel did not suffer the presence of the enemy.

And make no mistake, Shades by the scores liked to hang out in graveyards. Knowing it was an unnecessary risk, I flexed my inner eyes and went to Netherview.

The somber gray sky turned to a roiling mixture of purple and black. Any measure of peacefulness that existed in Earthveil dissolved into spiritual chaos. Pale, luminous Shades stirred and careened around the ethereal, mist-shrouded atmosphere. Dozens of them perched on gravestones like carrion birds waiting for something to die.

Yes, the gravestones and other monuments were still there. No massive, turreted castles or fortresses existed here in this place. Just the graves and the stone structures that marked them. But they were no longer whitewashed. Now their surfaces were sickly yellow or marrow-toned, strewn with all manner of creeping green lichen.

"Enough," I muttered, chiding myself back into Earthveil. Painting a bull's eye on one's self was not wise when one is surrounded by guided missiles.

Shades loved to hang out in cemeteries. It was a place where they could do their most insidious kinds of damage. After all, broken, hurting people came with great frequency to cemeteries. It was a place where Shades could torment and terrify; one place where Shades would be so bold as to appear to the living.

Heartless, cruel miscreants, I thought, grinding my teeth. Some Shades even went so far as to masquerade as the deceased. Pain, terror, and false hope were equally effective tools for the gouging of Soulmarks. Far too many agonized mourners arrived at a cemetery alone and departed with an invisible, malevolent hitchhiker. Or more than one.

The road forked half a dozen times, and I followed the path in my memory. The cemetery grounds became less open and sprawling, and thickets of spruce and pine took more territory. Grave sites became more grandiose and more secluded.

I slowed the car and waited for a bunch of pure white geese to waddle across the road in front of me. That gave me a moment to notice how the road curved wickedly ahead and disappeared as it climbed a wooded hill.

This was the place.

I followed the path, found the dead end I remembered, and parked. A slightly jarring symphony of frogs and crickets awaited me when I got out of the car. The tree cover overhead

GHOST

cast a night-like darkness over the hill. Here and there, a forlorn firefly blinked to life and extinguished.

At the top of the hill, in the deepest shadow, stood a single cylindrical mausoleum. It was tall, maybe thirty feet, and domed, supported by austere ionic columns. The widest gap in the columns opened to a seldom trodden path that ended at the dead end where I'd parked.

I took the path to the Waypoint of Anthriel.

Shadows cloaked me as I came. The crickets and frogs muted their music. I approached the columns and stepped over the threshold. If I had been just a visitor to the cemetery...maybe, in my grief, wandering aimlessly until I found myself curious about this structure, I would have discovered a shadowy vault with a very high ceiling. I would see seven evenly spaced statues standing in their private recesses in the walls. I would find bronzed placards beneath each statue with long messages engraved in an ornate foreign language that I wouldn't recognize. And I would feel as if all seven of the statues were staring down at me, their weighty, empty gaze urging me to leave this place. And I would have departed as quickly as my legs could carry me...only to forget the entire event just moments later.

If I had been an enemy and crossed that threshold, I would have suddenly found licks of hungry, white fire climbing over every inch of me, burning and tearing at my flesh until my mind and body were incinerated.

Thankfully, I was neither a stranger nor an enemy. I was on the right team. Nothing happened to me. I went forward, and found an impossibly long hallway rising on a slow but relentless incline. Antique lamps and strange, gilded oil paintings adorned both sides of the hall. I would never forget this hallway. The paintings were a test.

A test I had failed miserably the first time.

This time, I refused to so much as glance at the paintings. I actually do learn from my mistakes...sometimes.

As I neared the end of the hall, I felt the weight of the scroll in my coat pocket. Maybe six ounces, but it felt like a metric ton.

At the very end of the hall, a massive curtain fell from high ceiling to floor. I waited to be summoned.

"Come, Horseman!" came a voice from beyond the curtain.

Horseman. I hadn't been called by that name for a very long time. I didn't much care for the name. It was a derogatory misnomer based on the kind of missions to which I am called. And, in a way, it was a slight to those who rightfully bear that name. For they are as far above Anthriel's pay grade as Anthriel was to me.

There was no throne room or mighty chair for Anthriel. He wasn't that type. Just maps. Great, vast, detailed maps—they were posted on the concave walls; they were strewn across half-a-dozen strategically placed tables; and many more were still rolled, at the ready, in designated barrels beside each table.

Anthriel was not garbed in armor—though I knew that, with a thought, he could be. Today, he wore fatigues like a commando. But the many pockets on his shirt and in his pants and in the belts across his shoulders and waist did not hold clips of ammunition or grenades. His pockets were filled with a variety of writing implements—and figurines.

The same sort of figurines that were spread in clumps across the map Anthriel labored over now. His hair was long and, because he was leaning over the map, it hung over his face so that I could not see his eyes. That hair was white as cream but, here and there, was striated by ribbons of amber wheat. It curled devilishly at the ends. Another interesting irony.

"It is not often that one of your...cadre...graces me with a visit," Anthriel said without looking up. "You are not under my command, directly, and I have no need of your particular skill set. I trust you have ample reason for intruding upon my plotting?"

I scanned the map in front of Anthriel. It might have been a map of Florida, but the border was irregular and stretched over large bodies of water. There was also a peculiar translucent territory seemingly hovering just above the main. And scattered across its entirety, were hundreds of the figurines. Some were silver. Some were black. Many were shaped like arrowheads. Others like tripods. And still others looked more or less like small shields.

It looked like an otherworldly game of Risk, but I knew the players and the stakes were much more serious.

Anthriel looked up at last, and his silver eyes fixed me with pulsing intensity. "Well?"

I bowed slightly and then said, "I apologize for the trouble, but I bear a message."

"We have couriers for such things," Anthriel replied, his eyes glinting, orbs of silver fire, as they shifted restlessly across the map.

"The source of the message," I said, "is a little unconventional. On my current mission, I found myself at the mercy of Forneus the Felriven."

The Knightshade's name, when I spoke the words, came out flat and brittle like thin, impure metal that, when struck with a hammer, would shatter into a thousand jagged shards. And the hammer fell.

"FORNEUS FELRIVEN!" Anthriel's pale skin flared white-hot, like a light bulb pushed beyond its wattage. He slammed a fist down onto the map and two things happened: dozens of the tiny figurines, both silver and black, went flying; and Anthriel's garb flickered, the many-pocketed fatigues blinking intermittently with hard plate armor. He seemed to master himself because his skin returned to its less smoldering color, and any sign of his armor vanished. He asked, "What mission could possibly put you into contact with one of the Highfallen?"

Great, I thought. *Time to beat myself up all over again.* "It wasn't exactly part of my mission. I was trying to piece together a theory, and I staked out an abortion clinic. I witnessed some rather disturbing events there, lost control of my rage, and went ballistic."

Anthriel surprised me then. Rather than castigate me for foolishness or loss of control, he said, "I hope you dismembered every Shade in that vile place and sent them in agony to the Abyss."

I blinked. Anthriel and I would never hit the town and shoot pool together, but he'd just risen fifty spots on my respect meter. "I took out my fair share," I said. "But, when I went inside the stronghold, thinking it would be just a random Knighshade, I found Forneus instead. He could have ended me—probably would have except he mistook me for a Guardian. He released me with the condition that I deliver a message to you and to you only. He took my tools as collateral."

"That seems a shame."

"I'm touched by your empathy," I said.

"What?" Anthriel thundered, his skin flaring. "Careful, Horseman, you forget yourself."

He was right, of course. "I'm sorry," I said. "I get glib when I'm frightened."

That seemed to amuse Anthriel. He went back to his map and began putting the tiny figurines back into their places. "And what was the message?" he asked.

"I don't actually know," I said, reaching into my pocket and removing the scroll. "He didn't tell me the message. He wrote it on this." I held it up.

Anthriel froze. "You brought a handwritten message from Forneus Felriven into a Waypoint? You realize the threshold might have ended you for even having such on your person?"

"I actually hadn't thought of that," I muttered. "Glad they let me pass. May I?"

He gestured for me to approach, and I handed him the scroll. He started to pull at the parchment seam, cracking the seal of black wax. "Uh, wait a minute, please...sir."

"What is it?"

"Look, sir," I said. "You know this level of business far better than I do, but even I can tell Forneus is up to something. There's a gravity to it that feels...well, epic. Like opening this scroll is going to set wheels in motion that will change things."

Anthriel's silvery gaze flickered from me to the scroll and back. "I feel it also," he said quietly. He glanced down at his map. "It is not merely that the pieces are in motion. The pieces are always in motion. But now, it feels as if the board itself is about to shift."

"There's one other thing," I went on. "Forneus told me not to deliver the message to anyone but you. That, if I did, that recipient would feel compelled to end me."

Anthriel seemed to weigh that information for a while. "It was wise of you to bring it directly to me," he said. "But I think I will wait until you have departed to read the message. Just in case."

"No argument there," I said. If the message put Anthriel in a rage, he could end me with a sneeze.

"You'll have to return to Sintryst, you know," he said. It wasn't a question.

"Or go without my tools."

Anthriel looked off to the side, seemingly deep in thought. "If you return, he will most likely end you."

"Most likely," I said. "He bears a Soulcleaver."

"Does he?" Anthriel asked, his voice still distant with thought. "Then, he has risen within his order. I wonder at this."

I bowed slightly, turned, and began to walk away.

"Be careful out there, Horseman," Anthriel called after me. "As I said, there are many pieces in motion. Some of them are pursuing you."

"Thank you," I said. "I'll be as careful as I can."

As I stepped back over the threshold and left the Waypoint, I considered Anthriel's warning. I thought I understood it. I thought he'd meant the FBI or La Compania.

I was wrong.

{ Chapter 26 }

AGENT DEANNA REZVANI felt like she was trapped in one of those time-lapsed movie scenes where a whole day's worth of activity buzzed around her at high speed while she stood still.

The FBI had commandeered a recently built office building in Pensacola. Most of the Jacksonville Field Office's personnel and a third of Mobile's manpower occupied the office now. Deputy Director Barnes ran the Smiling Jack Task Force like an orchestra conductor...if said conductor used a sledgehammer rather than a baton.

Barnes didn't micromanage. He macromanaged. His philosophy was simply: *Know your job, do your job, don't screw up, and stay out of my way.*

And for a composite built from two field offices, the Task Force seemed to be living up to Barnes' maxim. Everyone had something to do, and everyone seemed feverishly bent on completing their tasks. Everyone except Agent Rezvani.

She stared at her computer screen, continued to squeeze the pencil she'd broken, and clenched her teeth. Bad habit #209, she thought. Each and every teeth cleaning, her dentist told her the same thing: You're a grinder. You're wearing down your teeth.

And the recommendation was always the same. *Heck with that,* she thought. *They'll be selling snow cones on the sun before I wear one of those overnight mouth guards.* She'd tried that exactly once, and her breath the next morning had laid waste to her potted plants. Not like the overnight guard would do much good anyway. Most of her teeth-grinding was on the job. Like today.

Except today, she'd been grinding so hard for so long that it had blossomed into a magnitude 6.5 tension headache. The muscles at the base of her neck stiffened, and a rod of pain lanced up into the back of her skull. Not content to cause manageable agony, the throbbing ache blossomed out to her temples like electrified moose antlers. Rez clamped her eyes shut and rubbed her temples, but earned precious little respite. She went to her purse and found the prescription strength ibuprofen her doctor had given her. It usually worked...to a degree...and not right away. But it was better than nothing.

She popped a pill, downed it with Diet Dr. Pepper, and went back to thinking. Or, at least she tried.

"Headache?" came a broadcast-quality male voice from behind her.

Rez spun around and found a Ken doll in a well-tailored, dark suit standing a little too close for comfort.

"Can I help you?" Rez asked, lacing her tone with a little, *Back off, loser. I bite.*

"Actually, I might be able to help you," he said, jutting out a hand. "I'm Ted Klingler, top cop from Mobile, well in my division anyway."

Klingler, Rez thought. She'd heard the name. He'd been pivotal in solving a few high-profile cases in the last year. Against her better instincts, she shook his hand. She regretted it immediately. Klingler's hand was feverishly hot, like he'd been holding onto a light bulb.

"I saw you shrugging your shoulders and neck," he said. "Tension headache?"

"Yeah," I replied. "And I think it's getting worse."

He ignored the slight and said, "I happen to be a licensed masseuse. Why don't you turn around and I'll—"

"Lose the use of your hands permanently?" Rez interrupted. "Because that's what's going to happen if you put those meat hooks near my neck."

"Meat hooks?" he echoed, looking down at his hands. "Who talks like that?"

"Look, Klinger—"

"Klingler," he corrected. "Klinger was on M.A.S.H."

"Whatever," Rez said. "Where I come from, we don't give each other neck massages in the office, okay? Now, if you'll excuse me, I have work to do. And I'm sure, being top cop and all, you do too."

Klingler backed away. He looked like a German-shepherd that had just been hit on the nose with a newspaper. But as he stepped out of Rez's line of sight, she heard him mutter, "...ever right about her. Ice queen, through and through."

That's right, Rez thought, the pounding of her headache reaching new percussive heights. *I'm an ice queen, especially to smarmy, self-inflated...* She never finished the thought. It wasn't worth it. She had too many other things to think about. Chief among them was how she was ever going to earn her way back into Deputy Director Barnes' good graces.

Barnes had gone out of his way to keep Agent Rezvani marginalized. He'd made sure she cut ties with John Spector and then thrown her a never ending pile of paperwork loosely related to Smiling Jack. In D.C. he'd have never pulled something like that. He'd always respected her work, even pulling strings to get her involved in some of the most intricate or sensitive cases.

And now? She thought, snapping the pencil into more pieces. Now, even though it was my legwork that turned up the new leads in the Smiling Jack case, now he throws me on the sideline. He doesn't trust my judgment.

The more Rez thought about it, the more she understood—and hated—her boss's conclusions. After all, she had demonstrated questionable judgment oh, about a dozen times since arriving in Florida. And, each and every instance, had to do with John Spector. Why had she trusted him? He claimed to be working her side of the fence, only for an agency well above her pay grade. But what real evidence did she have that Ghost had anything to do with a government agency?

He had high tech weapons. That was one thing. But he didn't even have his own cell phone. He had sharp investigative skills. He was good in a fight. But then, there was the miraculous healing ability. How could he have survived the gunshots? Wasn't that evidence of being involved in some hush-hush, ultra black agency?

And what about the websites, the articles, and the creepy photos? The truth was, she didn't really know anything at all about John Spector, aka Ghost. And she had entrusted him with details of a critical ongoing FBI case. It was a lapse in judgment. A big one.

So why don't I feel like I screwed up? she wondered. This John Spector, whoever he was, felt like a good man. He felt like someone she could trust. He'd freely shared all the Smiling Jack leads he'd discovered. And he had saved her life. But aside from that, there was some intangible quality about him that she couldn't quite describe. It was as if he somehow radiated trustworthiness. No, it was more than that. Bigger than that. Ghost had a rare purity about him. He didn't smoke or drink. She hadn't heard so much as a 'darn,' in his vocabulary.

He was like a wall. That was it...or at least as close as she could come to an apt description. An implacable, noble wall. Unlike so many men she'd worked with, Ghost didn't vacillate under pressure. Some men would make a decision and then look to her as if to say, "Is that right? If it's not, I can do whatever you think is best." Rez didn't need that kind of second-guessing nonsense. She needed someone who knew what was right and did what was right.

A commotion from behind walloped Rez out of her thoughts. A door slammed. Someone cursed. Ten voices argued at once. Rez leaped up, strode past half-a-dozen cubicles, and joined the throng in the floor's largest conference room. She found a room plastered with maps, crime-scene photos, and brainstorming pads. There was a large gray table, a half dozen computers, and enough cigarette smoke to curdle milk. There was also an angry horde of agents.

'That's a bunch of crap!" Field Agent Cadens shouted, the cigarette hanging precariously from his lower lip. "We were all over Louisiana in the first place. This guy's making it up."

"Looking for his fifteen minutes!" blurted a squat, toad-like agent named Addams.

"How'd he know about the birthmark then?" Special Agent Garcia asked, her question and tone as sharp as her facial features. The room went silent.

"Maybe *he's* Smiling Jack," someone muttered. Rez couldn't see who. But that sent the room back into spasms of argument.

Rez spotted the Ken-doll-agent, sidled his direction, and barked a whisper, "Klingler, what's going on?"

"Oh, now you want to talk?" he replied, rolling his eyes.

Rez fixed him with a glare that would have melted iron. Klingler blinked and said, "You got problems, Rezvani. You need help." He gave an exasperated laugh and shook his head.

"Nothing like the problems you're going to have if you keep stalling," Rez said. "I need you to tell me what's going on."

"Probably nothing," Klingler muttered. "Some nutball says he's the father of the recent vic."

Rez sucked in a gasp. "The woman from Fort Pickens," she whispered. "We got a name? Where's he now? Got anybody en route?"

"If you'd shut up a minute," he replied, "maybe we could find out."

"...next closest Field Office is Little Rock," someone said.

"Nah, Dallas is closer."

"I'm still saying it's a waste of time," Addams muttered.

"Send some plain clothes over there to pick'm up," Cadens suggested. "We got bigger fish to fry here."

"Exactly what fish do we have to fry here, Leonard?" Deputy Director Barnes thundered. "We got an unidentified body cooling in the morgue, and nothing but the cause of death and a few footprints in the sand. We got no trail. We also got no time to waste. Brookheart?"

"Sir?" a narrow, dark-skinned Special Agent bounced from his chair.

"Get on the horn to Little Rock," Barnes commanded. "Dallas has too much going on with that serial poisoning case. Little Rock's got the new choppers; they can get there in what?"

"Forty minutes, give or take," Brookheart replied.

"And we need someone on the ground there too," Barnes said. "Dagget, you and Klingler get over to the chopper. The rest a' you, get back to work!" When Deputy Director Barnes pounded his fist on the conference table, the room cleared out as if someone had dropped a grenade.

Agent Rezvani had to flatten herself against the door to avoid the stampede. As the torrent turned to a trickle, Rez rounded the door and stomped over to Deputy Director Barnes. "How long, Sir?" she demanded.

Barnes looked up suddenly and whisked away his reading glasses as if embarrassed to show a chink in his granite armor. But, nonetheless, he glared at her with his usual intimidating confidence. "Did you say something, Agent Rezvani?"

"With all due respect, Sir," Rezvani said, mentally weighing her career against speaking her mind. For a wildly insane moment, speaking her mind appeared to tip the scales. So, she plowed on. "With all-due-respect, your hearing hasn't gone yet. You heard my question, and you know precisely what I'm asking."

He folded his hands and, for a split heartbeat, Rez thought she saw the hint of a grudging smile crack his brickish jaw. "Until the killer is caught," he said.

"I've never known you to waste resources, Sir," Rez said. "I know the Smiling Jack case as good or better than anyone in the Agency. You know my fieldwork. Why are you wasting me?"

"You know why."

"Spector?"

He nodded.

"For crying out loud, Sir. You forced me to spend my own vacation time to follow leads I believed were there. Then, as soon as I find something, you freeze me out. Spector gave me my best leads. The camera—photos, video—he gave that to me. And...in the meantime, we took out a La Compañía heavyweight."

"Temporarily," Barnes said.

"What do you mean by that?"

"Lawyers got Ramírez out. Four million bail."

That stunned Rez for a few ticks. She remembered Ramírez' threat to Ghost. She shook her head to focus on the matter at hand. "I just don't understand why, Sir? I mean...*really* why?"

"Agent Rezvani," he said, "you are a very capable investigator. What do you think happens when a case gets reopened? When a major case gets reopened?"

"It makes people wonder why the case was closed to begin with."

"Bingo," Barnes said. "It's a great big dunce cap for the FBI. And not just people. Press. Certain members of the journalistic community are very interested in publicizing such an embarrassment, and certain people in our organization are rather sensitive about such things."

The dot-to-dot picture suddenly formed a clearer image. Rez sighed.

"Right," Barnes said. "Now suppose that an enterprising reporter for a national news agency does a little digging and discovers that, just before the case gets reopened, the only agent who was still interested in the case was forced to investigate on her own time, and then a body shows up, finally—finally—legitimizing the case?"

"Crap."

"You need to be out of the public eye," Barnes said. "Or someone's going to paint that dunce cap fire-engine red. You don't want to see that happen, do you, Agent Rezvani?"

"So Director Peluso's willing to shelve me and take the risk that—"

"I asked, do you want to see that happen, A-Gent-Rez-Va-Ni?" He glared at her as he sharply enunciated the syllables.

GHOST

She squinted back at him, not understanding. This wasn't his *My Final Word* routine. "Nossir," she said at last.

"See, now I knew you were a team player," Barnes said. He stood, strolled to the conference room door, and shut it. He returned to his seat and leaned forward. "So, you're officially off the Smiling Jack case," he said, his voice strangely thin. "Present here in only the most cursory support capacity. So you wouldn't want to have anything to do with a Mr. Paul Graziano who claims to be the father of the victim left at Fort Pickens."

"Nossir," she said, shaking her head comically.

"So an address in Shreveport of 618 Bay Avenue would be of absolutely no interest to you."

"Nossir," she said. "As a matter of fact, I've got so much meaningless paperwork to complete that I can't afford to take any more of your time, Sir. I apologize for the intrusion."

"Thank you for your understanding, Agent Rezvani," Deputy Director Barnes said. "One thing more: if something gets done, and you get this guy, you know who gets the credit."

Rez didn't say a thing, but she knew.

"Uh, huh," Barnes said. "But, if this gets screwed up any worse and it gets public?"

"Siberia?" she asked.

Barnes turned on his *Final Word* grimace. He said, "If you're lucky."

***   ***   ***   ***

"The choppers are all gone," Rez muttered. "The cavalry's already en route to Shreveport. What the heck am I supposed to do?" *Maybe that's why Barnes threw the info my way,* she thought. *Just enough information to get me off his back, but nothing I could really do anything about. Not really.*

{ 277 }

She'd tried calling Mr. Graziano, of course. She'd tried six times and got no answer. She'd used the Bureau's digital files, up to her clearance level anyway, to see what she could find out about the guy. Paul Louis Graziano was a retired mill worker. He had divorced four years ago; never remarried. He didn't have much of a record. Late on his taxes a couple times. There was a flag in his file, but when she clicked on it, nothing came up. That usually meant it was something recorded before the FBI completely overhauled their databases in 2001, after the Y2K scare. Citizens who were categorized as "low risk" didn't get a lot of love from the FBI data geeks.

Rez leaned back in her cubicle chair and thought about the murdered young woman. She'd been in her early twenties when Smiling Jack took her life. If Graziano was actually the woman's father, why didn't he have a missing person report filed?

Of course, she knew there could be a thousand reasons. Maybe he was just a scumbag. He was divorced. Maybe the wife had custody. Maybe father and daughter were estranged. Maybe she'd run away from home and become one of the nameless many to disappear into the sexual cesspool in and around Hollywood.

Rez shivered. She couldn't shake the image of the dead woman. If the ME's report could be trusted, she'd been violated and had her throat cut...bled out most likely from the vaginal wounds...wounds that might be consistent with an abortion. She'd been used up and slaughtered, left in that blasted fort, and arranged to lie in the fetal position. She'd looked innocent when they found her, almost like she was sleeping. But there was blood: stark red blood against her skin. So pale she looked ghostly.

Crap, Rez thought. *I'm an idiot.* She yanked out her cell phone and started dialing.

GHOST

*** *** *** ***

Halfway back from the cemetery in Jackson, I'd pulled into a parking lot of a truck stop called the 231 Bistro because I'd had an idea. I couldn't believe I hadn't thought to look earlier.

Assassins were a secretive lot. When I'd initially searched his car, I'd found an arsenal of weaponry. I could have probably pawned those for all the money I'd need. But I'd dismissed that idea, knowing that the guns would end up in the wrong hands...more or less because of me. I'd destroyed the weapons, but I'd never thought to snoop around the car a little more.

I opened the glove box, found a little magnetic key box stuck to the side. When I opened it up, I found a wad of hundred dollar bills. "I'm an idiot," I muttered, thinking of all the Waffle Houses I'd passed up in the morning.

When I'd thought I had no money, I'd willed my hunger away. But now, my body woke up and demanded food. I didn't think I could bear to drive south again to search for a Waffle House. I practically jogged into the truck stop.

Surrounded by a bunch of burly, bearded guys wearing flannel shirts with the sleeves cut out, I ordered two T-bones, double mashed potatoes and gravy, and a salad.

The waitress brought the food a short time later and set it out for me: all four plates worth.

"Sure you got room for all that, honey?" the waitress asked.

"Oh, yeah," I replied. "I'll have room for dessert too. You have dessert, right?"

"Best Pecan Pie you ever had," she said. "Butter brickle brownie cake too."

"I'll have both," I said.

I was halfway through the first steak when one of the truckers clapped his hands. "Now that is one manly meal!" he said. "Yes, SIR!"

Another trucker chimed in. "Shoot, he might just beat Otis' record."

I turned and nodded politely.

"A man's meal," the trucker repeated. "Yes, sir!"

That's when it happened.

I am sixteen going on seventeen; I know that I'm naive.

Of all the times.

I dropped the silverware and dug around in my pockets and found the phone, but not before its ringtone belted out:

Fellows I meet may tell me I'm sweet, and willingly I believe.

I hammered the green button. "What do you want, Agent Rezvani?" I growled, feeling the truckers' stare, heavy with accusation. "I thought you weren't going to contact me anymore."

"Fine," she said. "You don't want a lead, I can just—"

"No, wait!" I said. "You've got something on Smiling Jack?"

"The victim's father," she said. "Where are you?"

"Halfway back to Panama City, why?"

She cursed. "This isn't going to work."

"What do you mean?" I asked. "You're not making sense."

"The guy's in Shreveport," she said. "Bureau's already choppered out to the airport. That would have been...almost two hours ago. Best guess is they'll be there inside of forty minutes. Once they get there, you won't have a chance to talk to the guy. I don't guess you can pull any strings, get someone there first, huh? No, of course you can't. That's not how it works."

I pushed aside my plate. Left a hundred dollar bill and started out the door. "I can make *something* happen," I said. "Give me the address."

"Wha—you can?" she asked, and I could hear the thrill in her voice.

"I'll make it happen," I said. "But what about your orders? What about the 'arrest on sight' bit?"

"I can't promise anything," she said. "I'm...I'm uh, not exactly working by the book on this."

"I understand."

"But, Ghost, listen," she said. "Don't leave me out of the loop on this. Don't cut me off."

"Whatever I find out," I said, "is all yours. Plus some other things I've learned since we last spoke. Now, give me his name and address."

* * *   * * *   * * *   * * *

I stood in the shade of an ancient magnolia tree at the end of a driveway. The tarnished numbers on the white clapboard house told me I'd arrived at 618 Bay Avenue, Shreveport, Louisiana. I dropped to one knee and gasped for air. I couldn't help it. Pushing myself the way I had was very dangerous. On most missions, I refused to utilize *surging* unless it was a matter of life and death. The drain on my entire body was immense and long-lasting. I wouldn't be back to full strength for days. A cold shower would help but initially, just in a cosmetic way.

Still panting like an overheated German Shepherd, I stood up and tried to collect myself. I might have fifteen minutes before the FBI arrived, maybe less. Mr. Graziano had an old bird bath in his weedy front lawn. It was chipped and stained and covered in some kind of pale lichen, but there was rainwater in it. So I splashed my face a few times, pasted my hair back, and breathed a regular breath at last.

I knocked on the front door and got no answer. I knocked again and waited. Nothing. I was about to knock a third time when the door creaked open and a sunken eye blinked at me.

"Whaddaya want?" he asked, his voice ten years of pack-a-day hoarse.

"Mr. Graziano?" I asked, holding up my ID and badge. I could see him squinting at my credentials. No way he read it all. "I'd like to ask you a few questions about your daughter."

He cursed, widened the door enough to lean out and spit a wad of something just left of my feet, and said, "You're fifteen years too late."

Something in the pit of my stomach turned very cold. "Mr. Graziano," I said, "you contacted the FBI, said you recognized the victim we found in Florida. If she is your daughter, then any information you could give us might save other lives."

"She's my daughter all right," he said. He swung open the door and stepped aside. "My little Erica."

I followed him inside and realized that Mr. Graziano and the house were one. He was thin, gaunt even. The house had narrow rooms with nothing on the walls except for water stains. His skin sagged and drooped in wrinkled folds. The furniture looked like it had been out of style forty years ago. The upholstery was faded, sunken, and threadbare. But the greatest and saddest similarity was the pervasive emptiness I felt from him and the house. This was a shell of a man living in the shell of a home.

Mr. Graziano motioned me to a chair. I sat, sinking down so that my knees were way higher than comfortable. He pulled a wobbly chair from the card table I suspected he used for meals. He sat down and asked, "Whaddaya want t'know?"

Pangs of pain washed through me. I didn't want to grill this man about his daughter. I wanted to tell him how sorry I was for his loss. I wanted to offer a thousand comforts. But I had to wade in. I didn't have much time, and I wouldn't get another chance. "Mr. Graziano," I said, "could you begin by explaining how you knew the victim was your daughter?"

"I told'em on the phone," he said. "It was the birthmark on her right thigh, just above the knee." He pointed out the spot on his own leg. "Coupl'a blotches, looked just like a bunny jumping over a log. Erica was my little bunny."

"How did you see the birthmark?" I asked. "Did the FBI show you...did they let you see her?"

"No," Graziano said, his eyes welling up. "The article online had a picture of her face, and I didn't really think much of it, 'cept she sort'a looked like my ex-wife. That's the only reason I kept reading the article. When I read there was a birthmark, I about had a heart attack. I called you guys, described my little Erica's birthmark, and well, here you are. What do you think, Mister...uh?"

"Spector," I said, my brain too busy elsewhere to hide my name. Much of what Graziano had said left me puzzled. What had he meant by fifteen years too late? Why did he keep calling her my little Erica? "Mr. Graziano," I said, "Could I have a look at your most recent photograph of Erica?"

He nodded and disappeared around a corner. I heard a drawer open and close, and then he reappeared carrying an old photo album. "I dug it out already," he said. "Figured you'd want to see."

He handed it to me with both hands as if it was a jeweled crown upon a velvet pillow. He nodded, letting me know that it was okay for me to take it. I held it reverently for a moment and wondered. Just looking at the dust collected on the frilly lace, I thought something was wrong. When I opened the album I became certain. The first few pictures were of a toddler who apparently liked to wear princess dresses. She was a beautiful child: dark hair and eyes, skin so pale she almost looked porcelain, and the cutest dimply smile I'd ever seen. I flipped through the pages and watched the little girl grow up...a little.

There were birthday parties and pony rides. There was Christmas morning where she'd been given a Lite Brite toy. There were bubble baths and puppies. And finally, as I came to the last couple of pages, there was a little girl getting ready for her first day of kindergarten. She had a pink backpack, and there was her mother, helping her step up onto the bus. The chill in my gut flash-spread all over my torso.

I remembered the pale-skinned brunette...dead, left curled in the fetal position in the sandy catacombs of Fort Pickens. The little girl and the young woman: too many features matched. The mother too, even more so because of her adult features. But the dead young woman at Fort Pickens couldn't be the mother. Mr. Graziano hadn't called the FBI to identify the victim as his ex-wife.

"I'm sorry, Mr. Graziano," I said. "But don't you have more recent pictures of your daughter?"

"Mr. Spector," he said. "Those *are* the most recent pictures of Erica. She was taken away from me and her mother fifteen years ago. She was only five."

{ Chapter 27 }

If Rez's estimate was accurate, I wouldn't have much more time before the cavalry arrived. And this cavalry would be none too pleased to find me on their turf, questioning their suspect.

"Mr. Graziano," I said, "our meeting here today is a preliminary. Other men, agents from the FBI, will be here soon. They will likely want to take you in under protective custody."

"Protective custody?" Graziano said, blinking. "You think I'm in danger?"

"It's purely precautionary," I said. "You have information critical to an ongoing investigation. What you have to tell us may save lives."

"I hope so," he said. He stared at the ground, and then he started shaking. "She...she was all I had, y'know? Sunshine in my life, and it all fell apart after she...after she was gone. All this time...after I'd given up hope...to know she was alive—I gave up on her. How could I? How could I?"

"From what you told me," I said, "you and your wife did everything you could. This falls on the FBI's shoulders, not yours.

This is a failing of law enforcement and an act of pure evil by the person or persons responsible."

"Who could do such a thing?" Graziano asked, wiping messy tears off his face. "Take a little girl away, keep her for years, and then kill her?"

"You don't have words for that kind of evil," I said.

"You gonna get this..." He uttered a blistering string of anguished curses. "Promise me that you're gonna get him!"

"Mr. Graziano," I said, "Erica's blood cries out, and this time, it hasn't fallen on deaf ears. I promise you: Erica's killers will fall."

***   ***   ***   ***

I had wandered two blocks up from Bay Avenue when a convoy of FBI-standard-issue SUVs rounded the corner and headed for Graziano's place. The manpower they brought, and the way they tore into the neighborhood, you'd have thought they were securing a beachhead. *Whoosh, whoosh, whoosh*—they sped past me without so much as a tap on the brakes. Just as well; I had no time to trifle with them. Too much on my mind.

I followed Bay Avenue, turned a corner and found two bridges crossing the bayou that ran behind Mr. Graziano's neighborhood. One was steel and new stone, rising on a high arc over the water, and open to traffic. The other was a pedestrian thing that was in such a state of flaking disrepair that it looked like it had been hewn from sandstone. No cars on this one. There was an old guy fishing about sixty yards away but no one else. I took a seat on the bridge and shoved my legs through an opening to dangle. I spent maybe ten minutes trying to corral my unruly thoughts, reeling with new information. Once I had it catalogued enough to speak on it, I opened the phone and dialed Rez.

"Rezvani," she said. "Hold, please."

I frowned. *Hold, please? Really?*

Thirty awkward seconds later: "Ghost?" she said. "Sorry. I had to get out of the office. Too many ears. Listen, I have news. Tracy in Speech and Language finally got back to me. You were right. The victim on the video, the redhead, she was talking just before Jack killed her."

"Anything useful?"

"Not certain," Rez said. "Tracy's one of the best, and she said a lot of the vic's speech was repetitive, like mumbling or...or singing. But she did make out one coherent string: 'Lucy, Lucinda, come braid my hair...before the doctor comes.'"

"Some kind of nursery rhyme?" I wondered aloud.

"None that I've ever heard of," Rez said. "We're working on it here. What about Shreveport? You couldn't organize something fast enough, could you?"

"I got to Graziano," I said.

She made a triumphant growling sound and said, "Finally! Flexed a little higher-than-the-FBI-muscle. Sweet! Who'd you send?"

How to answer that? If I told her I'd gone to Shreveport, there'd be too much time wasted with new questions I could not answer. "A trusted agent," I said finally. "No one I trust more."

"Good, good," she said. "What's the deal? Is Graziano on the up-and-up?"

I was about to answer when I heard a strange warbling beep. I looked at the phone's display and saw the little battery icon blinking. "I think this battery's about to die, so I'm going to give it to you fast. You have something to write with?"

"Yeah, yeah, just a sec," she said. I heard a lot of muffled noise. "Got it; go ahead."

The battery warning beeped again. "Erica Graziano is the victim we found at Fort Pickens," I explained. "She was taken from her parents when she was just five years of age. She—"

"Five?" Rez blurted. "That can't be right. Medical examiner said she was twenty-two years old."

"I said she was taken when she was five. She was killed fifteen years later." Silence from Rez. The battery beeped again. I didn't have time to let Rez puzzle it all out. "Agent Rezvani, I need you to track with me here. Erica Graziano is the Fort Pickens victim. Your FBI buddies will confirm this when they compare DNA with the sample Mr. Graziano will provide from an old hairbrush, a lost tooth, or...or something. She was kidnapped from a local daycare center and never seen again...until the Smiling Jack pictures."

"Son of a..." Her voice trailed off. "That's how he did it!"

"Smiling Jack took them young," I said. "Somehow kept them out of sight and off the grid as they grew up. When they were old enough, he killed them for the whole world to see and got away with murder."

"No missing person reports," Rez muttered. "No one to recognize the victims."

"Because they were all fifteen years older," I said. "The reports were filed, but they were for children, not adults." The battery warning beeped again.

"So Smiling Jack and his accomplice had us off track from the beginning," Rez said. "But why? Was this just all about beating the cops? Is Jack some egomaniac getting off playing Dr. Moriarty and making fools of the FBI?"

"No," I replied. "There's more, but I haven't pieced it all together yet. But remember the weapon. We're talking a turn-of-the-century abortion knife. That's the key. Listen, I've—" The battery warning. "Agent Rezvani? You there?"

"Yeah, yeah, I'm still here. You know, you can just go buy a charger. Radio Shack or Walmart probably have a generic that will work."

"Noted," I said. "But for now, just get this: the knife is the key. Smiling Jack is sending a message related to this weapon. Now, I made a contact at Panama City Beach Hospital Center. He's a cardiac surgeon, and he's done some legwork for me. Turns out the old abortion knife is something of a rarity; only a few are known to still exist. Doc might have a list of potential owners, or maybe your crew can dig one up."

"Holy smokes!" Rez said. "Could it be that simple?"

"Maybe," I said. "If you can get the list, look for ties. See if any of the owners lived in Louisiana fifteen years back. Also, get someone searching out kids who went missing fifteen years ago. If there was a burst of disappearances, especially if they're geographically close, there's a better chance they're related."

"Fifteen years," she muttered. "Wait, something I'm not getting here. What's the time connection?"

"What do you mean?"

"There are two sets of Smiling Jack murders," she said. "Separated by four years. If he takes the victims as kids and lets them grow up, what is his trigger? What happened twenty-three years ago to kick this all off?"

"Twenty-three years?"

"Yeah," Rez said, "assuming he did the same thing, right? Figure he takes them at five years old or close to that, waits, and then kills. The first set of pictures appeared eight years back, so fifteen years or so before that—gives you twenty-three. Was there a tragedy, twenty-three years ago? Maybe something related to abortion?"

"And why the four years of silence in between killing sprees?"

"There's a bigger picture we're missing," she said.

"I know. But we have important pieces. So, you'll follow up with Doc Shepherd, get that list of anyone who owns a Cain's Dagger. Get the Bureau resources combing for related kidnappings occurring around the Graziano abduction. You got that?"

"On it," Rez replied. "It's all going to hit the fan when my team finishes with Graziano. You know that, right?"

"I am not very popular with the Bureau," I said. "I won't forget."

"Forget...I can't believe it," Rez grumbled. "I almost forgot to tell you. Ramirez, the La Compañía boss we put away, he got out on bail. Watch your back."

"I had a little run in with La Compañía already," I said, remembering the rest stop incident. "I'm good."

"Okay," she said, hesitance brittle in her tone. "Still, don't underestimate them."

"I won't."

"I've got my game plan," she said. "What...uh, what are you going to do?"

I was about to answer when the phone made a whooshing sound. I looked at the display and watched it shut itself down. *Just as well*, I thought. Rez didn't need to know my game plan. She didn't need to know that I had six hundred miles of traveling to do to get back to Florida.

*** *** *** ***

"Anything back from Shreveport?" Rezvani leaned into the conference room and asked. But Deputy Director Barnes wasn't there. She swept down the hall and ducked into the newly dubbed command center, a little closet of a room filled with computers. She found Barnes there, bathed in electronic hues of blue and green. She started to speak, but he held up a hand.

The phone smashed between his ear and shoulder, Barnes scribbled something on a notepad and said, "I understand. No, not a coincidence. No, not a chance. I want it pushed through." He paused a few moments and as he did, his granite chin became more set, his gray brow lowered like a storm's mantle. "You tell Seavers that he can get me the results within the hour or he can flip burgers for a living!" He slammed the phone, looked up at Rezvani, and snarled, "What?"

"I can come back." She tried to duck away.

"Here. Now."

Rezvani trudged sideways into the room full of computers. "Bad news from Shreveport, I take it?"

"How'd he do it?" Barnes demanded.

"How did who do what, Sir?" Rez asked.

"You don't wear stupid well," Barnes said.

"And you don't wear vague well, Sir," Rez fired back. "What are you talking about?"

"Your boy," he said. "Your consultant, Phil Spector."

"John Spector," Rez corrected.

"John, Paul, George, or Ringo, I don't care. How in the great cauldron of Hades did Spector get in to see Graziano before our team?"

"I told you," Rez said. "He has connections higher up."

"Connections, Agent Rezvani? Like who? Scotty on the Enterprise?" Barnes' face purpled.

"I...I uh," Rez stammered.

"I called in a favor," Barnes explained. "Our team choppered straight to Eglin Air Force Base where a twin-turbofan C-21 was already fueled and waiting. They landed in Shreveport within two hours. They were at Graziano's door twenty minutes later—and your man Spector had already been and gone."

"That's not possible, Sir," Rez said. "Spector was in town when I spoke to him, and that was two hours after our team left."

"Maybe he was already en route," Barnes said. "Maybe he lied about where he was. Whatever, but he got there first."

"He didn't...uh. He didn't mess anything up, did he?"

Barnes shook his head. "But you already know something, don't you? And may I remind you, Agent Rezvani: if you withhold any information—"

"I know, Sir," she said. "Graziano's the victim's father."

"Great Scott!" Barnes exclaimed. "Spector got a DNA test done that fast?"

Rez didn't answer directly. "Graziano is the victim's father. Her name is Erica Graziano, and she was taken from the family when she was five years old."

That stopped Deputy Director Barnes short. His jaw snapped shut with an audible click. Rez told him everything Spector had shared.

"This changes the entire span of the investigation," Barnes said. He cursed inventively. "You know what this means?"

"It means that the FBI gave up," Rez said. "It means that somewhere between twelve and eighteen women were held captive, likely tortured, and then murdered on our watch."

Barnes cursed again. This time something about Director Peluso giving birth to several unlikely things.

Then, Agent Rezvani told him about the murder weapon. "That's impossible," Barnes replied. "We had experts, we scoured every journal, every database."

"Spector's source is better," Rez said. She didn't know if that were true or not, but so far, Ghost's resources had proved incredibly accurate.

After an invective related to the improper treatment of circus animals, Barnes stormed to his feet. "This is unbelievable!" he thundered, casting around the command center. "Couldn't happen at worse possible timing. Where is it? Where is it?" Then, he darted toward a flatbed scanner. "Here. Here it is." He handed a newspaper to Agent Rezvani. "Go ahead, read the headline."

It was the *Miami Herald*, and Rez noted it was today's edition. She read the headline: *The Wait May Be Over.* The photo showed several hundred protesters, some looking strangely overjoyed. Then she read the caption and understood at last: *Pro Life organizers march outside of the Supreme Court where in just a few days the landmark abortion ruling Roe v. Wade is expected to be overturned.*

"See what I mean?" Barnes grumbled. "Sweet mother, this is going to stir them up. I can hear Senator Esperanzo now."

"What do you mean?" Rez asked.

"He's already must-see-TV," Barnes said. "He's leading the Dems in the polls by close to thirty percent. That's unheard of."

"So?"

"So, Esperanzo is *Pro Life*," Barnes said as if the phrase was unpleasant. "If he gets wind of Smiling Jack and the abortion knife—and somehow I think he will—he'll shine a ten-thousand watt spotlight on it. He'll blame the FBI's failures on the current administration. But it'll come back on us."

Agent Rezvani left the command center feeling sick to her stomach. *Four years,* she thought. *Four years between killing cycles.* Her mind reeled, even as she sat at her computer and began her search. She typed: *Presidential Candidates and Elections to Present.*

{ Chapter 28 }

"RESTROOM, PLEASE!" I GASPED, holding my hand at an angle so that, hopefully the woman behind the counter couldn't see my face. The condition I was in, one look and she'd probably call an ambulance...or the police.

"Sir, the restrooms here are for paying..." She stopped that line of thought. "Oh, mannn, uh...yeah, it's back there behind the chip rack. Use the second door. The men's sign is too faded to see."

"Thank you," I mumbled, hurrying around a tall wireframe rack of gourmet potato chips. I stumbled into the second door on the right and heard a shrill sound that wasn't quite a scream but more of a startled squeak.

A wide-eyed brunette, twenties, maybe a college student stared at me. Then she glared at me. "Uhm, wrong room!" she said. "Duh."

Out I went. I must have been completely waxed from the surge. I'd gone in the first door on the right. The Ladies Room. This time, I made sure. I saw the faint, faded stencil of the word MEN, and ducked into the room. The door had a latch lock. I rattled it into place and went to the sink. I smacked cold water on and glanced into the mirror. I found myself looking at a Hollywood zombie version of my face. The skin sagged horribly and capillaries had burst all over, streaking my flesh with jagged streaks of crimson lightning. Both eyes were dilated, and the whites were bloodied. I'd pushed myself too hard for too long.

What I really needed was a shower or a submersion, a proper resetting. But I needed to make do. I cupped my hands under the flowing cold water and splashed it all over my face, my neck, my bare arms. The first dousing vanished as my flesh absorbed the resiliency-giving water and began to rebuild. The feeling was like knobby cables untangling beneath my skin, spreading into something linear and smooth. My eyes stung, but I knew that to be a good thing: a cleansing of contaminated blood, a clearing of visible imperfections. Again and again, I splashed myself. I didn't care how soaked my shirt and cargo shorts became.

Finally, I stoppered the sink and let it fill. I bent at the waist and plunged my face in, ten-twenty seconds at a time. I repeated the dunking once, twice, a third time. Then, I gasped for air. I breathed deeply, slowing down a bit between each breath, letting my heart rate return to normal. When I looked into the mirror again, I found that I could pass for normal again. Sixty-hour work week, anxiety-ridden, three hours of sleep a night—normal, but good enough.

"Thank you, so much," I told the woman behind the counter. I slapped a hundred dollar bill on the counter. "I need a computer code and the biggest mug of the best coffee you've got. And please, keep the change."

The woman blinked at the bill and then back at me. "Are you kidding?" she asked. "That's like eighty dollars change."

"Please," I said. "It's the least I can do. I kind of splashed a lot of water in the restroom."

GHOST

"Oh," she said. She eyed me more closely. "You okay?"

I nodded. Then, I made a show of sniffing the air. "I'll be even better when I get some of whatever smells so good."

She laughed, and slid me a tiny slip of paper. "Here's the internet code," she said. "I'll get your coffee."

I wandered over to a computer and slid into the chair. I exhaled, and it seemed a lifetime of exhaustion flowed away into the air with that breath. The waitress—or was she a barista? Serving girl, hostess, bartender, shopkeep? It was an Internet Cafe, and they served coffee. So I had no idea what to call her. All I know is she brought me a massive, steaming mug of coffee.

"You have no idea how much this means to me," I said, closing my eyes and inhaling the aromatic blend of Costa Rican coffee beans, almondine, and cacao.

"Been traveling?" she asked. "Long road?"

"Six hundred miles," I muttered, taking my first sip of brown paradise. "Mmmm, this makes it worth it."

"There anything else I can get you?" she asked.

I opened my eyes from the coffee-induced euphoria. I finally figured out what to call her: Melanie. Her name tag said so. "You've already done me a service I will never be able to repay." She laughed. I wasn't joking. "But, if you'll bring me another mug of this...this heavenly nectar...say, every half hour, I will most assuredly leave you a tip that will make your day."

"You don't need to leave any tip," she said. "Your last one already made my day." Melanie laughed again, a musical, trilling giggle that reminded me of how important my mission was...how precious these people are.

As she walked away, I used the cafe's code to login to the computer. It was a high-end Mac, and it was fast. Since I didn't have my silver case and the splendid drives within, I needed all the speed I could get. I wouldn't have access to law enforcement files. I wouldn't be able to break down firewalls. I'd have to search this out the way everyone else did.

"Browser," I muttered, "looks like it's just me and you." I began searching child abductions in the Shreveport area in and around the time Erica Graziano had been taken. Then I began sifting the results for anything meaningful. It wasn't a needle in a haystack, but it was close. I hoped Agent Rezvani was having better luck.

* * *   * * *   * * *   * * *

Agent Rezvani was sitting in Doc Shepherd's office when he arrived early in the morning. "Well...uh, hello," he said, raising a bushy eyebrow. "When the nurses told me an FBI agent was in my office, I was kind of expecting someone else."

"Spector?" Rez asked.

"Precisely."

"I'm Special Agent Deanna Rezvani," she said. "But, ah...Spector's not with the FBI," Rez said.

"Not FBI either," he said. "I found out the other day he wasn't local law. You know, Agent Rezvani, I don't much appreciate being lied to."

"Spector wasn't lying," Rez said. "At least not in the sense you mean it."

"I wish I could believe that," Shepherd said, his tone still pleasant. He parked behind his desk and folded his hands. "Mr. Spector flashed a badge and let on as if he were some kind of official investigator."

"He is," Rezvani explained. "Just not FBI. He's higher up than that. Heck, he's at a clearance level I've never encountered before. If he misled you, you can be certain that it is because he is not permitted to reveal certain details about his occupation."

Doctor Shepherd leaned back a few inches and twirled his mustache. "Spector's above your pay grade?"

"Far above."

"Now, that's a stitch of a different color," he said, a twinkle in his ice-blue eyes, "And, I must confess I am glad to hear that. Very glad. I've always felt I was a good judge of character. Spector seemed like an honorable man, but I thought he'd put one over on me. You've done me a service, Agent Rezvani, and I appreciate it. If you ever need a heart procedure, you'll let me know, won't you?"

Rez paused. "Uhm, hopefully that won't be necessary, but if I do, I'll remember you."

"That's fair. Now, why have you come to see me, Agent? Are you working the case of the young woman murdered recently, a series of killings, wasn't it?"

"Yes," she replied. "Spector and I were—are—working together on it. Have you heard of the Smiling Jack killings?"

"Smiling Jack," he said, nodding wistfully. "Spector named the case for me, and I've followed it some. The Bureau declared it a hoax, but Spector said it was real."

Agent Rezvani frowned. "We had no physical evidence," she said. "We had no missing person's reports. No one identified the alleged victims. All we had were photographs. I'm quoting the party line, you understand. Truth is, we never should have closed the case."

"The young woman at Fort Pickens?" Doc Shepherd asked. "She was in those awful photographs?"

"She was," Rezvani said. "And now that we have a body to match with the photos, the Bureau is putting all its muscle into catching the killers. And that's why I've come to you."

"The weapon," he said.

"Spector said you have special insight about the knife. It's surgical, turn of the century."

"Not what I would call surgical," Shepherd corrected. "It was used for abortions. Cain's Dagger, it was called. Do you understand the reference?"

Agent Rezvani vaguely remembered the story of Cain and Abel. Cain murdered Abel, hadn't he? She couldn't remember why or any other details. She chose not to answer the question. "Spector said that the knife is quite old and quite rare, that you might have access to a list of owners."

Doc Shepherd eyed her for a few silent moments. He reached up and twirled his mustache. "Agent Rezvani," he said, "I come from a long line of surgeons. We've spent generations trying to save lives and inventing better ways to do so. If information I can provide will help you save the lives of other young women, then I will be in your debt for the opportunity. But, if what Mr. Spector told me is true, the practice of abortion is somehow mixed up in this whole thing. And that concerns me greatly."

Agent Rezvani swallowed. She couldn't afford to cut off this source, but she needed to be up front. "Doctor Shepherd," she said, "are you saying that you might withhold information depending on the political slant of this case?"

"Absolutely not," Doctor Shepherd said, each word a scalpel stroke. "I'm going to assume that you deal quite frequently with political agendas, with that manner of power-brokering vacillation in the FBI?"

"Almost daily," she said.

"Then, I will forgive your insinuation. I will give you everything within my power to give." He paused, reached into a drawer, and removed a piece of paper filled, margin-to-margin with text and numbers. "This is a list of every known Cain's Dagger knife, its original owner, its purchase history, and its current owner. If my source is to be believed, there are only six knives surviving."

"Who is your source? That is, if you don't mind my asking."

"My Uncle Timothy," he said, straightening his lively turquoise bow tie. "He was once an orthopedic surgeon of some renown. Ninety-two now but still razor-keen intellect. He's a bit of a collector of surgical implements. He knew just who to call in Europe to find out about the blade."

"In Europe?"

"That's where the blade was made," Doc replied. "A collector associate of Uncle Tim's put him on to it straight away."

"May I have the list?"

He slid the paper to Rez. "I would like you to promise me something."

Rez took the sheet. "It's hard for me to make promises," she said, "when I'm in my official capacity, that is. I'll do my best."

"Very well," he said. "I'll accept that. This is what I ask: Smiling Jack used a nineteenth century abortion implement to murder young women. I think it's clear the weapon was chosen for a purpose. He's promoting a message of some kind, and it's not clear, to me at least, what manner of message he's trying to send. But Agent Rezvani, make no mistake, Smiling Jack wants everyone to know what he's doing and why. He wants press. He wants attention. All I ask you is this, whether Smiling Jack is some sick Pro Lifer or something else, will you do your best to make sure that his message does not get heard?"

Agent Rezvani blinked. Doc Shepherd surprised her.

"At this point," she said, "I'm not sure. I've recently entertained the idea that the killing cycles match the rise of Pro Life Presidential candidates. But whatever his message, Smiling Jack is a murderer. If there's anything I can do to mute his message, I will do it."

"Thank you, Agent Rezvani," he said. "And please, when you see Mr. Spector, pass along my apologies for a misunderstanding. And do let him know that I'd like to see him again before this is all over."

"I will," she said. She stood up with the list, scanning it as she started to leave. Then she froze. "One of the Cain's Daggers," she said, "it's owned by a doctor in this hospital."

"I'm aware of that," Doc Shepherd said. "Now, if you'll excuse me. I have a valve replacement to prepare for."

***   ***   ***   ***

The only good thing about the Internet cafe was the coffee. My search results had proved utterly fruitless. Nearly all of the remotely similar child abductions in Shreveport had resulted in a body being discovered or the lost child returning, found, or rescued. There were a handful of unsolved disappearances, but five of those had been male children. The rest had been girls already in their teens. I couldn't completely rule out the girls, but they didn't seem to fit Smiling Jack's MO.

I was disgusted. The whole case had been like this. Every promising start, every revealing clue, led to a dead end. I lifted the great mug to my lips and drank deeply. When I lowered it again, the man who called himself Mr. Scratch sat across from me.

"Dear, oh dear," he said, feigned distress dripping from his words. "I do believe I have seen you looking better."

"I've had better days," I replied, playing along. I still had no clear evaluation of this man. His eyes showed no sign of being taken, and yet there was definitely something unwholesome about him.

"Better days? Better weeks is more like it, wouldn't you say?" he asked, crossing a leg and leaning back in his chair. It was the same black pinstripe zoot suit. But his tie was even more obnoxious than last time: light blue background with a dazzling array of multicolored butterflies, all with a metallic sheen.

"What's with the garish tie?" I asked.

He grinned, the painfully white teeth lighting up against his deep tan. "That's for me to know," he said, "and for you, to find out." He paused, leaned forward, tented his fingers. "I tell you, Ghost, I cannot for the life of me understand why you insist on doing things the hard way."

"Maybe you could help me do things the easy way?"

"Oh, most certainly," he said. "I already have, of course, many times."

"I told you before: I don't remember you."

"Pity," he said. "I certainly cannot imagine why you would wash away memories of someone like me. Doesn't it trouble you at all? This isn't the first time you've *forgotten* me, you know."

"Actually, it does bother me," I said.

"Such admirable honesty," he said. "One thing I can count on from—"

"It bothers me because I don't wash something from my memory unless it's deeply disturbing, corrosive even. You know what else bothers me?"

"Pray, do tell." He tugged gently at the brim of his fedora. Honestly, the man seemed to be made of jazz. Every movement was stylishly graceful.

I lowered my voice to a caustic whisper. "It bothers me that you know something about Smiling Jack that you aren't telling me. It bothers me that you sit here wasting my time with your punk smug routine while innocent women are dying."

"Are you not thankful for that dreadful tool of yours that I so generously returned?"

I blinked a glance down. The Edge was in the top left hand pocket of my cargo shorts. It was a great comfort. "Changes nothing," I said.

He laughed jauntily. "Oh, yes," he said. "Yes, it most certainly does change things. I have helped you twice now and asked nothing in return."

I ground my teeth, tiring of his nonsense. "Your advice was lousy," I muttered.

"What you mean to say is that your intuitive faculties were too limited to unravel my advice in a...timely manner."

Sometimes the way forward is the way back. What kind of stupid, cryptic—then, it dawned on me. "Graziano," I whispered. "Smiling Jack took them as children."

"Ah, there now, you see?" Scratch said, "that was useful, was it not? My advice is always useful. Useful and rich, layer upon layer of meaning."

Melanie appeared at the table. "My shift is over," she said, gesturing to my mug. "Can I get you anything else before I go?"

"No, thank you," I replied. "You more than earned your tip."

"What about your friend?" she asked.

"Brilliant young woman," Scratch said. "Here just a moment and yet, she intuits that we are indeed friends. Splendid." His left hand sliced a velvet curve in the air and ducked beneath the table. When it returned, he had the gold pocket watch. "But I am afraid that I don't have time for coffee. Thank you, dear, for the courtesy."

Melanie blushed and left the table.

I watched closely as Scratch twirled the pocket watch once on its chain and then replaced it. "That's an ugly scar on your wrist," I said.

"What?" he snapped. And I saw again that lightning glimpse of pure hatred.

I decided to press him. "Your left wrist," I said, nodding. "The scar. Looks like it must have been painful."

He uncrossed his leg and leaned forward, the very first bit of motion from him that didn't look like ultra-slick dance. His dark eyes smoldered, the irises tremoring slightly as if boiling in the whites. His glare was painful and searching, and I found myself holding my breath.

"Have you remembered...something?" he hissed.

I didn't answer. The question didn't make sense. I'd seen the scars on his wrists the first time we met. You didn't forget that kind of thing. It didn't seem like that could be what Scratch meant. I did my best to glare back.

Suddenly, like the switch of a light, his face melted back into smooth. "No," he muttered. "I thought not. You know, Ghost, it's a shame you had to get nasty. I could have given you a great deal of assistance tonight. A real shame." He stood up and, in turn, pulled taut the cuffs of his shirt. He walked slowly past our table but stopped near my side. He whispered, "Another will die tonight because of you."

Rage bubbling up inside, I spun out from my chair and took hold of his forearm. At least...I thought I had. With speed that shocked me and that easy fluidity, Scratch shook off my grasp and moved a step backward. He wore that sharkish grin when he said, "Perhaps, it was good for you to forget about me. Perhaps, I ought to forget about you, as well."

"Wait," I said, the rage draining. "Please, tell me what you know. Tell me something. How can I save her?"

He shook his head and made a tisking sound. "Too late for that, my dear Ghost," he said, and his eyes flashed with that horrible malice. "I have borne your stupidity with graciousness.

But no more. How dare you offer me such effrontery and then beg for help."

"I'm not begging," I said, the words gone before my thoughts could caution me against using them.

Scratch blinked. "To think I came prepared to bail you out...all manner of information to share. I even dressed for your benefit."

It was my turn to blink. Dressed for my benefit? What kind of ridicu—the tie. Something about the tie. Butterflies?

"Hmph," he said, the sound somehow thoughtful...calculating. "Perhaps, you aren't as dull-witted as I feared. Good luck, my dear Ghost." He turned his back on me and swayed toward the cafe door. He paused there and gave his head a half turn. "Just remember," he said, his voice taking on a saw's edge, "the next time we meet, things will be different. This is three times I have given you aid. Your side of the ledger is ruefully empty."

He turned the corner. I went after him, but when I set foot outside the cafe, there wasn't a zoot suit to be seen.

{ Chapter 29 }

"NO, NO, NO!" I yelled at the cell phone, getting all kinds of concerned looks from the nice folks behind the cafe counter. Thanks to the new car charger I'd purchased at a local Radio Shack, the unit had power. But no battery in the world could force someone to answer. "Come on, Rez. I'm trying to keep you in the loop here." I kept muttering, kept mashing the redial button, and kept getting Rez's answering service.

But there was nothing for it. She wasn't answering. Maybe her phone was dead. I couldn't know. That left me with two options: contact someone else in the FBI or search it out on my own. No contest. If I called the FBI, I would waste precious time with red tape and run around as some junior agent tried to figure out who I was and whether I was credible or not, and, *Oh-by-the-way, Mr. Spector, was it? Did you know you're on a special list here at the FBI?*

The bottom line was: even if I could somehow persuade them to use their computer muscle to find the place Mr. Scratch hinted at—a butterfly place?—the place where the killers might strike again, the FBI would never share that information with

{ 307 }

me. I'd be left in the dark while they scrambled black SUVs to come pick me up. Fact was, I needed the FBI's help, but not at the risk of their interference. I hoped to save the remaining captive girls, but I had less constructive plans for Smiling Jack and his accomplice.

I pounded the computer keys, searching out: butterflies, Panama City Beach, butterfly farm, insect zoo, and everything else I could think of that might connect me with the link I needed. I skittered through a dozen unsuccessful results, modifying my search terms again and again. At last, I came up with a few viable options: exactly four.

Gulf Coast Insect Zoo, Bug Crazy Museum, The Butterfly Conservatory, and The Butterfly Refuge. The first two were close to Panama City. The other two—much farther away—but closer to the original Fort Pickens crime scene.

Four.

Twenty minutes for the first two. An hour for the others. That's enough time for the killers to get in, leave their victim, and get out. More than enough time for a young woman's life blood to leak away.

If I drove.

I finished writing the directions to all four locations onto the back of a real estate flyer. I didn't know how much more my body could take, but driving was out of the question. Time was not my friend. Even if I got lucky and found the killers at the first location, I could still be too late to save lives.

Besides, I don't believe in luck.

***   ***   ***   ***

"We should have had this list YEARS AGO!" Deputy Director Barnes raged.

"Yes," Rez replied, rolling her chair a few inches back, "yes, we should have. If we'd correctly identified the knife to begin with, maybe we would have gotten the list years ago. Maybe we would have saved lives."

"Cain's Dagger," he muttered. "What a name for a thing." He typed into the term field and pulled up a photo of the abortion tool from a surgical museum. Then, he brought up a weapon isolation shot from one of the Smiling Jack photos. Finally, he pulled up a third knife image: the turn of the century abdominal blade that FBI forensics had declared a match for Smiling Jack's weapon. He brought all three images together, side-by-side. Then superimposed.

"Can you tell these things apart?" Barnes asked, rolling his chair away from the HD monitor.

Rez leaned in. "The woodgrain is a little lighter on the abdominal blade. But that could be from age or maintenance. Something looks a little different on the blade's edge too, but...I'm not certain."

"No wonder they missed the ID," Rez said. "But a collector would know, especially a collector who is also a surgeon."

"Unbelievable." Barnes muttered a string of curses, this time, something about the unclean habits of alien life forms. "If this gets to the press—"

"Screw the press!" Rez shouted. She glanced through the command center's windows and saw other agents popping up from their cubicles like prairie dogs. *I may have just gotten myself fired,* she thought. But she was already committed, so she said, "Really, Sir, with all due respect to you, we should be about saving lives, not saving face. When did the Bureau lose track of that—"

"I know when I did."

"What?" Rez thought she'd misheard. At the same time, her cell buzzed in her suit coat pocket. *Poor timing.* She ignored it and said again, "What?"

"It was when I took this ridiculous promotion," he said. "Deputy Director, hmph. I thought I could brace myself. Do the job without political trickle-down from the Director, but it's like a slow-acting poison."

"Sir?"

"I'm saying you're right, Agent Rezvani," Barnes said, leaning back, his eyes still combing the list of knife histories. "Never thought I'd see the day that a woman would grow a pair bigger than mine."

Rez stifled a laugh. "Sir, that could be considered sexual harassment."

"Stow it, Rezvani!" Barnes growled. "My Clara wouldn't believe it for a second. Now, why are you still here?"

Rez bounced up out of her chair. "I...uh...?" She looked at him blankly.

"Scan this list," Barnes commanded. "Get it out to every field office within fifty miles of these last-known addresses. These two in the U.K....get on the horn to Scotland Yard. Ask for Chief Inspector Cornell, and tell him I'm calling in the chip he owes me. And, for Heaven's sake, handle the Florida knife owner yourself."

"But, Sir, the Director gave you orders to sideline me."

"Whatever," he replied curtly. "Maybe she'll bust me back to Senior Agent. Might be where I belong."

"Thank you, Sir!" Rez said, half-tempted to salute. She turned to leave, but he called her back.

"Not so fast," he said.

"What?"

Barnes stood up and glowered at Rez. "Do not take this personally," he said. "It's for the good of the Bureau."

Agent Rezvani looked up questioningly. "Uhm..."

Deputy Director Barnes' face turned as red as a cut watermelon. His eyebrows beetled like knotted caterpillars, and the creases on his face deepened to fault lines. When his mouth opened, Rez felt like she'd been caught in the wash of a dragon's breath. He unleashed a series of condemnations the likes of which Rez had never heard before or imagined.

He blasted her for her incompetence on every case she'd ever had the gall to work on. He questioned her work ethic, her drive, her personal code of conduct...and her ancestry. And mingled with all the caustic phrases were enough sonic expletives to wilt Holland.

Rez didn't have to try hard to look browbeaten. She felt like she'd just been inducted into the Marines and been welcomed by a bunch of soldiers with tube socks full of soap bars.

The cell phone still buzzing off and on in her coat pocket, and still ignored, Rez trudged out of the room, her head bowed, shoulders drooping.

She was defeated...and triumphant.

* * *   * * *   * * *   * * *

Like I said, I don't believe in luck. That probably explains why I don't have any.

I struck out at Gulf Coast Insect Zoo and Bug Crazy Museum, the two local places. I'd wasted a total of seventeen minutes in the process, plus another forty for travel to Pensacola.

I stood outside The Butterfly Conservatory. It was a glassy building that stood between two thatches of swaying palms. The moon was behind clouds, and the nearest streetlight was at a skate park across the street, so there wasn't a lot of light.

I trod up to the front entrance, a surprisingly modern-looking, brushed-silver pair of doors covered with surprisingly cheesy-looking butterfly stickers. I found no signs of forced entry, ran around back, and found nothing there either. I did, however find a couple of concave, bubble windows that gave me a pretty good look at the interior of the building.

Inside, there were dozens of tall glass cubes, presumably full of slumbering butterflies. Did butterflies sleep? I really didn't know. A useless waste of thoughts. I stopped, leaned my forehead up against the off color glass and exhaled a hot breath. I had been ignoring the nagging pricks of reality since I'd left the Internet cafe.

I was painfully aware of how futile this hunt was. I didn't know Mr. Scratch. Therefore, I couldn't trust him. For all I knew, he could be Smiling Jack's accomplice. Or, he might be something worse.

But even if Scratch was altruistic, accurate, and reliable...even if his information was spot-on, I was still fighting a losing battle. A young woman was going to die, and there wasn't a solitary thing I could do about it.

The timing was the most vexing variable. Did Scratch offer me the hint because the killers were leaving a new victim tonight? If tonight, when exactly? The killers might be slaughtering a young woman right now and leave her at one of the insect zoos I'd already visited. It was equally possible that, the moment I depart the Butterfly Conservatory of Pensacola, the killers could emerge, leave the victim, and escape without any interference from me.

So be it. If traveling back-and-forth between the four locations all night long, gave me my best shot at catching the killers, then I would do just that...until I collapsed from utter exhaustion. I'd made a fool of myself for lesser things.

I had one stop left before I repeated the path: The Butterfly Refuge in Navarre. I'd have to—

The crawling, itching sensation that passed through the glass to my flesh was otherworldly and frightening. It traveled like a stinging electric current onto my fingertips, my forehead, and even up through the soles of my shoes. Any piece of me in contact with the physical surroundings, felt this intense, skittering surge.

I snapped away from the glass and flexed my still tingling fingers. But I still felt it. In fact, it was slowly increasing its voltage. Something was drawing near.

It wasn't a Shade. It wasn't a Knightshade. Not even Forneus the Felriven had generated such a threatening aura. I found myself backing away from the building, my hand reflexively going to the Edge in my pocket.

I crossed the alley, clambered up onto a dumpster, and used it to get to the roof of the thrift store next to the conservatory. Then, I ducked down next to a whirring air intake and waited. The crawling electric current continued up through the roof's gravel, the metal of the intake, and now even the air around me. It intensified yet again and made my teeth feel strange.

I really didn't want to stay. Every impulse told me to get far away as fast as I could. But if what I felt was Smiling Jack arriving, it was a game-changer. I had to see. I had to know just what I was up against...because it wasn't human.

My heart stroking a deep staccato, I watched the other end of the alley. My eyes had adjusted to the low, moonless light, and I could see a few crates piled against the far corner of the Conservatory. A recycling dumpster jutted out from the base of the thrift shop.

At the opening of the alley, a thin road ambled by, and across the road, a line of palms stood sentry. What I saw in the air above the road, left me breathless. A kind of darkling mist appeared there, maybe nine or ten feet above the road, and rapidly thickened to a writhing inky wound. A viscous dark fluid, like black blood, spilled out of it. It reached the surface of the road and began to pool. Irregular shadows rose up from the growing puddle. Slowly, like a vortex of wood smoke, the shadows coalesced into a tall figure. Its edges were still indistinct, and the shadows seemed to whirl around it like a cloak. The streetlight at the far end of the alley flickered and blinked out.

The headlight of a passing truck vanished as it went by the alley. The charge traveling up from the rooftop doubled. It was all I could do to stay still and silent.

When the figure, cloaked in murk, strode forward into the alley, I panicked. I rolled backward as if I'd been struck, scrambled to my feet, and sprinted across the rooftop. This was not Smiling Jack. This was something I had heard whispers about long ago, something that supposedly had gone out of the world. It was something I could not hope to face and win. I reached the far end of the roof and dove.

* * * * * * * * * * * *

Rez looked down at the name on her phone display. "Dr. August Garrett Malcolm." It didn't strike her as the name of a killer. Few names did until after the killer was caught. And then, the name would be seared into the national consciousness forever as obviously wicked.

Rez strode purposefully into Panama City Beach Hospital Center, stopped at the desk, and learned from the receptionist that Dr. Malcolm's office wasn't in the hospital's central structure. There was an outpatient wing, she'd said, and Dr. Malcolm's unplanned pregnancy clinic was the octagonal facility at the end of the wing.

The outpatient wing stretched out like a true wing from the hospital proper. It was a long, slightly kinked hallway with offices, clinics, and waiting rooms opening up on either side for more than a hundred yards. The hall bustled with hospital personnel: orderlies sliding past with carts layered with gowns, towels, and thin blankets; nurses guiding unsteady patients from one room to another; and, of course, a plethora of doctors skittering from chart-to-chart.

Rez found that the hall grew more desolate as she approached the unplanned pregnancy clinic. No one in sight for thirty feet. Just two flat gray doors at the very end. Just as Rez came to the doors, there was a muted buzz. The doors swung open. Rez stepped back as two figures emerged. There was a young woman, maybe seventeen, Rez thought. She had brown hair cut in a pixie-like bob. She might have been very cute, but her skin was so pale, her dark brown eyes so huge and haunted that she seemed almost ghostly. Her eyes, staring straight ahead without the slightest movement, really unnerved Rez. That and the way she kept rubbing her elbow and upper arm as if fighting off a determined chill.

Rez looked to the other figure. A startling contrast. This was a woman who meant business. She was older, likely the mother, but her skin showed fewer wrinkles than was natural. Her hair was perfectly styled half-updo, lush black streaked through with gray. Her makeup was heavy and bold. No, fierce was a better word. Blood-red lips, heavy black eyeliner, bruised blue eye shadow. Her eyes were dark like her daughter's, also staring straight ahead but simmering with indignant anger.

"That's far enough," the severe woman said.

"But I'm tired," the teenager replied. "Tired and hurt."

"You brought this on yourself."

"I know."

"So walk."

Rez watched in disbelief as the young woman stood from the wheel chair. She wobbled a few paces, stumbled, caught herself, and kept going. The woman in the business suit eyed her watch. "We're going to have to pick up the pace."

"Yes, Mother."

Rez watched them drift slowly up the hallway: the daughter draped only in a thin robe; the mother an expensive burgundy business suit and heels. Something congealed in Rez's stomach. It was far too easy for an investigator's mind to conjure story lines for this forlorn pair. Rez blinked. Someone had said something.

"Can I help you?" came a voice from inside the office doors.

Rez turned to find an African-American woman seated behind a very modern acrylic desk. She was a thickset woman, but not fat. She wore an expression that might have revealed boredom or exhaustion or detachment...or a little of all three. "Can I help you?" she asked again.

Rez stepped forward and said, "Yes, sorry. A little lost in thought." She flipped open her badge and ID. "Special Agent Rezvani. I made an appointment to meet with Doctor Malcolm."

"Got it right here," the woman at the desk said. She pressed a button on her keyboard and spoke into a headset mic, "Dr. Malcolm, the FBI woman is here to see you. Should I send her back?" She nodded a few times, apparently attending to the speaker's questions. "Tight as a drum. You know Clarence. He does a good job. Uh, huh, clear 'til three. Okay...right." Her eyes refocused on Rez. "You can go on back." She pointed. "Third conference room on the right."

Wondering about the receptionist's cryptic conversation, Rez followed her directions. She was counting doors on the right when she noticed a steel gray door on the left. She only noticed it because of the bright orange biohazard sticker on the wall next to the door handle. There was a small, vertical rectangle window just above the lock mechanism. Rez glanced inside...and then, wished she hadn't. The room was dark but illuminated by several eerie green digital numbers that appeared on displays in the two visible corners. And in that green light, Rez could see a row of thick metallic canisters, each one emblazoned with its own biohazard warning.

Rez shuddered involuntarily and turned away from the room. She'd never considered herself Pro Life. No, not even in the same zip code. But, while she emphatically supported a woman's right to choose, she'd never been altogether comfortable with the abortion practice.

She came to the third conference room, turned the corner, and found a very stern-looking man in a bleached-white doctor's coat. With the blockish shape of his head, protruding brow, and sallow complexion, he reminded Rez of Herman Munster...well, minus Herman's perpetual grin.

"Doctor Malcolm?" she asked.

He nodded and motioned for Rez to join him at the table. "Yes, yes, Agent," he said, every word clipped as if he was in a hurry, "what's this about anyway? If it's the constant death threats from those right wing fanatics, I've already given a statement."

"Not about that," Rez said as she took a seat. "But since you mentioned it, are you still getting threats?"

"All the time," he said, entwining his long, knobby fingers. "I don't take them seriously, of course, but some of my personnel do."

"How many threats in the last year?"

He paused. His eyes flitted under heavy hooded lids. "Three, I believe," he said at last. "But listen, if this isn't about the threats, why are you here? I run a very busy practice."

"There doesn't seem to be too much traffic in here today," Rez said flatly.

The corner of Dr. Malcolm's mouth twitched. "That...is because I cleared my schedule for you, Agent. Well, except for one procedure, but that was rather an emergency."

Rez blinked, thinking of the staring young woman in the hall and her austere mother. "Thank you for making time for me, Dr. Malcolm," Rez said. "The reason for my visit is that it seems you're a member of a rather exclusive club."

"Which one?" he asked without the faintest hint of a boast. "Garnier's Marina and Yacht? Bayshore Links? El Castador Cigar Lounge?"

"None of those," Rez said, removing a glossy photo from her briefcase. She slid the picture across the table. "It's a knife club. Do you recognize the blade in this photograph?"

Dr. Malcolm flinched at the shoulder ever so slightly, but Rez had caught it. He went on to study the photograph for a ten count. His hooded, deep-set eyes came up, and he said, "Before I answer your question, I'd like to know: am I a suspect in a crime?"

"No," Rez said. She waited, watched the good doctor relax a little and then said, "You're more of a person of interest."

He stiffened again and let the photo fall back to the tabletop. "I don't like semantics," he said. "And I don't like surprises. Suppose we do this another day, a day when I have my lawyer with me?"

Rez balled her hand into a fist beneath the table. "We could do it that way, Dr. Malcolm," she said. "But I'd hoped to save you the trouble."

"What trouble?"

"The trouble of a much higher profile questioning," she replied. "You answer my questions here and now, and I don't think of you as an evasive person of interest. I don't have to come back wearing my bulky navy blue jacket with the giant yellow FBI letters and take you out of here in cuffs. But if you'd rather answer the questions in an FBI holding tank...with your lawyer present...that's fine. We can do it that way."

Dr. Malcolm's lips went very thin. "What do you want to know about the scalpel?"

"First," Rez said, careful to hide the smugness she was feeling, "do you know what the knife is used for?"

"Was used for," he corrected her. "It was used for abortions more than a hundred years ago."

"Where did you get the blade?" she asked, unfolding a sheet of printer paper. "There aren't many of them still in existence."

"Look, Agent," he said. "I'm guessing you know exactly where I got the instrument. I suspect it's written on the paper in your hand."

"Humor me."

"I bought the blade directly from the original manufacturer, Eugene Lacy Company out of London. It came from their private collection, and I paid close to forty grand for it. That would have been..." He leaned back in his chair, "...about 1996, I think. I was at a convention."

"1997," Rez corrected.

"Whatever," Dr. Malcolm replied curtly. "Now, Agent, why don't you ask me something not printed on your sheet."

Rez placed the paper face-down on the table, tilted her head slightly, and raised on eyebrow. If this doctor thought his god-complex was going to intimidate her, he was far dumber than he looked. "Doctor Malcolm," she said, lowering her voice and sharpening the syllables with her best Miranda Rights pronunciation, "the blade, often called Cain's Dagger, has been used in an ongoing series of serial murders. Young women are getting their throats cut with the blade."

"M-my blade?" he asked. Rez watched the color of his face change from ashen gray to pallid white.

"Or one just like it," Rez said. "So the question I'm wondering about is why do you own such a blade? Why go to all the trouble—why pay so much for it? What is a blade like this to you?"

Whatever discomfort Dr. Malcolm had felt disappeared. He seemed to regain his stern man-of-medicine arrogance. "Agent, I purchased the blade because I collect antique surgical implements. Some people collect teapots or spoons. I collect blades, especially blades related to my line of work. I take great pride in what I do. Women in all kinds of trouble come to me. They are burdened and face uncertain futures. I help them find freedom again."

"Just the same, Dr. Malcolm," she said, "I wonder if you know where your blade is right now?"

"Of course I do," he replied. "It's in a display case overlooking the pool table in my basement."

"You won't mind if I send some technicians around to have a look? Run a few tests?"

"They may test away," he replied. "But they had better not damage the blade. As you know, Agent, the Cain's Dagger did not come cheaply."

"You can afford it, right?" Rez asked, edging her voice menacingly. "You did say *business* is booming, didn't you?"

Dr. Malcolm folded his hands and grinned for the first time. *Huh,* Rez thought, *he really does look like Herman Munster.*

"I don't know what you think of me or what I do," he said. "But I'm not your bad guy. I've made a career out of helping women...not hurting them."

Rez thought again of the pale young woman in the hall and thought, *Yeah, you're a real humanitarian.*

{ Chapter 30 }

"I believe you missed your calling," Jack said, extending the cold fingers of Pamela's already stiffening hand.

"How do you mean?" Dr. Gary asked. He stepped carefully over Pamela's outstretched left leg, stooped down, and bent her right knee so that her foot would disappear into the ground cover ivy.

Jack tilted his head. "You could have been an artist," he said. "Just look at the way you've positioned her here. Except for the wound, Pamela could be a renaissance maiden in one of Botticelli's masterpieces."

"Surgeons are artists," Dr. Gary replied. "But I thank you nonetheless." He stepped back to admire his work. A red light from the security panel they'd disabled cast a ruddy glow onto Pamela's pale body. And just at that moment a monarch butterfly, one of hundreds flying free within the Butterfly Refuge in Navarre, Florida, landed on a knuckle of Pamela's left hand. "Now," he said, "that is art."

***   ***   ***   ***

Treading unsteadily toward the Butterfly Refuge, I couldn't help looking over my shoulder. I could still feel the muscle memory echo of the crawling, itching sensation that inundated that alley. It couldn't have been coincidence that the shadow-shrouded dark figure appeared outside the Conservatory just after I arrived. It was one piece of evidence I couldn't ignore, and all the more reason to look over my shoulder.

Nothing there so far. Just a palm festooned neighborhood full of darkened ranchers and the odd colonial. I sighed. *Good.*

If I somehow managed to complete this mission, I'd have to contact Anthriel and ask him about what I'd seen. It couldn't be what I'd first thought of. Couldn't be.

The Butterfly Refuge sat adjacent to an L-shaped strip mall. Most of the mall's store spaces were empty, ready for lease, and the only thing open this late at night was the 7-Eleven at the top of the L. Feeling the strain from all of the night's traveling but still amped up on fear-induced adrenaline, I stalked closer to the Refuge.

The gravity of my mission poured back over me like a lead shower. I had to push past the freak encounter and get to the business at hand. From the outside, the Butterfly Refuge seemed, at once, more professional and less kid-friendly. It looked like it had once been a large family home but had been retrofit with the broad windows and sculpted plaster of a business suite. They'd built a bank of flower gardens outside, creating a meandering path to the front door. In the dark, if felt like wandering through a South American jungle. Small plaques displaying standout examples of the order Lepidoptera jutted up from the soil in each of the flower gardens.

I noticed two things at that moment: the *shoosh* of the Gulf of Mexico and an inconsistent trail of dark splotches on the walk. I thought about the Gulf being near as I knelt. I put my fingertips to the dark spot, and they came back up wet with crimson.

I had the Edge in hand and slithered out of the flower gardens and up to the entrance. It was too dark to see inside through the little panel windows. I tried the door and found it still locked. But the blood was fresh, and I was out of patience.

I flicked on the Edge and jammed it into the locking mechanism. There was a muted crackling and a fount of white sparks. What was left of the lock didn't do its job. I raced into the Refuge and nearly lost my feet, sliding in blood on tile. I regained my footing on the corner of an observation center. Then, I stood very still...listening. Some part of me registered that the temperature inside was much colder than the Pensacola night outside. But I was too tuned to a strange sound. I'd hoped for shouting or footsteps or even a gunshot, but instead, there was only a peculiar, thin clicking sound.

Whatever it was, it was all around me...faint but persistent. I crept forward warily, eyes adjusting to the darkness as I went. A fair number of sleeping computers offered a little digital twilight, luminous green or slowly pulsing white. Security consoles on half a dozen support beams cast a more prominent ruddy light to the mix. Something flittered by my face. I ducked.

And then, I wanted to hit myself with a hammer. *Butterflies, duh.* The light clicking sound. The Refuge was home to several thousand insects, most flittering around inside glass or clear plastic enclosures.

I continued forward until I heard a faint trickle of water. It sounded like the quiet melody of a tiny brook. As I moved forward, the Butterfly Refuge became much more of the naturalist's museum. The interior had been painstakingly crafted to look like a wooded glade. The support pillars had been encased in realistic-looking tree trunks, complete with a variety of boughs and foliage. The tile floor gave way to cobblestones and ground cover ivy. I saw a little waterfall.

And then I saw the body.

I was too late again. The rage boiled up, and I tasted something bitter in the back of my mouth. The victim was young, maybe early twenties like the others. In the reddish light, I couldn't be certain, but her hair looked like a dark auburn. She was long and lithe, her limbs supple with young feminine muscle. And, of course, she was very pale. All the victims had been. Not surprising if they'd spent their childhood locked away from the sun and from prying eyes.

Unlike Erica Graziano's cause of death, the killing stroke here was obvious: a cut throat. There were no lower body wounds visible. And unlike Erica, this victim hadn't been left in the fetal position. The killers seemingly had taken time to arrange this young woman in a strangely artistic pose.

She was nude, reclined as a woman might lie by a pool: one arm raised, canted by her head, the fingers extended in a carefree gesture; she had one knee slightly bent, the other leg extended gracefully; her head was tilted back, resting on piles of thin stones; and her lush hair had been fanned out behind her as if gently moved by a cool breeze. But then, there was the ghastly wound: as with Erica's, this cut was far deeper than necessary to sever the artery; clumped with dark, half-clotted, bloody gobbets; and gaping to the point of revealing bone.

I shivered...half from the cold and the grim discovery. A buzz on my thigh startled me, and I heard music. Before Liesl could utter a fifth syllable of song, I snatched up the phone.

"It's about time!" I growled into the phone. "I've called you forty times!"

"So, so sorry," Agent Rezvani said. "I've been busy following up leads on the knife. Your Doc Shepherd came through. Only six known Cain's Daggers still around, but so far...no guarantee any of them was the murder weapon. I met—"

"Rez," I said. "There's another body."

The line went silent for a few ticks then, "What?"

"Smiling Jack killed again," I said. "I'm at a place called The Butterfly Refuge in Navarre, about fifteen minutes east of Pensacola."

"How in the heck did you know? Wait, why didn't you tell me?"

I wanted to crush the phone in my palm. "You need to listen, Rez," I said. "I tried to contact you, tried to let you know...hold on a second."

It got very cold. I killed the phone and looked up just as a massive shadowy form barreled into me and crushed me against the wall.

* * *   * * *   * * *   * * *

Fuming about Spector, Agent Rezvani checked her weapons. She sat beside Deputy Director Barnes in the SUV. Agent Klingler, rising star of the Mobile office, drove. Agent LePoast, who'd flown in that morning, rode shotgun. Rez checked the safety and slammed a clip into her Sig Sauer.

"How many times you going to do that?" Barnes asked.

"Helps me think," she replied. And it did, but it also helped with her nerves and her anger. She wasn't mad at Spector, not really. How could she be? He'd tried to reach her, seven times based on her phone's log of missed calls. No, she was furious that she'd missed those calls; furious that she'd missed a huge opportunity; and a combination of furious and terrified that something was happening to Spector and she wasn't there to back him up.

Rez caught a street sign flash by. They'd hit Navarre in two miles. She holstered the Sig Sauer beneath her jacket and then went to work on her Glock 27.

*** *** *** ***

"We've not long to wait now," Dr. Gary called over his shoulder from the yacht's wheel.

Jack ducked under the boom and stood at his partner's side. "Perhaps, we've been overestimating them," he suggested.

Dr. Gary smiled humorlessly. "That was with one body," he said. "One body reveals only the beginnings. But two? Two bodies will reveal patterns...our patterns. And there, our beloved technology will become our undoing."

"You sound so certain," Jack said. "But we were so careful."

"Meticulously careful," Dr. Gary agreed. "But technology will shrink the nation like a noose, and someone will come calling."

Jack stared out at the water. During the day, the Gulf of Mexico was a sparkling turquoise. At night, with no moon, it was black.

*** *** *** ***

"Sweet mother of Judah," Special Agent LePoast muttered.

"FBI!" Klingler cried out dramatically.

Rez rolled her eyes. Whatever had happened at the Butterfly Refuge was over and done with. Rez shook her head, taking in the destruction.

"Get the MEs in here!" Barnes barked, windmilling his arm. "Get the body sealed off! But, for cryin' out loud, watch the blood on the tile! Bloody footprints all over!"

Rez grimaced. Another young life taken by Smiling Jack. But looking at the interior of the Refuge, there was a lot that didn't match up with the killers' MO. The body positioning was different, but more than anything else, why all the destruction? Other than the area immediately around the body, the rest of the place was trashed. Display cases and terrarium's shattered, glass everywhere, and peculiar scorch marks on some of the walls. It was almost as if the cause of the mayhem had purposefully avoided the body. Why? And why trash the place in the first place?

"Deputy Director?" Klingler called, his voice hollow. "You want to take a look at this?"

Watching her step, Rez followed Barnes toward the building's rear entrance where all manner of debris covered the tile.

"You thinking bomb?" Barnes asked.

"I don't know what I'm thinking," Klingler mumbled. He pointed up. "Look."

Rez was half-afraid to look up. She didn't want to see another body, this one carved up and swinging from the ceiling. But when she let her eyes drift upward, there was no body at all. The cathedral ceiling looked to have been more than twenty feet high, but a five-foot section of it had been torn out: drywall, joists, insulation, and shingles—blasted right out as if someone had launched a rocket.

It didn't add up. And that, Rez thought, probably meant Ghost was behind it.

{ Chapter 31 }

I NEEDED WATER and I needed it badly. I was so emptied, so wrung-out exhausted that I barely made it back to Panama City Beach. The fight against the shades had very nearly ended me...very nearly ended the mission. There had been so many—haunts, roamers, and prowlers—that they forced me to my last resort. They forced an unmasking.

When I unmask, things get messed up. I get messed up. If anyone saw me now in the condition I'm in, if anyone got a good look at my face, there would be trouble. Forget zombie. My face looked like *zombie-in-a-blender*. I limped to the assassin's car, drove to the nearest hotel with a pool, and just before sun up, I slithered over the hotel property's fence and fell into the pool.

It was with a strange combination of utter relief and abject fear that I sank beneath the water's surface. Water is my friend and water is my enemy. It allows me to heal and, at my current level of injury, it was the only way I could be healed. I had so many wounds: gouges from long, curving talons, jagged tears from cruel uneven teeth, bruises, and even fractures. And in the state of exhaustion I was in, the resetting wouldn't begin without total submergence in water.

But, as brilliant white light blazed out of my wounds, and the familiar tightening of my flesh began, there also came teeth-rattling terror. I gasped for air and found only water coursing down my throat. I gagged, forced a gout of air to clear my lungs, and writhed. I was maybe two...three feet beneath the surface, and yet, to me, it felt like I'd just been expelled from a bathysphere near the ocean floor a thousand feet down. The pressure clamped me like a vice. My ribs felt like they would collapse and crush my organs. My ear drums popped, and my skull throbbed. I could bear it no longer. With whatever breath I had left, I screamed.

The sound underwater was alien and garbled, but still fierce and deep like a mortally wounded beast. I shot up from the water and sucked in enough air to fill a blimp. I swam rapidly to the shallow end, struggled to my feet, and gasped. I inhaled precious breath after precious breath. In reality, each air intake probably tasted like chlorine, but to me it was the rich scent of a meadow full of lavender and fresh cut grass.

Standing in the "kiddie" end of the pool, breathing like I'd nearly died, I felt a little like an idiot.

"Uhm...sir," came a timid voice behind me. "The pool doesn't open until 9:00 a.m. And, uh...we don't allow skinny dipping."

I turned and found a smallish man wearing green coveralls and wielding a pool skimmer. He was staring at me awkwardly...as if he didn't really want to look. Then, I felt a lot like an idiot.

I realized then that the sun had crested the horizon while I'd been submerged. And in the light...I discovered that the few shreds of clothes that had survived the Shade attack were now floating on the surface of the pool's deep end. I was butt naked. And yes, at that time, I felt like the king of all idiots.

I looked back to the pool maintenance guy and muttered, "Sorry. The mood just strikes sometimes, y'know?"

"I wouldn't know about that, sir," he said sheepishly.

"I don't suppose you could grab me a towel?" I prodded gently.

He was a kind soul. He placed two towels on the edge of the pool near the ladder. And then, he disappeared into a shed near the fence. I saw him peek around the shed doors a couple of times, most likely hoping I'd be gone.

Okay, so two towels are a great help, but I had destroyed my wardrobe completely. I could manage to wrap my waist pretty well, but I would need new clothes and right away. I left the motel pool grounds, slid carefully into the assassin's car and drove to the nearest fast food. In my present garb, drive-thru was the only real option. Thankfully, a Smack Burger was just up the road.

I think I stunned the employees with my order because their initial response was a rather rude suggestion that seemed anatomically and pragmatically impossible. I assured them that I wasn't kidding about the order, drove around to the window, and paid for the massive bill up front. The Smack Burger manager apologized profusely for the initial response but, since the order was so large, I had to pull around and wait.

Waiting wasn't a problem as I needed to kill a couple of hours until a surf shop might open to allow me to get some new clothes. I spent the time thinking of what I'd learned from the second body. Number one: Smiling Jack wasn't through sending messages. The way the victim had been posed this time, but for the gaping wound, a scene of startling beauty and peace—it was juxtaposition with some kind of nasty point. I had some suspicions about the message of the first body at Fort Pickens, but this one had me stumped.

Number two, and this was the most troubling aspect: Smiling Jack no longer cared if he got caught. For whatever reason, he'd run out of patience. The pictures and websites were no longer enough. He wanted to give us flesh and blood and, with that, he sacrificed his anonymity. Sooner or later, we would learn his methods and his patterns. And then, we would track him down.

But Smiling Jack had proven to be too cagey not to know that. Few things are more dangerous than a serial killer who no longer cared about getting caught. I blinked back memories of the photographs, the young women Smiling Jack had penned up like animals. If the pictures accurately represented the number of captives, there were only two women still alive. I'd already failed miserably, but I'd rather have my wings clipped than—

A sharp rap at my window. A disheveled looking man with a Chaplin mustache and a gaudy orange and red Smack Burger uniform stood there. "Sorry to keep you waiting," the manager said. "We've never had to drop that many hash browns before." He handed me half a dozen white paper sacks each emblazoned with the equally gaudy orange and red Smack Burger logo and, of course, Sir Smacks-a-lot the burger-eyed clown.

Resetting uses up every spare nutrient in my body and, when food nutrition is absent, will even consume muscular tissue...tissue that I could ill-afford to lose. So after such a full overhaul, I need to plow down thousands of calories. Smack Burger wasn't so nutritious, but it was filling and full of some of the major macronutrients. And...I couldn't wander into the local grocery store in a towel.

After nine sausage, egg, and cheese English muffin sandwiches, fourteen bags of hash browns, and three boxes of cinna-chomps, I felt like I had enough fuel to start the day. I let out a contented burp and noticed the cell phone on the passenger seat. In my hurry to flee the Butterfly Refuge and in my depleted, semi-clothed state, I wasn't certain if I'd remembered the phone. "Thank God," I muttered. I checked the display, and it flashed two pieces of information: low battery and nineteen new messages.

All from Rez. I hit her number. She picked up before I heard a ring.

"Ghost, what the heck did you do?" she asked, her voice hushed but urgent.

"I...I...uh, what do you mean?"

"The Butterfly Refuge looks like a bunker-buster missile hit!" She muttered something completely unladylike under her breath. "The place is wrecked. There's a hole torn out of the roof for cryin' out loud!"

"I didn't have much choice," I said. "I had some trouble."

"I guess so," she said. "But listen. This doesn't look good. Evidence is scattered all over the place. They know I got the tip from you. They're going to wonder if you had something to do with this."

"I'm going to guess I'm not real popular with Deputy Director Barnes right now."

Rez replied with an additional unladylike comment. "It'll be a miracle if they don't put out a warrant for your arrest," she said. "Seriously, Ghost, bloody footprints everywhere! Could you have been more careless?"

"I get reckless when I'm tired...and when things are trying to tear my head off."

"Whatever," Rez said. "Just tell me you got something. Tell me the reason the place is wrecked is because you were taking down Smiling Jack and his accomplice."

"I wish I could," I said, releasing a sigh like a flat tire. "The killers were already gone when I got there."

"Then who the heck were you fighting?"

"Remember the guy you shot in the alley?" I asked. "The guy with the invisibility suit? You called him a kind of terrorist. Well, there were a lot more of those guys."

The next thing Rez said was not only unladylike but it bordered on startling. Then, she said, "Four year intervals."

"What?"

"Smiling Jack's killing cycles came at four year intervals...you know what else does?"

"It wasn't four," I said. "It was four, then eight, right?"

"Divisible by four, then," Rez grumbled. "Look, I did some hunting around, and each killing cycle so far coincides with the impending election of U.S. Presidential candidate who happens to be Pro Life."

"Wait," I said. "What about four years after the first killing cycle?"

"Pro Choice."

"Possibly still a coincidence," I said.

"Possibly." I could hear her muffle the phone with her hand. Then I heard muted conversation, but I couldn't make out the words. "I gotta go," she came on suddenly. "Don't leave town."

The line went dead. I stared at the phone and noted that it was still blinking two messages: low battery and, this time, one missed call. I didn't recognize the number but pressed call.

"Panama City Beach Hospital Center," answered a mellow southern voice. "To whom may I direct your call?"

Then, the phone died.

Doc, I thought. *Had to be.*

GHOST

I fired up the assassin's car, wondering what Doc Shepherd had to say. We hadn't exactly parted on good terms.

*** *** *** ***

"Rezvani!" Deputy Director Barnes thundered. "Get in here!"

Rez hustled into the conference room and found Barnes, as well as Agent LePoast huddled in front of a computer screen.

"Sir?" Rez said as she stepped closer to the backs of their chairs. They didn't answer.

"Scroll up," Barnes said. "There. Do you see?"

LePoast leaned closer to the screen. His head went very still. "Son of a...how'd you see that with your old eyes?"

"Careful, LePoast," Barnes warned. "I might replace you with Rezvani here."

Rez looked back and forth between the two men and the wide, flatscreen monitor. There was a morgue photo, the victim from the Butterfly Refuge. There was also a scan of an old newspaper article. It had a black and white photo of a young girl in what looked like a school portrait. The girl couldn't have been more than six or seven. She wore pigtails and freckles and had big bright eyes that somehow looked blue even in black and white.

"Seriously," LePoast said, "Now that I see them side-by-side, I get it. But how'd you see this out of all those articles?"

"It's the smirk," he said. "Right corner of her mouth...that mischievous little curl."

"Yeah, yeah," LePoast said. "It's hard to see it on the vic because...well, you know." He cleared his throat. "Still, we'll need the DNA. Gotta be certain."

"It's her," Barnes said, using his Final Word tone. He leaned away from the monitor for Rez and said, "Special Agent Rezvani, meet Pamela Katherine Kearney of Anchorage, Alaska."

***   ***   ***   ***

If there were no complications, Doctor Shepherd was expected to be in surgery for the next six hours.

This was the news I got from the Nurse Pelagris at Panama City Beach Hospital Center's cardiac floor. Six hours. I'd stood in a towel at quite possibly the last pay phone on planet earth...and six hours was all I got for my trouble.

I'd already wasted time eating and then trying to digest my ridiculously large breakfast—and that just to get to ten o'clock so I could find a place to purchase new clothes. Now, it looked like I'd have to wait some more. If something went wrong during surgery, there was no telling how much more the wait might be increased. I sighed, buckled up, and pulled out onto Front Beach Road.

A few miles from Smack Burger and just a stone's throw from the sun-dappled Gulf, I found Mad Monk's Surf Shop. Colorful kites sailed high above the store, and the front door was propped open by a faux conch shell the size of park bench. Getting out of the low slung sports car without losing one of my two towels was no easy task. I managed, but it was a close thing. And, in the process, I learned just how chilly the morning air off the Gulf could be.

I decided to play it like I'd just walked in off the beach, that the towels were just to keep a wet swimsuit from dripping all over the shop's floor. Then, I'd start browsing, pick up what I need, and duck into the nearest changing room. I'd wear the stuff to the register, pay for it, and move on. No scene. As little attention as possible. Low key.

The moment I set foot in the store someone shouted, "Dude! What happened, you fall into a pool of bleach?"

Against my better judgment, I froze in place and looked left and right, as if he might be talking to someone—anyone—else. I saw the guy then, at the counter. He had corn rows, a tan two shades darker than chocolate, and enough shell necklaces to outfit a hydra. He looked like he was born to work in a surf shop. And he looked like he was thoroughly content to draw attention to me.

"Seriously, boss," the tan man continued, "you just fly in from Siberia, or what? Never seen skin so white."

So much for low key. A teenage couple near the dressing rooms laughed it up. A little girl pointed me out to her father. The look on her face made me want to lock myself up behind bars. Poor kid. I kept my distance from the other customers as I browsed. The loquacious shopkeeper was another matter.

I found a pair of long cargo shorts with a rope-tie belt. It looked to be about my size. I was browsing through a rack of button-down shirts when the guy with cornrows appeared right in front of me.

"Hey, bro," he said, "you have like a skin condition or something?"

"Something like that," I replied.

"Oh, hey, you know I was just messing. If I'd known, I would'na said Jack. I'm totally into affirmative toleration, y'know?"

"You always insult new customers?" I asked.

"Pretty much," he said.

"Make a lot of sales that way?"

"People come in here expect a little crazy," he said. "I'm Mike the Mad Monk, man."

"You have a gift for alliteration," I said. I held up a black shirt decorated with electric blue stick figures. "You have this in a 3XL?"

"Big dude, huh?" he asked. His eyes widened as if he hadn't really looked at me before this moment. "Whoa, you are a big dude." He took the shirt. "Back in a flash."

Mad Monk Mike returned moments later with a different shirt. It had a lot of black in it, but the collar, tails, and sleeves all bled from black to a kind of vibrant sea green. "So, dude, the one you got is XL only. But this one is 3X; thought it would look better on ya' anyway. The green'll make you look less shockingly pale, y'know?"

"You've really got this sales approach down," I said, taking the shirt.

"Hey, thanks, bro," he said. "That's mighty white of you." He burst out laughing. "Hey, hey, sorry, man. Couldn't resist."

I rolled my eyes and strode to the nearest dressing room. The shorts and shirt fit well, and I found a pair of rugged-looking sandals. I paid Mad Monk Mike with more of the assassin's money and went back to the car. The temperature had gone up twenty degrees in the last half hour. The car's interior was baking, so I was grateful to have something substantial between flesh and upholstery.

The cell phone had charged up two bars, and again, the missed call symbol blinked on the display. "This is getting ridiculous," I muttered, checking the number. It was Rez. I dialed.

"Special Agent Rezvani," she answered, her tone professional and disinterested. Before I could say anything, she said,

GHOST

"One moment please." I heard her cover the phone with her hand. A few moments later, she asked, "Ghost, where are you?"

"I'm in town," I said. "As directed."

She ignored the jab. "We've got a name on the second victim," she said. "Pamela Katherine Kearney. We found her folks. They still live in Anchorage, Alaska. They took her when she was four. Four years old, Ghost."

I couldn't find words. But I smoldered plenty. It was a reality that I could not escape. Evidence that another little girl had been torn away from her family and then kept captive like an animal for more than fifteen years. I thought about the myriad terrors she must have felt, the screaming ache for her parents...for someone to come rescue her. Only no one did. Smiling Jack and his accomplice murdered her.

"Ghost?"

"I'm here."

"Shreveport and Anchorage," she muttered. "Not exactly sister cities."

"Smiling Jack went mobile," I thought aloud. "That's an angle we'll need to explore. What else you got?"

"The doc at Panama City Beach Hospital—"

"Doc Shepherd?"

"No," she said, "an abortion doc off the list Doctor Shepherd gave me, the list of Cain's Daggers still known to exist. I visited Dr. August Garrett Malcolm."

"But he's not Smiling Jack?"

"But he's not Smiling Jack. He all but rolled out the red carpet for our forensic team. They tested the implement every way possible."

"Maybe that's part of his con," I said, grasping at straws. "Just like he was putting those videos up for years, rubbing it in the face of FBI and everyone else."

{ 341 }

"I wondered the same thing," Rez said. "But he's got an airtight alibi. He lectured at a local college, went out with colleagues for cigars and drinks until 3:00 a.m. It all checks."

I slammed my fist on the steering wheel. "He's here, Rez," I growled. "Smiling Jack and his accomplice are here in town somewhere! We've got all the photos. We've got the camera. We've got the video clips. We know the murder weapon. We've got two bodies. Why are the killers still alive?"

"You mean free, don't you? Why are the killers still free?"

I didn't answer. "You'll let me know if the Bureau gets closer...if you find out anything new?"

She took too long to answer. "I'm talking to you right now, aren't I?"

"I've...I've got to go," I said. "I need to clear my mind. I need to think."

We hung up. My focus on the conversation had led me to drive unconsciously. I obeyed all the traffic signs and signals, but I had no idea where I was driving or why. I'd left Front Beach Road behind, that much was clear. Suburban homes sprung up all around me. One street sign told me to slow down. Another street sign told me there was a playground near.

I pulled up close to a rounded corner and put the car in park in the shadow of a huge weeping willow tree. Across the street, a little horde of children chased each other through a sprinkler designed to look like an inverted octopus. Even sixty yards away, I could hear the kids giggling. The average person put in my position would wonder what kind of monster could take a child, hold a child captive, torture, and murder a child? But I don't wonder.

I know such monsters...all too well. Over a great many years, I have found myself repulsed and shocked, mentally and emotionally wrecked by the savagery of mankind. Unimaginable horrors are possible when there is no concept of how rare and matchless each human life is. And unlike some teenagers desensitized by ultra-violent, photorealistic video games, I never get used to it.

Even now, I can feel the Smiling Jack murders gnawing at my mind, shredding the fringes, and threatening far worse if I don't wash them away. I crushed my eyes shut, remembering my silver case hidden away in Forneus Felriven's sepulchral halls. One way or the other, I would finish this mission, and then I would have to face Forneus and his soulcleaving blade. If I did not, if I resolved myself to flee, and resigned myself to live with the images I'd seen and would see...I'm not sure what would happen to me. My greatest fear was that my mind would fracture to such a point that...I would become like the monsters I pursued.

But I would not flee. It was not in my nature. So, I watched the children play and thought. Smiling Jack and his accomplice had taken the young women when they were children, five and four respectively. If the pattern fit their approach to all of their victims, how had they done it? While it was tragically true that children are taken every day, at least half the time the perpetrators are caught, usually within a very short time of the taking. So how did Smiling Jack get away with it?

Sure he was clever...and diabolically patient. By taking the young women as children and not performing the murders until they were adults, he'd had the FBI chasing ghosts. In fact, Smiling Jack had outwitted the FBI at every turn. But still, sooner or later, the law of averages would have caught up with Smiling Jack.

I watched the scene in front of me. The little blond girl in pigtails had picked up the octopus sprinkler and was giving her friends a good soaking. Then, I saw a face appear in the screen window several feet above the playful children. The face disappeared. Moments later, a woman appeared bearing an armful of towels. She wrapped the dark haired girl about the shoulders and kissed her cheek. Then she gave her a gentle shove toward the backyard. The women dropped a towel on top of the towheaded boy and gave his head a good rumpling. While she dried him off, she glanced up and glared at me.

She'd seen me sitting here in the car. She'd wondered why a man would sit in a hot car parked so close to where her children played. Her protective instinct had taken over. And she'd come for her kids. Smiling Jack might have outwitted the FBI, but there was no way he could have totally outperformed parents' protective instincts, again and again, without ever been seen. Unless he was seen. Unless he was known.

Statistically, the kidnapper is most often someone the kid knew: a disgruntled spouse, ex, or step parent. Maybe that's how Smiling Jack did it. No, but that didn't make sense. Shreveport, Louisiana and Anchorage, Alaska? And what about all the other victims from the photos. They could be all over the country, maybe all over the world. Smiling Jack couldn't know each all of them personally...could he?

I watched as the woman herded the last of the three children into the back yard. She gave me a withering glance as she shut the gate. I put the car in gear and proceeded slowly down the road. I drove exactly the speed limit, but due more to my distracted mind than to propriety. If Smiling Jack and his accomplice did not know the children or their families, all it would have taken to get the killers caught was one child's scream...one nosy neighbor. As if on cue, I passed an old guy pushing a lawn mower. He had a very round pot belly and a floppy fishing hat with a beer logo. He watched me drive by. He didn't wave or smile, but he did raise an eyebrow.

I passed a small park nestled protectively beneath a canopy of broadleaf trees. Kids bobbed up and down on the seesaw. I watched a child clamber up a sliding board and then *whoosh* back down. The swings were occupied by kids as well. But for every clump of children, there were adults watching. Some wandering aimlessly over the chipped wood path; some in animated conversation on park benches; others just standing and staring—maybe lost in the magnificence of childhood—but all of them were watching. If I set foot in that park without a child of my own, every adult in the area would scan me up and down. They'd begin questioning my motives. Some would have their cell phones at the ready.

The park in my rearview mirror, I drove on. I passed a mailbox, a fire hydrant, and a couple of kids hard at work drinking the lemonade from their own stand. Sure enough, a parent sat on the front stoop. I felt like I had just a few more pieces to find to complete a large complicated puzzle, but the person who put the puzzle away last lost the very piece I needed. I knew the sort of piece to look for; I knew its general shape and the types of sockets it had to fill. But it just didn't seem to be there.

The clock on the dash read 12:40. Still hours before Doc Shepherd might be free. I drove on, planning to exit the neighborhood by the next through street. Then, I heard a familiar jingling tune. I slowed and pulled to the curb, waiting. The chiming tune grew louder; it was a springy version of "Do Your Ears Hang Low?" A white truck pulled around the corner. Kids trailed behind it at a safe distance. A few moments after the truck came to a stop, a large side window slid open, and a man with a fuzzy grey mustache leaned out.

The Ice Cream Man.

No, I thought. But it seemed to fit the puzzle. The driver of an ice cream truck wasn't someone parents knew as a general rule, but the appearance of an ice cream truck was as accepted as a thunderstorm. Sometimes it came; sometimes it didn't. Either way, no one really cared, except for the kids. And kids really did care...a lot.

All it took was a few distant jingly notes, and kids from all over the neighborhood would burst from their doors at mach speed. They'd leap fences, cut through yards, and even dodge traffic to get to that white truck. And then, they'd wave cash at the driver. They were doing it right now. Right in front of me.

Smiles everywhere. Smiles from the kids. Smiles from the parents. Smiles from the Ice Cream Man as he handed frozen goodies to the kids. It fit. Kids in every state would throw caution to the wind for the Ice Cream Man. They might even follow the Ice Cream Man into the back of his truck. I grabbed the cell phone, scrolled down to Rez's number, and almost pushed send.

Almost.

The thought scratching at the backdoor of my mind hadn't quite coalesced just yet. Half-conscious of what I was doing, I put the car in drive and made a slow u-turn. I glanced at the crowd still gathered around the Ice Cream Man. It was a good puzzle piece. The colors on the fringes matched, and it seemed to have the right shape. But it didn't quite fit. Smiling Jack and his accomplice might have used the guise of an ice cream truck vendor to bring the kids running. But, if they did, they would also bring witnesses.

I drove back the way I came, passing the lemonade stand, the fire hydrant, and mailbox. I passed the park, now less populated, due to the Ice Cream Man no doubt. When the bells of an ice cream truck rang, lots of people came. Little kids, sure. But also, there were teenagers and even parents. Lots of people liked ice cream.

If little Susie disappeared and the last time anyone saw little Susie was around the ice cream truck, it wouldn't take long for someone to go ask the Ice Cream Man a few pointed questions. Parents would remember their kids blasting out the door. Heck, most of the time that was preceded by kids begging their parents for money to buy ice cream. No, the Ice Cream Man puzzle piece didn't quite fit.

There was something about the little group of kids playing at the sprinkler. Something I had seen but still missed. I knew they wouldn't be there when I returned. The wary mom had tucked them into the backyard and out of sight. But still, I needed to revisit, to see if even the tiniest strand remained for me to grasp. I rolled to a stop at the curb directly across the street from the yard where the children had played.

As I suspected, the sprawling Bermuda grass lawn was empty. I left the car running, scanned the yard, and let my thoughts meander. I figured I had about five minutes before the eagle-eyed parent noticed me again and got nervous enough to call the local police.

"Big family," I muttered, recalling the children bobbing in and out of the sprinkler. A redhead, a couple of brunettes, a blond, a towhead, a...*a diverse family.* That thought arrived, and it felt like a strand, so I pulled. Come to think of it, the woman who came out to keep the kids safe didn't really look much like any of the kids. Maybe the brunette girl. She and the woman had the same long, coltish limbs. But I didn't notice any overt similarities in the rest of the kids. Most of them looked about the same age too. So maybe not a family? Then...then it smacked me in the forehead.

I knew it before I read the little sign in the front yard.

"Little Miracles Family Daycare."

I jammed the car in gear and had the phone dialing Rez in an instant.

She picked up. "Agent Rezva—"

"Daycare," I said. "That's how he did it."

"What?"

"Smiling Jack," I said. "That's how he's done it all these years. He runs a daycare."

"Ghost, that's insane," she said.

"Go back and look at Erica Graziano's file," I said. "She was snatched from a daycare."

"I remember that," she said, "But she was taken *from* the daycare not *by* the daycare."

"You sure about that?" I asked. "Did you crosscheck with the Kearney girl? She was four when she was taken, not quite school age, but perfect—"

"Perfect for daycare." Rez was silent a few tics. "Okay, I'll check it out. But think about this: most daycares are run by women. Sexist as it is, a lot of moms wouldn't trust their kids in a daycare run by men."

{ Chapter 32 }

I THREW THE ASSASSIN'S CAR into park while it was still moving, so it jerked to a stop at the curb. I knew Agent Rezvani would find a way to get the FBI's trillion gigahertz engines to work, but I couldn't leave it just to them. I returned to the Internet cafe where Mr. Scratch had appeared with the butterfly clue. I ducked out of the car, realizing I hadn't noted the cafe's name when I'd come the first time. No small wonder as I was severely diminished by a lengthy travel.

The Bean Machine. Not very clever, but I guess it didn't matter when their coffee was that good and their data transmission rates were that fast. I was grateful to find Melanie again behind the counter. Her lively eyes brightened when she saw me.

"Hey, mister," she said. "You aren't going to slosh the restroom again are you?"

"I wouldn't dream of it," I replied. "Listen, I need a code and more of that incredible coffee you brought me last time? Same deal work for you?" I slid a hundred dollar bill across the counter. My last one. After breakfast, the surf shop, and this, I was officially broke again.

"You got it," she said, blinking and shaking her head. "You just paid for my Econ book next semester."

I sat at the same computer and typed in the access code Melanie had provided. My fingers flew over the keyboard. I searched both the Graziano and the Kearney abductions. And I searched out the most recent Smiling Jack photographs. I found the original article on Erica Graziano and scanned down the page. There it was.

Erica had been playing in the yard at Small Favor's Daycare Center when she'd been taken. The daycare's owner, Martina Palmer, had been quoted as saying, "I'd just called all the children in for lunch. It was grilled cheese, Erica's favorite, so I wondered when she didn't come running."

I finished the article, noting once again the photo of little Erica and her parents. But there was no picture of Martina Palmer or the daycare center. Then, I clicked and browsed a dozen articles on Kearney's abduction. Two years and more than four-thousand miles away, and the two articles were nearly identical in content. Pamela Kearney had also been taken while under the not-so-watchful eye of a daycare provider. This time, her name was Elizabeth Borden of Little Eskimo's Family Daycare. The article's author described Ms. Borden as heartbroken and visibly disturbed by the loss. In fact, Ms. Borden had closed the daycare in order to seek psychiatric help.

As Rez had suggested, both of the daycares were run by women. But on a whim, I searched Little Eskimo's Family Daycare and Borden. Then I clicked on the images search filter. There were several photos: an Easter Egg hunt, a birthday party, a grand opening. One of them showed Elizabeth Borden straight on. She had long hair, pulled back tightly, distant darkish eyes—I couldn't tell the color—and a grim smile. She also looked very familiar to me.

I tabbed to the Smiling Jack photos. I zoomed in on the bottom half of Jack's face, all that was visible. I put it next to Elizabeth Borden. I increased the zoom on both. I shook my head. The chin had a dimple, maybe a cleft chin like Jack's. Maybe. Nothing conclusive. The Smiling Jack photos had more detail, visible wrinkles, what appeared to be a very light 5 o'clock shadow. I began to wonder about Smiling Jack's accomplice. Siblings?

Melanie appeared and blessedly refreshed my mug of dark bliss. I hoped I managed to pop up a new window in time to cover up the Smiling Jack images. Melanie walked away with a normal posture and pace, so I figured all was well. I tilted the computer's thin screen a little and went back to scrutinizing the photos.

I was relatively certain that the FBI had some facial recognition software that could potentially check the features of Elizabeth Borden's face with the lower half of Smiling Jack's face, but to show what? That they are siblings? Rez was right: many parents wouldn't entrust their young children to the care of a man. Too many male predators in the news. That left me with more questions about the daycare providers. Were they just innocent victims like the children who were taken from their centers? Victims like their parents?

There was something else to check, I realized. Something I should have checked first. I minimized the window with Elizabeth Borden. Then I searched: Martina Palmer, Small Favor's Daycare Center. I clicked the filter again for images. I clicked through several shots that didn't seem to have anything to do with the daycare itself: a summer camp with the same name, a snow cone shop, a May Fair at a local elementary school. I refined my search by putting in the name of the city. Similar results. No portrait of the provider herself. Then I added the victim's name and the word abduction.

There was a photograph of interest.

The reporter had snapped the shot from the other side of a waist-high picket fence. Two uniformed police officers stood on the front stoop and, between them, partially obscured by the policemen's broad shoulders, was a woman. She was somewhat gangly, wearing a petite dress that exposed her arms to the shoulder. Her hair was cut in a short bob and, even in black and white, she seemed to be wearing heavy make up: dark lips, plenty of blush, and stark eyeliner. But it was those eyes that struck me.

I zoomed in, but too far and it blurred out the detail I wanted to see. I pulled back and moved the window to the side. Then I brought back the window for Elizabeth Borden. I put them side-by-side.

"Brimstone hammers," I muttered. "It's the same woman."

I didn't need the FBI's facial recognition apps to know for certain. If you've ever seen eyes like these, you don't forget them; you don't mistake them. They were cold eyes; brutally cold and intelligent. Killer's eyes.

I couldn't say whether this woman was Smiling Jack's assistant or if she was actually the killer in all the photographs, the killer we'd always assumed was a man. But I now knew the face of one of the killers. As I dialed Rez to give her the information, I glanced back at the face on my screen. I felt a peculiar tingle trickle along my spine. It wasn't déjà vu, but it was something close. I'd seen her before...somewhere.

*** *** *** ***

"This is brilliant work!" Deputy Director Barnes bellowed, smacking his palm on the conference room table. "LePoast, get in here!"

"Sir?" he said. A line of sweat already trickled down his forehead. He saw Rez and averted his eyes.

"Agent Rezvani made a breakthrough," he said. "We can tell the geeks we have a new angle for Smiling Jack."

"Geeks, sir?"

"Aw, crap, LePoast, don't get all PC on me now," Barnes grumbled. "The techno weanies downstairs and their Big-Blue-wannabe computers!"

"Right, Sir," LePoast said. "What's the new angle?"

"Tell him," Barnes said.

Rez exhaled and said, "He's snatching them from daycares."

"From daycares?" LePoast repeated. "The Smiling Jack killer preyed on daycare kids?"

"Think about it," Barnes said. "Easy surveillance. He can pose as a prospective parent, look around the place, figure out a plan. Then, when the kid's not being watched, he's got her."

"But, Sir," Rez said. "It's not just that the victims were both taken as children from daycares. The daycare providers of the two victims...I'm almost positive they're the same person. We need to go all points on this woman. She's—"

"That's crap, Agent Rezvani," Barnes said bluntly. "But you got it right with the daycare angle. I can feel it. LePoast, tell the geeks to narrow their search to kidnappings that occurred at daycares in and around the dates they already have. Then get'em to do some of that digital aging nonsense to see if we can match up more of the Smiling Jack photographs with missing children."

"Yessir," LePoast replied and was gone.

"Sir, with all due respect," Rez said. "We're missing an opportunity. We've got a photo of Smiling Jack—"

"So Smiling Jack is a woman?" Barnes barked. "You know the odds in serial murder. So there's a woman out there kidnapping girls, raising them, and then cutting their throats? Oh, and wait, this same woman ran the daycare in Shreveport and in Anchorage? So, what's she do, Rezvani, open a daycare for each victim she takes?"

Rez opened her mouth but let it snap shut. *No way he'll buy into the Presidential election theory,* she thought. She spun on her heels and darted out of the conference room.

"Where you going?" Barnes voice demanded from behind her.

"I have a call to make," she growled back.

*** *** *** ***

"Thank you for not holding an old man's idiosyncrasies against him," Doc Shepherd said. "I was out of line before, Agent Spector, and for that I apologize."

"No apologies necessary," I said. "You've a sharp mind and a keen eye. I'm glad you're on our side. Oh, and technically, I'm not an agent. I'm more of a utility officer."

"You must have a broad definition of utility," Doc Shepherd quipped.

"I'm more of a Swiss Army Knife," I said. "I do things that need doing with whatever I have available. I'm hoping you have something for me today."

Doc Shepherd adjusted his bow tie, this time DayGlo green with navy blue squiggles running through. "I'm not certain this will be of use to you," he said. "I suspect you know that I gave Agent Rezvani the list of Cain's Dagger owners. And...I suspect at this point, you've already delved deeply into their histories and current owners."

"The FBI has," I said. "Unfortunately, we haven't discovered any evidence to implicate anyone in the crimes. Not yet, at least."

"Yes, well," Doc said, giving his handlebar mustache a twirl, "I wondered if I might expand my search a bit. I paid my Uncle Timothy a visit, and he discovered something that could possibly be of use."

"Another Cain's Dagger owner? One we didn't know of before?"

"No," Doc replied. "A bit more than that. You recall our initial conversation about the Cain's Dagger blade?" I nodded. He went on. "My Uncle Timothy did some digging in the company that created the original. Turns out, the company went under at the turn of the century."

"I thought they were still in operation today."

"That's what I thought initially," Doc said. "The original owners of the company had no choice but to sell out to a competitor. The competitor went on to use the original blade and the company name. When the economy in England improved, they...if you'll pardon the expression...they made a killing."

"Not sure if I can pardon that one."

"Granted. It was poor." Doc smiled ruefully. "In any case, Uncle Timothy, he may not be able to get up and around very well—arthritis stole his legs—but no one I know can scour the digital landscape like he can. He set to work tracking down the original owners of the company. It was family owned for more than a hundred years."

"I don't suppose there are any living descendant living here in the States? Descendants who might have access to a Cain's Dagger?"

"As a matter of fact, there is such a person. Three as a matter of fact. They are Winifred Lacy Drew, Captain Arnold Lacy USAF retired, and Dr. Garrison Albert Lacy, but you might want to take a particularly long look at Dr. Lacy."

"And why's that?"

"Dr. Lacy is an abortion pioneer of some renown in the Floridian medical community," Doc Shepherd said. "Strike that. Renown is far too kind a word. Notorious is more accurate. I met him once. Garrulous, arrogant man."

"Where can I find him?"

"I suspect you'll find Dr. Lacy at the Pryiam Regency Convention Hall in Pensacola at about 7:30 this evening." Doc Shepherd twirled his mustache and raised an eyebrow. "You'll find me there as well, but for very different reasons. It's the Medical Innovators Awards Ceremony. Regrettably, Dr. Lacy will likely be receiving the board's highest honor: the Agnes Armistice Award."

I thought for a moment, glanced at the clock, and then thought a bit more. "I don't suppose you could acquire two tickets to the awards event for me, could you?"

Doc Shepherd looked as if he'd been waiting all day for me to ask. His frosty-clear blue eyes twinkled as he slid an envelope across the desk to me. "I thought you might ask," he said.

"Again, I'm glad you're on our side," I said.

"Thinking of bringing a date?" he asked mischievously. "It should be a marvelous party."

Laughing softly, I said, "I have someone in mind."

***   ***   ***   ***

"You what?" Agent Rezvani's blurted response practically burst from the cell phone.

"Is it so hard for you to imagine?" I asked, keeping my voice flat. "I'm asking you to a dance."

"Look, Spector," she said, "I am five minutes from my hotel room where I fully intend to pass out. What are you playing at?"

I told her what I'd learned from Doc Shepherd. I told her about the MIAC event and the guest of honor.

"I'm in," she said.

"It's formal," I said.

"Meet me at the mall in Pensacola."

***   ***   ***   ***

"Some date you are," Agent Rezvani said. "Making me pay for your tuxedo isn't very chivalrous, you know."

"I trust you're billing this to the Bureau?"

"Yes," she replied, frowning. "My gown as well, but that's beside the point."

"If I had the means," I said, "I would pay for it all."

"Holy smokes," she said. "I just realized: you don't have your silver suitcase."

I tried to hide the grimace I felt coming on. "It doesn't go well with a tuxedo," I said.

"What happened to it...really?"

"It's a long story," I said, closing the subject. "And we have work to do."

{ Chapter 33 }

WE SAT IN THE PARKING LOT of the Pryiam Regency, Pensacola's posh hotel and convention center, and disagreed.

"We don't engage," Rez said flatly. "We don't antagonize. We have a theory; that's all. Dr. Lacy could be as innocent as a lamb."

"Hardly," I bristled. "He's performed thousand of abortions."

"Leave your politics out of this," Rez said.

"I don't have politics."

"Whatever. I'll do the talking. We'll measure him, figure out what we can, and then...then, we'll go from there."

"We'll need to push him," I argued. "How else are we going to get anywhere?"

"We stir something up in there," Rez said, "and we'll have Pryiam security escorting us outside in a heartbeat."

"And what if everything falls into place? What if we can make a positive ID?"

Rez looked at me as if I'd just said something in Swahili. "If we...?" she spluttered. "If Dr. Lacy is Smiling Jack...we call it in. We take him down in the parking lot after the ceremony."

I sat still and silent for several halting heartbeats. I needed to swallow back the rage, needed to keep any trace of it from my words. "Agent Rezvani," I said, "when we began this case, I told you, I don't subscribe to the usual channels. I don't follow the usual protocols. If we've got the right guy, and we mess this up, other young women will die. I will not risk losing the opportunity."

Maybe it was my imagination, but it seemed like I was watching the chill ripple up Rez's limber arms. I watched her eyes in the glow of the dash. They seemed to harden as if frozen in the pale blue light. She blinked once. Her eyes darted a moment, and then she looked up at me again. I thought maybe she'd reached some kind of decision, and I wondered if she'd tell me what it was.

"We don't attempt the takedown inside," Rez said firmly. "No matter what. Even if we're certain that we've got Smiling Jack, we don't spook him. He might start shooting or take a hostage. We don't risk that. If we play it cool, we'll have a chance to get him here in the lot, after the ceremony."

I nodded approval, but I didn't think we were anywhere close to the same page.

The Edge felt strange in the baggy tuxedo pants. It slid in the pocket over my thigh as I climbed out of Rez's SUV. Rez told me she had her Glock on her, but I couldn't tell where. She wore a sleek, dark crimson gown that tied decoratively at her right hip. The material had a kind of shimmer to it, like running water under starlight, and it undulated as she walked. Glided is a better word. Even in formal heels, she moved effortlessly. The little purse in her palm—that had to be it. Had to be where she'd hidden the Glock.

"Take my arm," she said. "You are my date, after all."

GHOST

I did as I was told. I noticed two things: the muscle in her arm was very taut, and her skin was quite cold.

*** *** *** ***

The Pryiam Regency was the size of a Roman cathedral. We entered its cavernous atrium and blended into a sea of formal evening wear. It was a distinguished-looking crowd. Lots of 140+ IQs and lots of money. I noticed more than a few of the gentlemen guests allowing their eyes to drift from their dates to Agent Rezvani. One of them, an older man who looked a little like Colonel Sanders, took a sharp flick to the ear from the woman on his arm.

At the ballroom entrance, a monstrous gilded sign declared we'd arrived at the 33rd Annual Medical Innovators Awards Ceremony. White crystal chandeliers blazed from the high vaulted ceiling inside. Silken drapes framed rows of floor-to-ceiling windows on the far wall. And a lively buzz mingled with jazzy notes from the nattily garbed swing band off to the side of the stage. Given the decor and the atmosphere, it felt more like an international event than a celebration of Florida's best and brightest.

I handed the tickets to one of the two burly ballroom attendants standing at the door. "Guests of Doctor Shepherd," he said, giving me a brief once-over. He handed back the tickets. "Welcome to the Pryiam Regency. Your table is nineteen A." He gave Rez a once-over as well, but not what I would call brief.

We made our way to the table and found Doc Shepherd and a handful of his guests actively engaged in conversation over a variety of hors d'oeuvres and beverages. His eyes twinkled up from the rim of his champagne glass. "Ah, Dr. Spector," he said. "And this must be your lovely wife."

Rez shot me a sharp look. I decided to be a perfect gentleman. "Yes, yes," I said, making a sweeping gesture with one hand. "Allow me to introduce Dr. Deanna Spector. We met in medical school, you see. Our eyes met over a cadaver, and we knew it was love."

We sat down amidst jovial rolling laughter. I didn't look at Rez and, maybe I imagined it, but it felt as if scorching beams of flame were torching my neck and shoulder on Rez's side.

Doc Shepherd made introductions. "This is my lovely wife Aurora," he said, putting his arm around the shoulder of a slender pixy of a woman. She wore her silver hair down with a single French braid curling around back like a velvet rope at a theater. She might have been older than her husband, but the wrinkles she bore seemed to be from frequent smiles and laughter, giving her a girlish look. Her dark eyes glistened with enthusiasm. Her relaxed posture and easy smile spoke of rich contentment. She and Doc were quite a pair.

He went on with his introductions. "This is Doctor Kane and his wife Doctor Kane," he said. "The preeminent cosmetic surgeons of Florida, two time winners of the Triple A, and known the world over as tops in their field."

"Triple A?" I echoed.

"The Agnes Armistice Award," Doc replied. "Reason we are all here. Who will win tonight, I wonder." He gave me a subtle wink. After introducing us to the rest of the table, successful surgeons all, he leaned in close and whispered, "I believe the doctor you're looking for is seated at the table near the front, closest to the bar."

I didn't want to draw unnecessary attention by darting up from our seats so soon, so I decided to sample the platter of cheese and crackers that served as the hub of our table. I recognized Muenster, pepper jack, smoked cheddar, and Havarti, but

GHOST

there were several cheeses that I'd never tasted before. One of them, a mustard yellow cheese with a golden brown rind, tasted of creamy butter, garlic, and onion. I found it remarkable.

"Darling," Agent Rezvani said, sounding as if she'd spoken through her teeth, "you might want to save some cheese for everyone else."

I realized I'd stacked my small plate like an Aztec pyramid. It had attracted some attention from the other guests at our table.

"You eat all that," the male Dr. Kane said, "you might need to come see us."

The female Dr. Kane laughed and said, "Yes, our lipo techniques are state-of-the-art."

"Sweetheart," Rez said, "you're blushing."

"Touché," I whispered.

An hour later, the meal was punctuated with a variety of splendid cheesecakes. I pushed my chair out from the table and said, "Deanna, I think I'll indulge in an after-dinner drink. Care to join me?" I stood and held out my arm. She took it and we made our way toward the bar.

The bartender was a tall angular woman with a glistening stud in her nose and her dark hair tied back so tightly it looked painful. Rez flowed up to the bar and ordered a cranberry juice and a ginger ale. She took the drinks and handed me the ginger ale. Then, she gestured at the table behind us and asked the bartender, "Do you know which one of these doctors is Dr. Lacy?"

The bartender smirked and said, "Dark red wine...the guy with the Drew Carey glasses."

Rez thanked the bartender and turned back to me. "How'd you know to ask?"

"I didn't know," Rez said. "But I figured, a swank event like this, management would make sure the help knew all the big-shots." She shrugged and made a wide circle toward the table. I followed.

We stood, our backs mostly to the stage, but at a natural angle for conversation. I scanned the table and found the man with the Drew Carey glasses and the dark red wine. In spite of the frames, Dr. Lacy looked anything but comedic. He had a square jaw and thin lips set somewhere between grim and thoughtful. His cheekbones were bony and prominent. His hair was close cropped, a dark brown flecked with sand and gray. His thick brows and mustache seemed darker, almost black, and his eyes were striking: dark and intense, exuding confidence. His tanned face was weathered and might be considered handsome in an avant-garde, middle aged kind of way.

But there was nothing aged or weak in his build. It might have been the cut of his tuxedo, but everything about the man looked broad and strong. Even his hands looked powerful: skin taut, knuckles large and knobby, fingers thick. It looked like with the barest squeeze, he could shatter the wine glass he held.

To his right was an older gentleman who seemed unable to speak without laughing at the same time. A chair waited empty at Lacy's left, and satin-haired beauty wearing an emerald gown sat a seat away.

"May I help you?" someone asked, the voice low and gritty without sacrificing crisp diction.

"I'm sorry," I said, turning to face Dr. Lacy more directly. "Was I staring?"

"You certainly were," he said. "You appeared so entranced I feared you might be having a petit mal seizure." There was a ripple of knowing laughter around the table.

I swiveled to Agent Rezvani. "See," I said, "I told you he'd be here."

GHOST

Agent Rezvani played her part beautifully. "Are...are you Dr. Lacy?" she asked.

"I am," Dr. Lacy replied. He wasn't nearly as puffed up as I thought he'd be. He seemed studious and a little annoyed.

"Dr. Garrison Lacy?" she asked. "The abortion surgery pioneer?"

That apparently hit closer to the mark. "The very same," Dr. Lacy replied, a hint of a smile appearing briefly. "What can I do for you, miss...?"

"Deanna," she said, then blinked and shook her head. "I mean, Doctor Deanna—Doctor Rezvani, I mean. I was...well, I was hoping I could visit your clinic some time. I'd very much like to observe your post operative patient care."

"Just post operative?" he asked, the smile vanishing instantly.

"Well, no," Agent Rezvani said. "I didn't mean to imply that, really...it's just—"

"Dr. Rezvani," Lacy said. "This really isn't the time or place. Why don't you make an appointment and we can discuss a time for you to come and observe."

"Yes, of course," Rez said. Color me impressed. Rez could blush on cue. She ducked her heady shyly and started to turn away, but then said, "Oh, and I just wanted you to know that I am so very appreciative of your stance. You are a true champion of a woman's right to choose."

Dr. Lacy didn't smile on cue. He simply gave a curt nod of the head, his dark eyes never leaving Agent Rezvani. It seemed to me that there was far more than lust in that glare. I started to say something to the good doctor, when Rez took hold of my arm. She smiled sweetly but hissed, "Come back to the table!"

I followed closely behind her and we passed awkwardly through several dozen doctors and their dates dancing. We found our table empty. The moment we were seated, I demanded, "Why'd you rush? We didn't pin him down with anything."

Rez scowled darkly. "Look," she said, "I don't know how you rose up through the ranks in your organization, but I worked my tail off to make Special Agent. I don't suck at this."

I exhaled loudly. Pride was a waste of time. I needed information. "What did you get, then?"

"He's not Smiling Jack," Rez said. "Did you see a cleft chin?"

"No," I admitted. "I focused on his eyes. Smiling Jack definitely had a cleft chin. That why you made an early exit—he's not our guy?"

"He might still be," she said. "Not Jack, but the accomplice."

"But you didn't push," I said. "He didn't say anything."

"It wasn't what he said," Rez explained. "I thought his reactions were off. Here he is at the biggest awards ceremony of the year, and he's likely to win. When I approach him like some star-struck groupie, he ought to be delirious with pride. That's not what I got from his glare. You?"

"Suspicion."

Rez nodded approvingly. "He knew I was acting," she said. "But he doesn't see that, doesn't catch on, unless he's running everything through a certain filter." She took another sip of her cranberry juice. "Not enough to be sure."

It wasn't enough for me to be sure either. But at this point, I'd had all I could swallow of uncertainty. I said, "I'm going to go find out."

I stood and shook off Rez's cautioning touch. "I won't hurt him," I said. "I won't even threaten him...overtly." She started to speak, but I cut her off. "Look, Rez, I didn't get this mission by accident. I don't suck at this either."

I left her, open-mouthed and fuming. I leaned forward and charged across the dance floor. When I reached Dr. Lacy's table,

GHOST

there was a woman in the previously unoccupied seat next to him. Her back was to me. Dr. Lacy seemed about to say something to the gray bearded man on his right, but then his eyes met mine and he scowled.

And when I say *scowl*, I do not mean the garden variety scowl: slight displeasure, lips downturned, eyebrows slightly beetled, and a disdainful tilt of the head. No, this was full-on malice. His eyes bulged, emphasizing the darkness; brows furrowed near the point of meeting over the bridge of his nose; his lips, all the muscle of his cheeks and clenching jaws combined in the sort of snarling, tilted sneer you save for lifelong enemies.

"What...do...you...want?" Dr. Lacy asked, practically spitting each word. "Wasn't one interruption of my evening enough?"

"I know this isn't the time or place," I said, determined to play the role to the end. "But I'm only in town for a few more days, and I'd heard that you're the local authority on abortion procedures."

"This is true," he said. "Shame you have to depart so soon." He went to turn away, but I held him with my eyes.

"Ah...well, you know how it is," I said. "Anyway, knowing your expertise and your history, I thought you might have an interest in something that has recently come into my possession."

"And what might that be?"

"It's a turn of the century surgical knife that was used for abortions," I said, watching his eyes carefully. "I believe it was once called a Cain's Dagger."

If his expression changed at all, it was a mellowing of the scowl to something closer to relief. That and his eyes. They seemed to shrink a little. He didn't reply immediately at least, not to me. He whispered to his left, and the woman turned around.

{ 367 }

A fist of bile leaped up into my throat. My right hand went involuntarily to my pocket, and I found my fingers wrapping around The Edge. *Not here,* I told myself urgently. *Too many people could get hurt.*

"May I introduce my beloved partner Jacqueline Gainer," he said.

She looked up at me expectantly and smiled. "Call me Jack," she said, holding out her hand demurely. "Everyone who knows me does."

Smiling Jack. There he was, or rather *she* was. Cleft chin...cleft chin and killer's eyes.

Red herring after red herring...Smiling Jack had gotten away with murder for more than a decade by feeding law enforcement what they thought they knew and sending them searching for wild geese that they'd never find.

I took her hand properly and gave a slight nod. Before I released her hand, I gave it a not-so-proper squeeze. "Partner?" I said, then releasing her from my grip. "As in at the clinic?"

"No, as in life," Dr. Lacy said. "Marriage is such an antiquated notion. Who needs God or man to sanction the love we share?"

I started to answer, but a finger tapped a microphone, sounding like a subwoofer-rattling bass drum on the too-loud PA system. "Good evening," said a slight, bespectacled man on stage. "Welcome to the fifty-seventh annual Medical Innovators Awards Ceremony." Loud applause. He started to tell more than I ever wanted to know about the ceremony and former doctors recognized by the award.

I waited for a brief pause, caught Dr. Lacy in my gaze, and asked, "What do you think about Senator Esperanzo becoming President?"

"I try to stay out of politics," Lacy hissed.

GHOST

"Think about the knife. I'll be in touch."

Dr. Lacy replied, "No, you won't." And the PA speaker began again.

I walked slowly back to Doc Shepherd's table, and I could feel the killers' eyes on my back and neck, unpleasant and hot. I stopped walking.

You're gonna burn.

The realization hit me like a comet. I had had her right at the start. The camera hadn't washed inland from the Gulf. She had gone to that stone jetty and tossed it into the turquoise water herself. I laughed at myself. I'd seen her crouching there and had even mistook her for a man, initially.

Jacqueline Gainer. Smiling Jack.

As much as I wanted to slug myself in the jaw, I couldn't afford to dwell in the past. There had been no way for me to know, or so I told myself. I sat down at Doc Shepherd's table a little heavier than I meant to.

"Dr. Spector, are you well?" Doc Shepherd asked. "You look pallid, like you've seen a ghost."

I looked up at Doc and forced a smile. "I'm fine," I said. "I think all that cheese is catching up to me."

Doc laughed and turned back to his wife. Rez looked at me intently. "What did you do?" she demanded, a little too firmly for my comfort.

"I didn't *do* anything," I said. "But I confirmed *everything*. Dr. Lacy is the accessory. Smiling Jack is his wi—partner. She came back to the table. It's them."

"She?"

"His partner is Jacqueline Gainer, but she goes by Jack."

"How can you be sure?" Rez asked.

I told her. I told her all of it: the dialogue, the exchanged recognition, the strange smiles—even the cleft chin.

"That's not a lot to go on," Rez said, though with little conviction.

I said, "It's enough for me."

"What are you going to do?" she asked.

"I'm going to wait until the ceremony is over, and I'm going to take them down."

"Into custody?"

"For a time," I said. "I need to find out where they have the other girls...if they're even still alive."

"And how are you going to get them to tell you that?" she asked.

I stared at her.

Rez stared at her empty cranberry juice glass. We sat in uncomfortable silence. Well, silence between us. The PA announcer went on and on and on. Now, he was beginning to speak the praises of this year's winner, making vague references that I thought sure were meant to describe Dr. Garrison Lacy.

Rez excused herself to the restroom and returned moments later. "Okay," she said. "I'm with you. But promise me you won't...you won't do anything permanent until we have the other victims safe."

I promised, and she seemed content.

***   ***   ***   ***

This year's Medical Innovator Award went to Dr. Garrison Lacy. The bile in my throat was viscous and burning.

Rez and I waited through his acceptance speech. We waited through two hours of dancing. We waited and watched as the hall began to empty. Dr. Lacy and his partner seemed in no hurry. That surprised me.

GHOST

But with the clock hitting midnight, their table began to disperse. We said our goodbyes to Doc Shepherd and his friends and followed our quarry. They did not exit by the Pryiam Regency's main entrance. They took a side hallway and headed past scores of rooms toward a distant glowing exit sign.

"This way," Rez whispered. "We'll cut through the pool exit and circle back to them."

She held open the door. I walked into the pool room, steamy with humidity and sharp with the smell of strong chlorine. We rounded the pool and strode across the concrete to the exit.

Rez darted through the door ahead of me. I followed. The moment I cleared the doorframe, I felt a gun barrel pressed up against my neck. There were at least a dozen men in dark suits around me. Each one: weapon drawn, Weaver stance, ready to fire at any unusual move from me.

"John Spector," came a deep voice. "You are under arrest."

{ Chapter 34 }

BETRAYAL.
In my line of work, it comes with the territory. My boss had to deal with it. My boss's boss had to deal with it. Shoot, even the creator of the whole branch had to deal with it, and his was the worst I'd ever heard of. I knew I wasn't going to be exempt. Still, it didn't prepare me for the event itself and all the complications it presented.

I'd just barely had enough time to hit the custom safety on The Edge before the FBI agents cuffed me and took the weapon from me. As they shoved me unceremoniously into the back of a black SUV, I thought maybe I should have left the safety off. Serve them right to cut off a few fingers.

The truck roared away, and I jounced around the back seat. "Whatever happened to Serve and Protect?" I groused.

"That's police," came the driver's rough voice. "Fidelity, Bravery, and Integrity, that's us. Now shut it!" The agent in the passenger seat as well as the two in the second seat got a hearty chuckle out of that.

I nodded. *Right, right.* Rez had told me that already. It was the lack of integrity she'd shown in turning me in that threw me off. "You mind telling me the charges?"

"Felony interference with a Federal case, for starters," the agent closest to me said. He had coppery hair cut high and tight and wore sunglasses. It was past midnight, and he was wearing sunglasses.

"Maybe accessory to murder too," the passenger agent said. He had dark hair in a tight tail and a smirk that never seemed to disappear.

"I get the interference," I said. "But accessory to murder? That's a stretch."

"Not if the evidence at the butterfly place pans out," Pony Boy replied. "Agent Rezvani said the evidence would put you at the scene. Footprints in the blood."

Ouch. That stung even more.

"What about the suspects?" I asked.

"What suspects?" Sunglass Man asked.

"He means the doc and his arm candy," Pony Boy said. "Rezvani was all uppity that we take them into custody."

"Did you?" I asked, probably sounding too eager, too desperate.

"Playing your part till the end, eh?" Pony Boy asked. "Whatever. Nah, they shook our tail. We lost'em. But we got you."

For fifteen minutes, I fumed there in the backseat. The Smiling Jack killers knew me. They knew I knew them. Whatever they had planned, whatever their timeline, it had just been shoved into overdrive. And it was my fault. Maybe they'd immediately kill any captives they had left, or maybe, they'd just disappear and start over. I considered my options. There weren't many.

GHOST

I could ride with the FBI, let them book me, and then attempt an escape. Or, I could completely blow my cover, escape now, and be the subject of paranormal news media for a decade. Or, I could wait and see: let them book me and see if the FBI could manage not to screw up the takedown of the Smiling Jack killers. I shook my head and released a steamy, exasperated laugh. Any of the options could jeopardize my mission. For all I knew, it could already be too late.

"Here we are!" the driver announced cheerily. "Your new home for awhile awaits."

I looked out the window at a multiple story, gray stone building that looked like an architect's attempt at modern art—that failed—actually resembling a child's attempt to stack blocks. I read the low spot lit sign in the front lawn: Pensacola Police Department. "Police?" I asked. "What's the matter, no room at the FBI inn?"

"Funny guy," said Sunglass Man as he stepped out into the blazing glare of starlight. "If there's no local FBI field office, we often make use of the local police department. Their accommodations might be a little less comfy, but I suppose you don't mind."

I didn't mind at all. Escaping a police jail was bound to be easier than breaking out of an FBI holding tank.

Processing went quickly, I thought. Mostly, the agents just flashed badges and moved me through the building. Just a skeleton crew was on duty at the Pensacola P.D. I counted nine officers from the help desk all the way to the cell blocks. One of the nine, the staff sergeant on duty, an officer named Barker, led us through the building.

"You have a special place in the jail for Mr. Spector here?" Sunglass Man asked.

"We prefer to call them incarceration facilities," Barker said, feigning an English accent. "We are rather full tonight, but yes, we shall find him a spot."

Somehow, everyone but me seemed to discover humor in my capture and confinement. We ascended a flight of black stairs, our shoes creating a strange staccato echo that followed us into a wide hall. Two guards were posted at the cellblock gate. One of them buzzed us in.

"12 A," Barker said as we passed through.

Dim recessed lights made an eerie trail of light and shadow between the cells that lined both sides of the hall. Just my luck. All the inmates seemed to be very interested in the new arrival. A woman with stringy hair and a pinched face struck a pose behind the bars. "Hey, baby," she cooed.

I looked away and found myself staring into the bloodshot eyes of a massive African-American man in the adjacent cell to my right. When I say massive, I mean he was four hundred pounds if he was an ounce. He looked at me like I was a snack.

The next cell contained what I took to be a sleeping vagrant. A Hispanic man wearing a very well tailored, expensive gray suit paced in the opposite cell. In the span of moments it took me to pass by his cell, he glanced at his wristwatch six times. Maybe he was due to be bailed out soon. Maybe it was just a nervous habit.

The third cell on the left held a wispy young woman with strawberry blond hair. She looked up from her weeping just long enough to meet my eyes. Inexplicably, I read her. Why her? I don't know. I never know. But I said the first thing that came to my mind: "He hears you." She wept even louder then.

"What'd that mean?" Barker asked.

"Stick around my cell for a bit," I said. "Happy to explain."

Barker shrugged, and we continued down the long hall.

GHOST

I didn't know at the time why all the inmates on that floor left such an impression on me. They just did. All eleven of them.

There was the angry young man with all the tattoos who cursed at me; the African-American woman who stood in the corner of her cell and mumbled; black-leather-chapped biker who could have been stunt double for ZZ-Top; the guy with huge, bulging eyes who stared at me from the shadows of his cot; the Dominican bodybuilder whose cell could scarcely contain him, much less his white undershirt tank; and finally, there was the nervous man. He looked to be in his middle forties. He spent half the time shaking his head; the other half running his hands through his thinning hair. He looked like a family man, maybe a guy who had one too many at the company party and tried to drive home anyway.

"Here we are," Barker said. "Your penthouse awaits. We call it 12 A."

I stepped into the cell, and I must have been smiling because Pony Boy said, "Get that smug look off your face."

Sunglass Man added, "Think you know something we don't?"

"Doesn't much matter," Barker said. "You're gonna be here a while."

I said nothing. The truth was, I did know something they didn't know. I knew those cell bars wouldn't hold me, and I knew exactly what it would take for me to free myself.

The cell door slammed home. I heard the lock mechanism trigger. Barker and the Feds left me. I saw the family man across from me staring. As soon as our eyes met, he looked away, started rocking on his feet, and ran his hands through his hair again. I felt bad for the man. I felt bad for every person I'd seen. While I'd never discount a person's personal responsibility for his actions, I also knew that many people had rougher starts than some others. And many a rough start led to a rough path and a rough end.

I waited my best estimate of five minutes after the cell block gate closed. I stood up and inspected the bars of my cell. It was 16 or 18 gauge stainless steel. I wrapped my fingers around the bars and felt the tension. Definitely steel.

"Thinking of breaking out?" the family man asked.

I just looked at him and smiled. But my smile vanished instantly. The steel bars began to vibrate.

***   ***   ***   ***

"Judge Deacon came through!" Culbert shouted as he emerged from the FBI's temporary offices. "We got the warrant for search and seizure."

"It's about time!" Barnes thundered. He nodded to the task force commander, a sniper named Kelly Phippen.

"Phipps," as they called her, made a propeller motion over her head, and her squad of sixteen poured into the waiting vans and SUVs.

Agent Rezvani watched with fascination as the hornets' nest of activity raced around her. But, as the group thinned, it seemed that each agent had a designated task. Rez had waited patiently, assuming she'd be riding shotgun with the Deputy Director. But when he hopped into the lead SUV and hadn't even glanced in Rez's direction, she knew something was wrong.

"Not again," she hissed. She ran up to the SUV just in time for the door to shut in her face. She rapped hard on the window.

Barnes rolled down the window. "What are you doin', Rezvani?"

She stammered, "Well, I...you...I thought—"

"Get in!" Barnes growled.

Rezvani blinked. "Oh," she said. Without another moment's hesitation, she jumped into the second seat and slammed the door.

***   ***   ***   ***

It was a faint vibration at first, passing from the stainless steel bars into the flesh of my palm. I flung my hands back from the bars.

"Shocked you, did they?" the family man said, wringing his hands together. "I know those guys don't screw around, but electrifying the bars? That's just wrong, man."

I shook my head. "It wasn't them."

"Huh?" The guy blinked at me. "Whaddaya...whaddaya mean?"

"Sir, I don't know what you've done—"

"DUI," he said.

I raised a hand to shush him. "Sir, there's about to be a serious problem here," I said. "Your life depends on you hiding now. Get under your cot and make yourself as small as possible."

This man was nobody's fool, save perhaps when he'd been drinking. I didn't have to tell him twice. Almost before I finished my sentence, he dove beneath his cot. His hand shot out and grabbed the corner of a jacket so that it draped over the end of the cot. Unless you went into the cell and looked around, I didn't think you'd see him.

"Stay down," I said. "Don't make a sound." I cringed. The itching, electrical aura penetrated the soles of my shoes and clambered up my shins.

The overhead lights began to flicker. "Blood and brimstone!" I muttered in disbelief. I didn't understand this thing that was happening. A small rational part of my mind identified the threat, but I couldn't rationalize that something out of ancient legend could be real. I'd seen what I'd seen outside the Butterfly Conservatory. I'd felt it then as I did now. But this time, I was completely trapped.

But I knew my priorities. I'd save as many of them as I could. Frantically, I searched my cell. There wasn't much to work with. I did the only thing I could think of to do: I tossed the top sheet and the meager mattress onto the floor and tore the cot's metal frame from its old anchor points on the wall. Then, I raised a spectacular ruckus.

Again and again, I slammed the cot's frame across the bars. The sound was a combination of grating metallic shrieks and trembling clangs. In between, I heard the other inmates stirring.

"Listen to me!" I cried out. "Shut up, right now, and LISTEN!" I'd allowed my voice to alter on the last word to a decibel just above thunder. The cellblock became silent.

"I don't have time to explain!" I yelled. "Something's coming in here, and if you don't hide, you are going to die!"

"Guards!" an inmate roared. "What's this lunatic on?"

"Yo, Parker, get yo—"

Then came the gunshots.

And the screams.

***   ***   ***   ***

Rez was glad to be out of the evening gown and into tactical gear. That slime Klingler had tried to cop a look from the rear view mirror as she changed, but Barnes had cuffed his ear. Hard too, and the memory gave her a bit of sadistic joy.

She took the little Glock from her purse and tucked it into the waistline of the black utility pants at the small of her back.

She missed her Sig Sauer, but was familiar enough to be effective with the Beretta 9 mm. Barnes had provided her.

"This is it," the Deputy Director called from the front seat. "Phipps goes in first. We follow."

The SUV ground to a halt. Four doors opened, and all four passengers rushed out into the teeming night. A single streetlight burned overhead...for a moment.

Phipps took it out with one shot from a silenced handgun. She made numerous signals with her hands, and her team fled like spirits toward the home of Dr. Garrison Lacy and his partner in life, Jacqueline Gainer.

Watching the tactical team work, Rez wondered if she hadn't sold herself short by taking the investigative career path. Phipps had her team moving with mechanical precision. No, it was better than that. It was the organic precision of a human body, the deliberate inhaling and exhaling, the fueling of blood cells with oxygen, and the fluid motion of those life-enriched cells coursing to their destinations. In moments, the tactical team covered every possible exit from the house.

Rez knelt by the SUV's back bumper and took a deep breath. This was it: the moment for which she had worked and waited all those years. She'd tied herself in knots over the Smiling Jack killings. First, with the agony of the young women being slaughtered; then, with the dueling barbs of inadequacy and frustration at the paucity of evidence; and finally with the exasperation of having it all declared a hoax—Rez had dwelt in a living hell. Sure, there had been dozens of other assignments, but the Smiling Jack case was always there in the back of her mind, lingering like a black spider in a dusty corner.

Rez switched her Cobra 2-way radio on and popped in the earpiece. There wouldn't be much chatter until they were inside, but Rez didn't want to miss a moment. Several heartbeats passed. There was a single click. Then, Armageddon.

Glass shattered. Flash-bang grenades overwhelmed the darkness with phosphorus white and ruined the silence like a host of wrecking balls. The next thing Rez knew, the tactical team had bludgeoned their way through the front door of the home.

"Den, clear."

"Living room clear."

"Kitchen and dining room, clear."

"First floor clear."

It went on like that for several seconds as the team scoured the home. But, with each territory cleared, Rez began to wonder. There were no shots fired. No loud commands of "Get down on the floor!" The icy finger of doubt slid down her spine.

"Bedroom one, clear."

"Second floor, clear."

"Wait," someone said. "I've got an elevator shaft. Back of the kitchen by the pantry."

Another voice: "Door's stuck open on an overturned trash can."

"Caution, Phipps," Barnes said. It startled Rez because his voice was right behind her *and* on the 2-way. She hadn't seen him circle back around the SUV.

"Roger that, sir," Phipps returned.

Rez shivered from more than the chill in the night air. She could only imagine stalking around the home of serial killers in the dark.

"Elevator panel shows there's a basement level."

"No stairs?" Phipps asked.

"Negative. Take it?"

"Barnes?" Phipps asked. "Your call."

GHOST

"You have a plan?" the Deputy Director asked.

"Yes, sir," Phipps replied.

"Do it."

For nearly a full minute, Rez heard nothing but a few clicks. Then: "Some kind of combination of turns," someone said.

"Turning what?" Phipps asked.

"Key," the other returned. "There's a key in the lock. One moment. There, got it."

Rez wondered why Lacy and Gainer would leave the key.

Thirty seconds later: "Basement clear."

"House is empty."

"But we got the cages," Phipps said. "This is the right house."

"You would not believe the tech gear they've got down here," someone said. "It's a freakin'—hold on."

Rez tensed.

"I'm picking up some kind of..."

"...it's cycling higher," someone else said. "Do you hear that?"

He kept the channel open, and Rez heard something faint in the background. It reminded her of the cooling fan in her computer when it ramped up. "Barnes," she said over her shoulder. "Barnes?"

"Phipps, get your people out of there!" Barnes yelled. He looked to Rez like he might crush the 2-way in his fist. "Phipps!"

"You heard the man," Phipps said. "Clear out!"

"Dear God," someone said. "...elevator's locked out."

"Run a by—"

FOOM!

The flash lit the entire suburban neighborhood. The explosion wasn't a thunderous thing but rather a sudden vacuum of all sound.

{ 383 }

Rez picked herself up off the ground and blinked stupidly at the scene. Bloody fire and a gargantuan vomit of smoke boiled up into the night sky. Rez's ears rang so fiercely that she didn't hear the chunk of burning debris that hit the sidewalk just a few feet from where she stood. She saw it though and leaped backward, crashing into the arms of Deputy Director Barnes.

She shuddered, turned, and backed away from him. There was blood on his forehead, dribbling over his brow and down his cheek. She could see his mouth working, but couldn't hear him.

She turned back to the burning home. She'd seen all kinds of explosions before. She'd even caused a few. But this seemed different. The house had not exploded outward. The outer structure was still intact. But the roof was completely gone. It was as if the force of the blast had come from below and was channeled upward. Even now, the fire looked more like a focused torch, belching its fiery breath into the sky.

The ringing began to subside, and Rez heard a man shouting. It was Klingler. She turned and found him walking in slow circles, shouting the same question over and over again: "What happened?"

Rez strode to him and grabbed him by the shoulders. "Are you hurt?" she asked. He didn't answer but blinked as if not recognizing her. "Are you hurt?"

"N-no," he mumbled. "No, I don't think so."

"Give me the keys," Rez demanded.

"What?" he asked. "Why?"

"Klingler, you give me the keys or so help me I will knock that sorry excuse for a hairpiece into the Gulf!"

The burning house reflected in Klingler's uncertain eyes. He blinked and then held out the keys.

Rez snagged them from his hand and ran to the SUV. She rammed the keys into the ignition, cranked the engine, and got on her cell. "This is a police emergency," she said to a 911 operator. "There's been an explosion. There are multiple officers down, and the fire is still burning." She gave the address and her best estimate on casualties. She ended the conversation by invoking all the authority of the FBI to get rescue and fire to the scene as fast as possible.

"This is Sanderson," came a voice suddenly from the two-way radio.

Rez tossed her cell onto the passenger seat and snapped up the radio. "Go ahead, Sanderson," she said.

"Phipps is down," he said. "I repeat, Phipps is down. I've got Gray, Karchek, and Marks with me. Three more are on the east side of the structure."

"I've got this, Rezvani," Deputy Director Barnes said, his voice a little shaky on the radio. Rez stared out, and there he was, on his feet. She caught his eyes. "You sure?" she asked.

Barnes nodded, a little trickle of blood still oozing down his forehead. And then, Klingler was there at the window.

"Look after the Deputy Director," Rez told him. "He's hurt."

"Wait a minute, Rezvani!" he whined at her. "Where are you going?"

"To see a man who can help us," she said. "A man I had thrown in jail."

{ Chapter 35 }

I COUNTED FIVE SHOTS: three from one gun; two from the other. The screams were high on the register, strained, and cut ominously short. And then, the inmates started to scream.

"Shut up!" I roared, again projecting my voice. "SHUT UP OR YOU WILL DIE!"

I pressed my head into the space between two bars and tried to see up the hall. There was no way to turn my head, but in my peripheral vision, I could see the cellblock's door. Maybe it was the angle, but I couldn't see anything through the thick glass window on the door. Then, an inky blotch appeared in the center of the door and began to spread outward malignantly. The flowing black engulfed the frame of the door, and I saw glowing embers appear along its outline. No flicker of flame or tongue of fire. Just voracious bloody orange embers–they consumed the door. A gout of black liquid spouted from the center of it all like crude oil gushing from a vertical wound.

I'd been a fool. Legend or not, this thing was coming. And it was coming for me. I had no choices left. I'd need to unmask. But could I harness enough concentration? The crawling, itching, electrical aura of the thing intensified greatly as it drew near. I could barely think straight, much less call all of my body's systems into perfect symmetry.

"No! NO!" It was a woman's voice, shrill and desperate.

I slammed into the bars, straining to see, pushing my face until my skull ached. I saw the shadow form, a writhing, cloaked apparition. It stood before the first cell, and a searching, smoking tendril surged across the distance and drove through the cell bars.

There was a dire scream and then, a wet gurgling groan. Transfixed, I watched the smoky tendril withdraw and heard a sharp suck of air, a lifeless gasp, and a sound like a gallon of paint splashing across the floor. Then, the cell block exploded in a cacophony of shrieks and screams as the other inmates recognized the approaching cloak of death.

"What are YOU doing!" I cried out through the bars. "You came here for me!"

There came no answer, but the shadow figure, a storm that walks, came forward. I threw myself to my knees and gasped for air. I was dangerously close to hyperventilating. I needed to think, needed to find an inner calm...a void where I could transit to my unmasked form. It took form in my mind like an undulating blue horizontal plane. I could feel the pulses of energy begin to throb. I was almost there.

The man's scream hit me like a physical blow. I fell backward, nearly popping the ligaments in my knees. Whatever calm concentration I had mustered, it was destroyed now. And the man continued to scream. It was the death cry of a big man, deep, wrenched up from his gut and wrung out of him until there was nothing left.

I picked myself up and stumbled once more to my knees. I sought the calm but did not find it. I heard another scream, this

GHOST

one more of a dry, wheezing thing. Then there were curses in English...and in Spanish, followed by a sudden, defiant yell. A single shrill cry came next. Then, a wretched, gargling throaty shout.

The walking shadow was killing the inmates one-by-one as it came, sluicing through the bars and leisurely ripping their lives away. In a corner of my cringing heart, I felt stricken with guilt. I'd given the inmates false hope. There was no way to hide from this thing.

The biker cursed it before crying out his last. The next death, there was no scream at all; only a vicious tearing splatter. Now the shadow shape was visible, just a cell away from my own. The bodybuilder put up a fight, which is to say, he banged around in his cell before groaning and falling silent.

Legs of black vapor strode forward, and it was there just outside the bar. The writhing oily black smoke seemed to coalesce in part, becoming a being of scaly, silver-blue flesh. All doubt scattered and was gone. The legend was no more. The Nephilim lived and walked the earth. And now, it leered at me with pestilent yellow eyes.

The voice that warbled out from its lips might have been the sound of a locust swarm devouring a field or the bleating of a thousand lambs being slaughtered at once. It might have been the silent cries of untold millions of unborn killed in the womb. It sounded like all of those tragedies together and yet, I could understand the speech as clearly as my own.

"I...have brought you...your tool."

His right arm rose, and I leaped backward. Then I saw: he had The Edge and held it out for me. I shuddered to think of what had become of the FBI agents who had relieved me of The Edge in the first place. But...why would the Nephilim give me a weapon? Mr. Scratch had been one thing, a bargaining chip or a favor to call in later. But I could not discern the Nephilim's purpose.

"I...savor...the hunt."

Sport. The Nephilim wanted more sport from me than he'd gotten from the defenseless. I resigned myself that, it might be my very last act upon this earth, but I would give him a measure of sport before I went.

I darted forward, in one motion snatching The Edge from his hand, flicking it on, and slashing his upper arm. The ethereal blade flashed to life and neatly severed his right arm just below the shoulder. The limb fell bloodless to the floor but vanished in a column of roiling black smoke. When I looked up, its right arm was there as if I'd never landed the blow. The Nephilim smiled lecherously and backed away from my cell bars. He turned at an angle and leaned toward the cell across from mine.

"NO!" I commanded, but it was too late. Its right arm became a vortex of darkness. It spiraled into the cell and found the man beneath his cot. There was a strangled cry, several sharp cracks, and a pressurized pop. A tide of blood washed out from under the cot and spread quickly across the cell floor.

The rage burst from me like a solar flare. I lunged, dragging The Edge across the top of the steel bars. I spun, cutting across the bottom of the bars and continuing the momentum with a sharp sidekick that raked out the section I'd cut. I leaped through and slashed the Nephilim, executing a barrage that would have eviscerated and all but filleted a man. I whirled away and turned back...only to find the Nephilim seemingly unharmed, tendrils of vaporous darkness surging over every wound until the scaly flesh was completely restored.

"Long...have I searched for you...Horseman."

"What do you want with me?" I asked, failing to hide the desperation in my voice. "I've done nothing to you!"

The Nephilim laughed, but it was a terrible, mirthless sound like the dry grinding of old bones. "It...is not what...you've done. It...is what you...are."

In that moment, the most ridiculous thing popped into my mind. While on a mission in Japan, I had seen a sketch artist's pencil cartoon that had left me aching with laughter. It was called Godzilla versus Bambi.

It was a very short cartoon.

I guess it came to mind because I faced a similar dynamic against a legendary power like the Nephilim. Given that, in the analogy, I was Bambi, there really wasn't anything all that funny about my situation. But the memory and the inner laughter relaxed me. My breathing slowed. My heartbeat hammered out its regular rhythm. Even as I brandished The Edge, threatening another run at the Nephilim, I focused inwardly. I saw the endless blue plane stretch to the horizon and beyond. And this time, it raced toward me, crashing over me like a wave.

I saw golden light. I could unmask, at last.

* * *   * * *   * * *   * * *

Agent Rezvani roared onto Keystone Lane and came to a violent, screeching halt in the parking circle in front of the Pensacola Police Department. As she leaped out of the SUV, she expected to find at least a half dozen startled officers streaming out of the blocky building's door. But no one came out to investigate the tire-burning ruckus she'd made.

"Well, it is 1:00 a.m.," she muttered, taking the steps two at a time. "Maybe they relax things after midnight down here."

She threw open the right hand door, plunged inside, and skidded to a hard fall on the wet floor. Whispering a few choice words under her breath, she rolled off her side and pushed herself up. That was when all words left her. She had slid in blood. Not just a splash or puddle, but a flood.

Deanna Rezvani, the FBI Special Agent, ceased to exist. In her place stood a young woman confronted with a horror beyond understanding. Thick crimson blood pooled from the base of the information counter to the opposite wall and spread all the way down twenty feet of hallway.

She turned a dazed circle and blinked with little comprehension of the incoming detail. Shreds and hunks of bloody pink meat, some embedded with shards of stark white bone, lay strewn all over the office. Every glass dividing panel, every window, every wall had been splattered with all manner of gore. Blood dripped forlornly from counters, edges of desks, and from half-clotted gobs on the ceiling. Each drop sent slow ripples across the inundated floor.

Rez's Special Agent side returned, professional detachment rescuing the other side from shock and madness. She drew her Beretta and began a slow, careful exploration of the building, and clinical procedure took over. The physical evidence seemed to indicate that the police officers had been blown apart. The carnage was certainly consistent with bomb damage or a missile strike. But there was no sign of fire or the equivalent damage to furniture. It was just human destruction.

She had no mental file to open, no list of things that could do this kind of dismembering damage to human beings without an explosion. A butchering serial killer might be as violent but, unless he gassed the entire precinct, there was no way a killer could take out all of the police. Not like this. That thought gave Rez pause. She'd had the police scanner on the whole drive. There'd been no report. Nothing. A patrolman returning from a shift would have reported the scene.

GHOST

She caught a tensing chill. She slowed her movements and kept the wall at her back. Whoever had done this was likely still in the building...capable of doing to her what he had done to the others. *But who could...?* She couldn't shake the question. The Smiling Jack killers were ruthless and clever. They'd rigged their home to explode, killing who knew how many? Could they have pulled this off as well? It didn't make sense. That left a chilling possibility.

Ghost.

What did she really know about John Spector? He'd admitted that name to be an alias. He'd been secretive in dozens of ways. And what was in that silver case of his? More technologically advanced weapons? Something capable of the...the massacre she saw before her?

No, she thought, shaking the snaking logic from her mind. Spector might be a self righteous pain in the nether regions, but he wasn't evil. Still, she had to admit that Spector was likely the most recent prisoner brought into the precinct. All this...had some connection to him.

Rez moved on, taking sure, careful steps in the blood. She rounded a corner and found a bank of monitors. She scanned the screens and stopped at the cell blocks. The third floor cells were full to capacity, and the inmates in view were severely agitated. Each time the camera cycled, focusing on a new set of third floor cells, Rez saw people throwing themselves at the steel bars, screaming, and tearing at anything they could find. Then she went to the second floor screens.

The first camera view was unclear. It was black and white, but the tones seemed off. The cell floor looked black. Then she saw the human head.

Rez fought her physiology and held back the vomit. The camera blinked, and Rez stared. It was Ghost. Or at least she thought it was. He stood near the shadows at the end of hall of cells. The man was big enough, but his face was distorted. She remembered the websites, the fan photos, and all the blurring on his face. *That's him,* she thought, convincing herself but not quite there. And she saw the man she believed to be John Spector swing a sword forward in a menacing manor.

"That's his crazy sword," Rez whispered. But what was he swinging at? At first, she thought there was something wrong with the screen. A blotch of darkness swirled around Spector, and he seemed to be trying to fight it off.

She began to tear herself away from the screen when she saw...something that momentarily scrambled her senses. Something flashed on the screen, but not like a lens flare. It was on Spector as if the monitor's contrast had gone haywire. The skin of his arm kindled to blinding white. His blurred face too, shifted into a blooming explosion of light. There seemed to be a radiant glow burning all around his back. And then, the camera cycled away to a different vantage.

I'm losing it, she thought, frantically leaving the police offices and searching for the route to the cell block. Finally out of the blood, she had better footing, but unfortunately her sense of direction and the department's lack of signs left her taking several wrong turns before stumbling onto the cell blocks.

She hit the stairs to cell block two and did her best to shut out what she saw as she climbed. The top of the stairwell, the podium desk, and the gate to the cell block were all strewn with gore and painted in blood. She raced through the gate and skidded to a halt. It hadn't been the screen. Toward the end of the hall there was a mixture of writhing shadows and blindingly bright light. She blinked and held up her arm reflexively. Squinting, she saw that the light had shape, a human form, well...basically a human form. There were strange features Rez didn't understand.

Then, the figure of light turned and sped toward her. It covered the ground between them in heartbeats. Rez fired a shot, then two more. But the light surrounded her, lifted her from her feet, and...spoke.

"Tuck your head into my chest," it said, its voice an otherworldly combination of intensity and calm. "Keep your eyes shut until I tell you."

Rez did as she was told. The blinding brightness burned through her eyelids anyway, and she saw strange shapes and patterns. But that was nothing compared to the sounds. Wind and storm and rain—a violent raging tempest—screamed against her eardrums. There came a deep crackling boom, and Rez couldn't hold on. Her consciousness slipped away in a vortex of light and sound.

{ Chapter 36 }

"A GENT REZVANI."

Rez heard someone calling her, and that seemed odd. Who calls the dead?

"Agent Rezvani," the voice called again. "I need you to wake up."

Wake up? Rez thought. *I can't wake up. I'm dead.* Rez couldn't recall how she died exactly, but she must have. There had been so much blood, so many dead. And then: blinding light and crushing thunder.

Rez had always known she'd die while on the job, but she figured it would have been a gunshot or a car bomb or maybe even a high speed collision. It never crossed her mind that she'd be whisked to the grave by a supernatural living light—

"REZ, WAKE UP!"

Rez opened her eyes, blinked at the stars overhead, and felt sand between her fingers. "I'm not dead," she whispered. Light shimmered in her peripheral vision. She turned her head and gasped.

A figure made of starlight stood upon the sand just a dozen paces from her. Rez squinted, blinked, and even rubbed her eyes, and her vision became more acute. He was not made of starlight or even of light. He wasn't like the Human Torch in the Fantastic Four, but his flesh seemed molten like slow flowing lava, shot through with spidery cracks and gaps where pure white light shone through. Rez had seen that kind of pristine brilliance once before...when Ghost had spontaneously healed from the gunshot wound.

"Ghost?" she whispered.

The being turned his head, and she recognized the features. Rez caught her breath and went to one knee. "I'm still out," she told herself. "I'm unconscious. This is a dream. Only a dream."

"You...are not asleep," the light figure said, his voice—at first clear like a clarion trumpet—began to strain. As he spoke this last, the words became thin and weak. "You...know...me." He groaned, staggered to one knee, and collapsed onto his side.

"You're hurt?" Rez leaped to her feet, took a step and froze.

She stared, transfixed at Spector's back...his wings.

Wings.

One hand at her lips, the other pointing feebly and trembling, Rez leaped backward as one wing extended and fell, the tip just inches from her feet. No feathers like that of an eagle, no webbing like that of a bat—these were muscular wings, scaled with tough, fleshy plaits like those of a gladiator's skirt. At a guess, the wing was eight or nine feet in length, hinged not once but twice at powerful joints made knobby beneath the flesh by heads of muscle.

To support and power such immense appendages, Spector—it felt surreal to call this being by a familiar name—had dynamic upper body development. Where a particularly well-built football player might have thick neck muscle and a dense upper back and shoulders, Spector had more. Massive, triangular slabs braced his neck and met huge panels of upper back on either side of his spine. His shoulders were almost comically large, like ribbed cannonballs covered by that smoldering flesh. But, in spite of the potential power there, Spector's wings were now virtually motionless.

Rez ran around the outstretched wing and knelt near his face. "Spector," she said, "Spector, is that really you?"

His eyelids fluttered, sending out flickers of white light. "I am sorry, Rez," he whispered hoarsely. "No time to explain. Help me...help me get to the water."

Spector rose to a knee, and his wings folded onto his back. He coughed, simultaneously retching up a gob of brilliant white liquid and causing a spurt of the same from his midsection.

"Oh, oh my gosh, is that blood?" Rez didn't know what to do with her hands. She didn't feel heat from him, but still, the molten appearance, bright light burning out of a myriad miniature strokes of lightning...it seemed she'd incinerate herself by touching him.

"Got to get to...water," he groaned. "Please."

Grimacing, she took his elbow and found him lighter than she expected. Far lighter, but not for lack of mass. His flesh was taut with blocks of thick muscle. Rez speculated absently that he'd be three feet taller than her if he wasn't so bent over and wracked with pain. *He ought to weigh close to 300 pounds,* she thought. But he didn't. Supporting him now was like bearing a teenager or spotting an athlete.

She got him to the water's edge with relative ease. "What now?" she asked.

"Farther out."

She led him until the warm water was waist high. "Now?"

"Let...me go," he whispered. "Let me fall. Need to reset."

"Reset?" she echoed.

"Let me go under," he said. "Just don't go anywhere."

Rez loosened her grip, and he pulled free. The winged version of John Spector disappeared beneath the water with a deep gurgle.

Agent Rezvani staggered a few steps backward, almost falling into the surf herself. "What am I doing?" she asked aloud. But she found no other words. She'd had a dozen reasons for signing on with the FBI. But in the past 48 hours, each and every one of them had been taxed, stretched, worried, bent, and blown up. She'd seen things that would disturb any human being, the mind-fracturing scene at the Pensacola Police Department would haunt her memory for as long as she lived. But, beyond that, there were events related to John Spector, events that the mind had no recourse, no paradigm to reference.

As if on cue, light strobed out of the water where Spector had gone under. Dappled flares shone and sparkled. The water surged and rocked as if a school of especially large fish teemed just beneath the surface. Spector's head came up, and he gasped for air.

Rez dove forward and reached for him.

"No!" he spluttered. "Not yet!" He went under again.

He was gone for much longer this time, but when Rez stepped forward, he came up. And he was John Spector again...a normal, if haggard looking John Spector.

He tried to get to his feet but fell backward. Rez assisted and found him a cumbersome bulk this time. She struggled, straining against the water weight, but got him upright at last. When they got safely back up onto the sand, Ghost breathed heavily, punctuated by a distinct wheezing.

"What's wrong?" Rez asked. "I thought you did that healing thing."

"I did," he said hoarsely. "Wasn't enough, not after..." His voice trailed off.

"You look like hell," Rez said.

"You're not far off."

"When will you get your strength back?"

"N-not sure," he said. "Never been hurt like this before. Might be a while."

"Good," Rez said. She drew her Beretta and trained it on him. "Now, convince me that what happened back in Pensacola wasn't...wasn't you."

Ghost's eyes seemed to swim in their sockets. He blinked until he could focus his gaze. "You...you mean the inmates?"

"The inmates?" Rez practically shouted. "The inmates, the cops—they were...they were shredded! The whole place was a blood bath."

"You think I did that?"

"I don't know what to think," she said. "Tell me you didn't do it. Tell me I'm wrong."

"I didn't kill anyone in that police station," Spector said.

"Then who did?" Rez said, swaying as she spoke. "Who did...all that? Who could *possibly* do...all that?"

"The same thing that nearly gutted me," Ghost said. "But it's hard to explain."

Rez barked out a laugh. "Hard," she said. "That's funny." She lowered her gun and sat suddenly in the sand. "What is all this? What...what are you?"

***   ***   ***   ***

"Don't cry, Midge," Carrie said as she stroked a brush through the weeping girl's sandy brown hair.

"Carrie's right," Jack said. "There's no reason to cry. You are about to make your grand debut."

"What do you...mean, debut?" Midge asked, rubbing a finger in the corner of her eye.

"People," Jack said in a dramatic whisper. "At last, people will see you...and like never before!"

"Like in the movies?" Carrie asked, her hand lingering on Midge's shoulder. "Like the outside people?"

"Yes, just like that," Jack said. "Only more people will see your movie tonight than you could possibly imagine."

There was a muted thumping overhead, and Dr. Garrison Lacy descended the stairs. He wore dark all-weather gear that glistened in the cabin's recessed lights. "We're anchored," he said. "But the surf is choppy. Storm's coming."

"Nothing that will hinder our event?" Jack said.

"Nothing will hinder our event," Dr. Gary replied. "We've enough bandwidth, contingency server muscle, and redundant satellite coverage to broadcast from the bottom of the sea if necessary, though I rather hope it wouldn't come to that."

"Could I have another patch?" Carrie asked, rubbing the mocha colored skin of her bare shoulder. "I think I've lost the first one."

"In a moment, sweet Carrie," he replied. "You too, Midge?"

Midge blinked and smiled hopefully. "Can I?"

"Yes, yes," Dr. Gary replied, sliding off his jacket. He eased into a bench seat and woke the sleeping laptop. "Tonight is a special occasion. Jack, would you see to their refreshments."

Midge grinned and clapped.

"Thank you, thank you," Carrie said.

"I'll get the liners too," Jack said, stopping just outside the fore cabin. "We can't take chances, especially with two."

Dr. Gary looked at Jack sympathetically. "We won't be needing plastic this time," he said.

Jack looked up sharply. "But don't you think...I mean, if we return to the marina, we don't want to be obvious."

"It won't matter," Dr. Gary said. "The cop knew."

"FBI," Jack said.

"No doubt. They were sniffing around in feigned vagaries, but they knew." He sighed. "We gave them a trail, and they followed. Even if they hadn't, someone would very soon."

"Isn't it possible that we might have one day yet?" Jack asked. "Are you certain we cannot run? We've enough provisions to sail out of U.S. jurisdiction—"

"Our broadcast tonight will shine a global spotlight upon us. The authorities would track us down and apprehend us even before we return to port."

"And if they do?" Jack asked, voice weakening to a whisper.

"We will let them board," Dr. Gary said quietly. "As many of them as will come, and then, I will end it."

{ Chapter 37 }

DEPUTY DIRECTOR BARNES had seen a lot of carnage in his day. He'd served as a Seal and been employed in dozens of unfriendly, forward locations. He's seen what an IED could do to a Humvee. He'd seen what a bomb could do to a shoddily constructed office building. Worse, he'd seen the dead and injured from the explosion at Dr. Lacy's house.

But he'd never seen anything like this.

"For the love of God, go across the street!" Barnes shouted as he emerged from the Pensacola Police Headquarters. Several of his Special Agents and a score of other policemen were scattered around the property getting physically ill into and onto the landscaping. "Klingler, Culbert, you guys know better! C'mon, you're contaminating the area!"

Klingler wandered away from a patch of bushes and unsteadily made his way to Director Barnes.

"Don't you dare puke on my shoes!" Barnes barked, blood and sweat mingling on his face.

"No, no, sir," Klingler muttered, wiping his mouth and chin with a handkerchief. "Nah, I think I'm okay. It's just...well, I didn't see any evidence of fire...no physical damage—to the interior, I mean. What..."

"What could do that to human beings?" Barnes said, his words empty of his usual ironclad certainty. "I...I don't have the first damn clue."

"What...what do we do with this?" Klinger asked, his eyes wide and shocky.

Barnes remembered himself then, remembered his job and his role. He took Klingler by the shoulders. "We do what we always do," Barnes said, firming his voice as he spoke. "We are the very best in the Bureau. *THE* Federal Bureau of Investigation. We know what to do. We have the tools. Make it happen."

Klingler stood a little more steadily. There was a bit of an arch in his back now, a trace of his cocksure demeanor had returned. "Yes, sir," he said, whipping a radio from his belt as he walked away.

Whether the speech had cleared his mind as well, Barnes wasn't sure, but he was thinking like an investigator again. He was thinking like a cop. And that's what the victims in that blood-washed building needed. They needed someone to find out what happened in there, someone to make sure the guilty parties didn't get away with it or, worse, repeat the massacre somewhere else. Director Barnes stood very still and ran variables through the labyrinthine possibilities. Nothing made sense, not yet.

But there was a variable sticking out like a weed: whatever had killed those police officers, whatever had happened, it had happened just after John Spector had been put in a cell here. And, as far as they could tell from the carnage inside, Spector's remains were not among the others. His cell had a section of bars cut out.

Coincidence? Maybe. But Barnes never liked coincidences. Life was never as random as it sometimes seemed. This Spector fellow had turned up in some awfully interesting places. He'd known some details he shouldn't have known. And, if Rezvani was right, Spector had done some pretty remarkable things. But murder all those cops? All by himself? That didn't seem possible. Maybe the vid-techs would shed some light on it once they arrived to access the police department's interior surveillance footage. But to Barnes, the details could wait. All the theories could be tested later, once they captured Spector and grilled him. Dr. Lacy and Gainer too.

They would find them all. Barnes would make sure of that. The bastards would answer for their actions. The call he was about to make would alert or mobilize every agent of law enforcement in Florida and every bordering state. With more than a dozen slaughtered policemen—their brothers in arms—the searchers would find John Spector, Dr. Garrison Lacy, and Jacqueline Gainer. They would find them or die trying.

***   ***   ***   ***

Somewhere on the ghostly illuminated white sands along the Gulf of Mexico, I found myself confronted by Special Agent Deanna Rezvani and...at a loss.

I rubbed at the loose flesh on my temples. The resetting had been far from complete. I'd need much more time in the water to accomplish that. But I didn't have time. Any time at all. And to give Agent Rezvani what she wanted would demand time. It would also mean crossing a line.

"Agent Rezvani," I said. "I—"

"Don't 'Agent Rezvani' me, Ghost!" she said.

The gun was still at her side, but her words felt like a gun barrel pointed at me anyway.

"That's what you do when you want to push me away. You make me sound like a professional contact as if you don't owe me anything more than courtesy."

"You are a professional contact," I said. "But...you're right. I do owe you more than courtesy. And I have one more favor to ask, so I'll owe again. But, Agent—Rez, there's only so much I can tell you, and we can't spend much more time here. There are still lives hanging on our action or inaction."

"So tell me what you can," she said. "And talk fast. I'm all ears."

"I really don't think you want to know," I said.

"Why not?" she said, her face a sarcastic mask. "Wait, let me guess: you could tell me, but then you'd have to kill me."

"No. But it will mess with your categories."

Rez shook her head as if I'd just insulted her mother. "After the last few weeks, Ghost, I don't have any freakin' categories! So tell me what you can, or so help me, I'm going to shoot something!"

I hadn't realized how much recent events had pushed her towards the edge. It would be a thin line between revealing too little and too much. I'd need to tread carefully. "I told you that I work for a branch of government higher than the President," I said.

"Yeah, I got that much before. Go on."

"I didn't explain how high."

"Okay, so who? Black Ops? A deep NSA branch no one's ever heard of? Or maybe the Illuminati?"

"None of those."

"Then who? How high?"

I paused. "The Most High."

GHOST

"What?" she blurted, her brows knitting in frustration. "What does that mean, the most high? As in—"

"As in *the* Most High," I explained. "I work for God."

Rez muttered a curse and then began a low roll of grinding laughter. She bent over at the waist, lowered herself by collapsing her knees, and sat hard on the sand. "You...work for God?" she blurted, her voice high and thin, almost manic. "God's detective, right? God's private eye!" She covered her eyes with a hand and let out a series of breathy, gasping laughs.

"I am one of the Euangelion," I said, watching her carefully. If she was going to crack, this would likely do it. "It's a special force of warrior angels, and I—"

Rez coughed, and the sound was sickly and unpleasant. "Son of a—" she spat. "You...you're an angel?"

She began to shudder out great waves of laughter, and I could just imagine the visions of little chubby, haloed cherubs dancing in her mind's eye. "Rez," I said. "It's not what you think of when you..." I cut off my own words. Agent Rezvani's laughter had changed tone and pitch. In fact, it wasn't laughter at all. She was sobbing.

It was the low, aching cry of those who mourned. It was a desperate plea of emotion, gushing out from her soul. I took a step forward, but Rez shoved herself backward and held up a hand as if to ward off a blow. "Stay away from me!" she cried. "Just...stay...away."

"Rez," I pleaded, "I'm not messing with you. It's all true. It's—"

"You idiot!" she cried out. She was practically wailing now. "Don't you see? Don't you get it? I know you're telling the truth. I know it's true. I can feel it...like fire in my bones. I've known all along you were, well...other. It all makes sense, except...none of it...makes sense. You...you had wings!"

"I was unmasked," I said. "You saw the reality of what I am. Back at the police station, did you see the other thing, the shadow being?"

She nodded. "I saw something," she said. "A lot of darkness. Was it another angel or...a demon? Wait, are demons real too?"

"They are the Fallen," I said. "But this thing is different. It is Nephilim. Stronger, utterly ruthless. It killed all those people back at the police department. It would have killed me...but I ran. I'm telling you this because it might come back. It's chasing me. Do you see?"

Rez nodded, but I could tell she wasn't covering all the bases. How could she? "What I'm explaining to you, Rez, is that so long as you are with me, you are in mortal danger. If the Nephilim returns, it would kill you without so much as a glance in your direction. I don't know if I can protect you. I would try, you know, but...it's out of my class."

Rez's tears had dried up. Her face became, not quite serene, but business calm. Determination was writ large in the set of her jaw. "What about Jack?" she asked. "We found the house, but they rigged it with some kind of bomb. No way to know whether they were in it."

"I don't think they would be," I said. "Not yet. We haven't heard their message."

"What message?" Rez asked.

"The point of it all," I said. "Whatever warped excuse for murder they've rationalized...they're going to make it much more clear."

"What will they do?"

"They'll kill again," I said. "And soon. They know they're out of time. They know we're on to them, and they know, sooner or later, they'll be caught. Whatever their message is, they will have to get it out before they are caught or killed."

"But where are they?" Rez asked. "They blew up their house. They eluded us at the convention hall."

"I believe they've gone back to the Gulf," I said. "Think of the body dumps, both just off the shore. And the killing photos. They kill out on the water. If I'm right, can you find them? Their ship will be registered."

Rez didn't answer but started dialing her cell. "This is Special Agent Deanna Rezvani," she told the phone. "Branch confirmation code: *0-1-niner-alpha-foxtrot-zulu.* Yes, that's right...out of D.C. We're in Florida investigating...uh, huh, right, you heard. Okay, so you know we're in the middle of a lot down here, and I need you to do something for me PDQ."

I listened as she went through one channel after the other. In three minutes, she had Dr. Garrison Lacy's ship: a 62-foot Oyster 625, purchased three years before. In two more minutes, she had their berth.

"It's the Four Season's Marina," she said.

"Unbelievable," I muttered. "What about—"

She held up a hand and said, "Yes, for that, I'll wait." Ten ticks later, she said, "Yeah, I understand. But that's pretty close to what you'd expect, right?" She paused again. "Okay, great. Can you give me the relative location, something I could—uh, huh. Exactly. Got it, got it. Thank you. You're a lifesaver."

"What?" I asked. Did I mention that I hate to wait?

"I got through to the Mobile field office," she said. "Seems like just about every office owes Deputy Director Barnes a favor, so I pulled some strings with the local Coast Guard. A couple of their cutters are picking up contacts that might match Lacy's boat. It's no sure thing, they said, but I've got the coordinates."

"The Coast Guard's not headed out, are they?" I asked.

Rez eyed me strangely. "Not yet," she said. "Why?"

{411}

Before I could reply, her phone buzzed. When she answered, I could hear the deep-voiced shout from where I stood. Her face went sheet-white. "No, Sir," she said. "No, now look...it wasn't him. I was there, just after it happened. I saw...well, never mind what I saw. It just wasn't Spector." She held the phone away from her ear, and that was probably a good thing because a searing burst of curses erupted from the speaker.

When the tirade was over, Rez put the phone back to her ear. "Think what you want, Sir, but if you want to catch the Smiling Jack killers, if you want to get the guys who put down our team, you need to listen." Remarkably, Rez paused, making sure she had a respectful audience. Gutsy move, considering who she was likely talking to.

When she spoke again, I was two seconds too slow to react. "Sir, the two killers are on a ship in the Gulf. I got the coordinates from the Coast Guard, and—"

I took hold of Rez's wrist. I gently removed the phone from her hand, and then, not so gently, I heaved it far out into the water.

"What...Ghost?" Rez said, blinking like a startled doe. "Why did you—"

"We're going after Smiling Jack and the doctor," I said. "But we aren't going there to arrest them."

{ Chapter 38 }

IT HAD TAKEN US HALF AN HOUR to hail a cab and another fifteen to drive to the Four Seasons Marina. We jogged passed the gatehouse. Rez had flashed her badge, but neither the Slickster or Redbuzz or anyone else seemed to be there. The gatehouse was dark. I guess the marina cared about their patrons up to a point but definitely not at o-dark thirty.

"Wait, the reason you ditched my phone," Rez blurted breathlessly, as she raced a step ahead and tried to cut me off. "You...you're going to just kill them?"

I sidestepped her and kept going.

"I thought angels protect people," she continued, unfazed by my silence. "Guardian angels, right? You've heard of those?"

"I am quite familiar with Guardians," I said, glancing over her shoulder at the flicker of heat lightning on the horizon. "But I am not that kind."

"So, what kind are you, then? Are you like God's hitman?"

That stopped me in my tracks. "If you had any concept of holiness," I said. "Even the faintest glimmer of understanding of pure, untainted good, you would not even begin to suggest anything like that about the Most High. We don't have time for me to explain."

"I've heard that kind of thing before," Rez said. And in that moment, I got a read on her that suggested several reasons for her skepticism and anger. "It's like what a lot of those Bible thumpers say when they get caught doing something they shouldn't be doing."

"No," I said gently. "That is not what this is like. In the Most High, there is no darkness at all."

"Right, no darkness," she said, her knuckles burrowing into her hips. "Explain this to me then: you said you work for God, right?"

"I serve, yes."

"And by 'serve,' you mean you take people out...right?"

"That is not always my mission," I replied. "But there are times such—"

"You can't have it both ways," Rez said indignantly. "What kind of God sends angels to kill people?"

I replied, "A patient God."

"Patient?" Rez scoffed. "I mean, don't get me wrong. If God wants to rid the world of a few serial killers, more power to Him. But to call it patience is a mockery of the word. You—"

"*You* are finite," I said firmly. "You see through blurred glass and weigh right and wrong on a broken scale. Understand, there is no one so patient as the Most High. Every breath of mankind is a grace gift of patience. If your standards were put to ultimate use by the Most High, there would be no choice for the beings of this world, no hope, and no love."

Agent Rezvani's flare of anger diminished to an amber glow. "I...I don't understand," she said. "But wouldn't it be more patient to let the police get these guys? Let us take them into custody, put them on trial, and see it through?"

"The Most High allows your authorities power to weigh and measure," I explained. "He gives your authorities the sword. But there are times when your authorities are overmatched, times when your authorities turn away, times when your authorities forget their charge. In those times, I—and others of my kind—take missions of singular importance."

"IF that's the truth," Rez said bitterly, "then God has a lot to explain about Hitler, Stalin, Pol Pot, and the rest of history's villains."

"Or, perhaps, history has a lot to explain," I said.

"Come again?"

"Where and when have these vile men come to power?" I asked. When Rez didn't answer, I finished the thought. "I will tell you. They came to power wherever and whenever mankind abandoned the Most High. But can you say for certain how each of those villains met their end?"

Rez stared at me hard, and I could see the gears and tumblers spinning. When they clicked into place, her eyes widened. "Are you trying to tell me—"

"Agent Rezvani...Rez, I will say this and then nothing more: what you have seen...what you have learned, it changes everything. Your world just expanded by dimensions, and you will be disoriented for a time. But even once you've adjusted, you will still see only the faintest hint of all there is to know. Trust for now in the infinite mind of the Most High. And trust me."

Rez blinked at me for several seconds. "I...I don't know if I can," she said at last. "But...if there's a chance we might still save those women...I'll try."

I felt sure that was the best I was going to get from Agent Rezvani, and that would have to do. But as I turned away from her to tread up the dock, I caught the faintest glimmer of something in her eyes. Clinically described, her lids closed a bit, her pupils grew, and a slight crinkle appeared between her brows. The net result was a thoughtful expression that bordered on cunning.

I turned my thoughts to other matters and scrambled on. We came to berth 22A, the Adderlys' berth, and I held my breath as we climbed aboard the *The Sirocco*. This was more than a long shot. This was desperation.

The yacht looked as still and silent and unoccupied as I thought possible. The cabin had a security door, and it looked like it was hermetically sealed.

Rez rapped on the door. "Mr. Adderly, this is Agent Rezvani of the Federal Bureau of Investigation. Please answer the door."

I thought I heard a hint of pleading in Rez's voice. Or maybe, it was just how I felt. We waited in empty silence. Not quite empty. I thought I heard a very low growl of thunder off in the distance. Maybe it wasn't heat lightning after all.

Rez rapped again. And we waited again. I'd already considered my options if this didn't pan out. And they paraded through my mind again, each one with a lesser chance of succeeding than the other.

I could go airborne, but in my still-depleted state, I wouldn't make it far without plummeting into the Gulf. Saltwater never rejuvenates as fully as freshwater, and after the pummeling I'd taken at the hands of the Nephilim, I just wouldn't have enough in the tank to find Smiling Jack.

We could call in the FBI cavalry. Or, we could go directly to the Coast Guard ourselves. But the time required for either to be effective frightened me. Whatever Jack had planned for his remaining victims, it wouldn't keep much longer. And, of course, bringing in the FBI or the Coast Guard would complicate the mission in other ways.

Rez sighed audibly, and I saw her shoulders slump. "Looks like they're out," she said. "Probably just do the sailing thing on weekend—"

Something muffled and unintelligible came from the other side of the door. We heard a metallic clicking, and the door opened. There stood Darcy, rubbing her owlish blue eyes and looking pretty, in a sleepy kind of way. Her hair was bed-tossed, and she wore little or no makeup. She had on cutoff shorts and a lopsided sweatshirt that scarcely covered her midriff and slid off one shoulder. She smiled when she saw us. But I bet her smile wasn't nearly as broad as mine.

"FBI, you're back," she mumbled. "Hey, Paul, the FBI guys are back."

She was joined at the door by the thin man with the captain's beard. Adderly beamed. "Well, I did not expect to see you all again," he said. "What's up? Got a drug lord for us to hunt down on the Gulf?"

Rez and I took turns explaining what we needed. "But understand the danger involved," Rez said. "This—"

Adderly held up a hand. "Are you kidding me?" he asked, tugging Darcy close to his side. "We wouldn't miss this for the world. Helping you get those La Familia guys...most exciting night of my life."

"We can't go in a club around here without someone buying us a round," Darcy said.

"That's something too," Adderly added. "With all the bloated windbags yachting around out here, spouting off about regattas and all that, ha! They'll never top my stories. Let's cast off!"

*** *** *** ***

"They're ready," Jack said.

Dr. Gary watched Midge and Carrie. Their eyes were open, seeing but not seeing. The anthenol-laced patches had done their work. "How about it, Carrie? Midge? Are you ready to make your movie?"

"Moo-vee," Carrie mumbled lazily.

Midge stretched like a cat in a sunbeam. "I'm ready...ready, ready, me."

Dr. Gary swung around to the main camera. "Satellite uplink is strong," he said, gazing warmly at Jack. "Initiate the protocol. Let's release our Manifesto."

Jack woke the sleeping laptop. The Manifesto file had been preloaded into the encryption breaking virus. The remote servers had been busy for more than a year, cycling through the government's cyber-warfare security systems, adding hitchhiker data and withdrawing bits of code for emulation. Jack had field tested the delivery agent a week prior.

It was just a rudimentary thing to confirm that the hack would work for the Manifesto release. It had caused a relatively minute percentage of government employees to receive an email that made it appear as if the last email sent from that account had bounced, returned to sender. It had worked like a charm. And no one noticed. No cyber watchdog caught the code or even attempted to block it.

Jack took a deep breath. So much had led to this night. He knew...no, wait. No more masquerade. No more being forced into the mold. *She* would send the Manifesto as *she* really was.

She looked down at the screen, the blinking connect button. One click, and the Manifesto would go forth. It would bind to ten thousand government email accounts. Then a million. It would flood the Internet's most popular servers, and it would establish a pathway for the video uplink.

It would set the web on fire.

*** *** *** ***

Adderly called the travel time forty-five minutes to the Coast Guard's nearest yacht-sized contact. Within ten or twelve miles, he'd explained, we'd pick up the contact ourselves...if it was still there.

Rez and I sat below, and I felt the weight of her stare heavy on my shoulders. It wasn't the only weight.

The Nephilim. It had found me twice. It could find me again, and I had no idea how it was tracking me. I shook my head at my own inadequacy. Forneus the Felriven, the Nephilim, and the entire FBI...I'd really outdone myself this time.

"I saw your website," Rez said.

The comment hit me like a foam sledgehammer. "My...website?" I said. "I don't have a website."

"Yes, you do," she said. "Dozens of them. But one in particular seems to be a kind of hub. I read some of the articles. You're a folk hero, you know that?"

"Don't believe everything you read."

"I don't," she said. "But there were too many stories, from too diverse an audience to discount. You've helped a lot of people."

"I've failed more than I've helped," I said.

"Not from what I've read," she said. "That's why I'm still here. That's why I didn't run to the nearest phone and call down FBI fire and brimstone on you."

"Interesting choice of words."

"Sorry," she said. She paused a breath. "On those websites, there were photos of you."

I knew where she was headed.

"And on the closed circuit monitor back at the police station," she said, "I could see you, but your face, your flesh was distorted. Did you do that?"

"Not on purpose," I said. "It's actually a beneficial byproduct of my kind. It's a little hard to explain, but because I am knit together of...otherworldly flesh and blood, cameras can't cope. Even with the ultra-high speed shutters, they just can't reconcile the strange light reflections. It's called dimensional blurring. It's how I got my nickname."

"We've got the contact!" Paul Adderly's voice, made tinny by the intercom. "Took longer than I thought. We're seven miles out."

"Almost there," I said.

"What about the nickname?" Rez persisted. "Blurry photos?"

"Ghost," I said. "The first time I used the alias John Spector, a guy I helped out took my picture with his young son. When he saw it, he said, 'Man, this looks like a ghost pic.' The name just stuck."

I watched the wheels turning in Rez's expression. "You...wait," she said, "you mean to tell me that...all the ghost pictures, all that paranormal stuff—"

I nodded and said, "Angels: my side, and the Fallen. There are other things out there as well, but not ghosts anyway. That reminds me...Rez, something you should know. If things go badly, don't hesitate to shoot, and I mean shoot to kill. When we were at the surgeon's dinner, when we confronted Doctor Lacy and Jack: I felt sure they were taken."

"Taken?" she echoed.

"Overcome," I said. "When a person dwells so deeply and so often in darkness, a crack can form in his mind. That crack can be exploited by the Fallen. People can become...well almost like puppets."

"You mean like...possessed?"

I nodded. "That is the common phrase, yes," I said. "But it is vastly overused and almost completely misunderstood. But, in this case, I believe Jack and Dr. Gary are taken. If I'm right, that will make them very strong. It'll raise their tolerance for pain. It'll make them absolutely ruthless. If all goes well, you won't have to deal with them. But if not, if you find yourself standing against them, don't bother with rights and speeches. Kill them."

{ Chapter 39 }

"WHOOPIE!" MIDGE EXULTED in the ship's motion. "Wee bump," Carrie cooed. "This is such fun."

Jack looked questioningly at Dr. Gary. He was the real seaman of the two.

"No problem," Dr. Gary said. "Storm's not on us yet, but even if it breaks overhead, we'll be fine. This is a thin line of thunderstorms; not a hurricane." He laughed. "It'll roll through and be gone."

Jack's mouse hovered over the connect button. "This is it, then," she said.

"Do it," Dr. Gary replied.

Jack clicked the button, and Dr. Gary exhaled. As Jack had explained it, there would be no status message, no progress bar. This wasn't an upload. It was a command of release, as if tens of thousands of caged wild animals were simultaneously turned loose.

"We've done it," Jack whispered. "We really have."

"Why are you crying?" Midge asked.

"This isn't a time to be sad," Carrie mumbled, swaying slightly with the motion of the boat.

"No," Dr. Gary said. "Carrie's right. This is a time for celebration."

Jack wiped away her tears. "You're right, of course." She minimized the connection window, and checked a few graphic gauges. "Signal strength couldn't be better," she said.

"Time to go live," Dr. Gary said. He stood and in turn, placed a hand on Carrie and Midge's shoulders. "Well, girls," he said, "are you ready to meet the world?"

"Oh, I am!" Midge said, eyes glimmering.

"Me too," Carrie replied. "Can I go first? Can I?"

"I don't see why not," Dr. Gary said. He nodded at Jack.

She stood, went to a port-side drawer, and withdrew Cain's Dagger.

* * *   * * *   * * *   * * *

I stood on the deck of *The Sirocco* and gazed out into the darkness, waiting for Adderly to pass me the binoculars.

"Yup," Adderly said. "That's an Oyster 625. Bet my life on it." He handed me the binoculars, and said, "See the bank of vertical windows at midship, kind of rounded rectangles, right? That's an Oyster thing. Beautiful ship."

Between the rolling waves and, in the intermittent flashes of lightning, I saw what Adderly was talking about. They weren't round like typical portholes, not like La Compañía's customized Sun Odyssey. But Adderly seemed certain about the ship being an Oyster.

"It's them," I whispered, lowering the binoculars. "Rez, it's them."

Thunder rumbled ominously. "Mr. Adderly," Agent Rezvani said. "Anchor here. And I mean, stay anchored here until we flash a light three times. If—when—we do, it'll mean that everything is secure, and we'll need you to come alongside."

"Got it," he said. "Don't worry, I'm nobody's hero. But the guys at the yacht club won't know that. Heh."

Darcy slapped him playfully on the shoulder. "You old sea dog," she said.

"Easy on the *old* talk, Darce," he said.

Shrugging out of my tuxedo jacket, I turned to Rez. "We need to go."

"Like that?" Adderly asked, incredulous. "I mean, she looks ready for a fight, but ah, you look like a penguin."

"We didn't really have time to prepare," Rez explained.

Adderly winked at Darcy. "Take the wheel, would'ya, Darce?" he asked. "I need to take Special Agent Spector down below for a moment."

She winked back mischievously and padded over to the wheel. Rez hung back with her, and just before we disappeared below, I thought I caught that canny glimmer in Rez's eyes.

Below deck, Adderly took out a ring of keys and opened a very new, very secure-looking footlocker.

I grinned. "Mr. Adderly," I said. "Have you been shopping?"

"Well...after those La Compañía types got all upset," he said, "threatening me, my family, and my family's family, well, I figured I needed a little something more. For home protection...you understand."

Adderly's footlocker looked like it might have been lifted from a Navy Seal supply depot. "That's a Benelli Super 90," I said, pointing to the sleek black 12-gauge, semiautomatic shotgun.

"Already loaded," Adderly said. "Cost a bit, that one."

I took the shotgun. I had The Edge, but not everyone recognized the threat of my weapon right away. Shotguns had a nice way of getting people's attention. I also took the Navy Mark 3, 6.5 inch combat knife. Most often called the Ka-Bar, the Mark 3 sported a non-reflective black oxide finish so as not to reflect light. The handle had a blunt face that could be used to smash things...if such a need arose. I recalled Dr. Gary's smug grin and thought smashing might be useful indeed.

    I took a Beretta M9 pistol and three clips for Rez. I knew she had one already...since she pointed it at me on shore, but extra firepower couldn't hurt. I took a black Condor tactical vest and leg rig. I picked up a pair of neoprene water shorts and a set of fins.

    "Mr. Adderly," I said. "You might have just earned yourself a crown in heaven."

    He laughed. "Well, that's the best news I've had all day," he said. "Good thing, that crown. Heaven knows I've got a lot of..." He coughed. "...a lot of regrets. Things...well, let's just say I have a bit of a past."

    "We all do," I said, putting a hand on his shoulder. "We should talk some time...after all this."

    "I think I'd like that," Mr. Adderly replied. He left me then to change into the gear.

    A minute later, I came topside and involuntarily ducked at a crack of lightning that split the sky overhead.

    "That was too close!" Darcy said.

    Rez stared up through the rain to the mantle of darkness above. Then, she looked at me. "Where'd you get all that?" she asked. "Mr. Adderly?"

    He shrugged.

    "Here, this is for you." I handed her the Beretta and the clips.

    "Locked and loaded!" Darcy said, making an awkward attempt at a Weaver stance.

GHOST

Rez zipped the weapon and ammo into her vest. "I'll keep it close to my heart," she said.

"Same as last time," I said. "We make sure the women are safe first, but after that..."

Rez nodded. The set of her jaw was firm, but her eyes seemed restless. They flicked south to the Oyster; then north over my shoulder. I glanced. There were plenty of lights on the distant shore, but also a couple running out on the Gulf.

"Anything you need to tell me?" I asked Rez.

She glared at me but said nothing. My mind churning with new variables, I slid over the side of *The Sirocco* and dropped into the water.

{ Chapter 40 }

D R. GARY SAID, "WE'RE ON IN FIVE..." He counted the rest with his fingers.

The green light lit on the remote camera. "Good morning," he said. "My name is Dr. Garrison Lacy. I am a board-certified obstetrics surgeon with twenty-two years of experience in the field. You may find my research articles and their findings in JAMA, including the salient abstracts...well, you'll find those in your email boxes and on all relevant social media sites. I am a human rights proponent. And given the terrible direction of our federal government, you might even call me a revolutionary."

Dr. Gary paused, and Jack spoke on cue. "I am Jacqueline Gainer. And I am a victim of the oppression supported by this nation's leaders and lawmakers. At age thirteen, I became pregnant, but due to the ignorant laws then, as well as, the fanatical beliefs of my parents, I was denied the right to do with my body as I pleased. I was denied the right to a legal abortion, and so, I sought help at a local college. Unfortunately, the med students who performed my procedure lacked the training and equipment. I was maimed and nearly died. In an emergency hysterectomy, my uterus was removed. Motherhood was stolen from me."

Dr. Gary spoke again. "Over the last two decades, we have witnessed a periodic shift in this nation's politics, a tragic shift to barbarism, manipulation, usury, and criminal ignorance. During such times, we have waged a silent war against the so-called Pro Life agenda. And through our good works, we have won back the rights for all of mankind's women to control their bodies. But, they turned out to be short-lived victories. And now, we stand on the brink of the worst travesty in American History since the first slaves were forced onto this continent. If current trends are not reversed, then the landmark of liberty, Roe v. Wade will be repealed."

"By taking away our right to choose," Jack continued, "you steal a woman's sovereignty. You gouge away our humanity, just as my womb was torn from me. When you take away our right to choose, when you take away our humanity, you take our lives. And so tonight, we will deliver our final act of revolution: a protest written in the blood of women."

Dr. Gary used the remote zoom and focused in on Midge and Carrie. Jack continued to narrate: "I'd like to introduce two young women this nation gave up on a long, long time ago. In unconscionable hypocrisy, a so-called Pro Life nation, abandoned these two daughters...left them for dead. And dead they will be...to show you, to teach you, what a backward culture does to its people. Ladies and gentlemen, these women are modern martyrs. Do not forget their blood."

* * *   * * *   * * *   * * *

GHOST

I stayed submerged for as much of the swim as I could. Once, I surfaced for air and thought I heard a strange buzzing sound, but a thunder blast obliterated any chance of identifying it.

In the darkness and murk, there was no way to tell if Rez was keeping pace. I saw no sign of her on the surface, so I swam on. The water gave me some additional rejuvenation but, as much as my body ached for it, I could not stop, could not open up to the resetting I really needed.

I surfaced near the heaving keel, paddled around to the transom, and waited. Rez appeared a moment later. Lightning flickered and slashed overhead. The thunder crashed and rolled and never seemed to end. In the span of our several hundred yard swim, the weather had gone from threatening to murderous. The irony was not lost on me.

Rez and I exchanged grim glances but said nothing. It was no small task to clamber up the landing's half ladder in the rolling Gulf. With the storm raging, we found the deck predictably empty. But through the sheets of rain, lights gleamed angrily ahead.

We moved as quickly as we could across the lightning-strobed, endlessly tilting deck; which is to say, we didn't move quickly at all. By the time we reached the door to the main cabin stair, it felt like we'd crossed the yacht's 62.5 feet six times.

Unlike the movies where ships seemed to somehow have multiple ways of ingress and egress, there were only two ways in. And the cabin stair was the only way we could enter standing up.

I wiped the rain out of my eyes only to have the wind toss another bucket-full right into my face. I glanced at Rez. With her gun raised, her hair plastered to her dark and rain-streaked flesh, she looked like a Comanche Indian warrior. I wondered briefly about the wisdom in letting her stay behind me, but there was nothing for it. I raised the Benelli Super 90 with my right hand, opened the door with my left.

Getting down the stair without slipping was a chore, but we took it slow. We found ourselves in a spacious living area, lit warmly in the corners and with recessed lights above. Bench seat couches lined both sides of the room and a dining table cozied up to the couch on the right.

I was a little surprised to find no one in the room. Even in a luxurious 62ft., yacht there was only so much living area. Beyond the living room, there was a very narrow, very short hall...and light beyond. I nodded to Rez, tucked the shotgun into my shoulder, and crept forward.

The door just ahead was cracked about two inches, and I couldn't immediately tell what was on the other side. But I heard voices. One of them sounded slurred, drunken.

"My turn, my turn, myyyy turn."

The other voice was low and gritty but clear enough.

"...if the Supreme Court cannot recognize the inherent authority of a woman over her own body, it has left the path of reason. A woman with no choice is reduced to chattel, enslaved...breathing but still dead. Antiquated monotheistic ideologies must not be permitted to once again dictate the rule of law. This determined initiative to overturn Roe must be defeated utterly. Let the blood of..."

That was all I could bear. I kicked open the door, stepped inside and, in an instant, took in the entire scene. It might once have been a bedroom, but it had been retrofit to become a studio. There were bright lights overhead and digital lights blinking on banks of electronics ahead. Nearest us, was a large digital motion picture camera, and in its view, there sat four people.

Dr. Garrison Lacy was on the left. Smiling Jack on the right. Not Smiling Jack as he...she'd portrayed herself in all the photos and videos. This was Jacqueline Gainer: hair down, make up on, and a shirt tight enough to reveal the bosom she'd kept hidden. In that stunning moment, I felt just a flash of pity...wondering why she had chosen her tragic path. All pity vanished when I saw the Cain's Dagger in her hand.

Jack held the knife to the throat of a young African-American woman. The other young woman who sat between the doctor and Jack had long, sandy brown hair that had been intricately braided. Both young women wore sheer white camis and the same ghastly grin as the other women in the photos. The women who were about to die.

All that, in an instant. And before my next breath, I realized my mistake. The shotgun, as intimidating as it was, left me at a huge disadvantage. It lacked precision. Dr. Lacy sat too close to the sandy-haired woman; Jack far too close to the dark-skinned woman.

Firing on either killer with the shotgun risked hitting the innocent as well. I could only hope Rez would make the same assessment and train her M9 on Jack.

"Rezvani, is it?" Doctor Lacy asked, adjusting his thick-framed glasses. If he was shocked by our sudden appearance, he showed no sign of it. Thunder growled ominously outside. "But not a doctor, after all. Shame. Had you a clinical perspective, you might understand."

"I understand that you are both murderers," Rez said, her voice tight, words clipped as if she was biting them as they escaped her lips. She stepped beside me and raised the Beretta to aim at Jack, just as I'd hoped she would.

"Murderers," Jack said slowly, as if chewing on the term. "That's what people like you call all who support a woman's right to choose, isn't it?"

{433}

"It is their rhetorical stance," Dr. Gary said. "And yet they come to kill us. Justifiable, they might say. Just as we justify what we are doing on behalf of womankind. Why don't you come before the camera, officers? We are broadcasting live to hundreds...of millions."

My shotgun blast shattered the moment...and the camera. Its black, modular casing splintered into jagged, smoking shards. What was left of the camera jolted from the tripod and clattered up against the far bulkhead. In that same moment, there was a clap of thunder. Only it wasn't thunder.

Rez had fired her Beretta. As I tossed the shotgun away and ripped The Edge from my vest, I saw blood erupt from Jack's shoulder. *The head,* Rez! I screamed mentally. *You should have shot her in the head!*

But the Cain's Dagger fell from Jack's limp left hand. The young women swayed slightly and held their hands up to cover their ears.

"Move away from the girls!" Rez yelled. "NOW!"

"It's far too late," Dr. Lacy replied, his dark eyes flashing malevolently. "The message has gone out. The world knows."

"I said, get up and move away from the girls!" Rez fired and put a dark hole not ten inches above the doctor's right ear.

He didn't even flinch. His upper lip curled into a snarl beneath his bristling mustache, making him look like some cornered feral animal. Now, I could see it plainly. I didn't need to engage Netherview. Dr. Garrison Lacy had been taken by something more than a Shade.

Then, the lights went out.

{ Chapter 41 }

"REZ!" I CRIED OUT, lunging forward. "Protect the girls!"

Something barreled into me hard. I was thrown against the bulkhead. Blinking at the abject darkness, I tried to roll to a knee. But blunt force struck my side, and I toppled. The next thing I knew, something sat astride my chest and had a hand on my throat. A single hand.

But that grip was more than human. It was devastatingly strong, and I had little bodily strength to fight it off.

But I had The Edge.

And then there was light.

The words appeared as brightly in my consciousness as the weapon's incandescent blade in the darkness. I carved a weak slash through Jack's elbow, but it was enough. She shrieked and fell away from me. She rolled into the darkness.

I grabbed her dismembered forearm, pried her hand from my throat, and tossed the limb away. But Jack wasn't finished. Her pale face and crazed dark eyes came out of the black. Her teeth flashed and she took me in an animal embrace that made it impossible for me to strike with The Edge.

I felt a sharp, stinging burn on my neck...an agony-inducing pinching of flesh as she bit into me. I dropped The Edge and tried to roll her. She clamped down even harder, and we fell backward into the cabin wall. I pushed at her shoulders, but it only caused the pain of her vice-like bite to intensify exponentially. If I forced her away, she would tear out my throat.

So I did the only thing I could. I wrapped my arms around her back and shoulders and thrust her into an even tighter embrace. My hands found her spine at last. I felt the bony knobs of vertebrae under my fingertips. I probed and prodded until I found the pressure points. Then I drove the points of my fingers in hard.

The stilling touch.

Her jaws lost pressure, and she went limp. I rolled her to the side. She wasn't dead. Not yet. But I couldn't linger. I grabbed up The Edge and cried out, "Rez!"

There was no answer. That's when I saw the square of lesser darkness. A hatch had been opened in the ceiling above the corner where Dr. Lacy had been. In the bluish light of my weapon I saw the two young women laying side-by-side and clutching each other.

"Rez!" I yelled again. "Rez, where are you?"

"Up here!" came a voice from above. But the voice was muffled and distorted by the storm. It could have been anyone for all I could tell.

No way, I'm sticking my head up through the hatch, I thought, my mind racing. That was not going to be a part of any plan.

I glanced down at Jack. Her eyes found me, and somehow, I could feel the smile in her consciousness. I so wanted to pry the Shade out of her right then and there, to strangle it in my bare hands...but I couldn't. Not yet.

GHOST

I left her lying there, and went to the two girls. They whimpered softly watching the Edge in my hand. I switched it off for a moment, picked up both young women from the bench, and carried them aft. I left them in an alcove behind the cabin stair. "Stay here!" I commanded them, using a little Netherview to deepen my voice. And I flicked on the Edge. It was just enough for a glimpse, but I saw the blazing red Soulmark on each young woman. I prayed for their healing, turned, and left them.

I took the stairs and thrust myself out into the storm. Lightning lit the back of the sail craft. No one was there, but I saw something large out on the water. There was a pale shape and a red light, but that was all I could make out through the pitch and yaw of the waves and the windblown curtain of rain.

The boat leaned suddenly, and I was thrown to one knee. An icy cold blast of water smacked into me. I stumbled forward, spun, righted myself with a slick rail, and spun around. "Rez!" I yelled into the wind.

I heard something in reply, a cry maybe. Nothing intelligible.

I plunged forward, half-sprinting, half-sliding. I ducked under the boom and came face-to-face with a nightmare.

{ Chapter 42 }

IN THE ETHEREAL BLUE LIGHT of The Edge, I saw Dr. Garrison Lacy holding Rez from behind. It was an eerily similar pose to all the Smiling Jack photos.

But no one was smiling.

The doctor looked as if he'd taken a sledgehammer to the face. His nose was mashed to one side, obviously broken. His left eye was swollen near to the point of being shut. Blood ran in rivulets from his temple, from the corner of his other eye, and like a flood from his ruined nose.

Somehow, Rez looked worse. Her cheeks, forehead, and jaw bore the swollen and bloodied abrasions that could have only come from being bludgeoned with the butt of a gun.

The same gun that Dr. Lacy now held with the barrel pointed under Rez's chin.

"You...sssee," he said, his gritty voice all the more choked with gobbets of gore. "It isss...too late."

Just then voices came out of the night, and a dozen suns blazed around us. Or, so it seemed.

"SAILORS ABOARD OYSTER SIX-TWO-FIVE, BY THE AUTHORITY OF THE UNITED STATES COAST GUARD, YOU ARE COMMANDED TO STAND DOWN!"

Even in the raging storm, the voice sounded like a cannon blast. My eyes darted left and right. A large cutter heaved and rolled on either side of us.

"You called them," I said. "Didn't you, Rez."

She looked up at me weakly and gave the slightest of nods.

"John Spector!" came another voice from the speaker of the portside cutter. "This is Deputy Director Barnes of the FBI! Put down your weapon!"

I didn't move a muscle. I stared ahead and saw three tiny, bright-red dots appear on Dr. Lacy's neck and face. I looked down and found three more dots darting around my chest. I was certain a couple danced on my head as well.

Laser sighted rifles in the hands of trained snipers. It was over. I deactivated and dropped The Edge.

{ Chapter 43 }

"DOCTOR GARRISON LACY!" Barnes bellowed from the speaker. "You are marked. Drop your weapon immediately!"

I watched the doctor look left. He tried to move Rez's body as a human shield, but then he saw the red dots dancing on his right side. It didn't matter which way he turned. The other would have a clear head shot.

He held out his right arm, let the gun dangle from a finger, and then, with a flick of his wrist, sent the weapon careening overboard. But he did not let go of Rez. He kept her pressed tight to his left side.

"Release Agent Rezvani!" Barnes commanded. "Now!"

"Even better," Dr. Lacy said, lisping. He glanced down at the deck as if thinking. "A very public trial...weeksss on end. A new platform for our message."

Our? What is he talking—I saw movement. A head emerged from the hatch just a few feet away. Smiling Jack slowly clambered out. Her hair was wild and soaked, but it was her. She was missing the lower half of one arm, and the other arm, strewn with dark blood, hung uselessly at her side. Still she came up.

"You there!" came Barnes' voice. "Don't move!"

I cringed inwardly. Barnes couldn't tell if Jack was a victim or something else. He wouldn't fire, not unless Jack did something provocative. But Jack did nothing like that. She stumbled out of the hatch, got to one knee, and stood just to Dr. Lacy's left.

Then, I watched Dr. Lacy turn his body, so that Rez was now shielding his right side. I knew what he was doing. And I knew what I had to do.

"You know what your trouble is, Rez?" I called out.

"What's that, Spector?" she groused, her voice just a thin cry.

"You just don't listen!" I said.

"Everybody, get down on the deck!" Barnes bellowed.

I thought maybe Barnes saw too, and thought maybe, he didn't like the positioning either.

"Get down on the deck!"

"I listen when it makes sense," Rez said, glaring at me. I saw a glimmer in her eyes, that same cunning I'd seen before, but now with a hint of mischief.

I heard boots on the deck far behind me. The Coast Guard, the FBI—whoever—they were boarding. Time was running out.

"Nah, Rez," I continued, tensing my legs. "You don't listen at all. First, I told you this was all beyond your pay grade. You didn't listen. I told you to protect the victims. You didn't listen."

"Lacy was getting away!" she barked back at me. "What was I supposed to do?"

"Get down on the deck, NOW!"

"Worst of all, Rez," I said quietly. "I told you to kill him, not fight him."

"You do it!" she cried out. In that moment, several things happened.

Voices behind me cried out, "Freeze!" and "Get down on the deck!"

Machine gun fire erupted from somewhere, knocking out four of the Coast Guard's spotlights.

Lightning flashed, and Rez drove her head back sharply, slamming her skull into Dr. Lacy's pulverized nose. He staggered backward, and the little red laser dots scattered and disappeared. Rez bolted toward the starboard rail.

I thought I heard someone shouting in Spanish amidst the chattering gunfire, but I rushed forward, sidestepping the open hatch and a knot of rigging. I took Jack under the arm, hoisted her off her feet, and kept going.

"You cannot win," Dr. Lacy cried out, but it was not Dr. Lacy's voice. It was not a single voice. A chorus of hideous, rasping voices slithered out from his lips, "...not against us. We are Legionnnn! We are—"

"Save it!" I barked, barreling into Lacy and charging toward the port rail. "I've heard it before. '*You are many.*' Like I care. I'm taking all of you down!"

With machine gun rounds raking chunks out of my shoulders and upper back, I took the Smiling Jack killers overboard and down, down into the dark, storm-tossed water.

{ Chapter 44 }

IT IS NO SMALL FEAT to drag two semi-buoyant human beings beneath the water and propel them into the depths. I squeezed them both at the ribs, forcing the air from their lungs. They struggled against me, and their combined strength was formidable. Too formidable for what I had left in the tank. It might end me, but I took a chance.

I went to that deep inner place, and let my mask fall away. It wasn't easy, and there was no massive burst of energy or light. But I felt my wings free. Using their propulsion, I kept going down.

As the pressure in my ears increased, so too did the realization of what I was doing. I had never extended The Offer to Garrison Lacy or Jacqueline Gainer, and I was taking them to die. Somewhere in the far corner of my consciousness, it was suggested that the two killers had lived long enough on the earth, that they had each had other offers and had refused them repeatedly.

I had to hope in that because I wasn't turning back.

I felt the fleshly structures in my ears burst, but I kept going down. I squeezed the killers and squeezed again, and I began to feel the last reservoir of my strength draining away.

I held on but felt the acidic burn from exertion in my arms fade into something closer to numbness. I wondered if I would black out before the killers would die.

But then, they stopped struggling and went very still. I watched a single translucent appendage emerge from Jack's open mouth. It was like a thick jellyfish tendril, but it had eyes and teeth, more like an eel or a leech. It wriggled free and fled into the murk.

More than a dozen Shades likewise burst out of Dr. Lacy's body. They came from his eyes, his nose, and his mouth. They scurried away in the water.

My vision graying out at the edges, I smiled at the thought of the Shades that deep in the saltwater. They hated water worse than I did, and better still, they have no sense of direction. They might never find their way to the surface.

My last thought as I lost consciousness was, *Neither will I.*

{ Chapter 45 }

I DIDN'T DROWN.
But I'm not altogether sure what happened as I sank deeper into the Gulf of Mexico. My best guess is that my body completely reset while I was unconscious. Rejuvenated and unmasked, I must have flown...somewhere. When I awoke, I thought I might be in a jungle, on a new mission.

But I wasn't. I still had all my memories of Smiling Jack. And the jungle was actually a landscaped thicket of bushes near Great Progress Clinic for Women. And it was night, early night. The sun had all but disappeared in angry red smear at the horizon.

I wasn't sure how that could be unless I'd been unconscious for close to a whole day. Maybe I had been. The kind of washed out I was, it would take that long for a complete resetting. All I knew for certain was that I had reset, unmasked, and flown here to the clinic. I flexed the muscle in my arm, shrugged the cables of muscle in my neck, and flared my back. Best resetting I'd had in years. I felt brand new. I felt strong.

The Edge! I had dropped it on the ship's deck before diving over the rail. But, when I patted my tuxedo pants pocket, I found the weapon there. I blinked, trying to remember flying to the coast, searching for Smiling Jack's Oyster 625, and then taking back my weapon. But there was nothing there to remember. Just a gaping gray sea. Still...having my go-to weapon back was a big plus.

But unfortunately I was going to be ended anyway.

Forneus the Felriven waited for me inside the clinic. He had my silver case. I needed it for Memory Washing and...well, just because it was *my* silver case. My tools were in there. I needed my tools.

So, feeling surly and grim, I emerged from the bushes and strode towards the clinic. I switched over to Netherview immediately, and the spiderish building became a fenced-in stronghold teeming with Shades.

I ducked under the gnarled limb of a leafless ethereal tree and kicked the iron gate in. It swung open and slammed against the other side of the fence with a resounding clatter. The Shades looked up. They saw me. I didn't care.

With my fists balled and hanging at my sides like leaden hammers, I strode up to the Shades and glared at them. They slithered and clambered around their buttress perch. They scowled and sneered and even spat. But they didn't attack.

A roamer had the nerve to leap into the walk in front of me. It danced around and wagged its elongated head at me. I hit it so hard in the face that its neck broke. Its head swung back like a sack of coins in a sock, and it collapsed at my feet. I stepped over it without looking down.

The misshapen gatehouse waited for me, and I ducked under its cruel portcullis. I found the formidable iron door open as before. And as before, it slammed shut behind me...and locked.

I felt the supernatural chill in the air and strode forward. My breath must have been hot because I exhaled great, roiling clouds with each step. The Shades that lined both sides of the long, narrow hall made no move to interfere, but they leered at me as I passed.

"Sintryst welcomes back, the Horseman!" a deep voice boomed. Hisses of approval from the myriad Shades whirled around me. I cringed inwardly. Forneus had called me Horseman. He no longer believed me to be a Guardian. He knew me. Any hope of Forneus simply handing me my case and allowing me to leave vanished like the whorls of my breath in the cold air. I shrugged off the chill and went forward.

"I delivered the message to Anthriel!" I called out. More hisses answered. "He wouldn't read it in my presence."

"Pity," Forneus' low voice rumbled out. "He might have saved me the trouble of ending you myself."

"Look," I said, continuing on. "I did what you said. I know Anthriel did read the message. I just came back for my case."

"It...is...here."

I came to the throne room and found its twin staircases lined with a virtual army of Shades and its mighty seat occupied by something worse. My resolve melted a little when I saw him.

Forneus the Felriven.

Muscle. Armor. Fur. Hooves. Wings. His mere appearance was enough to knock the wind from my lungs, but I masked it well enough and summoned enough gall to scowl.

"I must admit," Forneus said, standing and flexing his vast wings, "I really did not believe you would return. It is courage, Horseman...or bravado. I respect both. Come, your silver case awaits." He turned, and the black sword swayed at his side like a pendulum. He gestured with his thick arm, and there, at the foot of his throne, was my silver case.

I learned long ago: if someone offers you a gift, you accept it. I stepped forward, following a direct path to the case. I was under Forneus' shadow when his massive hand blocked my way.

"Lo, Horseman," Forneus said, "are you so eager to depart? You who wrought such carnage here in my domain? You who led me to believe you were a harmless Guardian? Your deceit alone is worthy of my wrath."

Shame on me. I'd also learned long ago: there's no such thing as a free lunch. I tried to keep my swallowing from being obvious. But, fire and blood, his hand was huge, the palm alone covering my entire chest.

Forneus loosed his Soulcleaver and held it horizontally for me to inspect the blade. "This is a sabeline sword," he said, as if I didn't know. "It is a volatile substance, Horseman. It has longings. Do you know what it wishes of thee?"

I had several guesses, all quite unsavory. I kept my mouth shut.

"It wishes to drink thee, to consume thee...to end thee. Goodbye, Horseman."

In his yellowed eyes, I saw a hint of regret...as if he might have wished me some other fate. But unfortunately, the rest of his countenance communicated deep-seated malice. He lifted the blade back behind him. No ceremony. No preface. He was just going to cut me down.

The Soulcleaver rang in the air as it came, but I wasn't standing still. I wasn't going to sit there like a block of wood or some sad sack waiting for execution. If I was going out, I was going out fighting.

My Edge buzzed to life, and I blocked Forneus' stroke. You couldn't actually call it a block. It was more of an anguished deflection. The Edge bounced away from Forneus' blow, and the recoil almost struck my neck. I stopped it just in time, spun, and lashed out low. That was the way to attack a much taller foe: cut out its foundation.

The Edge struck the top of Forneus' right hoof and bounced. But it bounced upward and carved a divot into the shaggy fur of Forneus' shin. There was a spray of hissing black steam, and Forneus roared.

When I say, he roared, you need to understand that an adult lion would shrivel up and die if it heard the sound Forneus made. It felt as if the entire throne room shook. I fell over on my side and clutched my ears. My heart raced so hard, I feared it would rupture.

Forneus kicked me.

The stunning blow made my ears ring and catapulted me across the throne room. I crashed into something hard and lost consciousness for a moment. I came to in the midst of Forneus' thunderous rage. He stood something on the order of sixty yards away. His kick had launched me that far.

"...dared to strike me?" Forneus yelled as he lashed out with his Soulcleaver and took out a column of stone as if it was made of papier-mâché.

I'm really—really—glad that Forneus hadn't used that stroke against me.

Suddenly, I found myself speaking. "Oh, get over yourself!" I choked out the words, tasting blood. "You're just a Knightshade! Sure, you might be an ancient Knightshade with an infamous reputation and legendary conquests, but you're still just a Knightshade!"

Forneus' head fell back and the hall filled with his suffocating laughter. "Oh, Horseman," he said, each word weighted with heavy rolls of his mirth, "you are defiant till the end! You should have been one of the Fallen!"

"Nah," I said. "The Most High has a better retirement plan."

That might not have been the best thing to say. Like the flick of a switch, Forneus' laughter ceased. "You spratling!" he hissed, using a curse I'd heard only once before. The Guardian who'd spoken it before had been cast out...forever.

"You speak of what you do not know!" Forneus growled. He stepped forward, each deliberate step vibrating the floor. He was coming to finish me.

"Speaking of what I do not know," I said, beyond caring at this point. "What was in that message you had me deliver to Anthriel?"

Forneus stopped his approach just twenty yards from me. "It was not for your eyes, little one," he said. "It was meant for your betters."

"Okay, I get that," I said. "But since you're about to ruin me, you could at least give me a hint."

"Very well then," Forneus said. "A dying wish. Know this, Horseman, with that scroll...I have started a war."

"So? The Euangelion and the Fallen have been at war for ten thousand ages."

"Not a war between our kinds," Forneus said, and he stepped forward. "You may take that knowledge to Oblivion!"

I rose to one knee, and found that The Edge was still in my hand. I wouldn't cower. I wouldn't close my eyes. I held the blade defiantly...and shivered.

If the room had been cold before, it dropped suddenly to sub Arctic now. Just then the Edge started to buzz in my hands. It rattled with such a tremor that the hand holding it felt numb.

Of all the times for the Edge to act up—No! I suddenly knew the sensation for what it was. The ground, still shuddering with each of Forneus' thunderous footfalls, began to surge and pulse with electricity. Tiny spiders of voltage clambered up the flesh of my knee and thigh.

GHOST

The air between Forneus and me seemed to melt, and a black wound formed. The wound bled tendrils of night, and the Nephilim formed from the pooling darkness. Continuing to coalesce into that livid silvery-blue flesh, the Nephilim stood tall, blocking Forneus from my view.

"You...keep running...from me," it said, in that voice of ten-thousand murders.

"Out of my way, smoke thing!" Forneus thundered. And suddenly, his massive hand thrust the Nephilim to the side. But the Nephilim's movement wasn't a fall so much as a reconstitution of its form. The flesh melted into black vapor and reformed. Its disease-ridden yellow eyes leered back at Forneus.

"Felriven..." the Nephilim whispered. "I...have heard...of thee."

"Stand aside," Forneus said. "My quarrel is not with you."

"Oh...yes. Yes...it is." Smoke curled around the Nephilim's limbs. And when it spoke again, I thought I saw flames. "The Horseman...is my...quarry."

Forneus drove his Soulcleaver at the Nephilim, carving a scathing stroke through its midsection.

If the Nephilim felt the blow, it made no cry. There was an instantaneous splattering of dark gore where the blade had swept through, but then, the Nephilim was whole again. It lifted both arms and its hands became twin vortices of oily black mist. They drove into Forneus' chest and began to churn. Shreds of armor, fur, and flesh began to fly, and Forneus unleashed such a cacophony of agony that I swooned.

"Run...away now...Horseman," the Nephilim said. And, even as it continued to rip at Forneus, it turned its head and gazed at me. "I...will come...find thee...later."

That was all I needed to hear. I leapt up on wobbly legs, made a wide berth around Forneus and ran for the throne. I had to duck and dodge dozens of Shades who'd only just begun to fly to the aid of their master. If my earlier count had been close, there must have been near a legion of Shades in and around Sintryst. I hoped they smothered the Nephilim, and I hoped they ended each other.

I grabbed up my silver case and ran. No, I sprinted. Actually, I drove my legs so hard that both hamstrings popped. I practically fell through the gatehouse door. I hit the turf at a crawl. But then, I flew.

{ Chapter 46 }

I FOUND THE ASSASSIN'S CAR at the mall in Pensacola and drove it on fumes back to the Four Seasons Marina. I spent the better part of the afternoon visiting with the Adderlys. We had us a good conversation.

I found out from Paul Adderly that the chaos the other night had been caused by a La Compañía gunboat that had been sent to hit *The Sirocco*. When the Coast Guard showed up, the mafia gunboat opened fire. Fortunately, the U.S. Coast Guard is not to be trifled with. They sent the gunboat to the bottom of the Gulf and, together with the FBI, rounded up the floaters who survived.

Adderly couldn't tell me anything about the two young women, Smiling Jack's final intended victims. But, he did say that I was deemed "lost at sea." They thought I had drowned.

So much the better.

I answered a few questions for the Adderlys before I left. They were good questions. The answers were even better.

I ran out of gas on the way to Panama City Hospital Center. I walked the rest of the way.

***   ***   ***   ***

Doctor Shepherd shook my hand and led me to his office. We sat. He twirled his mustache a bit. Then he held up a finger. "Ah, just a minute," he said. "I have to make a quick call."

He picked up the hospital phone and dialed exactly eleven numbers. An outside line. An area code. A phone number.

"This is Doc Shepherd over at PCBHC," he said. "Right. Looks like I've got a slot available for you for the procedure you requested. Uh, huh. Right. I'll see you then." He hung up.

"Now then, Agent Spector," he said. "Where were we?"

"Remember, I'm not an agent," I said. "Not really."

"Right, right. Old habits die hard." He laughed self consciously. "So, where were we, Mr. Spector?"

"I was saying goodbye."

"You were?" he said. "Work all finished here?"

I nodded. "I was wondering if you had a card, something with your contact information? And I was wondering if I might be able to call you in the future if I have...issues...on other cases."

"I'm a cardiac surgeon, not a detective," he said. "Ha, sounded like Dr. McCoy there." He fished around in his desk drawer and retrieved a card. "Not sure what help I can offer, but such as it is, you have it."

"Thank you," I said. I stood.

"That it then?" Doc Shepherd asked.

"I have another mission."

"Can you tell me?" he asked. "Did you get the killer, Smiling Jack?"

"There were two killers," I replied. "And yes, I got them."

He nodded thoughtfully. "I don't care for any loss of life," he said. "But this...this was different. I read their Manifesto. Have you?"

I shook my head.

"Well, don't bother," he said. "It's the most heinous diatribe I've ever encountered. Is it true they were going to kill those women on TV and online in real time?"

I nodded. "In their twisted logic," I said, "they saw it as a sacrifice for the greater cause."

"Sick."

"I agree."

I took Doctor Shepherd's card. We shook hands again. And I left.

When the elevator doors opened onto the first floor. I found Agent Rezvani waiting for me.

She didn't look happy.

{ Chapter 47 }

"Am I under arrest?" I asked.

"You son of a—"

"Careful," I cautioned.

Suddenly, Deanna Rezvani, Special Agent of the FBI, was hugging me. I felt the wetness of tears on my neck.

"I...I thought you were dead," she whispered.

"Came close," I said. "Several times. You had Doc Shepherd working for you, right? He called you?"

She laughed, drew back, and wiped tears. I left the elevator, and we walked through the atrium. I glanced up the silly cherubs one last time. I think Rez noticed. She followed my line of sight and laughed.

"So are you going to arrest me?" I asked as we departed the hospital.

"No, I'm not going to arrest you," Rez replied, making a face. "You're clear of the killings at the police station. The closed circuit shows...well, it shows some strange stuff, but it's pretty clear you didn't kill those officers or the inmates. The whole state—shoot, half the nation—is still screaming for an arrest.

Barnes still wants to bring you in for questioning, but he can suck an egg."

"Can you give me a ride, then?" I asked.

"Where to?" she asked. "Wanna get a drink, maybe?"

"That would be nice," I said. "I could use some coffee, but I need to be somewhere."

"Where?"

"The airport."

The first ten minutes of the drive were curiously silent, but I felt an electric tension in the air, all radiating from Agent Rezvani.

"We wouldn't have gotten them," she said at last, her eyes fixed on the highway. "Without you, I mean."

"The girls? Please tell me they made it."

"Yeah, yeah they did. They're reunited with their parents. There'll be a lot of dark days and nights...a lot of therapy."

I nodded. I knew there would be.

"Have you seen the news?"

"No," I said. "Why?"

"The bastards won," she said.

"What do you mean?" I asked. "Garrison Lacy and Jacqueline Gainer are dead."

"I know that," Rez said. "We fished their bodies out of the Gulf. But their message went out."

I closed my eyes tight. I knew I wasn't going to like the answer, but I asked anyway. "The Supreme Court?"

Rez whispered, "Roe v. Wade stands."

I inhaled. I exhaled. But I didn't understand.

"What's wrong with this country," Rez muttered.

"I thought you were Pro Choice."

"I...well, I was," she said. "But then...I met you."

GHOST

She took the first airport exit, but she was driving more slowly than she usually did.

"Is there something else?" I asked.

"There are a lot of something elses," she replied, releasing an exasperated sigh. "You're a freakin' angel."

"I don't think I can answer your questions, not all of them, anyway."

"But what about God?" she said. "I mean, if you're real...well, that means..."

"Yes," I said.

She opened her mouth to say something more, but closed it. She was silent until we got closer to the airport. "What airline?"

"Delta."

She cruised up to the Delta terminal. "I see you got your silver case back," she said.

"I try not to go anywhere without it." I opened the car door, stepped out.

"Hey," she called.

I leaned down. "Thank you, Agent Rezvani," I said. "Rez, I mean. You have no idea what an impact your deeds have wrought."

"Whoa, now that's some angel talk right there," she said. She was quiet a moment. Then, she said, "I don't suppose you want to tell me where you're headed?"

I smiled. "I'm not sure yet. I'll know when I get to the desk."

"Uh, huh," she said. "I'm not going to see you again...am I?"

"Probably not," I replied. "I don't maintain relationships well."

Rez laughed. "Neither do I." She smiled, and there was an entire novel unspoken in that smile.

I walked away.

{ 461 }

Wayne Thomas Batson

* * * * * * * * * * * *

When I came to the Delta desk, I found myself saying, "I need to book a flight to Atlanta."

"We have flights to ATL leaving pretty much all afternoon," the Delta rep said.

"What's soonest?"

"Flight 491 leaves in 30 minutes."

"Sold," I said.

I paid cash for my ticket to Atlanta. Seventy bucks. That was all. Not bad. That left me $523. And that was odd. Every mission, every time, cost me exactly what I'd been given...to the dollar. But I had half a grand left, and the mission was over.

I mulled that until I fell asleep on the flight to Atlanta, Georgia.

* * * * * * * * * * * *

I wandered Hartsfield-Jackson Atlanta International Airport, the world's busiest airport, and realized why it was called the world's busiest airport. I was surrounded at every turn by a sea of travelers. Still, I kept walking. A mission was certainly calling me but it wasn't quite clear. As I meandered, I reflected on the message of Forneus. *I have started a war...not a war between our kinds.* What did that mean? Somewhere, I'd need to find a waypoint. I'd need to talk with Anthriel again. I'd need to find out just what sort of war I'd catalyzed.

Speaking of war, I drew a couple of suspicious glares from the airport guards. I suspect they didn't care for my taste in carry-on luggage. I wasn't worried. When I switched on Security Mode, my silver case would radiate an image to any scanner or X-ray. They would see that I was merely a professional photographer carrying a high-end digital camera and an array of accessories.

Moments later, I drifted away from the crowd mass and found myself at the Iceland Air counter. "I need a one-way ticket to Scotland," I said, blinking in surprise at my own words.

"Edinburgh or Glasgow?" the Iceland Air associate asked.

I paused for a moment. Then, I asked, "Could you tell me which flight would cost exactly $523, including tax?"

The associate looked at me as if he'd just eaten something that he wasn't quite certain he liked. "Uh...let me check," he said. He tip-tapped on the keys a bit. "How...son of a gun, to the dollar! Edinburgh would be $523...exactly."

I smiled. It always works that way. "Looks like I'm heading to Edinburgh then."

* * *   * * *   * * *   * * *

"Ladies and gentlemen, this is your captain speaking. We're going to depart a little early. Trying to beat the storm out of here. Should be clear sailing once we get out over the Atlantic, but until then, you'll need to remain seated with seat belts in place."

I leaned toward the window. A pretty substantial wall cloud had formed just to our east. Lightning flickered beneath it. Thunder came fifteen seconds later.

As the plane accelerated down the runway, I leaned back in my seat. I had a rather impressive-looking pair of headphones on, the cord running directly into my silver case at my feet. I let the subtle music of the Memory Wash relax me. Soon, the death and sorrow of Smiling Jack would be gone. By the time the plane landed in Scotland, I'd have left all the psyche-shattering misery behind. But, I wondered about a decision I'd made.

It wasn't what I chose to forget. It was what I chose to remember.

The nose went up. The wheels left the ground. The plane leapt skyward. Thunder rumbled again as we climbed. I heard some of the other passengers muttering worriedly about the storm.

I didn't care. I love storms.

Divine violence.

The End

ABOUT THE AUTHOR

WAYNE THOMAS BATSON is the Bestselling author of ten adventure novels including the fan favorite DOOR WITHIN TRILOGY, the pirate duo ISLE OF SWORDS and ISLE OF FIRE, and the new 7-book fantasy epic DARK SEA ANNALS. A middle school Reading and English teacher for 22 years, Batson loves to challenge—and be challenged by—his students. So, when he began writing stories to supplement the school district's curriculum, it was his students who taught their teacher a lesson. Batson's students were so taken by one of the stories that, over a thirteen year span, they pushed him to make it into a full-length novel.

Wayne Thomas Batson

That story became The Door Within. Since then, Batson's students continue to be his frontline editors. Says Batson, "Two things you can count on from middle school students: Intelligence and Honesty. Kids are so much more perceptive than a lot of us 'Big Folk' give them credit for. And when something's not right in the story, they'll tell you about in very clear terms."

With over half a million books in print, Batson believes his books appeal to so many kids and adults because, at a deep level, we all long to do something that matters, and we all dream of another world.

GHOST

ACKNOWLEDGEMENTS

GHOST is my first solo eBook / paperback. It is also the first book I've written with adult readers in mind. It absolutely would never have happened if it weren't for the help of more people than I could ever hope to mention. If you helped me, and I neglected to mention you, remind me. The next round's on me.

TO MY WIFE MARY LU, you believed I could do it, and you struggled with me over the four years that led to GHOST happening. I pray the result is worthy of the love you've shown me.

To my four kids, now teenagers: **KAYLA, TOMMY, BRYCE, AND RACHEL**: Thank you for understanding why you know the back of my head so well. Thank you for sharing your Dad with a whole bunch of readers! I love you!

TO MOM AND DAD: over the years of my adulthood, you've fed me some pretty brilliant thriller writers to learn from. Thank you for your voracious reading appetite, your endless generosity, and your unfailing love.

TO LESLIE, JEFF, AND BRIAN: You guys rock. Thank you for memories past, present, and future. Siblings like you make life a story waiting to happen.

TO THE DOVEL FAM: I scored HUGE with in-laws like you. Seriously, thank you for friendship, fellowship, and support.

Wayne Thomas Batson

TO CHRISTOPHER HOPPER: my brother in arms and kindred spirit: I cannot thank you enough for all the writing sessions, advice, laughs, and commiseration. Here's to many, many more books from both of us. Schiiiing!

TO FRIENDS: DougS, DaveP, ChrisH, AlexD, MatD, DanS, WarrenC, ToddW, CameronS, DawnH, AlainaH, SusanM, ChrisS, NoelleD, and so many others...thank you for "doing life" with me.

STEVE POOLE & PHILIP GALLMAN: Thanks for the key information about marine radar.

ASTRID AND THE TEAM AT LITERATURE AND LATTE, the Gift-from-God company that gave us Scrivener, the best writing software on the planet: thank you for all the help with the eBook and CreateSpace versions of GHOST.

GHOST PATRONS: all my readers ROCK, but you all are a special kind of insane! • Jay Goebel • Declan Ross • Jadi Verdin • Elizabeth Hornberger • Morgan Babbage • Brent Ammann • and Lindsay Renea! Thank you for inspiration, enthusiasm, and relentless hunger for new books!

LAURA G. JOHNSON: for fantastic proofreading and some stellar creative input. Your meticulous efforts made the book much better!

CARL GRAVES AT EXTENDED IMAGERY: thanks for the incredible front cover for GHOST, books 1&2. Here's to ten more books!

Look For GHOST Book 2:

MINISTER OF FIRE

Fall 2014

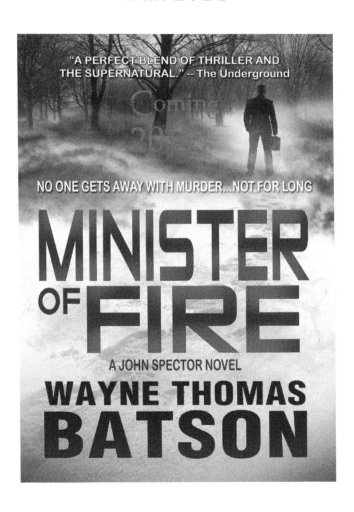

Made in the USA
San Bernardino, CA
13 December 2016